THE SCORPION'S TAIL

Also by Douglas Preston and Lincoln Child

Agent Pendergast Novels

*Relic**
*Reliquary**
The Cabinet of Curiosities
Still Life with Crows
*Brimstone***
*Dance of Death***
*The Book of the Dead***
The Wheel of Darkness
Cemetery Dance
Fever Dream†
Cold Vengeance†
Two Graves†
White Fire
Blue Labyrinth
Crimson Shore
The Obsidian Chamber
City of Endless Night
Verses for the Dead
Crooked River

Nora Kelly Novels

Old Bones
The Scorpion's Tail

Gideon Crew Novels

Gideon's Sword
Gideon's Corpse
The Lost Island
Beyond the Ice Limit
The Pharoah King

Other Novels

Mount Dragon
Riptide
Thunderhead
The Ice Limit

*Relic and Reliquary are ideally read in sequence
**The Diogenes Trilogy
†The Helen Trilogy

By Douglas Preston

The Lost City of the Monkey God
The Kraken Project Impact
The Monster of Florence
(with Mario Spezi)
Blasphemy
Tyrannosaur Canyon
The Codex
Ribbons of Time
The Royal Road
Talking to the Ground
Jennie
Cities of Gold
Dinosaurs in the Attic

By Lincoln Child

Full Wolf Moon
The Forgotten Room
The Third Gate
Terminal Freeze
Deep Storm
Death Match
Lethal Velocity (formerly *Utopia*)
Tales of the Dark 1–3
Dark Banquet
Dark Company

PRESTON & CHILD

THE SCORPION'S TAIL

First published in the USA in 2021 by Grand Central Publishing,
a division of Hachette Book Group, Inc.

First published in the UK in 2021 by Head of Zeus, Ltd

9 7 5 3 1 2 4 6 8

A catalogue record for this book is available from
the British Library.

ISBN (HB): 9781838931230
ISBN (XTPB): 9781838931254
ISBN (E): 9781838931261

Printed and bound in Great Britain by
CPI Group (UK) Ltd, Croydon CR0 4YY

Head of Zeus Ltd
First Floor East
5–8 Hardwick Street
London EC1R 4RG

WWW.HEADOFZEUS.COM

In memory of William Smithback, Jr.

IN PACE REQUIESCAT

THE SCORPION'S TAIL

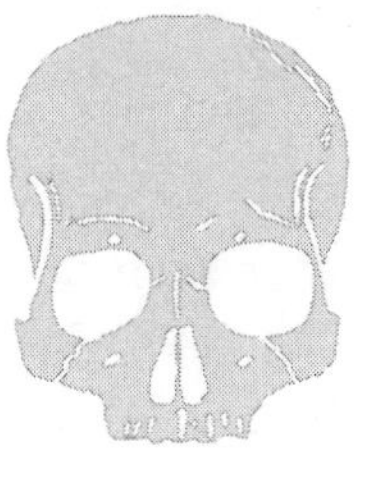

1

Since graduating from the Academy eight months before, Special Agent Corrie Swanson had learned to expect almost anything. Nevertheless, she hadn't expected to be serving warrants on bawling teenagers. As she rode back through the mountains with the rest of the FBI team, she felt relieved that a difficult day was almost over.

They were returning from the town of Edgewood, having served the warrant on a pimply-faced hacker who, when he answered the door of his mother's house, had broken down in tears at the sight of them. Corrie felt bad for the kid, and then felt bad for feeling bad—because, after all, he'd hacked into a classified network at Los Alamos National Laboratory "just for fun." Now his computers, external hard drives, iPhone, USB sticks, PlayStation, and even home security system were all loaded into the black Navigator with tinted windows that was following their vehicle with Agent Liz Khoury at the wheel and Agent Harry Martinez riding shotgun.

Corrie sat next to her boss, Supervisory Special Agent Hale Morwood, who was driving the least likely G-ride Corrie had ever seen: a late-model Nissan pickup, loaded, in candy-apple red with racing stripes and a Chinese dragon decal running diagonally across the hood. It was totally unlike Morwood's dry personality. When Corrie had finally screwed up the courage to ask her boss why he drove it, his response had been "I travel incognito."

"So," Morwood said, shifting into his mentoring voice. "Enough excitement for you today?"

Difficult or not, Corrie knew that the day had been a reward of sorts. She'd put in more than her share of desk duty, worked hard to impress Morwood, and even managed to play a major role in a recent case. To Morwood, no doubt this was the equivalent of a field trip.

Still, she knew he wouldn't like a display of gratitude. "I felt a little silly," she said, "wearing a bulletproof vest on a call like that."

"You never know. Instead of just yelling, that mother might have pulled out a .357 Magnum."

"What are they going to do with all that computer equipment?"

"The lab will look at it, find out exactly what he did and how, and then we'll go back and arrest him—and his life will be over."

Corrie swallowed.

"Seems harsh to you?"

"He didn't fit my idea of a criminal, to be honest."

"Me neither. Smart kid, stable middle-class home, straight-A student, promising future. That in a way makes it worse than, say, some kid who grows up in the inner city and starts dealing drugs because it's all he knows. Our boy is eighteen, he's an adult, and he broke into a system that holds classified nuclear bomb information."

"I get it, totally."

After a moment Morwood said: "It's good to have compassion. That's something a lot of agents lose over time. But balance it with a sense of justice. He's going to get a fair trial in front of twelve ordinary, commonsense Americans. That's how it works—and it's a beautiful system."

Corrie nodded. Morwood was a twenty-year agent, and his lack of cynicism continually surprised her. Maybe that's why he'd been tapped to mentor new agents during their two-year probationary period. So many of her fellow rookies—most of the guys, some of the women—were already trying on a tough, cynical, hard-boiled macho persona.

They were passing through the town of Tijeras, on old Route 66, when Morwood reached down and turned up the volume on the police scanner, which had been murmuring in the background. *Domestic, Cedro Peak Campground, report of shots fired...*

Corrie brought her wandering thoughts to attention.

Reports indicate a domestic dispute and shots fired in a camper, possible shooting victim, possible hostage situation. Location Cedro Peak Campground, New Mexico 252, Sabino Canyon turnoff...

"Well, I'll be damned," said Morwood, fiddling with his navigation program, "that's just around the corner. Looks like this is one for us." He pulled down his mic. "Special Agents Morwood and Swanson, Khoury and Martinez responding. We're passing through Tijeras on Route Six-Six, turning onto New Mexico Three-Three-Seven south. Ten minutes out."

Morwood accelerated, talking to the dispatcher and the agents in the following car. The tires squealed as he took the turn from Route 66 onto 337, heading into the foothills of the Sandia Mountains. As he did so, he reached for the dash, hitting the siren and activating the hideaway lights. The SUV followed suit.

The dispatcher relayed all the information she had, which was precious little. Essentially, others in the campground had called 911, reporting an incident in a pop-up camper—a loud argument, a woman screaming, shots fired. One said he thought he heard a little girl crying as well. Naturally, everyone in the campground had gotten the hell out.

"Looks like we're going to get some real action, not just a crybaby hacker," Morwood said. "We're the first responders. Check your weapon."

Corrie felt her heart accelerate. She removed her Glock 19M from the underarm holster, popped out the magazine, checked it, then reinserted and reholstered. Per standard procedure there was already a round in the chamber. She was glad to still be wearing the bulletproof vest.

"Domestics," said Morwood, switching again into mentoring mode, "as you probably learned at the Academy, can be the most dangerous of calls. The perp can be irrational, agitated, and often suicidal."

"Right."

The speedometer edged up to seventy miles an hour, which while not fast in itself was frightening enough on a mountain road with steep drop-offs and few guardrails. The tires gave a little protest of rubber at each curve.

"So what's the plan of action?" Corrie asked. This wasn't some pimply kid; this was real. This was her first active shooter call.

"They've called in a SWAT team and a CNU negotiator, and the FBI's got the CIRG on alert. So what we do is, we take up defensive positions, announce, assess, and de-escalate. Basically, we keep the guy talking until the pros arrive."

"What if he's taken a hostage?"

"In that case, the key is to keep him talking, reassure him, and focus on getting him to release the hostage. Unless it's a crisis, the less we do the better. The most dangerous moment is when we first arrive and the shooter sees us. So we go in nice and easy, no shouting, no confrontational stuff. Should be a cakewalk. Good experience for you." He paused. "But if things go south . . . just follow my instructions."

"Got it."

"Remind me of your shooting qualification score?"

"Um, forty-nine." Corrie reddened; that was barely above qualification, and followed weeks of practice at the range so intense her forearms had ached for days. Shooting just wasn't her forte.

Morwood grunted a nonreply and pressed still harder on the accelerator, the truck flying up the meandering two-lane road that climbed through piñon- and juniper-clad hillsides. Five minutes brought them to the turnoff for the Cedro Peak Group Campground in Cibola National Forest, and another five to a gravel road. Morwood eased back on his speed. In a few more minutes they arrived at the campground: a peaceful, grassy basin with picnic tables, a group shelter, and firepits set among piñon trees, with the great mass of Sandia Crest rising behind.

At the far end of a loop road, she could see a lone camper attached to a white Ford pickup. The rest of the campground was empty of people, with a few tents scattered around.

Morwood turned his truck into the right side of the loop and gestured out the window for Khoury and Martinez to go around the other way and converge at the far end.

"Keep down in case he shoots at us," said Morwood. "I'm going to drive in as close as I can."

He pulled the truck to within twenty feet of the camper. No shots were fired. The camper was one of the kind that fold open, with sleeping compartments on either side of a central living space, screened in with mosquito netting and white nylon. The thing was practically see-through—and Corrie could, in fact, see a man standing in the living space, holding a little child in a hammerlock, gun pressed to her head. She was sobbing in terror.

"Oh shit," breathed Morwood, crouching down in the seat and sliding out his weapon.

The man said nothing, did not move, keeping the weapon to the girl's head.

Corrie also reached for her gun.

"Get out on the far side and use the truck as cover. Stay behind the engine block."

"Right."

They both crept out and crouched behind the front of the truck. Morwood had grabbed the vehicle's mic cord and pulled it out with him. He now spoke into the mic, voice unhurried and neutral over the truck's loudspeaker.

"We're Agents Hale Morwood and Corinne Swanson, FBI," he said. "Sir, I'm going to ask you to please release the girl. We're here to talk to you, that's all. No one's going to get hurt."

There was a long silence. The man was backlit through the netting, so she couldn't see the expression on his face. But his chest was heaving and she heard the rasp of his breath. And then she noticed: blood was draining out the door and running in rivulets down the camper's steps into the dirt below.

"You see the blood?" Morwood asked.

"Yes." Her heart was in her throat. The guy had shot someone inside the camper already.

"Sir? We're asking you to release the hostage. Let the child leave. As soon as you do that, we can talk. We'll listen to what you have to say and work things out."

The man pulled the gun from the girl's head and fired twice at them. Both rounds missed the truck entirely.

I've been shot at before, Corrie thought. *I can handle this. Besides, he can't aim.*

Morwood spoke again, his voice steady. "Please, let the child leave. If there's anything you need from me in order to do that, tell me."

"I don't need shit from you!" the man suddenly screamed, so full of rage and gargling hysteria that the words were hardly intelligible. "I'm going to kill her! I'm fucking going to kill her right now!"

The child began to scream.

"Shut the fuck up!"

Morwood continued to speak, steady but firm. "Sir, you are not going to kill a child. Is she your daughter?"

"She's the *bitch's* daughter, and I'm going to kill her right now!"

Corrie saw him raise the gun and fire two more shots toward them, one of which slammed into the truck's rear side. Then the man pressed the gun back to the child's head.

"She's gonna die, count of three!"

The girl's tiny, terrified scream sounded like a metal blade cutting through tin. "No!" she choked out. "Please, Uncle, *no*!"

"One!"

Morwood turned to Corrie and spoke quietly and rapidly: "I'm authorizing deadly force. I'm going to the right to get a side angle on him. Cover me. If you get a clear shot—and I mean *absolutely clear*—take it."

"Sir."

"Two!"

The Glock felt like a block of heavy wet plastic in her trembling hand. *Calm down and focus, for fuck's sake.* She peered over the hood and then took a low shooting stance, bracing her arms. It exposed her, but the guy couldn't aim worth shit. She repeated it in her head: *The guy can't aim worth shit.*

She carefully drew a bead on the man's head and placed her finger lightly on the trigger. He was holding the girl in front of him, and ten yards was too far for a positive shot.

Morwood bolted from behind the truck and scrambled to a piñon tree thirty feet to the right, throwing himself down into a prone shooting position.

Corrie kept the man square in her sights. A head shot at this distance with her Glock 19M was still way too risky for the child. She glanced to her left and noted that Khoury and Martinez were behind their SUV, guns trained. Now she could hear the faint sirens of the SWAT team coming up the road.

Thank God—they were almost there.

"Three!"

Morwood fired his weapon, but Corrie instantly understood it was a decoy shot to distract the man, stop him from shooting the girl—and distract him it did. He pulled the gun from the girl's head and returned fire, two wild shots. And in that moment the girl twisted away and broke free of his grasp, lunging for the door but slipping and falling short.

In that moment the man was isolated, alone, and perfectly silhouetted against the netting. The girl was on the floor. Corrie had the man dead in her sights.

She squeezed the trigger.

The gun bucked, and the round, missing the head shot she was aiming for, smacked into his right shoulder instead. The hit spun him to the side; he swung his weapon around to return fire but was off-balance and aiming wildly. Corrie saw the flash and kick of the weapon just as the girl scrambled up, grabbing at the flimsy door of the camper. She tumbled down the steps to the ground, pigtails whirling, Princess Leia hair clips flying.

"You *bastard*!" Before she could think of what she was doing, Corrie charged the camper. Simultaneously, a fusillade of shots rang out from Morwood and the other agents. The rounds connected, and the man jerked back, his body a macabre imitation of a Raggedy Ann doll as he was thrown through the rear netting of the camper.

In a second Corrie had reached the girl and scooped her up, turning her own back to the shooter. The child was motionless, covered in blood. And then the SWAT team was suddenly swarming everywhere. Corrie looked up to see an ambulance screeching to a halt in a cloud of dust, the paramedics leaping out. She ran toward them, and they surrounded her, gently removing the girl from her arms and putting her on a stretcher.

One paramedic held Corrie's arm as she staggered. "Are you all right, ma'am?"

Corrie, paralyzed and heavily blood-splattered, merely stared at him.

"Are you injured?" He spoke loudly and distinctly. "Do you need help?"

"No, no, not my blood," she said angrily, shaking his arm off. "Save the girl."

Morwood was suddenly at her side, arm around her, supporting her. "I'll take over," he told the paramedic. Then he turned to her. "Corrie, I'm going to walk you back to the truck."

She tried to move her legs and stumbled, but he held her up. "Just one foot after the other."

Out of the corner of her eye she could see the paramedics madly working on the girl.

She followed Morwood's murmured instructions as best she could, and he eased her into the front seat. She realized she was hyperventilating and sobbing at the same time.

"Okay, take it easy, easy now, Corrie. He's gone. Take a deep breath. That's it, a deep breath."

"I fucked up," Corrie said, choking. "I missed. He killed the girl."

"You just take a deep breath now... Good... Good... You did nothing wrong; you took your opportunity, you fired, and you hit him. We don't know the girl's condition."

"I missed the head shot. I *missed*—"

"Corrie, just take a moment to stop thinking and breathe. Just *breathe*."

"He *shot* the girl. She's—"

"Listen to what I say. *Stop* talking, *stop* thinking, and just breathe."

She tried to follow his directions, tried to breathe, tried to stop thinking, but all she could see was the man's shoulder turning, turning, while he swung the muzzle of his gun to fire at her, the premature shot going straight into the girl instead... and then the little body sprawled on the ground, bloody Princess Leia hair clips lying in the dirt.

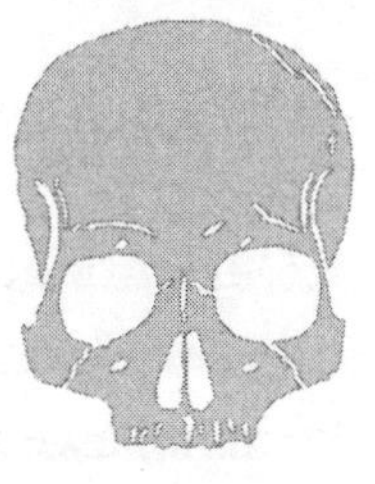

2

Two Weeks Later

As Sheriff Homer Watts reached the pass at Oso Peak, he paused to slip his canteen off the saddle horn and take a swig of water. The view from the pass was spectacular: the land fell away through piñon-clad foothills to the desert many miles away and thousands of feet below. September had brought a pleasant freshness to the mountain air, redolent with the scent of pine needles. It was Watts's first day off in a while, and it was a gorgeous one, a gift from the gods.

He gave his horse, Chaco, an affectionate pat on the neck, hung back the canteen, and touched the horse's flanks with his heels. Chaco moved forward easily, starting down the trail to the upper reaches of Nick's Creek. Watts had packed all he needed for a quiet day of fishing: his bamboo fly rod in an aluminum tube, a box of flies and nymphs, creel, knife, compass, lunch, flask of whiskey, and his grandfather's old pair of Colt Peacemakers, snugged into holsters almost as ancient.

He rode lazily down the trail, through shade and sun, past stands of ponderosas and glades of wildflowers, lulled by the gentle rocking of the saddle. On the shoulder of Oso Peak, the trees gave way to a broad meadow. Three mule deer grazed at the meadow's far side: a buck and two does. They were startled by his sudden appearance and bolted. He paused to watch them bound away.

Crossing the meadow, he glimpsed, far away to his left, a puff of smoke in the foothills, on a mesa extending from the base of the mountains. He stopped his horse again, took out his binoculars, and gave it a closer look. A fire at this time of year, when everything was bone dry, would be disastrous. But the glasses revealed it wasn't smoke at all, but irregular clouds of sand-colored dust raised by some sort of activity on the mesa. It was coming from a location he knew well, an abandoned mining camp named High Lonesome, one of the most isolated and unspoiled ghost towns in the Southwest.

Clouds of dust. What did they mean? Someone was up to something. And given the size of the clouds, it probably wasn't good.

Watts paused, thinking. To his right the trail would lead him to Nick's Creek and a peaceful day of fishing in a burbling stream, its deep pools and hollows flashing with cutthroat trout. To his left was a trail that would take him to High Lonesome and a day, perhaps, of aggravation and trouble.

Son of a bitch. Watts gently reined his horse to the left.

The land dropped away steeply, the trail switchbacking down the flanks of Gold Ridge. As the elevation decreased, the ponderosas gave way to juniper. As he rounded the side of the ridge, the ghost town came into view, a scattering of old adobe and stone buildings on the tongue of a mesa. He paused to once again glass the scene. And sure enough, it was as he suspected: a relic hunter. He could see the man shoveling sand from the basement of one of the ruined houses, a pickup truck parked nearby.

Watts felt his blood quicken. He knew High Lonesome well,

from the time his dad first took him there camping as a kid. The ghost town, remote and little known, had largely escaped the casual looting and destruction that had stripped most of the deserted mining towns in the state. There had been the occasional vandalism, for sure, mostly drunk teenagers from Socorro out for a weekend of fun in the mountains, but nothing on a large scale. The place wasn't even listed in any of the guidebooks to the ghost towns of New Mexico. It was just too hard to get to.

But here was some son of a bitch vandalizing the place.

He reined his horse off the trail and rode down through the piñon trees. He didn't want the relic hunter spotting him and taking off before he had a chance to collar the guy. While this was all Bureau of Land Management land and thus not his jurisdiction, he was the elected sheriff of Socorro County and he still had the right to arrest the bastard and turn him over to the BLM police.

After a while the slope leveled out. Moving his horse at an easy walk, he emerged into the open behind the town. The looter was at the far end, now out of sight because of the intervening buildings. Watts rode on through, keeping cover between him and the digger. A steady wind muttered through the ruins, and a tumbleweed came rolling by, just like in all the Westerns ever made.

As he approached, he got a good view of the pickup truck. He recognized the old Ford as belonging to Pick Rivers.

Pick Rivers. This was a head-scratcher, and no mistake. Rivers had once been a cocky little shit, fond of meth and known to sell relics to get it. But he'd cleaned up his act about two years ago—after a brief stint in the pen had scared him straight—and he hadn't been in any kind of trouble since.

As he reached the far end of town, Watts brought Chaco to a halt behind a building, dismounted, unlooped his lead rope, and tied the horse to a wooden post. He gave him another pat on the neck and a murmur of affection. He hesitated, then lifted the holsters from the saddle horn, removed the guns and checked them, reholstered, and buckled them around his waist. Just in case. Rivers was one of those dudes who was into open carry, and Watts knew he liked to go around with an S&W .357 L-frame strapped to his hip.

As Watts walked around the corner, he could see the building Rivers was digging in. It stood off by itself, a two-story adobe structure, the top floor mostly collapsed. The man was in the basement, heaving shovelfuls of sand out a broken window frame. And he was working hard, too. Watts wondered what he had found.

He approached cautiously, his hand resting on the butt of the revolver on his left hip. Rivers had obviously uncovered something, because he was now bending down and digging more cautiously. And as Watts watched, the man dropped to his knees and started using his hands to sweep away dirt and sand. He was so engrossed in what he was doing, and the basement so full of dust, he had no idea Watts was approaching from behind.

The sheriff moved to where he had a good view of Rivers through the cellar entrance, laboring away. Then he called out: "Rivers!"

The figure froze, his back to Watts.

"It's Sheriff Watts. Come out, hands in view. *Now*."

The man remained motionless.

"You gone deaf? Show your hands."

Rivers obliged, back still turned, holding his arms out to either side. "I hear you, Sheriff," he said.

"Good. Now get your ass out here."

"I'm coming." The figure began to rise—and then, suddenly, the hands disappeared and he whirled around, .357 Magnum gripped in both hands, aiming dead-on.

Watts yanked out a Colt just as Rivers's .357 went off with the boom of a cannon.

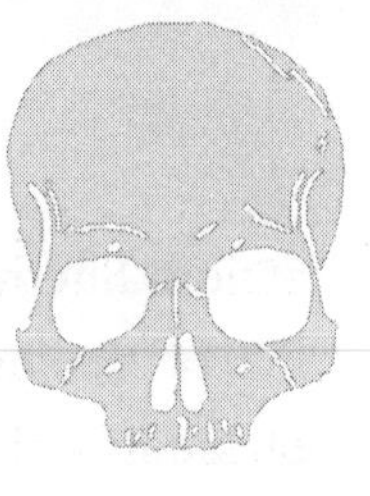

3

WHEN SPECIAL AGENT Swanson exited the bathroom, the two junior agents in the hallway fell silent just a little too quickly. She passed by them, not making eye contact, and headed back to her cubicle in the Albuquerque Field Office on Luecking Park Avenue Northeast. She took her seat and pulled the file she'd been working on closer to her. She was in the dimmest corner of the room, farthest from the windows. It was where the rookies were traditionally parked, and as they rose in the ranks they also moved closer to the wall of glass that had a panoramic view of the mountains. But Corrie was glad not to have to look out the window at the eleven-thousand-foot-high Sandia Crest, dusted with the season's first snowfall, because all it did was remind her of her failure. It was a bitter irony: up until two weeks ago, the sight of mountains had been a reminder of her biggest success as a young agent. Now she wondered if she would ever be able to look at that mountain again without feeling overwhelmed by shame and regret.

After the shooting, there had been an inquiry—expected and routine. Corrie hadn't received a reprimand or disciplinary action. She had even been verbally commended for saving the life of the hostage at the risk of her own. And thankfully—blessedly—the girl had only been grazed by the shot. A few stitches, and she'd been sent home to her grandparents the next morning, along with an armada of grief counselors. All the blood that had so terrified Corrie belonged to the poor girl's mother, who'd been lying dead on the floor of the camper.

Even so, Corrie couldn't forgive herself. She should have nailed that head shot—even at ten yards. She had a bead on him, she was focused. Her gun wasn't sighted wrong; she had established that at the range later. She had simply *missed*: missed at a critical moment. Even though she wasn't the best shot in her peer group, she wasn't the worst: forty-nine out of sixty on a QIT-99 was one point above the minimum score required, which wasn't great, but a quarter of her peers hadn't even passed. She should have made that shot—and then she would have saved the day, emerged with a commendation, elevated her profile further, cemented herself as an up-and-coming agent. Instead: ambiguity, sideways looks, and a single whispered *Nice shootin', Tex.*

She had fucked up, and everyone knew it. One senior female agent had taken her aside and told her it was wrong—Corrie had been unavoidably put in a spot where, basically, she shouldn't normally have been. But her fellow rookies were looking pretty smug, and it reminded her of that brutal saying, *It's not enough to succeed; others must fail.* Worst of all, Morwood was unexpectedly quiet on the subject, beyond making a passing suggestion that she put in more hours at the range. He didn't bawl her out, but he didn't praise her, either. Though it might be her imagination, he seemed to have become a little distant. And that stack of files from yet another cold case he had left on her desk sure felt like a punishment.

In the two weeks since the shooting, she'd been putting in an hour a day at the range after work. On her last go-around she'd scored fifty-one out of sixty: about average, and she believed that with hard work, she could push that up to fifty-two or even fifty-three. But when she told Morwood, he hadn't seemed impressed. "Anyone can score at the range," he said. "Put them in an active-shooter situation—that's where the rubber meets the road." The comment felt like another slap in the face. She had almost blurted out, asking him point-blank if he was referring to her performance at Cedro Peak, but then swallowed the comment and merely said, "Yes, sir."

"Corrie?"

It was Morwood, leaning in the doorway of her cubicle, his ID dangling. She noticed that the hair on his thinning crown was growing long. His smile looked a little forced. She was certain he was still disappointed in her.

"A moment?"

"Yes, sir."

She stood up and followed him out of the cubicle and down the hall to his small office, which also looked out over the Sandias.

"Have a seat."

Corrie sat, trying not to glance out the window.

"Well, well," said Morwood, folding his hands on the desk. "I've got a case for you. Right up your alley, in fact."

"Yes, sir," said Corrie. She was suspicious of his tone, which seemed a little too jaunty. If this were a good case, he sure as hell wouldn't be giving it to her. What was more likely to happen was that he'd put her "on the beach," in FBI lingo, starting the process with some meaningless case she couldn't fuck up and, even if she did, no one would notice or care.

"The sheriff of Socorro surprised a relic hunter yesterday, digging up some bones in the middle of nowhere. Human remains. BLM jurisdiction. There was a gunfight from which the relic hunter, a guy named Rivers, emerged the loser. He winged the sheriff and got his own kneecap shattered for his trouble. He's in the hospital, guarded around the clock and charged with the attempted murder of a law enforcement officer. The locals aren't too happy about it, and he's probably under guard as much for his own safety as to prevent an escape."

Corrie nodded without speaking.

"The remains Rivers discovered look twentieth century, based on the little bit of clothing visible. But the body doesn't look recent: maybe forty or fifty years old, at least, or so I was told. Could be anything—murder, suicide, accident. That's where your degree in forensic anthropology comes in, especially since it was found on federal land. The sheriff—who seems like a good guy, if a little dinged up—" He paused. "Socorro's a damn big county and he's the only sheriff, so he's happy to have our help."

It wasn't quite the shitty case she'd feared—after all, it involved the shooting of a law enforcement officer. Even so, it might turn out to be not a case at all, but just the bones of some old cowpoke who'd been kicked by a mule back in the days of J. Edgar Hoover. But she was in no position to complain. One thing she knew for sure was that she had to hide any feelings of doubt, work hard, and always project the façade of an obliging, cheerful, and *promising* rookie.

"Great. Thank you, sir. I'd be happy to look into it. It is right up my alley." She plastered on a smile. Socorro was an hour away. She had never been there but sensed it might be one of those hot, sad desert towns that dotted the state. "So, I'll be on my own?"

"Yes, until it becomes an actual case. First, you'll probably want to head over to Presbyterian this afternoon and question the shooter. Tomorrow, you're scheduled to liaise with Sheriff—" he rustled through his papers— "ah, Homer Watts. He'll drive you out to where the bones are. Apparently, it's way the hell out there and impossible to get to unless you know the route."

Homer Watts. Was this perhaps Morwood's idea of a practical joke? "And what time do I liaise with Sheriff Watts?"

"Eight o'clock, at the sheriff's office in Socorro."

That means a six o'clock wake-up. No, make that five thirty. "I'll be there. And thank you, sir. Thank you for giving me the opportunity!"

She noticed Morwood casting her a long, appraising look. "Corrie? I know what's going through your mind. And I just want to tell you one thing: you never know where a case might lead." He leaned back in his chair. "Remember Frank Wills?"

"Was he an FBI agent?"

"No. He was a hotel security guard. One night, he noticed that a couple of door latches had been taped open."

Corrie waited to hear more, wondering where Morwood was going with this.

"Seemed like a pretty small thing," he continued. "Doors get taped for convenience all the time in hotels. But Frank mulled it over and decided to notify the police—even if they laughed at him for calling them about something as stupid as a couple of taped locks."

He waited for Corrie's reaction, a small smile on his face.

"So what happened then?"

"Watergate," said Morwood.

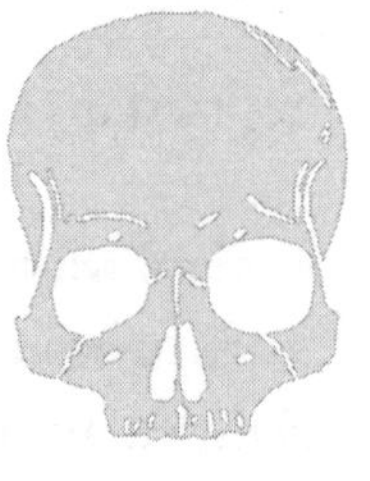

4

Corrie walked down a drab third-floor hallway of Albuquerque's Presbyterian Hospital. In her experience, hospitals were unpleasant places at best, and the corridor she found herself in was a model of neither efficiency nor cheer. Gurneys lined the walls like double-parked cars, most of them occupied by patients in various degrees of consciousness. IV racks and linen carts left here and there made her passage all the more difficult. The nurses' station was a mob scene, everyone either on the phone or in heated conversation. Corrie was about to stop for directions when she spotted what had to be her destination: a closed door at the far end of the hall with chairs placed on either side. One of the chairs was occupied by a law enforcement officer, and a folded newspaper and cup of coffee sat on the floor beside the chair.

Smoothing down her blazer with the palm of one hand, Corrie made her way through the chaos, which thinned out as she approached the closed door. The man in the chair glanced her way, and she saw from his uniform he was a ranger with the Bureau of Land Management. That made sense: the shooting had taken place on federal land, so the BLM would be in charge of guarding the prisoner. They had special agents, but few and widely scattered, so the duty would go to those a notch down on the totem pole.

"Special Agent Swanson, FBI," she said as she stepped up to him, showing him her shield in the lanyard dangling from her neck. "Here to question the suspect."

The ranger rose and looked at her shield and ID just long enough to be insulting. Finally, satisfied, he nodded. "Lots of luck," he said, handing her a clipboard with a sign-in sheet.

"What do you mean?" she asked as she filled out her information.

"Guy hasn't said a thing since he got here, other than a few choice words for the nurses when his dressing is checked."

He retrieved the clipboard, unlocked the door, let her pass through, then closed and locked it behind her. Corrie stopped just past the threshold to look around. The room was even plainer than the average hospital room. There were no paintings, television, or even a dresser. There was only an electric hospital bed, and in it—one wrist chained to the raised guardrail—the shooter.

Now Corrie stepped forward. She'd practiced interrogations like this before, and witnessed others, but this was her first time on her own. "Mr. Rivers?" she said. "Pick Rivers?"

The man looked at her without expression. He was in his late fifties, of average height, and thin. Although he had days-old stubble, his hair was cut short and groomed.

Once again, she took out her shield. "I'm Special Agent Swanson of the FBI. I'd like to ask you a few questions."

This elicited nothing. The man continued to look at her, his face betraying neither emotion nor interest. She waited a moment, mentally going over the course of questioning she'd laid out for herself.

"Your charge is attempted murder of a peace officer, with specific intent. And you did it on our turf, which makes it a class B felony. A federal felony. You did this with a deadly weapon—specifically, a .357 Smith and Wesson—which is an aggravating factor that will be taken into consideration when your sentence is determined. In short, you're looking at some serious time in prison. And as you probably know, there's no federal parole system, so you're going to do the full stretch. I've looked over your history, Mr. Rivers. I know you spent a couple of months in county lockup. But where you're going now is going to make that look like nursery school."

She paused to see what effect this speech had had on the prisoner cuffed to the bed. As far as she could tell, there was none. The man had run his eyes up and down her body—but that was all.

She took a few steps closer, so he'd know that his silence was not intimidating her. "But there may still be some things you can do to help yourself. Answering my questions, for one. Why were you digging up at High Lonesome?"

No response.

"Was anyone else involved, or were you working on your own?"

Still, silence.

"Did you have any reason to believe that you'd find a body there? Or did you come across it by chance?"

Still, only silence.

"You've cleaned up your act these last few years. What was so important about this discovery that it was worth attempting to kill a cop for?"

Rivers used his free hand to eject the contents of one nostril into a cup beside the bed, but otherwise kept quiet.

His cocky silence was becoming annoying. Corrie took

another deep breath, careful to keep her tone even and unmodulated, her face expressionless. "You've got one chance to help yourself, right here, right now. Otherwise, you're looking at some hard, *hard* time."

At last, the man's eyes showed a flicker of interest. For the first time, he spoke. "Hard time?"

Corrie tried not to show the excitement she felt at getting even two words out of the suspect. That was two more than anyone else had managed. "That's correct."

"Well, I'll tell you what," he said, his voice gravelly. "Maybe we can come to some kind of—accommodation."

"That would be smart." She pulled a digital recorder from her purse, turned it on in full view of Rivers. "You've been Mirandized, but just to remind you, anything you say can be used against you."

Rivers shook this off as if it were a gnat. "You mentioned hard time," he repeated, his voice unmodulated, confident.

Corrie nodded, glancing down to make sure the recorder was running.

"Well, that's a coincidence, because I've gotten kind of hard myself—a cute little bitch like you coming in here, me in bed and all. So I'll answer your questions... after you've sucked me off."

Corrie stared at him, temporarily speechless, mortified that the blood was rushing to her face. She made a huge effort not to show her anger, to remain cool.

"Oh, and uncuff me, so I can work your head with my hand." And now at last he began to laugh—quietly, provocatively.

He was still laughing a few seconds later when Corrie left the room, gestured for the ranger to lock the door, and strode briskly down the hospital corridor.

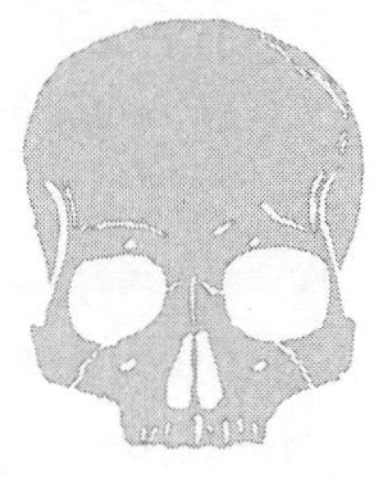

5

Socorro turned out to be not as bad as Corrie expected, with the Rio Grande flowing along one side, irrigated fields, and some dry mountains rising at the other end of town. But it was still a flat, hot grid of streets—damned hot, in fact—and as she approached the sheriff's office the desert wind bounced a couple of tumbleweeds across the street in front of her, as if to remind her where she was. As she picked up her gear bag and got out of the car in the parking lot of the office, the long wail of a train whistle underscored the feeling of desolation. This was exactly the kind of place she imagined FBI agents who fucked up were sent to. For the hundredth time, she reminded herself she'd been given a case that had some promise.

The sheriff's office, on the other hand, was an attractive adobe building, surrounded by a parking lot of cracked asphalt that had been dribbled on by more asphalt, forming a spiderweb pattern. Even though it was late September, her hiking boots stuck on the tar as she entered the building.

Sheriff Watts came out right away, and Corrie had her first shock of the morning. Instead of the jowly, mustachioed good old boy she expected, Watts was around her age—twenty-three—tall, fit, and handsome as hell, with curly black hair above a smooth brow, brown eyes, and a movie-star smile. Accentuating the look were the two antique revolvers he wore, one on each hip. A fat bandage was affixed to the bottom of one ear. He wore a fancy cowboy hat with a woven horsehair band, and he seemed as surprised at meeting her as she was at him.

As they exited the office, Watts suggested that they ride in his cruiser. He moved to open the Jeep's door for her, then appeared to think that might not be appropriate and backed off to let her open it herself. It was pretty clear she'd overturned all his preconceptions of an FBI agent.

"Agent Swanson," he said, sliding behind the wheel, "before we head out there, I'm going to swing by and pick up a fellow named Charles Fountain. He's a lawyer who knows a lot about local history—a real encyclopedia. I thought he might be able to shed some light on things, maybe answer a few questions."

Corrie hadn't expected a civilian to ride along, but she was hardly in a position to object. "Thank you, Sheriff."

He nodded and started the Jeep Cherokee, which was painted up and decaled as a cruiser with a big sheriff's star on it. Corrie wondered if she should invite Watts to switch to a first-name basis but decided against it. Better to keep it formal.

"I hear you spoke to Pick," the sheriff said as they drove slowly through town.

"I'm surprised you can call him by his first name, after he tried to kill you."

"Well, he didn't succeed, and I'm not one to hold a grudge," Watts said with a laugh. "He's a pretty poor shot. Guess he just got lucky."

"I'll say. Lucky he didn't get killed."

"Oh, that wasn't luck. If I'd wanted to hit the center of mass, I would have." This was said in an offhand way, with nothing of a boastful tone in it. Corrie considered this for a moment. Did it mean that Watts had actually let Rivers shoot first? She decided it would be impolitic to ask him directly. Instead, she said: "Speaking of gunfights, I couldn't help but notice those ivory-handled revolvers of yours."

Watts nodded again, this time with a touch of pride. "Colt .45 Peacemakers. Single-action, black powder frames. From 1890 or so. They belonged to my granddad. He refuses to tell me where he got them from."

"Why do you wear two?"

Watts shrugged. "They came as a set."

"And what's with the backward holsters? The handles are pointing forward."

"You never heard of a cross-arm draw? Guess they don't teach you everything in FBI school."

Corrie didn't answer. She'd take her own semiautomatic Glock over those relics any day—but she wasn't about to say so.

"I still can't figure why Rivers drew on me, though," Watts said. "He's had a spotless record for a couple of years now. Can't imagine what was so special about that corpse that would make him risk everything like that."

They pulled up in front of a modest, neatly tended house, and before Watts could get out, a man burst through the door. Looking at him, Corrie got yet another surprise. Instead of the devil-and–Daniel Webster country lawyer she'd expected, with a corncob pipe and red suspenders stretching over a capacious gut, Fountain was tall, perhaps sixty years old, and only slightly heavyset. He wore a dark green Barbour jacket—probably the only one within a hundred miles—so rumpled he might have slept in it. His face was clean-shaven, and his luxuriously thick salt-and-pepper hair was parted in the middle and hung down almost to his shoulders. He glanced from one of them to the other with faded blue eyes that sparkled with intelligence from behind gold, round-rimmed glasses.

Watts got out and shook the man's hand, and Corrie followed. The sheriff made the introductions.

"You're a lawyer, I understand," she said.

"Semiretired at present," Fountain replied in a quiet, melodious voice. "Probably for the best."

"Don't let him kid you," Watts said. "He's got a reputation that stretches across the state, and beyond. You won't find a sharper legal mind anywhere. Never lost a case."

"Is that true?" Corrie couldn't help asking.

"Only partly," Fountain said. "I lost a couple when I worked for the U.S. Attorney's Office."

"But none since he became a defense lawyer," Watts said. "It's the voice. They never see him coming."

"You might as well say it: voice *and* appearance," Fountain said with a laugh. "I prefer to call it a 'disarming presentation.'"

"He wears that disheveled look like a work uniform," Watts said. Being in familiar company seemed to have relaxed him, because this time he held the car door open for Corrie without thinking.

"I'm just coming along to add some background as an amateur historian," Fountain said as he got into the back seat. "I won't get in your way."

Watts put the A/C on full blast, and they headed out of town. "Where we're going," he said, "is a ghost town up in the Azul Mountains named High Lonesome. It's an old gold-mining town abandoned when the color played out in the early 1900s.

One of the prettiest ghost towns in the state—but hell to get to. We've got a two-hour ride ahead of us. It's not that far as the buzzard flies, but the roads are torture."

Two hours? Corrie thought. She'd be lucky to get back to Albuquerque before midnight.

"Music?" Watts asked, pulling out his phone and plugging it into the stereo.

"Ah, sure," Corrie replied.

"Any preferences?"

"As long as it's not Gregorian chants or rap, I don't care," said Fountain from the back seat.

Corrie didn't think Sheriff Homer Watts would have the music she liked. "You choose."

"You two can veto this." He fiddled with the phone and the sound of the Gipsy Kings came floating out of the car's speakers. It wasn't the music Corrie would have selected, but it wasn't bad, either, and it kind of fit in with the landscape.

Watts drove south toward a jagged line of mountains rising out of the tan desert. The Cherokee turned off on a Forest Service road. Corrie quickly lost track of the bewildering maze of dirt roads, one turn after another, with each more rutted and washed out than the last. The vehicle eventually slowed to about five miles an hour, bucking up and down, Corrie holding on to the ceiling grips to keep from getting thrown out of her seat. As they climbed higher into the mountains, the piñons gave way to ponderosa pines, which in turn gave way to Douglas firs and spruce trees. At the top of a pass, stupendous views opened up.

Watts halted the car for a moment and pointed.

"South of us, that's the Jornada del Muerto desert and the San Andres Mountains. That's all part of the White Sands Missile Range, where the army folks play with their weapons."

Fountain said, "In Spanish, Jornada del Muerto means 'journey of death.' The old Spanish trail from Mexico City to Santa Fe crossed that desert, over a hundred miles. The trail was paved with bones and lined with crosses."

Corrie looked in the direction he indicated, the tan desert, streaked with red and brown, stretching southward.

"Farther south and over the mountains," said Watts, "are the White Sands. Ever been there?"

"No, I was only assigned to the Albuquerque office eight months ago. Have you?"

"Many times. I grew up in Socorro; Dad's a rancher. When I was a kid I rode our horses all over the place. White Sands is one of the most amazing places on earth: dunes as white as snow, stretching for hundreds of thousands of acres."

"You grew up here?"

Picking up on her tone of incredulity, Watts laughed.

Fountain said in a pleasant tone, "Some people *do* manage it."

Corrie felt herself redden. "Are you from here, too?"

"Just north of Socorro," Fountain replied. "Place called Lemitar."

Corrie, not knowing where this was, simply nodded.

"It's not as bad as it might seem," the lawyer went on. "There's a lot to explore. On our right is Chimney Mountain and over there is Oso Peak, where Black Jack Ketchum and his gang used to hide out. He terrorized Socorro in the old days, robbed the railroad many times. When they hanged him, they botched the job and he was decapitated. They say he landed on his feet and stood for a while before falling down."

"Impressive sense of balance," said Corrie.

Fountain laughed. "And to the southeast of us is the Mescalero reservation. Beautiful country. That rez is where the last of

Geronimo's Chiricahua Apache band finally settled. Geronimo, Cochise, Victorio—those great chiefs used to roam all through these mountains."

Corrie could hear a strong love of the land in Fountain's voice, and oddly, it made her envious. She had no love for her own hometown of Medicine Creek, Kansas, and never planned to go back. She'd rather go to hell.

Watts eased the Jeep forward and over the pass, the road dropping down through switchbacks to a series of desert mesas projecting from the southern end of the mountains. They lost most of the altitude they had gained, winding down one bad road after another, until they were back in a piñon-juniper desert cut with arroyos and mesas. And then, suddenly, the ghost town appeared, perched on a low mesa above an immense plain, stupendously isolated. Watts drove down a few more eroded switchbacks, and in five minutes they were coming into town.

"Welcome to High Lonesome," he said.

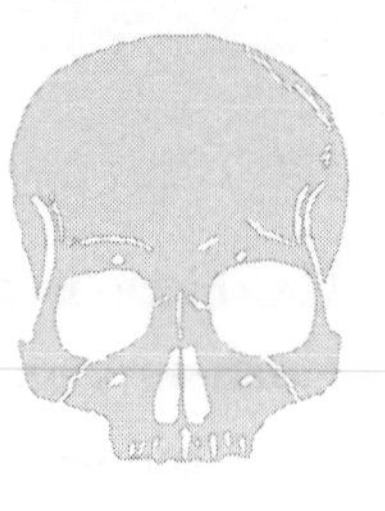

6

THIS PRONOUNCEMENT WAS greeted with a brief silence.

"It really lives up to its name," Corrie murmured. "What a view."

A single dirt street ran the length of the town, with ruined adobe and stone buildings on either side, some still roofed, others exposed to the elements. "That was the hotel," said Fountain, pointing to a two-story structure of rough-cut stone with crooked wooden portals wrapping around its façade. "Saloon, stores, miners' houses, church—this was a bustling town after gold was discovered down in the basin, back in the early 1880s," he continued. "At first it was a dangerous area, with Geronimo's Apaches roaming around. When they finally surrendered, prospectors came in and followed an epithermal deposit. The mine is actually in the cliffs below. Single horizontal shaft, hard rock. With the Geronimo Campaign over, there were plenty of discharged soldiers willing to work as miners. They processed the ore at a stamp mill back in the mountains, near a stream."

"How is it that a town like this could survive so long undisturbed?" she asked. "It could be a movie set."

"You saw the road coming in," the lawyer said. "And the town was built mostly with stone and adobe, instead of wood, so it isn't likely to burn. The whole place was abandoned rather abruptly, which ironically also helped preserve it."

Corrie saw the two men exchange a glance.

"What is it?" she asked.

Fountain cleared his throat. "Well, the history of the place ended up as ugly as its surroundings are attractive. When the gold mine started playing out, the owners pushed too hard to follow the dwindling vein. They didn't shore up the shaft properly. You can probably guess the rest: the shaft collapsed, trapping a dozen miners."

"Trapped alive, by all accounts," Watts added. "It must have been a slow and horrible death."

Fountain nodded. "If you walk far enough out of town, you'll come to what's left of the cemetery. A dozen tombstones with the same date are all in one corner. Of course, there are no bodies in the graves."

They passed through the town and came to a scattering of buildings nearer the edge of the mesa, with worn adobe walls and vigas lying splintered on the ground. Watts brought the vehicle to a halt beside one, and they all got out.

"I followed a pillar of dust to that cellar hole over there," Watts told them. "Can you see, beyond those other buildings, where the opening is?"

He walked in the direction he'd indicated, and the other two followed.

"After I'd cuffed and stabilized Rivers," he said, "I crawled in to see what was important enough to shoot me for. He'd cleared off the top of a skull, along with a hand. Another fifteen minutes, and he'd probably have yanked everything out of the ground and driven away."

Corrie pulled a headlamp out of her gear bag and put it on, along with nitrile gloves and a face mask. "I'm going to take a look in there, if you don't mind—alone."

"Be our guest," said the sheriff.

Corrie got down on her hands and knees and peered in. Splinters of sunlight striped the dark space. The cellar was still roofed, although it was caved in on the left. The basement had half filled with windblown sand. She could see where Rivers, the relic hunter, had crawled in, leaving his footprints everywhere. Quite obviously, he had dug a number of holes. Up against the wall to the right, where the most serious digging had taken place, she could see the cranium the sheriff had mentioned, along with the bony hand and the withered sleeve of a shirt and, partially covering that, a duster or oilcloth raincoat.

She crawled down and removed her camera, shooting a full set of images in the interior space. There was just enough headroom to walk around while hunched over. Approaching the bones, she knelt again, took a fresh set of pictures.

The first thing she noticed on closer observation was that the remains consisted of more than bones; there was still a lot of mummified flesh adhering to them. She pulled out a brush from her kit and whisked away the loose sand from the cranium and exposed the arm, with its ropy beef-jerky muscles that rattled like dry corn sheaves as she brushed. She could even see a downy coat of hair on the forearm, which, despite her training, she found faintly disgusting. Further brushing exposed more of the clothing, including a gingham shirt underneath, falling off in strings. The hand sported a gold ring on its pinkie finger.

Peering closely, she saw the letters *JG* engraved on it. Clearly this was an item Rivers hadn't been able to take before the sheriff caught him.

She cleared sand from around the skull and found more of the rotting duster turned up around the man's neck—it was definitely a man, judging from the clothing and the fringe of hair encircling the bald skull.

Corrie stopped. Getting these remains out of this pile of drifted sand was going to be a serious job. If he was a murder victim and she dug out the bones herself, she'd compromise the integrity of the evidence. Her background was in forensic anthropology; she wasn't trained as an archaeologist. She was qualified to analyze the remains in her lab but didn't have the expertise to dig them up properly in the field. On the other hand, if she called in the FBI's field Evidence Response Team, dragging them and their van all the way out here, three hours each way from Albuquerque over terrible roads, only for them to discover it was an accidental death... she would look like an idiot. What she needed, it seemed obvious, was an archaeologist who could excavate the bones in a proper manner.

She thought of Nora Kelly.

Kelly was a senior curator at the Santa Fe Archaeological Institute. Corrie had worked with her before—their collaboration, although unanticipated, had ultimately expanded into Corrie's first, and only, important case.

And it had been a success, as well. Her first—and only.

Crouching next to the skeleton, Corrie thought about the idea. Kelly had been supervising a dig in the Sierra Nevada a few months back when Corrie intruded on her camp, investigating a case involving murder and grave robbing. She and Kelly had locked horns initially, and the woman could be a pain in the ass at times—stubborn and a bit full of herself—but she was certainly qualified. If it came down to it, she would make a good expert witness. And Corrie was pretty sure Morwood, who knew Kelly from the same prior case, would approve of bringing her in. Kelly had what he would have called "sand."

Besides, the woman owed her one.

After taking a final round of photos and slipping the ring into an evidence bag, she came back out, blinking in the bright September sun. Watts and Fountain were standing there, chatting. They looked toward her.

"So what's the deal?" asked Watts, removing his hat and mopping his brow.

"Well," said Corrie, "we're going to need a little extra help here. I'm going to bring in a specialist to excavate the remains—just in case it's a homicide."

"Why a specialist?" Fountain asked. "If it's murder, whoever committed it is long dead."

"That may be the case, but we have to preserve the integrity of the evidence—and that means bringing in a professional archaeologist. And the sooner the better, too." She pointed to the ring. "This might not be the only valuable item."

"Good plan," said Sheriff Watts with a brilliant smile. He looked at his watch. "I'm starving, and we didn't bring any lunch. There's a nice café in Socorro, and if we hurry we can get there before it closes at three."

Corrie wasn't sure there was such a thing as a "nice" café in Socorro, but she, too, was hungry. And she was not looking forward to the long drive to Albuquerque, on top of another one just getting out of High Lonesome.

Fountain looked from one to the other. It was clear Watts hadn't included him in the invitation.

"Don't worry about me," he said laconically. "I'm on a diet, anyway."

"I'll drop you off at your office," Watts said. He put out a hand, and Corrie passed him the evidence bag. "Too bad the initials aren't *HW*," he said, peering at it and handing it back a moment later. "Looks like it might just be a perfect fit."

"That would be felony robbery of the dead," Fountain said as he got into the back of the car. "But don't worry, Sheriff," he continued as they set off on the long, bumpy ride back to civilization. "I could get you off."

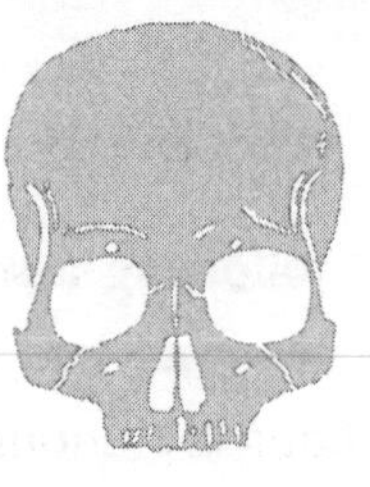

7

THE WALLS OF the small Pueblo cave dwelling had been plastered with mud and painted red, but the intervening span of six hundred years had taken quite a toll. Nora Kelly examined the back wall with her headlamp. It was stained with soot over a circular area that looked more thickly plastered than the rest of the interior. The longer she looked at it, the more she was convinced the plaster concealed a hole in the back of the shelter.

Her graduate student, Bruce Adelsky, entered and knelt, peering over her shoulder. "Funny-looking plastering job."

"Just what I thought." She reached out and, using the handle of her archaeological trowel, lightly tapped on the plaster. A hollow sound resulted.

"Holy cow," he said. "There's something back there!"

"I'm pretty sure it's a burial. Which means we don't touch it."

"Come on. Really?" Adelsky asked, his voice betraying his disappointment. "Just to take a look?"

"The new president is even more of a stickler about protocol than I am." Nora ventured a small smile. The reputation of the Santa Fe Archaeological Institute was currently in the toilet following a scandal involving the previous president. But the Institute had the money and power to climb out of that hole quickly enough—and, in the meantime, the current chief of archaeology was retiring in a month, and Nora was in line for the promotion. Securing the chief of archaeology position would be a big deal; it would put her in charge of the Institute's "dirt herd," as it was affectionately called, overseeing all the active excavations the Institute was engaged in. She had even allowed herself to think that, one day, she might be president herself. The current dig had been as much of a success as the last one was a disaster—ahead of schedule, no problems or controversy, strong support from the local Pueblo council, and beautiful results. And besides, none of the many problems that had occurred at the Donner dig could be laid at her door—her own work had been practically flawless.

"I find it interesting how they buried their dead right in their own homes," said Adelsky.

Nora smiled at him. This was another plus: Bruce had proven an excellent graduate student, meticulous and reliable, fully capable now of running a dig on his own. "The ancient Pueblo people liked to keep their dead near them," she told him. And she added, almost to herself: "It is interesting. But understandable."

Then she checked her watch. "Let's break for lunch."

The two crawled out of the low entrance to the cave. Nora stood up and looked about, massaging the small of her back. This cave was one of hundreds carved into the volcanic tufa of northern New Mexico, part of an ancient Pueblo settlement called Tsankawi. It was tangential to the Bandelier National Monument, a complex of caves, ladders, trails, and a mesa-top ruin. The view from the mesa was amazing—the ancestral Pueblo people really liked their views—looking across the valley of the Rio Grande to the Sangre de Cristo Mountains, twenty miles away, covered by a fresh dusting of snow. And all this, Nora thought, was a few scant miles from Los Alamos National Laboratory, where they had designed and built the first atomic bomb. The contrast between the ancient ruins of a vanished people and the birth of the nuclear age always gave Nora a creepy feeling of cognitive dissonance.

As she gathered up her day pack, she saw a figure approach along the trail. It was probably an intrepid tourist—a few did visit the Tsankawi ruins—but as it approached, it began to look familiar. More than just familiar.

"Damn," she murmured under her breath.

"Uh-oh," Adelsky said, staring. "It's that fed again."

Nora slapped the dust off her jeans with a sinking feeling as she watched Corrie Swanson approach. She wondered what the agent wanted now. She sure as hell hoped Swanson wasn't going to throw her current dig into the extended chaos she had with the previous one. Reluctantly, Nora climbed down from the cave entrance to meet Corrie beneath the tent shade set up on the valley floor.

Corrie approached with her hand extended.

"Hi, Nora," said Corrie, shaking her hand. "I hope I'm not interrupting anything."

Nora said, "Well, that depends."

"This isn't about the Donner Party site, if that's what worries you."

Nora took immediate, and instinctual, offense. *Do I look worried?* But she pushed the feeling away, telling herself she was being prickly.

"We were about to have lunch," she said instead. "Come into the shade and have some coffee."

"Great, thanks."

Nora led the way. She poured Corrie a cup from a large thermos and another for herself.

"Have a seat," she said. "Cream and sugar are over there."

Corrie eased herself into a chair, looking uncertain. Adelsky took a seat nearby and pretended to drink his coffee, while obviously waiting with his ears perked up to hear what the FBI agent might have to say. Nora thought with a certain amusement that Corrie still looked very much the rookie—she hadn't yet developed the air of authority and self-assurance law enforcement types usually displayed. And she looked so young. It couldn't be easy for her in an FBI office with a bunch of older guys. Nora certainly empathized with that.

So why did she feel such an urgency to speed Corrie on her way?

"How's your arm?" she asked, making an effort to be polite.

"All healed up, thanks for asking."

They sat in director's chairs around a plastic worktable. Nora's sandwich was in the cooler nearby, but she figured it would be rude to start eating in front of Corrie. Adelsky felt no such compunction, and he hauled out an overstuffed bologna sandwich and began to chow down.

Nora took a deep breath. "What brings you all the way out here, if not the Donner case?"

"I didn't mean to drop in on you like this. I would have called, but, well, you've got no cell reception—and I'm in kind of a hurry."

Nora nodded.

"I'll get to the point," said Corrie. "A body was found in a ghost town in the Azul Mountains. I need someone to excavate it properly."

"Someone. You mean *me*?"

"Yes."

All of a sudden, Nora realized why Corrie's appearance made her antsy. It was because, unconsciously, she'd been afraid of a request exactly like this.

"Doesn't the FBI have a team that does that sort of thing?" she asked.

"We do. It's called the Evidence Response Team."

"So why not use them?"

"The thing is," Corrie said, "we don't know yet if the individual represents a homicide or just an accident. In other words, it isn't an official case yet. It's a small job, something that could be done in a couple of hours. It doesn't require a big forensic team and a lot of fuss."

In other words, my time is less valuable than theirs. Nora pondered this for about one additional second. "I'm sorry, but I'm totally tied up here. Our permit expires October 15, around the time the snows start at this altitude. I have to have everything finished before then."

"I understand," Corrie said. "But it's only a couple of hours' work, and I just want to make sure it's done right and the evidence isn't compromised."

"I doubt the Institute would release me, even for a day."

"On the contrary, I'm pretty sure they would. Local institutions often lend their expertise to law enforcement. It's considered a courtesy."

"A courtesy." Nora felt slightly annoyed at the way she'd framed this, implying that a refusal would be a discourtesy. Rookie or not, Special Agent Swanson was proving once again that she could be a pain in the ass.

"And," Corrie added, "it would be good publicity for the Institute, which... could probably use it right about now."

And whose fault is that? Nora almost replied, swallowing her words. This damned FBI agent was like a dog with a bone. A lot was riding on the smooth completion of this project—for Nora personally. She took another deep breath. "Sorry. You make a good case, Corrie, you really do. But I'm telling you the truth. We're incredibly busy, on a short clock, and—" she fibbed— "behind schedule as it is." She gave Corrie a long, friendly smile of refusal. Maybe if she split her sandwich with the woman, she'd leave.

"Have you ever been to the ghost town of High Lonesome?" Corrie asked after a moment.

"Never heard of it."

"It's on a mesa, overlooking the Jornada del Muerto desert. Used to be an old gold-mining town. The buildings are fabulously preserved. There's a hotel, saloon, church, livery stables. And those mountains are where Geronimo and Cochise used to hang out. All in all, a pretty spectacular spot."

Nora shook her head. She was not going to take the bait.

"The body I mentioned was found by a relic hunter in the basement of a rather mysterious building, off by itself next to the edge of the mesa. It looks as if he took refuge there—or his body was dumped—maybe sixty, seventy years ago."

"No sign of foul play?" Nora asked, despite herself.

"Hard to say. The relic hunter only had a chance to uncover the cranium and part of the right forearm before being arrested. The body is mummified and covered in windblown sand. I'm no archaeologist, but it looks like he was crouching against the wall."

"Mummified?" She found herself intrigued—but only a little. Corrie was selling this pretty hard...but the fact was, she couldn't even consider it. And it would be better if she didn't hear anything more.

She shook her head with what she hoped was finality. "Your

salesmanship is first-rate, Corrie, but your timing is awful. My back's against the wall here."

Corrie looked at the ground for a moment, almost hesitantly, then looked up—first at Adelsky, then at Nora. "So is mine. Look, I really need this. I'm in a bit of a shit storm back at work." Another hesitation. "Actually, I'm drowning in one, to be honest. You heard about the shooting in the Sandias?"

"I did."

"I was one of the agents involved. I kind of fucked things up. So they dumped this case on me. I think it's sort of a penance. Or more likely, the first stop on a lateral arabesque to some desk job, investigating white-collar crime."

Nora frowned. "What do you mean, fucked things up? From what I heard, what happened in the Sandias was a success. They—you—rescued that little girl with barely a scratch."

Corrie winced, then waved a hand as if to shoo away something painful. "I can't go into the details." She glanced again at Adelsky. "But I hope what I've said will make it clear just how important this is to me."

There was nothing else Nora could say, so she remained silent.

After a moment, Corrie spoke again. "I just thought, you know, given what happened in the Sierras, when I, um…" She stopped. "Well, I hate to bring this up, but—not to put too fine a point on it, I *did* save your life."

For a moment, Nora was speechless at this brazen combination of honesty and lack of tact. Then, suddenly, her irritation vanished and there was nothing left for her to do but laugh. "You're relentless!" she said, shaking her head. "Wow, I guess you really must be in deep shit. Okay. Thank you, *again*, for saving my life up there in the Sierras. And by the way, you're welcome for my preventing *your* death from hypothermia."

Now it was Corrie's turn to say nothing.

Nora spread her hands, palms up. It was hard to turn down an appeal like that. And maybe, she thought, giving a little pro bono assistance to the FBI would help shine up the Institute's reputation and give her promotion an additional push. "Since you put it that way, how can I refuse? What the hell—I'll do it. When? With some fancy footwork I can probably squeeze in a day off sometime next week."

"The thing is," Corrie said, "we're worried about word getting out and other relic hunters coming around. Apparently they're endemic around here—but I don't need to tell you that."

This was true; Nora had seen more than her share of looted or desecrated prehistoric sites. "So you're saying you need this taken care of soon?"

"Like, um, tomorrow?"

"Tomorrow?"

Corrie flushed. "The sooner the better."

"Yes, but I just finished explaining that—"

"What's the point of your agreeing, if by the time we get there everything's been looted? Speaking of that—" and she turned to Adelsky— "everything you've just heard is privileged information, and if you repeat it, you risk, well, a felony."

"Repeat what?" Turning away, Adelsky busied himself finishing up his sandwich.

Corrie turned back to Nora. And, for the first time since she'd arrived at the mesa, she smiled. "Why not just get it over with? I'll pick you up at—say—seven thirty in the morning? It's a bit of a drive."

There was, Nora had to admit, real value in just getting it over with.

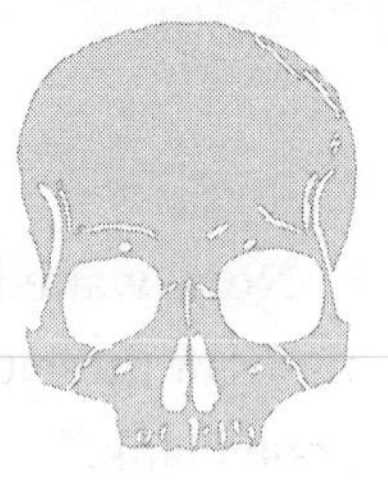

8

CORRIE HAD ARRIVED at Nora's apartment at dawn. She drove up in a big black Navigator with tinted windows—the quintessential FBI car—the rear filled with plastic evidence boxes and bags and containers. The "bit of a drive" turned out to be over four hours—two from Santa Fe to Socorro and then, Corrie warned her (belatedly), another two over bone-breaking dirt paths across the mountains. Nora felt a little aggrieved at the lack of prior warning—until she realized just how much additional time on the road Corrie would have to put in, picking her up and dropping her off, given that Albuquerque was itself another hour's drive from Santa Fe.

After passing through Socorro, they turned east and entered the mountains. Corrie had her GPS out and consulted it constantly, along with some hastily scribbled notes, as they bumped and lurched along one Forest Service road after another, each worse than the last, until Corrie halted the car at a fork in the track.

"Crap. No GPS signal."

"Are we lost?" Nora asked, her irritation rising.

"No, no! Just not sure . . . if this is the right turn."

Nora waited while Corrie fiddled with the GPS. "Damn, I thought these things worked with satellite signals. The map has gone blank."

"They do," said Nora, "but you have to download the underlying maps ahead of time if you're going out of cell range. It's a trick we archaeologists know only too well."

"Crap," muttered Corrie again.

Nora started to get out of the Navigator.

"What are you doing?" Corrie asked.

"I'm going to tell you which way to go."

She walked around the vehicle and examined the dividing tracks: one going right, the other straight. Then she turned and got back in.

"Take a right," she said.

Corrie stared at her. "How'd you do that?"

Nora couldn't suppress a smile. "Tire tracks. You were in here a couple of days ago, right? So I looked for the fresh tracks in the dirt. I mean, it's not likely anybody else is going to be out in this godforsaken place. So you keep driving and stop at each turn, while I figure out which way to go."

Corrie nodded, looking put out—whether at the discovery that she was lost or at not anticipating the ease of the solution, Nora didn't know.

They drove on, and at each fork Nora got out and examined the tracks, looking for a soft spot where tread marks would be preserved. Finally, around eleven thirty, they came around a ridge—and there, suddenly, was the town of High Lonesome, stretched out in front of them.

When Nora emerged from the vehicle, she was stunned. She'd seen her share of ghost towns, but nothing like this. All of a sudden, the drive seemed worth it.

"I can't believe a place like this could survive into the twenty-first century," she said, looking around.

"I thought you might say that."

As Nora walked down the main street, she paused to look at the buildings on either side, some with weathered signs still intact. There was a two-story hotel (HOTEL HIGH LONESOME, SALOON, ROOMS), a livery stable, a bath house, and at the far end of the street, a church. The first story of the church was made from stone and adobe. The spire was of weathered wood and remained standing, but crooked, like the tower of Pisa.

The town was perched on a mesa, looking out over a desert so vast it was like infinity made real. She could see, in the far distance, the immense expanse of the Jornada del Muerto, a brutally harsh desert patched in tan, red, black, and gray, running up against the mountains. It was a crisp fall day, the sky a robin's-egg blue, the air cool and refreshing. Nora was suddenly glad Corrie had talked her into this, and what was left of her irritation melted away.

"Not bad, right?" Corrie asked, brushing her short brown hair out of her face and looking around.

"Hell, no," Nora replied. And, after a pause: "This is why I love New Mexico. It's full of amazing places like this. You're lucky to have landed in the Albuquerque office."

"Think so? Albuquerque seems like such a dump."

"It has a few charms. You just have to find them. And look at the bright side—you'll never be bored, considering its sky-high crime rate, underfunded police department, and incompetent DA's office."

"Do I detect a note of disparagement?"

Nora laughed. "I'm not telling you anything that everyone in New Mexico doesn't know already."

They got back into the Navigator and drove slowly down the main street, veering right at the church. As if on cue, a conspiracy of ravens, disturbed by their arrival, flapped out of the belfry, croaking their annoyance. They passed a bedraggled schoolhouse overgrown with chamisa, surrounded by a picket fence. Reaching the end of town, they approached a building that stood off by itself, partially collapsed, its eroded adobe walls like so many rotten brown teeth. Corrie brought the car to a halt and they got out.

"I wonder what this big building was doing out here, all alone?" asked Nora.

"Whorehouse, I'll bet."

"You know," said Nora, "I actually think you're right."

Reaching into the rear seat, Nora pulled out the backpack containing her excavation tools, water, and lunch. She shouldered the backpack and breathed deeply of the fresh air. High Lonesome. If ever a place lived up to its name, this was it. Despite all the work still waiting for her at Tsankawi, this was going to be an interesting day—perhaps very interesting.

It was unlikely, she thought, that the body would turn out to be a homicide—it was probably an accident, someone who got lost and died of thirst or heat. She took a moment to examine the ruined building. Dry, split vigas lay strewn about where the roof had collapsed. A cellar door, half-buried in sand, opened on the basement, into which fresh footprints led.

"It's down through that cellar door," Corrie said, "against the far wall, partially exposed."

Nora nodded. "Okay. Let me take a look."

"Do you mind if I come down and watch? I promise to stay out of the way."

Nora hesitated. She didn't particularly like people breathing down her neck as she worked. "Looks kind of cramped down there."

"It's actually something I should do, as the agent of record on the case. If possible."

That was Corrie all over again, pushing the limit. "Okay," said Nora after a moment. "Watch out for rattlers."

She took off the backpack and pushed it through the old door, got on her hands and knees, and crawled through and then down the slope of sand. Once at the bottom, there was just enough headroom to stand up. Here and there, small holes could be seen: exploratory trenches or—more likely—the amateur relic hunter, digging for finds. As her eyes adjusted, she saw against the far wall an area where the drifting sand had been cleared away. She went over and saw an exposed skull and forearm.

"What do you think?" Corrie said, behind her.

Nora didn't answer right away. She felt a creeping sense of dismay. "Well, it's going to be quite a job. To do a proper excavation, I'd have to remove everything down to the basement floor around him. That's a lot of sand." She hesitated. "I'm not sure this is a job that can be completed in an afternoon."

"You can't just dig up the body?"

Nora sighed. People didn't seem to understand how archaeology worked. They'd seen too many Indiana Jones movies. "No. We don't just *dig up* stuff, and I thought you knew that."

Corrie looked disconcerted.

Nora went on. "You need to excavate down to what we call the 'horizon'—in this case, the cellar floor. There may be artifacts or items left on the floor around him. You have to go layer by layer—and with this loose sand, you'd have to do it with brushes."

"Okay, you're the expert."

Corrie sounded a little tense, and Nora wondered why. Probably the rookie thing again, trying to cover up her lack of self-confidence.

These sorts of explanations—of what she was doing and why—were one reason why Nora didn't like rubberneckers at a dig. But she kept this to herself. Now, eyes fully adjusted, she realized there was actually enough indirect light available, and she would not need a headlamp. She set her pack down to one side, some distance from the body, unzipped it, and laid out her equipment—Day-Glo string, stakes, measuring bar, trowel, brushes, kneepads, face mask, hair net, and nitrile gloves. She always brought extras and, as she put on hers, she nodded to Corrie.

"You too."

"Right. Of course."

Briskly, with a practiced hand, Nora measured out and set up a grid, staked it, and strung it—four square-meter quads. She took some pictures and sketched it in her notebook, then entered the data into an iPad loaded with Proficio, the archaeological software program she used for small digs like this. The program would not only record every layer and artifact in situ in three dimensions but also archive it all into a searchable database.

She took out a medium-size paintbrush and, kneeling, began to brush the sand away from the cranium. Working around the loose hair, she started uncovering the face. There was still a lot of desiccated flesh, and as she proceeded she realized this was in fact a mummy, preserved by the high desert air—and a fragile one, at that. Little pieces of flesh were barely clinging to the bone, requiring the utmost care. She felt that sense of dismay returning. This was no simple job. She worked slowly, trying to keep everything together, pausing from time to time to take pictures.

Inch by inch, the face came to light.

"Holy crap," Corrie said from over her shoulder. "Look at that face. He must have died in agony."

Nora, too, was taken aback. The man's demise was clearly written in his expression: the mouth open as if screaming, protruding tongue brown and mottled as a dried morel, desiccated lips drawn back from brown teeth in a rictus of pain and horror.

Nora worked on the remains for another hour, then sat back on her haunches and glanced at her watch. Almost two o'clock. Despite the grisliness of the task, she realized she was both hungry and thirsty.

"Lunch?" she asked Corrie.

"Okay."

Nora eased herself to a standing position, feeling her bones creak. Grabbing her lunch bag, she climbed out of the cellar and into the strong sunlight. She took a seat on a viga and removed a large roast beef sandwich, packed by her brother, Skip—they shared a house in Santa Fe, and Skip did almost all the cooking, in return for a break on the rent.

Nora took a bite and then glanced at Corrie, who was standing off to one side, looking away.

"No lunch for you?"

"No, no," Corrie said. "I'm, ah, on a diet."

Nora stared at her slim figure. "You mean, you forgot to pack one. Right?"

"Well, yeah, but don't worry. I'll be fine. I've just been a little distracted lately. You know, with work."

Nora took half of the sandwich, oozing mayonnaise and horseradish sauce, and held it out. "Here. I can't eat it all."

Hesitating, Corrie took it and sat down.

They ate in silence for a minute, and then Nora broke the news. "I hate to tell you this, but this isn't a day's worth of work. Not by a long shot."

"You can't hurry it up?"

"No," said Nora, annoyed all over again, "I can't. You yourself said you wanted it done properly. As I'm sure you've noticed, those remains are as delicate as paper."

"But... it isn't like it's a prehistoric burial. All I need to know is if it's a homicide or not."

Nora stared at her. "I'm doing you and the FBI a favor. If I'm going to do this, I've got to do it the right way—the way I know how. Okay?"

"So when can you finish?"

Nora really couldn't spare the time right now. She had to bring this to a close as gently as possible. "At the rate my own dig is going, I'd say in two weeks."

"*What!* Are you serious? My boss would have a fit."

"I don't give a damn about your boss and his fits. You've got a bigger problem."

"What's that?"

"Me. I'm up against a deadline—remember? I did you a favor, just rearranging things sufficiently to come out here today."

"I know that, and I'm grateful. But—" Corrie swept her hand toward the caved-in cellar in frustration— "you can see for yourself this is important."

Nora sighed. "It might be. It's also a four-and-a-half-hour drive from Santa Fe—nine hours round trip. And it's two o'clock already: we need to leave here in an hour, and even so I won't get home until eight. That's a lot of driving to get in three hours of work."

There was a silence.

"Here's what I propose," Nora said. "I can return to help after I've completed the dig at Tsankawi. The excavation is mostly complete, and we're moving on to documenting and stabilizing the site. I should be finished there in two to three weeks."

"Thanks," Corrie said after a moment. "But you know as well as I do that in two weeks, there's going to be nothing left here besides spade marks and boot prints."

Nora took a sip of water. She hadn't considered that, but Corrie might be right. Word could get out, or someone else might just find it. She looked around: at the remarkably preserved ghost town, at the magnificent desert view.

"You agreed to this," Corrie said. "Please finish it. You can't just leave me in the lurch."

Although Nora shook her head, Corrie's point struck home. And she had to admit; she was intrigued by that body and the expression on its face. She swore silently; she should have followed her initial instincts and said no right up front. "There is one possibility," she said slowly.

Corrie turned toward her.

"I come back tomorrow—with camping gear. That way, I can put in twelve to fourteen hours instead of three . . . and complete the work in two days." Adelsky, she thought, was ready to take charge at Tsankawi; he could deal with documenting the worksite: photography, artifact descriptions, database work. It would be good practice for him.

"Camping?" Corrie asked. "My supervisor isn't going to go for that at all."

"Well, you don't have to come. It's not as if you can help with the work, anyway."

"You can't camp out here alone!"

"I'll bring my brother. He'd love this place. And he's got a Remington twelve-gauge he's quite handy with."

"What about your dog? I couldn't allow him at the site."

"That's Mitty, Skip's dog, but he's temporarily staying with our aunt, who just lost her husband and needed companionship. Look, I can't promise. I'll have to get permission from the Institute's new president, but I think, if it's only two days, she'll be cool with it."

"But...I've *got* to be here with you. That's just the way the FBI works. I'll have to get permission, too."

"Well, hurry up and get it, then—because that's the best I can do." But even as she spoke, Nora's eyes crept back toward the cellar, and the mystery that lay within.

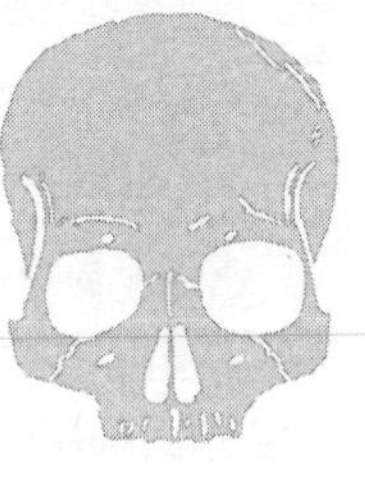

9

When Nora had called the president's office the next morning to ask about taking two days off to work for the FBI, the president's assistant had said brightly, "What a coincidence! I was just about to ring you. Dr. Weingrau wants to see you in her office at ten."

As Nora approached the hand-carved door to the president's outer office, she felt uneasy, but she wasn't sure why. Dr. Marcelle Weingrau had accepted the position after a long search by the Institute's board, following the scandalous disgrace and imprisonment of the previous president. She had arrived at the Institute only a month ago and hadn't yet introduced herself to the staff beyond a single formal meeting. Nora got the sense she was going to be a distant and chilly leader.

In her previous position, Weingrau had been a dean and professor of anthropology at Boston University, and Nora thought that maybe her formality could be chalked up to the culture of her New England background. Once out west, she might loosen up a little. Her CV had been circulated at the time of her hire, and Nora was interested to see that her PhD was in the anthropology of the Maya of the Guatemalan Highlands, where she had lived for several years, and that she was fluent in both Spanish and K'iche'. Nora had looked up some of her publications and found them respectable, if rather jargon-heavy, and she was curious to get to know her better.

"Come in and have a seat," said Dr. Weingrau's assistant. Weingrau's door was shut, but Nora could hear her talking to someone: a man with a deep voice.

Nora sat down, and a few minutes later Weingrau opened the door. "Ah, Nora, glad to see you. Come in."

Nora entered the beautiful old office. She had often been in here when it was occupied by a previous president, where it had been decorated with historic Pueblo Indian pots and Navajo rugs from the Institute's collection. But Weingrau had taken those out to make space for a wall of her diplomas, along with pictures of her among the Maya of Guatemala, interspersed with Chagall and Miró prints. While Nora liked those artists well enough, the images seemed out of place in the Spanish Colonial office.

A young man rose from a chair next to the desk.

"I wanted you to meet Dr. Connor Digby, our newest curator."

The man took a step forward. He had a square jaw and classic Ivy League good looks, with a blue blazer, khaki pants, and a repp tie to match. He held out his hand with a brilliant smile.

"Nora Kelly," she said, taking it. "Pleased to meet you, Connor." She maintained her smile. She hadn't been aware that appropriation had been made for another curatorial salary, although God knew the Institute could use the manpower.

"Connor is an authority on the Mogollon culture and did his fieldwork at the Casas Grandes site in Mexico." Weingrau continued, "Nora is our resident expert in the ancient Pueblo culture of the Southwest, and she also has extensive experience in historical archaeology, in both California and New York. I'm sure you will find you have a lot of interests in common."

"I'm sure we will," said Digby.

"Connor has just finished up working in Mexico for INAH," Weingrau said. "He'll be joining the Institute as a senior curator."

Senior curator? Suddenly things made more sense. That was her current title: if she got the promotion, that would leave an opening. So Digby would move into her current job. Did this mean she was getting the promotion? She tried to control her facial expression, remain calm and collected, not think too far ahead.

"Please, have a seat."

They sat in leather chairs on either side of Weingrau's desk.

Weingrau went on to describe Nora's work with the Institute, and then she explained to Nora in more detail Digby's experience and background, what he'd be doing, and why he'd be useful at this critical time in the Institute's history.

Nora listened, waiting to hear about her promotion and wondering to herself how the curators would feel about Digby being brought in for a senior position from the outside. But as Weingrau went on, describing how the two of them were going to collaborate, Nora began to realize that talk of the promotion might not be on this meeting's agenda, after all.

Now Weingrau was describing the office Digby was to have—next to hers, an office that had been vacant for a while. Nora would be glad, Weingrau knew, to show him around, introduce him to the others in the dirt herd, and help make space for him in the lab. She concluded: "You two will be working closely together. Not on the same projects, of course, but I imagine you'll find areas of synergy."

Smile plastered on her face, Nora nodded, careful to keep looking interested. But a new and disagreeable thought had just occurred to her. Did this mean that, instead of getting a replacement for her old job, she now had a rival for the promotion to chief? But no, that wasn't possible: even in the current political climate, promotions were largely based on merit and seniority. She had far more experience than Digby, had published a great deal more, and was at least five years older than him—she'd have to check his CV. Besides, there were her many years of service to the Institute to consider. She was just being paranoid... these days, not necessarily a bad thing.

Finally the meeting came to an end. Digby rose, shook her hand again, and went off to get a tour of the storage rooms. As Nora rose to leave, Weingrau asked, "And what was it you wanted to see me about?"

Christ, Nora had almost forgotten. "It wasn't anything really important," she said. "I went up to the site I mentioned yesterday—the one the FBI want excavated? It's way out in the Azul Mountains. It's a difficult location, and it's going to take two more days of work. Will it be all right if I complete it? Bruce Adelsky has got the Tsankawi excavation well in hand. Skip will join me, if you can spare him from the institute."

"Of course," said Weingrau. "Take the days—even more if you need them. This is just the sort of thing we should be doing to help rehabilitate our image with the community. Thank goodness," she added, "that we now have Connor to take up the slack."

Nora left the office with that last sentence ringing in her mind.

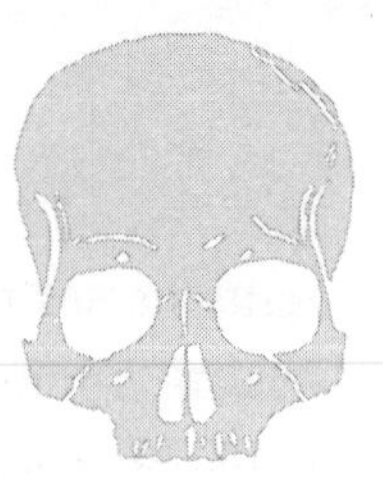

10

Corrie was surprised when Morwood readily agreed to her proposal—until it occurred to her that maybe he was just happy to get her out of the office for a couple of days. If that was the case, so be it: she'd treat this case as if it were the most important in the world, and not betray a hint of the dismay and frustration she felt. Nora had worked things out with her assistant, Adelsky, and saw to it he had a list of assignments that would keep him busy running the dig for at least a couple of days.

They had returned to the ghost town two evenings before, with all the necessary gear and food. Nora had worked from dawn until dusk the following day and had been at it again that morning at six. By sunset she'd finished uncovering the body and the surrounding basement floor. Now, at ten that night, they were sitting around a pleasant fire after consuming a well-earned steak dinner. Nora was an experienced camper, and her brother, Skip, had come along to cook, tend the camp, and provide musical entertainment. Corrie found him a decent enough guy, tall and gangly with an unruly mop of brown hair, poorly cut. He was an excellent cook, and the tents he set up were as tight as a drum. Corrie liked how he fussed around camp, making sure everything was perfect. And while his guitar strumming and renditions of old cowboy songs weren't likely to get him a recording contract, Corrie found it nice to be out there, under a bowl of stars by a dying fire, listening to unfamiliar melodies on an out-of-tune Gibson. His most endearing quality, Corrie thought, was an insatiable curiosity, and once he'd heard the story about the miners who had died trapped in the cave-in, he wouldn't rest until he'd visited the ruined cemetery, examined every tombstone, and asked dozens of questions, most of which Corrie couldn't answer.

Corrie was relieved that the excavation was finally done. Nora's painfully slow work on the corpse had almost driven her around the bend. For hours it was *brush, brush, brush*; then a few squirts of air from a finger bellows to clear away the sand; then more *brush, brush, brush*. But she knew the enormity of the favor the archaeologist was doing her and the long hours she was putting in. By the end of that day, Nora had uncovered the entirety of the body. It was a bizarre and gruesome sight, and it only deepened the mystery of what the man had been doing here and how he died. Tomorrow morning, after Nora finished documenting the site, they would remove the body and associated items, place them in evidence lockers, and drive it all back to Albuquerque. Corrie felt glad to have had these days away from the office: it was the first time since the shooting that she had felt somewhat normal. Still, she privately hoped the case would turn out to be nothing and—her penance complete—Morwood would move her on to something more relevant.

"All right," said Skip, sitting on a log before the fire, "now that we're off the clock, anyone for a little nip of sotol?" He fished a bottle out of his pack and held it up, sparkling in the firelight, giving it a little shake.

"Ugh," said Nora. "You know I can't stand that stuff."

"What's sotol?" Corrie asked.

Nora shook her head. "Trust me: just don't. Have a beer instead." She opened the cooler and pulled two Coronas from the ice, offering one to Corrie. The bottle looked tempting, with shavings of ice sliding down the frosty neck. Corrie considered whether she was, indeed, off the clock and decided she was.

She took it.

"Smart choice," said Nora, flipping the cap off her beer and taking a sip. "And, Skip, go easy on that stuff."

"I will, I will."

A silence settled as they stared into the fire.

"I wonder if the skeletons of those miners are right beneath us somewhere," Skip said at last. "That's roughly where the gold mine was—right? Think of it: a slow death of hunger and thirst. Or maybe suffocation—in pitch blackness, too." His voice lowered. "You know, people who die in awful ways like that don't stay quiet. Their spirits get... *restless*."

Nora threw her beer cap at him. "Don't start spinning one of your damned ghost stories, trying to scare us half to death."

"So," Corrie said. "Now that you've uncovered the body: What do you think?"

"Well, it doesn't look like we have a murder on our hands. Not an obvious one, anyway."

"Not obvious. But still possible?"

"It's hard to say. The fetal position of the corpse is very strange, as if he was poisoned or maybe freezing to death. Or, perhaps, hallucinating—if you look at his arm, it's almost as if he's pushing someone, or something, away."

"And that grimace," said Skip, who'd done his share of kibitzing from a distance. "A million dollars' worth of CG couldn't create a face that scary."

"We'll do a thorough workup back at the lab," Corrie said. "Toxicology, pathology, everything. If he was poisoned, we'll know."

"Maybe he died of bad taste," Skip said. "Did you get a load of that shirt he's wearing?"

Nora ignored this. "The artifacts I uncovered with the body do suggest a few possibilities for investigation."

"Such as?" Corrie asked.

"The rock hammer and folding shovel he was carrying? Looks like he might have been a prospector. I'm also curious to see what's in that satchel of his. Maybe some ID."

"We'll do a thorough inventory of his belongings at the lab," said Corrie.

Nora hesitated. "I had another idea. That canvas pack lying next to him? It isn't a backpack. It's a pannier used to pack a mule."

Skip gave a low whistle. "Are you thinking—?"

"Yes."

Corrie looked at Nora. "What is it?"

"All pack saddles have two panniers: one for each side. That means the mate to this pannier might be around here somewhere. And with it, maybe the skeleton of his mule."

Corrie shuddered. "Tomorrow, we'll search the town."

11

THEY GOT UP before sunrise—except Skip, who had overindulged in the sotol, despite Nora's warnings. As Corrie hauled herself out of her bag into the chill air, she was grateful Nora had risen earlier to build up the fire and make a pot of camp coffee. As she and Nora sat sipping the bitter brew, the sun climbed over the eastern mountaintops, throwing a lonely yellow light through the ghost town. It was like an Edward Hopper painting, Corrie thought, all long shadows and dark windows.

"Let's see if we can find our fellow's missing pannier," said Nora, setting down her empty cup. "And the bones of his ride."

"Right."

They decided to split up, Corrie taking one side of the town and Nora the other. As Corrie walked among the ruins, the ravens once again rose up and wheeled overhead, cawing and croaking. There were plenty of old fence posts and other places to tie a horse or a mule—almost too many, in fact.

And then she had an idea—why tie up a horse when you could just turn it out in a corral?

She headed over to the livery stables, and there—just as she hoped—was an old set of corrals behind the ruined building. Most of the posts lay on the ground; but half a century ago, the corral might have been intact enough to hold an animal overnight.

She went in and looked around. The corrals were overgrown with dead bunchgrass, and tumbleweeds had piled against the fences. The area was strewn with old trash—broken bottles turning purple in the sun, curling strands of barbed wire, rusted harness buckles and dried-up leather straps.

She paused. There, up against the far corner of the corral, was a patch of white. She went over and found the skull of a large animal, half-buried in sand. The remains of a leather halter were tied around it. She kicked aside some tumbleweeds and exposed more bones—the horse or mule had died at the fence. Nearby, at what had evidently been the gate of the corral, she found a piece of rotten canvas the same weight and color as the pannier in the basement. This was it, then—the missing pack animal. Some rotting clothes lay nearby, falling out of the remains of a canvas pannier.

As she poked around, she made another discovery: a coil of climbing rope and a loop of wire holding rusted pitons, chocks, and carabiners. Corrie had enough experience to recognize this immediately as rock climbing gear.

She called for Nora, who was across the way. The archaeologist came over.

"Poor thing," said Nora, peering at the scattering of bones. "What a way to die."

Corrie nodded as Nora knelt beside the bones. "Looks like we can start to reconstruct the subject's last day. He turned the mule loose in the corral and left one pannier and the saddle by the gate. He carried the other pannier back to his basement shelter. And that's where he died, evidently in agony—leaving the pack animal shut up in the corral to die as well."

"Maybe not," Nora said, as she swept away the sand that partially buried the skull.

"What do you mean?"

Nora pointed, and immediately Corrie understood. The archaeologist had uncovered the front of the skull, and in it, Corrie could see what was unmistakably a bullet hole. It had gone in the skull, but there was no exit hole.

Nora carefully shook the skull and heard a rattling sound. She peered inside and saw the bullet, distorted and flattened. "This mule was shot," she said.

"Why would he shoot his own animal?" Corrie asked.

"We don't know he did. We also don't know why he died in that strange position, all curled up. There are a lot of things here that don't make sense."

They fell quiet for a moment.

"What do you make of the climbing gear?" Corrie finally asked.

"I'll bet he was searching the old gold mine below the rim of the mesa."

Corrie nodded again. "Let's get all this stuff into evidence lockers."

By ten everything had been removed, packed, and sealed except the body itself. Skip had finally risen and cooked everyone a huge breakfast of blueberry pancakes, bacon, and eggs.

"Moving that corpse is going to be a challenge," Skip said, his mouth full of bacon. "The thing's as delicate as a butterfly's wing." He crammed another strip of bacon into his mouth and chewed noisily.

"It's going to take all three of us," said Nora.

After breakfast, they returned to the basement, bringing along a body bag and a large, coffin-like evidence locker. The man was curled up against the basement wall, dressed in an oilcloth duster worn over a checked shirt and canvas pants held up by leather suspenders. The clothes were so desiccated their edges were brown and crumbling to dust. Large sections of his skin were coming off in dry sheets. The remains of an old cowboy hat lay near his head. One hand clutched his chest and the other was thrown out as if pushing something away.

"All right," Nora said. "Here's how we're going to move the body. We're going to lay the open body bag on the floor next to it, and then the three of us will place our hands under the body and, on the count of three, lift it in one smooth motion and put it in the bag. Then we put the bag in the locker. Okay?"

Both Corrie and Skip nodded.

They slid their gloved hands underneath: Nora at the shoulders, Corrie at the hips, and Skip at the knees.

"One, two, *three.*" They raised the body up—it was remarkably light—and gently placed it on the unzipped bag.

A strange and unpleasant smell wafted up, reminiscent of very old cheese. Corrie tried to breathe through her mouth.

"Perfect," said Nora.

"Hey," said Skip. "Something fell out of his clothes." He pointed to an object lying on the plastic next to the corpse. It was about the size of a hand, wrapped in a piece of leather and tied around the middle with a thong.

Corrie bent down to look at it more closely. The leather was splitting, and she could see a gleam from inside.

"Let's open this up," she said. "Nora, you agree?"

"I don't see why not."

Corrie photographed it, and then Nora picked it up with her gloved hands. "Wow," she said, hefting it. "Heavy." She delicately picked at the leather knot, worked it open, and unfolded the stiff leaves of leather.

It revealed a spectacular golden cross, encrusted with what looked like gemstones, gleaming faintly in the gloomy light of the cellar.

"Sweet mother of *fuck*!" said Skip.

"Beautiful," Corrie murmured.

Holding it in one hand, Nora fished a loupe out of her pocket, put it to her eye, and examined it, turning the object this way and that.

"Is it real?" Skip asked.

"It's heavy," Nora said after a long moment, "and there isn't a trace of tarnish. No doubt about it—it's solid gold. The workmanship is incredible—the granulation and filigree work is so fine it's almost microscopic. And I'm pretty sure all these stones are real, as well—rubies, sapphires, emeralds, turquoise, lapis."

"Where did it come from?" Corrie asked.

Nora hesitated. "If I had to guess, I'd say Spanish colonial, probably seventeenth or eighteenth century. It's got to be one of the finest gold objects I've ever seen."

"So what's it worth?" asked Skip after another brief silence.

Nora scoffed. "You *would* ask. From an archaeological point of view, it's priceless."

"But if you *were* to sell it, what could you get?"

Nora hesitated. "I really have no idea. A hundred thousand? Half a million? This is unlike anything I've seen in a museum."

Skip whistled. "What was this old dude doing, schlepping around something like this out in the middle of nowhere?"

Damn good question, Corrie thought.

Skip suddenly grew animated. "Hey, maybe there's more treasure on him! Let's check it out!"

"*Whoa!*" said Nora sharply as Skip reached toward the body. "No searching!"

"We'll examine the remains back at the lab," Corrie said, "and if there's anything else to be discovered, we'll find it then. So let's put that gold cross into the box along with the body and get the hell back to Albuquerque. Having something like that in our possession way out here is making me really, really nervous."

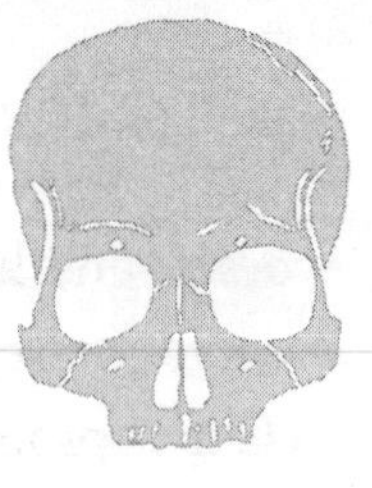

12

WELCOME TO MY pathology lab," said Nigel Lathrop, his plummy British accent filling the lab as he held open the door.

Corrie didn't much like the "my" in that sentence, but she kept a friendly smile plastered on her face as she followed him in. Morwood had dropped a couple of veiled warnings about getting along with Lathrop. The forensic pathologist had apparently been with the Albuquerque FO forever, and had acquired a reputation as a harmless eccentric of whom everyone professed to be fond. In truth, Morwood hinted he was a pain in the ass—and that one of Corrie's jobs was to win him over.

"He's a jack of all trades," Morwood had told her, "dating back to a time when forensic science wasn't so specialized. He handled the basics: a touch of fiber and hair analysis, fingerprints, some blood spatter analysis, blood typing—stuff that they wanted done fast and didn't need to be sent to a national lab." He was likely, Morwood noted, to be less than thrilled at her advanced expertise in forensic anthropology. And if he didn't like you, he could easily manage to slow things down or—

worse—find himself mystified by something easily identifiable to anyone else.

Corrie promised to get along with him at all costs. As a result, she was both curious and apprehensive as she shook the man's hand, as cool and dry as an iron railing. Lathrop was a small, lean man with a pointy gray beard, thin lips, and a springy step. He affected a hearty manner, but there wasn't much of a friendly look on his face.

They were in a drab laboratory space in the basement of the Albuquerque Field Office, surrounded by equipment that was not aging well. She followed him, edging past stacks of shipping boxes—delivered but not yet opened—and into the cramped, brightly lit operating theater. It was dominated by three rolling, guttered tables displaying the recent finds in High Lonesome: the mummified corpse, still zippered in a white body bag; another table with plastic boxes containing the mule skeleton; and a third spread with rotting artifacts.

Lathrop exchanged his tweed jacket for a white lab coat hanging from a rack. He pulled a pair of nitrile gloves from a wall holder, snapped them on, and tied on a face mask and a hair cover. Corrie followed suit.

"Well, well, what do we have here?" he said, approaching the large examination gurney. Bending over the body bag, he unzipped it swiftly and spread the opening wide, peering down with pursed lips.

"Help me transfer this."

She helped him with the bag. The mummified body was still desiccated in its fetal position, one arm raised, the other tucked underneath, covered in a duster. After they set it down, sand dribbled from cracks and fissures in its dried flesh and rotten clothing, forming little piles.

Lathrop circled the body, hands clasped behind his back, making various *hmmms* and *aaahs*.

He moved on to the other tables and glanced over the mule bones, the rotting panniers, and then paused at the cross, lying next to its former leather wrapping. He gently picked it up and turned it over, then held it up to the light.

"Impressive!" he said, laying it back down and turning to her. "Looks like I have quite a lot of work ahead. When would you like the report?"

Corrie cleared her throat. "Actually, I was expecting to work *with* you."

His eyebrows shot up. "Oh?"

Corrie suppressed a swell of annoyance. "I have a degree in forensic anthropology, which is why I was assigned to this case. Didn't Special Agent Morwood discuss this with you?"

"Ah, yes, yes! My apologies. Morwood did mention your background. I'm used to working alone, but I could always use some help. Delighted, perfectly delighted."

He seemed anything but delighted.

Corrie reminded herself that, even though as a special agent she outranked Lathrop, he was a veteran of the Albuquerque office, and she was a rookie... and one who had recently fucked up. It would not do to get into a pissing contest with him about who was in charge, especially given Morwood's warning.

"Well, this is a delicious little problem, isn't it?" Lathrop rubbed his hands together and smacked his lips, as if about to commence a meal, as he circled the gurney with the body. He was, she felt, genuinely fascinated: he was no burned-out case going through the motions.

"Let's get to work," he said. "I'll start on the body while you examine the artifactual evidence."

"My specialty," Corrie said, trying to muster some authority in her voice without sounding bitchy, "was biological anthropology. Perhaps it would be appropriate if I worked on the actual human remains, as well?"

Lathrop frowned. "I suppose so."

"But first," Corrie said, "would you suggest we look at the X-rays?"

"Naturally." Lathrop turned on the flat-panel screen and, tapping away at a keyboard, called up the X-rays. A silence settled in the room as they examined the images, grid by grid, starting with the skull. Corrie had wanted to do a CT scan, but Morwood had vetoed it because of the expense and the fact that there was as yet no official case.

"No dental work," said Lathrop. "Thus no dental records to help with identification. Pity."

Corrie tried to focus on the images. In her forensic training, she had been dismayed at how easily you could miss something that became glaringly obvious when it was pointed out. She was determined not to overlook anything Lathrop might notice, primarily because she didn't want him lording it over her.

"Look at that," Corrie said. "Isn't that a faint closed fracture in the frontal bone, and another in the sphenoid?"

"I see them," said Lathrop, manipulating the images to magnify and increase contrast. "Yes, indeed: very faint but distinct."

They moved on down the body.

"And here, too," Corrie said, pointing to a rib. "Another small fracture."

Lathrop peered in and magnified it.

"I see no sign of the formation of a fibrocartilaginous callus," said Corrie. "Seems to have occurred perimortem."

Lathrop grunted his assent.

"Look, another one," said Corrie. "And another. Anterior four, five, and six. Do you see?"

No sound from Lathrop.

"All these fractures are anterior," Corrie said, excited despite herself. "And perimortem. Looks like maybe he had a fall right before his death. What do you think?"

"Shall we wait for the physical examination before drawing conclusions?" said Lathrop, lips pursed, a sarcastic prickliness in his voice.

Corrie swallowed hard and pushed down on her irritation.

After completing the X-ray examination in silence, Lathrop turned to Corrie. "Let me show you how to set up the video recorder," he said, "for the gross examination."

This is better, Corrie thought. She watched as he turned on the video system and tested it, memorizing the process.

"Now we start work," said Lathrop. "We both speak the date, time, and location, and give our names and titles. And then, as we work, we say out loud what it is that we're doing. Are you clear on that, young lady, or would you like me to repeat?"

"I'm clear." She had practiced all this many times in her pathology classes at the John Jay College of Criminal Justice. Only at John Jay they had better equipment.

They started working on the body, one on each side. Lathrop began cutting off the duster while Corrie helped, snipping up one sleeve and down the front, so it could be removed in pieces without disturbing the brittle body. The duster was then folded up in an evidence container and sealed.

"A brown stain is noted," said Lathrop, "on the front of the shirt. There is more staining around the nose. It would appear the subject had a severe nosebleed not long before death."

Corrie was about to say that was more evidence of a fall but decided to refrain from commenting. She kept silent and let Lathrop do most of the talking for the tape recorder. After examining and photographing the bloodstains, they cut off the shirt, undershirt, and pants, again sealing them up in evidence containers. The boots were tricky, having shrunk and warped, and they had to be snipped off with great care. Even then, a piece of foot broke off, adhering to the boot, and had to be teased away from the leather.

Corrie was secretly hoping to find more treasure hidden in the clothes, a wallet or some sort of ID, but nothing came to light beyond some small change in the man's pocket. She removed the coins and laid them out: two quarters, five nickels, and four pennies. Lathrop went to put them in a container, but Corrie spoke.

"Shall we get the dates?"

Lathrop paused while Corrie sorted through the coins and jotted down the dates, which ranged from 1922 to 1945. That latter date was on an almost uncirculated penny, which she thought significant.

"Looks like a *terminus post quem* of 1945," said Lathrop, examining the penny with a loupe.

"He must have died in 1945 or later, but not earlier," said Corrie.

"My dear, that's what *terminus post quem* means," said Lathrop, peering down at her like a disappointed professor.

Asshole, thought Corrie, with a smile. Had she been daydreaming when that was covered in her John Jay lectures? She'd have to Google and memorize the damn term so as not to be caught again.

The body now lay naked and exposed. As she peered into the abdominal cavity, she noted that a rodent had built a nest there, lining it with grass and bits of cotton.

"Snug little cottage," said Lathrop, "with loads of hygge." He gingerly removed the nest in a single piece and placed it in an evidence container.

Corrie had no idea what "hygge" was, but wasn't about to ask. "We're especially interested in toxicology and pathology results," she said. "Particularly in light of the man's, ah, facial expression and position, which might suggest poisoning. I'd like to recommend we remove the stomach, liver, and kidneys for analysis."

"Noted," said Lathrop. He reached in and began snipping and crackling around in the abdomen while Corrie stepped back. Soon he had removed the organs in question, shriveled up like ancient apples. They went into separate containers.

"And a hair sample, please," said Corrie.

Snip, snip, and what small amount of hair still existed on the man's head went into a test tube.

"Do you need the heart, brain, or lungs?" asked Lathrop.

"Not at this point. In fact, I'd like to stop the autopsy now, if you don't mind, to keep the body as intact as possible for a CT scan later—on the chance this becomes an official case."

"Very well." Lathrop covered the body with a plastic sheet and arranged and labeled the evidence containers, while Corrie sorted through the man's effects and began picking them apart and laying them out. There was some more clothing, a soot-stained pot and dented frying pan, a grill, old matches wrapped in oilcloth, a split can of condensed milk and a few swollen cans of beans, a tin of Spam split open with a dottle of desiccated meat still inside, a broken compass, a can opener, a pocketknife, two empty two-quart canteens, and a hip flask of Rich & Rare Canadian Whisky, also empty. But no notebook, maps, ID—or treasure; nothing to indicate what the man had been doing. It all went into labeled evidence containers, and she moved on to the mule skeleton, which had been heaped into a large box. Unlike the person, the animal had not been mummified, probably because it was out in the open. She pulled out the skull, along with the bullet she'd retrieved from inside the cranial cavity that had caused the animal's death—a .22, sealed in an envelope bag—and placed them both on a gurney.

"Horse or mule?" Lathrop said, advancing with eyebrows raised as if he were administering a quiz.

"I always assumed a mule, but I actually have no idea," Corrie said.

At this Lathrop brightened. His frown vanished, and he leaned down to examine the skull, picking it up and viewing it from different directions, squinting at it first with one eye and then with the other.

"We had a case here some thirty years ago," he said. "A man stole a mule and was pursued and killed by the mule's owner. The animal was also killed in the fight. This happened deep in the Sandia Mountains, and the skeletons weren't found for twenty years. The man's skeleton couldn't be identified, but it was suspected it might be the mule thief. For that reason it was a significant clue to know whether the victim had been riding a horse or a mule. I undertook a little research project—a quantitative comparison of horse and mule skulls. It was something no one had done before—forensically, that is."

"How did you do it?"

"I got my hands on several dozen horse and mule skulls and took various measurements, then drew up a list of averages for each species. With that we were able to determine that the skull was indeed that of a mule—which was instrumental in solving the case."

"Clever," said Corrie.

"Now watch as I apply that data to our skull—sadly perforated, I see, but no less useful for that."

He rummaged in a drawer and brought out a pair of calipers, then began taking measurements along various parts of the skull, jotting them down on a piece of paper. This concluded, he brought out an old notebook and compared the measurements to others in the notebook. Clearly, Corrie thought, this re-creation of his long-vanished triumph had gone a long way toward dissipating his sour mood.

"Aha!" he said, interrupting her thoughts. "Now I know what animal this is." He paused dramatically, the point of his beard thrust forward.

"Which is it?"

"Neither."

Corrie paused. "Neither? What is it, then? A donkey?"

"A hinnie."

"A . . . what's a hinnie?"

"Well," said Lathrop, adopting the tone of the lecture hall, "in point of fact a mule is a cross between a mare and a jack donkey. A hinnie is a cross between a stallion and a jenny donkey. Hinnies are smaller than mules, more donkey-like than horse-like. This is definitely a hinnie."

Corrie couldn't imagine a duller taxonomic factoid than this. But Lathrop's beard was almost quivering with triumph, and realizing this was her opportunity she quickly seized it. "That's remarkable! I've never heard of such a creature. Have you published your research?"

"I've been working on a little paper for the *Forensic Examiner*. You know, just a note—nothing of any great importance." The tone of his voice belied the self-deprecation.

"I'm sure they'd love to read a story on your findings."

"The article just needs a bit of an edit, that's all. Another pair of eyes."

"I'd be happy to, ah, look it over—if you'd like."

"I say—really? That would be first-rate! I'll bring it in. And now, let's continue our perusal of the gentleman and his *hinnie.*"

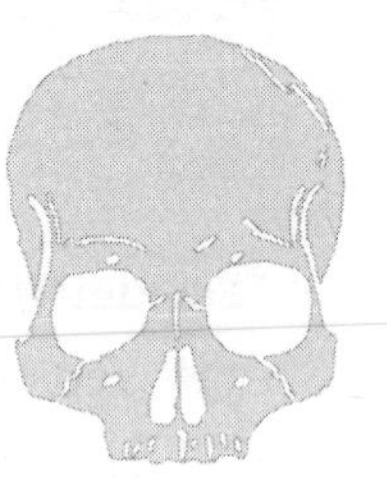

13

MORWOOD SAT ON the edge of his desk, arms crossed, his tie pulled down, top button unbuttoned—apparently, Corrie thought, his idea of Casual Friday. She noticed her report sitting on the desk beside him.

"Please, sit down."

Corrie took a seat, hoping her nervousness wasn't too obvious.

"I read through your report and found it quite interesting," Morwood said. "After giving it some thought, and conferring with the SAC, I think we're going to follow your recommendation and declare this an official case." He smiled.

"Thank you, sir. Thank you."

"That's two thank-yous too many," said Morwood. "This is not a favor. Even if I am putting you in charge."

Corrie bit off another *thank you*.

"We don't know if we're dealing with a homicide or not, but what we do know is that this gold cross is valuable, and as you point out in the report, the likelihood of it being stolen property is high."

"Yes, sir."

"I understand you've developed a working relationship with Sheriff Watts."

"Yes, sir. I think he'll be easy to work with."

"Good, good. As I've repeated ad infinitum, getting along with local law enforcement is always a top priority."

Because Corrie was still in the two-year probationary period for a new special agent, Morwood, her supervisor, was "ghosting" her as she worked her first cases. He now switched into mentoring mode, Socratic style. "What are your thoughts on how the investigation should proceed?"

"I'd like to turn the cross over to Dr. Kelly at the Santa Fe Archaeological Institute for a detailed analysis and possibly even an ID—if it was ever reported stolen."

Morwood nodded. "Good."

"Now that it's a case, do you think we could do a CT scan of the corpse? As noted in the report, we found evidence of injuries sustained at the time of death—fractured skull and ribs, a bloody nose. It doesn't seem nearly enough to be a cause of death, but there may be more injuries a scan will bring to light."

"You have my permission to proceed."

"And we need to identify the body. There was no ID with it, and no dental work. We could order DNA testing, although with a seventy-five-year-old corpse we're not likely to find any on file. We might get genealogical matches, but that can take months and it's a shot in the dark at best."

"As you well know," Morwood replied.

Corrie didn't respond to this veiled reference to her last—and to date only—big case. "Fingerprints are a possibility. There are a couple of techniques I learned at John Jay, which would require amputation of the fingers."

"Very good."

"If all else fails, I'll do a forensic facial reconstruction." She added, "It was one of my specialties at John Jay."

Another nod. "And now, what are your thoughts about the site?"

"What about it?"

"Don't you think it needs to be further searched?"

"The whole ghost town?"

Morwood waited.

"I suppose so." Corrie didn't like the idea, although she wasn't sure why.

"The man was carrying a valuable gold object. There may be more treasure hidden somewhere nearby. What would you think about calling in a field ERT?"

"Good idea, sir."

"All right, then. And..." Morwood's voice lowered. "How are *you* doing? I mean with regard to the Sandia shooting."

She colored. "I'm doing fine, thank you."

"Your first shooting is always tough, even if you didn't fire the, ah, fatal shot."

"Actually, sir, it's my second shooting. And that's the problem: that I didn't fire the fatal shot, I mean. I missed."

She realized Morwood was looking at her curiously. "You didn't actually miss, you know. You knocked him back with a shot to the shoulder, which allowed the other agents to rush in and take him down. His wild shot was purely random."

"If I'd hit him where I intended, there wouldn't have been a wild shot."

"True," said Morwood. "But that can be fixed by more time at the range, which I note you're already spending."

And then he paused. "Well?"

"Well what, sir?"

"Aren't you going to challenge that last observation?"

Corrie frowned. "I . . . I don't think I understand."

"You've had a quick comeback for every other attempt I've just made to lighten your guilt. That tells me you've been thinking about it—and a lot more than you should. I'm going to give you an assignment, and you might find it a difficult one. I can summarize it in two words: *don't brood*." He looked at her, hard. "Are we clear, Agent Swanson?"

"Clear as crystal, sir."

Morwood grunted. Then he slid off the desk, signaling the end of the meeting, and Corrie rose as well.

"At our weekly meeting, I'd like you to present your case to the office. It's got some unusual aspects to it the other agents would be interested in hearing about." He paused. "And if she learns anything of relevance, feel free to bring Dr. Kelly in to talk about that gold cross."

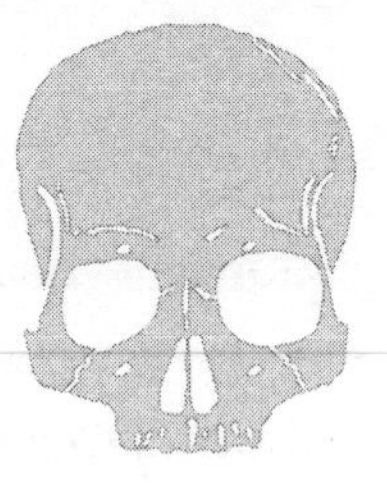

14

Specialist Brad Huckey, head of the Albuquerque Evidence Response Team, stepped out of the ERT van and transferred his shades from his Dallas Cowboys cap to the bridge of his nose in order to survey the area without getting blinded. The ERT photographer, Milt Alfieri, and a second crime scene investigator, Don Ketterman, climbed out and stood beside him, looking around.

"Wow," said Alfieri. "Could be a movie set."

The special agent in charge of the case was arriving in a separate vehicle, a Jeep Cherokee belonging to the Socorro County Sheriff's Office. It parked to one side, and the agent—it could only be the agent—got out of the passenger side, the sheriff getting out the other, wearing a big silver star.

Huckey could hardly believe his eyes. He'd never seen an agent so young. What the hell was the FBI coming to, hiring women like this who probably couldn't do five push-ups? One of those affirmative action hires, for sure. But at least she wasn't hard to look at.

He turned to Alfieri and gave a low whistle. "Check that out."

The special agent came over, pale skin and brown hair in a

short cut, along with the sheriff, who looked almost as young as she was. One of his ears was bandaged. He was a real piece of work, too—sporting six-guns on both hips.

The agent stuck out her hand, which—he noticed—was missing the end of one finger. "Corinne Swanson."

"Brad Huckey."

"Milt Alfieri."

"Don Ketterman."

"Homer Watts."

Homer. What a name. Huckey almost expected to see a piece of straw sticking out of the guy's bandaged ear. Looking at those guns, Huckey wondered if he'd heard of the internet. Or even electricity.

They all stood around in the sun shaking hands while ravens circled and croaked overhead.

"Thanks for coming all this way," said Swanson. "Not exactly the best road in the state."

"I'll say," said Huckey. "So where's the crime scene?"

She pointed to a ruined building just beyond the town. "The body was found in the basement. We're not sure yet if it's actually a crime scene, though."

Huckey's two associates began unloading their equipment. "Any idea what the building was?" he asked.

"Pretty sure it was a house of ill repute," said Watts.

Huckey gave a laugh. "Not much of a whorehouse, if you ask me. So what's the history of this town, Homer?"

Watts removed his cowboy hat, gave his brow a swipe with his forearm, and fitted it back on. "It was a hopping little place for a while, when the gold mine was producing. But then the gold started petering out; there was a cave-in with lots of victims, and the town was abandoned shortly afterward."

"Victims, you say?"

"A dozen men. Trapped inside."

Huckey nodded. He'd always had an amateur interest in gold mining. When this was over, it would probably be worth coming back here for a look-see. There might well be valuable antique or curio stuff here, ripe for the taking. And, given his day job, he was an expert at finding just that kind of shit. Take that old well, for example, in the shadow of what looked like the remains of a stable—people had no idea how many valuables got lost down a well. This one, of course, hadn't seen a bucket in probably a hundred years.

They walked to the ruined whorehouse and stopped at the entrance to the basement. It was half-blocked with sand. Huckey crouched and looked in, shining a light around.

"Hey, Corinne," he said, "give me the rundown here."

Swanson crouched next to him. "The body was over there against the far wall," she said. "You can see the excavated area. We've already removed and screened most of the sand."

Huckey turned. "Don, let's set up and rescreen it all—just in case."

He grabbed a shovel and descended, Milt following. Ketterman handed down shovels, a saw, a sledgehammer, and a screen on a frame. Huckey unfolded the screen.

"You guys, just shovel all this shit from one side to the other, through the screen."

Huckey pulled on a face mask and got to work, shoveling and tossing each shovelful through the screen. Dust rose up. He was damned glad it was a cool fall day; in the summer it would be hell down in that whorehouse basement. As the fine, dry sand fell through the screen, a bunch of stuff bounced up—broken bottles, cheap flatware, buttons, tobacco tins, nails—but it was all worthless, nothing contemporaneous with the body.

Suddenly, a bone bounced off the screen.

"Whoa there," said Huckey. He went over and picked it up, turning it over. "Look what we got here! A humerus!" He glanced over to where the FBI agent was watching them, at the cellar door. "Looks like you missed one," he called up, waving the bone at her.

She slid down the sand and came over, slipping on nitrile gloves. He handed it to her. She looked at it for a moment. "Um, I believe that's a sheep's tibia."

Huckey stared at her for a moment. Unbelievable, this FBI agent. He leaned back and let out a belly laugh. "A sheep's tibia? Are you shitting me? I've been identifying bones my entire life and, trust me, I know a human humerus when I see one." He turned. "Alfieri, bag that as evidence." He flipped it to Alfieri, who caught it and put it in a Ziploc bag, labeling it with a Sharpie.

Huckey turned back to the FBI girl with a grin. "Sheep's tibia, my ass."

She looked like she was about to talk back, but she managed to button it up—and good for her. It was her own damn fault she'd made herself look like an idiot.

"Okay, we're going to keep going. If you don't mind, we need some elbow room down here."

The agent stalked out, positioning herself once again in the doorway to watch them work.

In an hour they had finished with the sand, finding nothing else of interest. Huckey cast his eye around for places where something might have been hidden. Most of his work on the ERT involved bashing down walls, ripping out ceilings, and tearing apart furniture and cars, looking for drugs or money. But be the setting new or old, he had a sixth sense for where stuff was hidden—and it never failed him.

"Let's have a look in that." He pointed to a big coal stove in the corner, once used to heat the place. He tried to open the metal door, but it was rusted shut.

"Bring over the sledgehammer."

Ketterman came over, his sleeves rolled up, carrying the implement.

"Bust that open."

Ketterman loved bashing in stuff, and a few well-timed blows smashed the cast-iron top. Huckey knelt and, pulling out the iron pieces, sorted through the interior, finding nothing. He looked around. Where else might someone have hidden things in 1945?

"Something got walled up here," he said, pointing to an area where the adobe bricks had covered an opening.

Ketterman ditched the sledgehammer for a Pulaski and swung the spike side of it into the wall. A few blows busted through the adobe, revealing a space.

Huckey shined the light in, but there was nothing there but an old root cellar with broken mason jars.

A voice came down. "Excuse me?"

Huckey turned to see Swanson peering down through the open door.

"Yes?"

"What are you doing?"

"What does it look like? We're searching."

"Is it necessary to break things up like that?"

Huckey stared at her. "What do you mean?"

"This is a historic site."

"Jesus Christ," he said. "We're feds; we're searching a crime scene. This is how it's done."

The face vanished. Huckey shook his head, wondering why the hell she was so concerned about a ruined whorehouse. He couldn't believe what kind of agents they were minting these days.

They next chopped into a small closet, finding nothing.

"Let's go to the first floor."

Crawling out of the basement, they ducked through the ruined doorway into the ground floor. The ceiling had partially caved in, but there was still quite a lot to search.

"Watch out for the rotten floor," Huckey warned.

It was a pretty lame whorehouse, he felt, with a single sitting room, a bar, some busted chairs and tables, a lot of broken whiskey bottles and glasses, and an ancient upright piano. A staircase went up to the sky, the second floor having completely fallen in.

The piano was an obvious place to hide something. He nodded at it. "Hey, Don, make some music, will you?"

Ketterman, still wielding the Pulaski, walked over and, taking aim, gave it a tremendous blow in the side, at the joint. It made a huge jangling noise. He hit it again and again, the side piece finally breaking loose. He looked in with a flashlight.

"Wait a damn minute," said Watts, the sheriff, standing in the door, that FBI girl behind him. "What the hell are you doing?"

"What does it look like?" Huckey was now thoroughly annoyed at this kibitzing.

"This isn't some meth kitchen," said Watts. "Have a little respect."

"Yeah, we could unscrew and take apart that piano and be here all week, but that isn't how we operate. We do this all the time, and nobody's going to play 'Chopsticks' on this shit piano again."

"This is a remarkably well-preserved ghost town, and it shouldn't be damaged any more than necessary. Just because it's federal land and you're feds doesn't mean you can do whatever you please."

"Let me explain something to you, *Homer*," said Huckey. "You've got your jurisdiction. I've got mine. I'm head of this FBI Evidence Response Team, and this is how we do things. You aren't the first to complain, okay? Nobody likes to see their shit smashed up. But this is how it's done. Why don't you go play with your six-shooters?" He scoffed. "Shit, the double-stack magazines in my Sig hold more rounds than your whole rig."

"If you shoot it right, it only takes one," the kid copper replied.

They stared at each other a moment in silence.

"But given your concern," Huckey said, suddenly going easy on the guy, "We'll be gentle with the piano. Right, Don? Go easy on the piano. What's left of it, anyway."

"Right."

They moved through the rooms, pulling up floorboards and breaking through lathe and plaster in areas where something might be hidden. But there was nothing. Huckey didn't like the way Swanson and Watts followed them around, monitoring what they were doing. And all this after having to get up at four in the morning, with a hangover no less, to get down here.

"Let's check the shitter," Huckey said.

It stood behind the ruins, a crooked rectangle against the blue sky. Ketterman went in with the Pulaski. With a few blows he knocked out the rotten foundation and toppled the thing like a tree, exposing a hole below, partly filled with sand.

"Gotta dig it out."

With the screen set up, they started digging. No actual crap was left, just sand and dirt, but as they shoveled, some interesting things appeared on the screen—some coins, a bunch of broken whiskey bottles, a pair of glasses—and then, suddenly, the gleam of gold.

"Hey, check this out!" Ketterman held it up while Alfieri photographed. It was a single Indian head gold piece.

Swanson and Watts came over.

"From 1908," said Huckey, taking it. "Looks like someone dropped it in the shit pile."

"We should put that into evidence," said Swanson, "even though it's probably not connected to the body."

Huckey put it in an evidence container and sealed it. Damn, he was going to come back here and really turn the place over. In fact, might be a good idea to pull back on the official search in order to leave some good stuff for later. He wished to hell he hadn't searched the shitter with all these people around.

"Now for the rest of the town. We can do this quickly—and, out of respect for your wishes, as gently as possible."

"Thank you," said the sheriff.

Huckey didn't answer. "Show us where the mule skeleton and saddle were found."

Swanson brought them over to the livery stables. Huckey could see where the mule bones had been dug from the ground. They set up a screen, and Ketterman began shoveling all around and tossing the dirt on the screen. More useless crap showed up, along with some bones.

Huckey held one up. "Another sheep?" he asked Swanson with a grin.

"No, that's a mule."

He tossed the bone away. "At least you got that one right."

They went through the rest of the town from one end to the other, photographing every room and searching the more obvious places, but nothing of note came to light. This time, Huckey made sure they didn't look too hard.

They ended up back at the van. Huckey consulted the search order. They were coming to the interesting part: the search of the gold mine below the mesa.

"Says here," Huckey read from the ERT outline—the one Swanson herself had written—"that the body was found with climbing and rappelling equipment. So they think he may have been down in the mine, or planning to go down. Also says here... Wait a minute. I'm going down with Swanson?"

"That's what it says," the girl said.

"Who the hell decided that?"

"I did. You did bring the gear, right?"

Huckey stared. "Sure, I brought the gear, but I thought Don and I were going to use it. You know how to rappel?"

Swanson nodded.

Huckey tried to hide his annoyance. "Well, I'll be damned. Okay, let's get the gear and have at it."

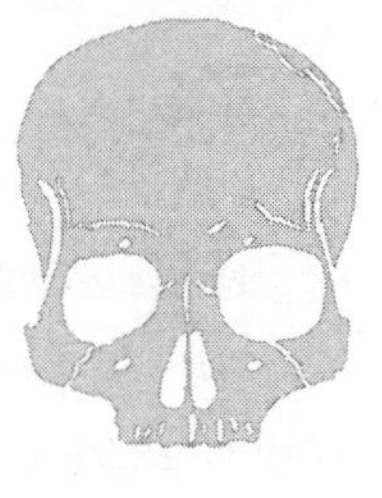

15

THE GOLD CROSS lay in a plastic tray lined with black velvet, below a stereo zoom microscope set at low power. Nora was moving the stage around, examining the cross. Orlando Chavez entered, his gray hair swept dramatically back from his patrician face, tumbling almost to his shoulders. A tweed jacket and a bolo tie with a chunk of turquoise heavy enough to sink a body announced him as both a professor and a westerner. Chavez was the Institute's expert in Spanish colonial history, and he was by far Nora's favorite person in the entire place. She had known him ever since she was a graduate student working on her dissertation.

"My, my," he said, smacking his lips as if contemplating a beautiful piece of cake. "How is it you're always in the thick of every ruckus around here? Let's have a look."

Nora yielded the eyepieces. He peered in, bushy eyebrows moving comically as he stared. Nora waited as he moved the stage around, examining the cross with minute attention.

"May I turn it over?" he asked.

"If you don't mind, I'll handle it. The FBI gave me strict

protocols." She pulled on nitrile gloves, turned the cross over, and peeled the gloves off, dropping them in the trash. She hated wearing those gloves.

More minutes of staring. Finally, Chavez eased back from the eyepieces, blinking, and expelled a breath of air.

"What do you think?"

"Well..." He fitted his thick black-framed glasses on once more and rolled back the chair. "Remarkable."

Nora waited. Chavez always liked to draw things out.

"Based on the style, technique, workmanship, design, and so forth, I'd say this cross was made in Mexico City and brought up into New Mexico via the Camino Real for use in a mission church. It probably dates back to before the Pueblo Revolt of 1680."

"Any evidence it's stolen property? That was something the FBI agent wanted to know."

"I would have known if a Spanish colonial artifact of this quality was stolen in recent times. But I've never seen it before. So I'd say probably not."

"What is it worth? The FBI wanted to know that, too."

"It's exceptionally fine work for its age. Historically it's of great value. I would say on the open market you could get at least a hundred thousand dollars for an artifact like this."

Nora whistled. "What else can you tell me about its history?"

Chavez smoothed his hair back with a knotted hand. "You probably noticed the cross is heavily worn."

"I did."

"Most mission artifacts aren't, you know. This was carried around a great deal. Maybe it belonged to a traveling friar as a personal holy relic. Or it traveled a lot for some other reason."

"And the gemstones? What can you tell me about them?"

He looked back into the stereo zoom. "The stones are beautiful but crudely finished. That's one reason why I say it's pre-Revolt. It looks to me like there's an emerald, some turquoises, a gorgeous jade, jasper, and a pigeon blood garnet of amazing quality. I would guess they are all of New World origin."

"Where did our man get it?"

Chavez shook his head. "It might have belonged to an old Spanish family. A Christian Indian might have hidden it during the Pueblo Revolt and it passed down secretly through his family—that's been documented. Quite a few Indians continued to practice in secret as Christians after the Revolt. In fact, many pre-Revolt religious items survive today in the Pueblos, closely guarded in the kivas."

At that moment, Nora felt a presence behind them and turned to see Connor Digby enter the lab. He greeted them and came over. "I heard about the amazing find. Mind if I take a look?"

"Of course not," said Nora, getting up from the chair so he could sit down. Digby had gotten rid of the blue blazer and repp tie pretty quickly, and now wore a casual jacket and open-necked shirt. Since his hire he'd been quiet and unobtrusive, getting his office in order, moving in his books and journals, and in general keeping a low profile. He had been friendly and quite deferential to Nora. He struck her as a genuinely nice guy who wanted to fit in and get along with everyone.

Digby peered through the eyepieces and gave a low whistle. "That is *something*. How old is it?"

"Pre-Revolt," said Chavez. "I would guess at least four hundred years old."

"Amazing." Digby got up. "Sorry to interrupt, but I just had to see what all the fuss was about. I'll get out of your hair now."

"No worries," said Nora, taking the seat again as Digby left.

She turned to Chavez. "Anything else I should tell the FBI in my report?"

Chavez pursed his lips. "Can you get them to donate it to the Institute after they're done with it?"

Nora frowned. The question of ownership of the cross hadn't occurred to her before. "Unless it's stolen," she said, "I imagine it belongs to the man's descendants."

"Ah, right, of course. Well, there's one other thing I wanted to show you. Turn it over again, might you?"

Nora complied.

"You see those stamps?"

Nora looked. There were indeed two sort of rounded stamp marks in the soft gold, symbols of some kind, almost worn away.

"Those are probably assay or fineness marks—if you could get a clear picture for me, blown up, I'll look into them. That should be most helpful in determining its date and provenance."

And he emphasized this observation with a furrowing of his bushy eyebrows.

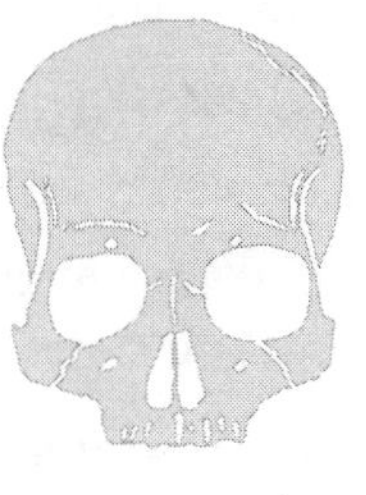

16

Corrie watched as Huckey dumped a pack loaded with rappelling gear at the edge of the mesa. He unzipped it and started pulling stuff out—two harnesses, rope, carabiners, belay and jumar devices. It was good equipment, most of it brand-new. A precipitous road had once descended from the rimrock to the canyon, but it was long gone in a series of landslides, leaving no way down except by rope. She could see, about seventy feet below, a huge pile of tailings forming a flat landing area, where the mine entrance was.

She stepped into the harness, clipped on the carabiners and descender, put on gloves and helmet. She watched as Huckey anchored the line to a massive juniper at the edge of the cliff and made sure he fixed the rope correctly. She didn't trust him at all and was determined to double-check everything he did.

The descent was a vertical face of hard igneous rock. They would land on top of the tailings pile, next to a rickety shaft house and cart tracks going out to the tip at the end of the platform.

"We're going to rappel down," said Huckey, "and jumar back up. You sure you know how to do that?"

"Yes," said Corrie. She had learned the basics in an elective course at Quantico and taken a couple of climbing courses in Albuquerque since, figuring it would be a useful skill. Now she was glad she had—although she wasn't exactly thrilled about having to partner with Huckey.

Morwood's words about getting along with everyone rang in her mind. Working with this jackass was a test she was determined to pass.

Huckey went first, and she saw, to her relief, that he did indeed know exactly what he was doing. In fact, he was so expert at it that she figured he must be ex-military. He certainly had the build. Maybe this wouldn't be so bad after all.

When he reached the bottom and detached, he signaled and she started down. A few minutes later, they both stood in front of the mine entrance.

"So you think the guy explored, or intended to explore, this mine?" Huckey asked.

"I do."

"Well, let's see if we can find what he was looking for. Maybe he was trying to get to the bodies of those miners."

They both put on headlamps and entered the tunnel. Huckey went first, and Corrie followed. It was a crude horizontal passageway drilled and blasted straight into the rock, with no timbering or bracing. A set of rails for ore carts ran down the middle.

"Imagine," Huckey said. "Trapped by a cave-in. No food, no light, no air. I wonder what got them first." He sniffed. "At least it doesn't stink in here. I was afraid it might smell like beef jerky." He snickered.

"A dozen men lost their lives," Corrie said. "Have a little respect."

Huckey muttered something under his breath, but his speculations on the fate of the miners ceased.

About fifty feet in, the natural light started dimming. Huckey stopped and shined his light around on the floor, covered with wind-blown sand and dust.

"I don't see any footprints. Doesn't look like anybody's been in here for a long, long time," he said.

Corrie nodded, then paused to take a few pictures with her FBI-issued camera.

They moved forward, Corrie stopping every few minutes to take photographs. Aside from the tracks, the tunnel was empty, until after about a hundred yards they came across a derailed wooden and iron cart, half full of rocks. Corrie took another series of photos and collected two samples of rock for analysis. Beyond the cart stood a rusted iron machine outfitted with a cylindrical hammer, screw, and lever.

"Bet you've never seen one of those before," Huckey said.

"What is it?"

"Portable ore crusher. You put a big piece of rock in there, turn the screw, and break it into pieces that can be lifted and sorted more easily."

"Right."

They went deeper, moving slowly. The air seemed to get colder and thicker, and the only light was now their headlamps: a gradual turn in the tunnel had put the entrance out of sight. They continued down the tunnel for another hundred yards or so before arriving at a massive cave-in. Here and there, Corrie could see the remnants of what looked like fruitless, almost pitiful attempts to dig past it.

She stared at the pile of wood and broken stone, at the collapsed ceiling, recalling what Fountain, the lawyer, had said back at the High Lonesome graveyard. The bodies, she knew, must still lie somewhere behind this rubble. Even though they were deep in the horizontal shaft, a chill wind seemed to stir her hair, and she shivered in the close and listening dark.

"Guess the jerky's beyond that rockfall," Huckey said. She could see him glancing sideways at her, waiting for a reaction.

She took a deep breath and managed to stay silent.

"Uh-oh." Huckey's flashlight illuminated a rotting wooden box, stenciled with ATLAS MINING CO. on the side, followed by TNT.

"This is probably the cause of that cave-in," Huckey said. "It's a cinch they wouldn't have tried using it to free the miners—that would have just made things worse."

He leaned over and gave the box lid a nudge with his foot. It came off, exposing decayed wax-covered sticks and bundles of wire.

"Jesus," said Corrie, taking a step back.

"Watch out," said Huckey, glancing at her. "It could go off at any moment. Let me move it."

"Wait...you're going to pick it up? I don't think that's a good idea—"

But Huckey was already hoisting the rotten box. Gripping it in both arms, he stomped across the ground past her...and then tripped on a rock, dropping the box at Corrie's feet. With a crash of splintering wood, sticks of TNT flew everywhere.

Corrie leapt back with a scream, falling in her panic to get away and ending up with her ass in the sand and her back against the fallen rubble—only to hear Huckey laughing uproariously amid the rising cloud of dust.

"What the *fuck*!" she yelled.

Huckey was laughing so hard it took him a moment to get enough breath to speak. "You should have seen the expression on your face when I dropped that box! You looked like a sheep struck by lightning!" He gasped and roared, doubling over. "I figured you didn't know squat about TNT—and obviously I figured right. That stuff isn't like dynamite; it won't go off without a blasting cap. And the older it gets, the more inert it becomes. Sure you don't want to spend another year or two at the Academy before venturing out here into the field, *Corinne*?"

Corrie steadied herself and got to her feet, the manic pounding of her heart quickly dying down, her terror rapidly replaced by an anger that could no longer be contained. She turned to face Huckey. "You bastard," she said.

"Hey, I was just having a little fun. Come on—because you're in the FBI, you aren't allowed to take a joke? If you're going to hang with the guys, you'd better get used to a little ribbing."

"The *guys*?" Corrie replied. "You mean, the ones with a dick between their legs? 'Cause that sure doesn't apply to you. Only a dickless wonder would find that schoolboy prank so hilarious, especially in a setting like this. You're pissed because I pointed out that bone you found was from a sheep—which it is—and you can't stand a woman showing you up. *You're* the one who'd better get used to it, because I'm going to be director of the FBI when your paleo-troglodyte ass is still digging up ancient shit piles and bashing down walls."

While she was busy ripping him a new one, Huckey's face had gone very, very pale. She halted, breathing hard, having run out of air and insults. He stared at her, balling his fists, and for a moment she thought he might knock her lights out. But he didn't.

"Now I'm going to finish the search," she said, moderating her voice. "Do me a favor and don't speak another fucking word to me."

While she completed a cautious examination of the cave-in, Huckey left the tunnel and waited outside. Heading back to the entrance, she went into the rickety old wooden building and peered around the sun-flecked interior, taking more pictures. A set of massive iron gears and other strange machinery loomed in the darkness, covered with cobwebs and dust. But there was no hint that the dead man had ever set foot down here, and no clue about what he might have been looking for. They went back to where the rope was dangling down the cliff. Corrie set up the apparatus and jugged her way back up, followed by Huckey, who remained silent and dark.

She found the other two agents waiting at the top. Watts was some distance away, strolling through the ghost town.

"Find anything?" they asked Huckey, who brushed past them without answering. He climbed out of his harness, pulled up the rappelling rope and coiled it, and shoved it and the gear into the bag. He slung it over his shoulder.

"Let's get the fuck out of here," he said to his companions without turning around.

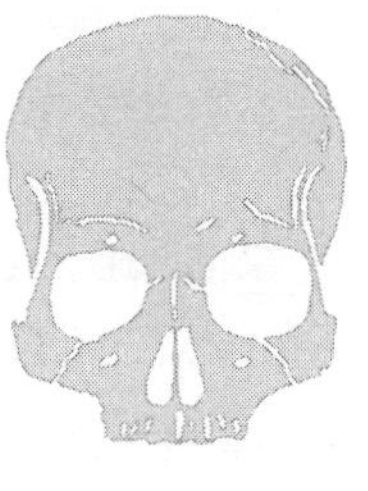

17

IN THE CRAMPED, quiet atmosphere of the pathology lab, Corrie paused and stepped back to admire her handiwork. This was the first time she had done a real facial reconstruction, outside of class, and she was pleased with how it was turning out. Even more, she was dying of curiosity to see the end result—to look on the actual face of a victim seventy-five years gone, brought back to life. It gave her a strange, almost religious feeling to be able to resurrect faces of the dead.

Every other method of IDing the body had failed. She had gotten good fingerprints, but there were no hits in the database. The man had had no dental work, and he seemed to have taken pretty good care of his teeth. The preliminary pathogen report showed no signs of disease beyond a touch of cirrhosis, and the toxicology labs came back clean. The DNA SNPs had turned up no hits, either, nor any intersections with commercial DNA databases. His racial makeup appeared to be generic Western European, most likely English/Scots/Irish. Reconstructing the face was a last resort—but she nevertheless had high confidence she could pull it off.

She had cast the cleaned-up skull in resin and used that as a foundation, filling in the undercuts with Plasticine, including the nasal cavity and orbital fissure. Then she'd put in clay eyeballs. Next came the key step—affixing twenty-one multicolored sticks vertically to precise points on the skull's surface. Each of these sticks showed the average tissue depths for a person of his race (Caucasian), sex (male), age (about fifty-five), and build (skinny). Then, using Plasticine, she had laid on the facial muscles in sequence—first the temporalis, then the masseter, buccinator, and occipitofrontalis. She worked with great care, making sure everything was done as precisely as possible, because even the smallest deviation could make a person unrecognizable. It was amazing how the human eye could pick up the tiniest variations in the anatomy of the face—millions of years of evolution at work, no doubt.

"What are all these plastic sticks?" came a voice behind her. She just about jumped out of her skin, then spun around to see Lathrop coming up behind her and peering over her shoulder, the smell of Listerine quickly filling her nostrils.

"You gave me a start," she said.

"You were working so intently I hated to interrupt. Now tell me what you're up to, Corinne." He indicated the many-colored sticks bristling from the skull. "Are those depth measurements?"

"Exactly," she said, struggling to project an offhand air. "I have a long way to go."

"Did you learn this at John Jay?"

"It was my specialty. Usually it takes two people to do this kind of thing—a forensic anthropologist and an artist—but I studied both in order to do reconstructions end to end."

"Impressive," said Lathrop. He pulled up a roller chair and sat down. "If you wouldn't mind, I'd like to watch. Back in the day, we didn't study forensic facial reconstruction—it was still in its infancy."

Corrie didn't especially enjoy working with people watching her, but she said as gamely as possible: "If you want to watch, that's fine."

"Do you use any particular methodology?"

"I follow the method outlined by Taylor and Angel in *Craniofacial Identification in Forensic Medicine*. It's old-fashioned, but I think it gives the best results—certainly better than the new computational forensics."

"Indeed? Why is that?"

"The computational algorithms suck, at least for now. It's not at all like the sci-fi forensic stuff you see on TV shows. The problem is, computer faces look too real, too specific. When you display them, they're so realistic people don't recognize possible variations. But with a model, they do. The slightly artificial, generic look of a model is actually an advantage, and it's easier for someone to look at it and say, 'Hey, that looks like Uncle Joe!' For now, at least, you can lay putty and clay over bone with your fingers in a way computers can't."

"Curious."

"We were lucky in that there was still some soft tissue on the face and more on the body. I was able to measure how much fat was present, which is extremely important for facial appearance."

"The fellow looked rather lean to me."

"He had no fat at all."

"Perhaps he was starving."

"Perhaps. But the man did have the remains of a last meal in his stomach—beef jerky, whiskey, and beans."

"Camp food," said Lathrop. "Breakfast of champions. Was there any poison? I haven't seen the tox labs yet."

"The first round came up negative. They're working on some of the more exotic toxins now."

Corrie realized she'd let her excitement get away from her and had gone on at greater length than she'd intended. Now she turned back to the model and finished laying on the muscles, while Lathrop breathed down her neck. She added little dabs of clay to build up the tissue depth to the precise point at each of the twenty-one markers, smoothing it out bit by bit.

"Amazing to see a man's face start to come to life," Lathrop murmured. "What's the full process?"

"I'll add eyelids and then sculpt the nose, lips, and soft tissues of the neck. Then I'll add the ears and age the face, putting in the wrinkles and sags you might expect to see on a fifty-five-year-old man. Finally, I'll paint it. That's when it really pops. We're lucky to know so much about this guy—that he was going bald; that his hair was brown and gray; that he had a deep tan and leathery skin from a lifetime outdoors."

"And you're confident we'll end up with a good likeness?"

"I'm sure of it."

"Capital." Lathrop checked his watch. He rolled his chair back and got up. "I've got to run on home and cook dinner, but I can't wait to see the finished product. Will it be done tomorrow?"

"I hope so."

From somewhere, Lathrop suddenly pulled out a folder and placed it on the table next to her. "My horse versus mule paper," he said, with a tone implying he'd only just remembered it. He leaned over her, once again just a little too close for her liking.

Corrie paused. She opened the file up to see a handwritten manuscript, full of mistakes, crossings-out, and scribbled additions. "You don't write with a computer?" she asked.

"It interferes with the creative flow."

"I see." The ideas had indeed flowed, Corrie thought—all over the page like diarrhea.

He gave her an ingratiating smile. "You agreed to jolly it into shape for me, right?"

Corrie swallowed. "Um, I'd be happy to edit it, but I can't work on it like this. It needs to be typed first. I'm sorry."

She felt a sudden coolness. "I beg your pardon, I thought you were going to help."

"I will," said Corrie. "But I'm not, you know, a secretary. Couldn't you please get someone else to type it first? I'm going to be up most of the night as it is, working on this."

Without a word Lathrop slipped the folder off the desk and turned and departed, leaving behind a most disapproving vibe indeed.

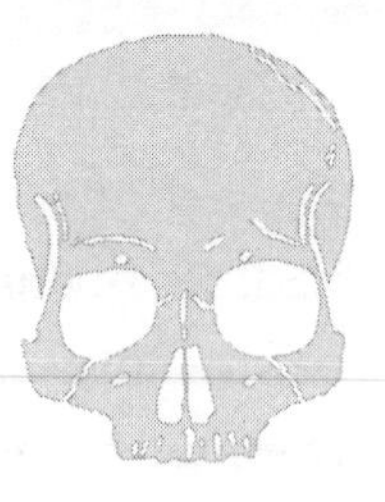

18

The Jeep lurched along a dirt road and passed through a ranch gate made of two tree trunks with a crosspiece, a longhorn cow skull nailed to the center, but a little crooked, having slipped awry. The dusty road led to an adobe ranch house surrounded by massive cottonwoods and a rail fence.

Sheriff Watts pulled up in a shady dirt parking area next to an old stock trailer. He got out, and Corrie did likewise. One of the rear doors opened, and Fountain, the lawyer-historian, hoisted himself out. Although he hadn't been able to identify the facial reconstruction himself, Watts had invited him along on the off chance his remarkable local knowledge might come in handy.

"Let's see what Grandpa has to say," Watts told her. "He's been here all his life, eighty years old, memory sharp as a tack."

"It was nice of you to volunteer your own family," said Corrie.

"They're going to love being part of this."

He clomped up the wooden steps to a broad porch and pushed through the screen door into a kitchen. It had been frozen in time, Corrie thought, somewhere in the midfifties, still spotless and bright, showing no signs of age. The linoleum floor with its floating rectangles of color, the curtains with images of cowboys and horses, the rounded Frigidaire and chrome-trimmed stove... everything was like a museum of midcentury modern. And permeating it all, the smell of coffee and fresh-baked cookies.

"Grandma and Grandpa, it's me, Homer!" the sheriff called out.

A plump woman in a gingham dress appeared in the kitchen doorway, threw open her arms, and gave Watts a big hug. He wriggled in her grasp, embarrassed, and she let him go. "And who's this?"

"This is the FBI agent I was telling you about, Corinne Swanson."

The woman was clearly surprised to hear this, but she covered it up quickly. "So good to meet you, Agent Swanson."

"Good to meet you, too, Mrs. Watts."

"Oh, and Mr. Fountain!" the woman said as she saw the lawyer enter the kitchen. "You all come into the den, where Mr. Watts is resting."

Corrie followed her into a cozy room with a stone fireplace, with plaques and trophies adorning the walls and mantelpiece. An old man was sitting in a BarcaLounger, wearing suspenders over a checked shirt. He pulled a lever, and the chair went into the upright position.

"Please don't get up," Corrie said, but he was already on his feet and shaking her hand.

"Edna, our guests need some cookies and coffee. Or milk, perhaps?"

"I don't need anything, thanks," said Corrie.

"I never say no to homemade cookies," Fountain replied with a smile.

"Good. Bring in the pot, please, Edna. And a few extra cookies, anyway." The sheriff's grandfather eased himself back down in the chair with the help of a nearby cane. "Have a seat over there, young Agent Swanson." Then he pointed to an overstuffed love seat. "And you, Mr. Fountain, take the place of honor."

"Thank you," Fountain said, blue eyes sparkling from behind his round glasses. "And I've told you: when we're outside of the courtroom, it's Charles."

"Speaking of courtrooms, I never did pay you for your time on that damn eminent domain business."

Fountain waved this off. "Anything for your family."

Corrie sat down, propping her accordion folder next to her chair. The sheriff took a chair on the far side as Mrs. Watts returned holding a tray laden with a coffeepot, cream, sugar, cups, and cookies.

"Maybe I will have a cup," Corrie said. She had been dying for more coffee all morning and it smelled heavenly, strong and black, not the weak-ass stuff you got in Albuquerque.

"I knew it," said the old man, pouring her a mug. "I took you for a coffee drinker the moment I saw you."

Mrs. Watts also sat down. "How's your ear?" she asked Homer.

"Fine. Just took off enough to leave a bit of a battle scar. Something to brag about when *I'm* sitting in that recliner someday."

"I still think you should have shot that no-good Rivers's head clean off," the old man said.

The sheriff laughed. "Federal prison will take good care of him."

There was a moment of silence. Corrie, making conversation, said, "That's quite an impressive collection of awards you've got. Were you a sporting champion in your youth? Football or something?"

Fountain chuckled to himself, while the old man guffawed loudly.

"Those ain't mine," he said. "Those are marksmanship awards, and they belong to Homer, here."

Corrie looked over at the sheriff to see, with surprise, that his face had gone a little red.

"You didn't know?" the old man asked. "Homer's a dead shot. Hell, he has three High Master awards from the NRA National Championships alone."

"Knock it off, Grandpa," Homer mumbled.

The old man laughed afresh. "All those trophies and things were just laying about his place, under the bed or in a closet, collecting dust. If he's not going to display them, I sure as hell will." The old man winked at his grandson. "Least he can do in exchange for my pair of Colts."

Corrie glanced at the pair of revolvers on the sheriff's hips with newfound respect.

Homer took a sip of coffee and sat forward, obviously eager to change the subject. "Agent Swanson has some pictures she'd like to show you."

"Yes, indeed, and I'm curious to see them." He looked at Homer. "Does this have something to do with that theory of yours?"

"God, no."

Corrie looked at them. "What theory?"

When there was no answer, the old man said: "Well, are you going to tell her about your crackpot ideas, or am I?"

"It's nothing," Homer said, almost shyly. "You know, we've always had a problem with looters and relic hunters here—like just about every place else in the remote Southwest. I keep an eye on the usual suspects. But recently, although there's been no uptick in looting, there's been an increase in antiquities hitting the market without any provenance."

"Could be a private collector who's short of cash," Fountain said. "Selling off pieces of questionable origin under the table."

Homer nodded. "Could be."

"Or it could be that my grandson has spent too much time with his head in the sun," the old man said.

"My head's just fine," the sheriff replied. "You called it a theory—I just call it curious. Anyway, this person we're trying to identify has been dead seventy years."

Corrie picked up her accordion folder. "Before I show you the pictures, I want to explain that what you're seeing is only a facial reconstruction, based on what we know from the anatomy of the man's skull. It almost certainly isn't going to be an exact likeness. But if it even merely resembles someone you knew, please tell me. Take as much time as you need."

He nodded. "When did the feller die?"

"We think around 1945 or a little later."

"I was five years old in 1945!" said the sheriff's grandfather. "How am I going to recognize him?"

"I realize it's a long shot," said Corrie.

"I'll do my best. Now, let's see the pictures."

Corrie slid the first one out, a full-frontal image of the reconstruction she had labored so hard over. She handed it to him, and he peered at it, frowning, his lips moving but making no sound.

"Here's another," Corrie said, handing him a three-quarters view.

He held them, one in each hand, looking from one to the other, lower lip protruding. A good minute or two passed. "Any others?"

Corrie gave him the profile. He peered at it. Then he gave a loud sniff. "Sorry, don't know him."

"You sure, Grandpa?" Homer asked.

"Never seen him before. I'm sorry to disappoint you, young lady."

Corrie gathered up the photos.

"Can you think of any other folks around here who might know him?" Fountain asked the sheriff's grandfather. "You know, old-timers who still have their marbles. Older than me. Older than *you*—if that's possible."

The man cackled. "That's a tall order." He was silent for a while, then tore a piece of paper off a nearby pad and started to write.

"There." He handed Corrie the paper, on which were written two names in a shaky hand. "Homer will know where to find these people. Both of 'em are eighty-five years or older."

Corrie drained her coffee, hoping to get a refill before they had to leave, and sure enough the sheriff's grandfather, without even asking, poured her another.

"Thank you, sir."

"Have another cookie."

They were Tollhouse, her favorite, but she managed a polite refusal. The lawyer, however, swiped a few as he walked past the plate.

"Even if Gramps didn't recognize it, that reconstruction you did was some piece of work," Homer said as they walked back to the Jeep a few minutes later. "Even the photo of it looks lifelike."

"Thanks. I always enjoyed working with clay in high school art class, when I got the chance. I never dreamed it might be useful in a law enforcement career."

The sheriff frowned at the paper with his grandfather's spidery script. "Clark Stoudenmire and Marilou Foss."

"We should also check the local paper," she said. "There might be some photographs in the back issues."

"The Socorro *Register* building burned down back in 1962, and it took all the old newspapers with it." Fountain shook his head sadly.

Watts was still examining the scrap of paper. "Foss is in town, but Stoudenmire is way the hell out in the foothills. I suggest we get him out of the way first."

"You're a most unusual man, Sheriff," Corrie said.

Watts looked up. "Why's that?"

"All those awards. I don't know how you resist bragging. I even heard you let that scumbag Rivers draw first."

For a minute, she thought he was going to turn red again. But then he scoffed. "Aw, heck. Practice and patience count for most of it. And you're not so old yourself—you've got time. How's your performance on the FBI range?"

"Sucks ass."

"Hell, it can't be that bad."

Corrie looked away quickly.

"What's the trouble there, Corrie?" she heard him ask in a quieter voice.

"It's not the marksmanship," she said, surprised to hear herself blurting it out. "It's—it's something else."

"You mean that little fracas at Cedro Peak Campground?"

She glanced back. "What did you hear?"

"I'm sheriff." And Watts shrugged, as if that explained everything. After a moment, he spoke into the silence. "How old was the girl?"

"What girl?"

"In the camper."

Corrie paused. "Seven."

"You were seven once. What was your father like?"

"Nice." Another pause. "It was my uncle who was the bastard. My mom's brother."

Watts sighed, shook his head. "Corrie, I'm not old enough to lecture you."

"Good."

"But I will say this: Pulling a gun on someone, with intent to kill—well, it can bring all kinds of stuff to the surface. Stuff you don't even know you remember. You can shoot five bad guys, but there'll be something about the sixth..." He paused. "Cops don't like to admit it, but it's true. I'll tell you something: If it ever stops mattering, you're in the wrong game."

This was followed by a silence. Fountain looked out curiously at them from the Jeep.

Corrie drew a slow, deep breath.

"Okay?" Watts asked.

"Okay." She looked at him, eyes narrowed slightly. "Did we ever have this conversation?"

"Hell no."

"I didn't think so."

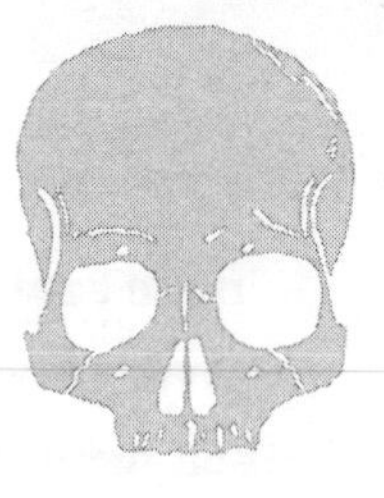

19

STOUDENMIRE LIVED IN a double-wide set upon a rise, surrounded by spectacular views. He didn't have a phone and so they weren't able to call ahead, but by the time they pulled up he was already standing in the doorway, a giant of a man with a barrel chest, narrow hips, and a bald, grinning head. As they got out, he held his hands up in mock fear. "You got me, Sheriff! I'm guilty! Slap on the steel! Whatever I've done, Mr. Fountain here will get me off!" And he gave a belly laugh as he shook the hands of both men.

Watts introduced Corrie, and Stoudenmire turned to her with the expression of surprise she'd come to expect. "FBI?"

Corrie shook his hand as he continued to stare.

"What brings the FBI out here?" he said.

"Shall we go inside?" Watts asked, pointing at the door.

"Of course, of course." They followed him into the dim and unappealing trailer, which smelled of old bacon, and took their seats in a shabby living room full of Scotch plaid furniture.

"Mr. Stoudenmire, do you know about that body they found in the ghost town up yonder?" Watts asked once they were settled.

"I don't get much chance to read the paper these days."

"Well, a body was found in High Lonesome, and we're investigating, the FBI and myself. We're trying to identify it, and Agent Swanson here has some pictures she'd like to show you. Just in case you might remember. The man died around 1945."

Stoudenmire nodded, his eyes lighting up with interest.

Corrie took out the first picture and handed it to him. He took it up as she gave him the spiel about not expecting a perfect match. After a lengthy pause, he tapped the picture with a long, dirty fingernail.

"Kind of looks like that old coot who was around here when I was a kid," he said. "I'm trying to think of his name."

"Here's another," said Corrie.

He took up the second picture, held it close up, then far away, squinting. "Yup, that's him."

Corrie felt her pulse quickening, thrilled that her reconstruction might have worked so quickly. "What was his name?" she asked.

"Jim..."

She waited.

"Jim what?" asked Watts, also on the edge of his seat.

Stoudenmire screwed up his face. "Damned if I can remember. He was an old feller, you'd see him in town from time to time. He had various half-baked ideas he was talking up, but none of 'em worked out. He bought a bunch of cashmere goats, but they all died. Then he thought he could make a business of buying and selling junk."

"But you don't remember his last name?"

He shook his head. "Everyone just called him Jim."

Corrie suddenly remembered the gold ring with the initials on it. "The last name began with G," she said.

"G," the old man repeated. "Jim G...Jim Gower. That's it, Jim Gower!"

Corrie leaned forward. "And you're sure of the identification, Mr. Stoudenmire?"

"You bet. Old Jim Gower. That's him." A decisive tap with the fingernail.

"What else do you know about this Gower?" Fountain asked.

"He scratched out a living on a ranch in the Jornada somewhere. That's hard country. After he lost the ranch you'd see him in town, sometimes drunk or sleeping on a park bench, or trying to sell some old coins or arrowheads and other useless relics. Harmless old duffer." He shook his head. "Jim Gower. Brings back memories, don't it?"

Watts raised his head. "There's a Gower out by Magdalena. Jesse. Young guy, writer or something. Do you know if they're related?"

The old man shook his head. "Don't know of any other Gowers in these parts, myself. I don't think he had much family, if any."

On the way back to Socorro, the sun cast a brilliant gold light across the prairie, setting the hills on fire. During sunset, the desert actually looked beautiful. The rest of the time, Corrie thought, it was just plain burnt-up.

"What do you know about this Jesse Gower?" she asked Watts.

"Not that much. He was from around here somewhere, went away to college. Lived in New York City for a while, then came back and settled at his old family place to write a novel. But that was ten years ago and I guess things haven't gone so well."

"Your guess is correct," Fountain said. "I heard he got his nose broken last year at a bar in San Antonio, spent the night in jail. My guess is he's taken to drugs or drink—or both. He may not be of much help to you."

"Maybe not," said Corrie, "but if they share a last name, we have to see him. I can't do it tomorrow morning—I've got to present the case at our weekly meeting—but afternoon is good, if that works."

"Fine by me," Watts said.

"Think I'll pass, myself," Fountain told them. "From what I've heard, visiting Gower won't be pretty."

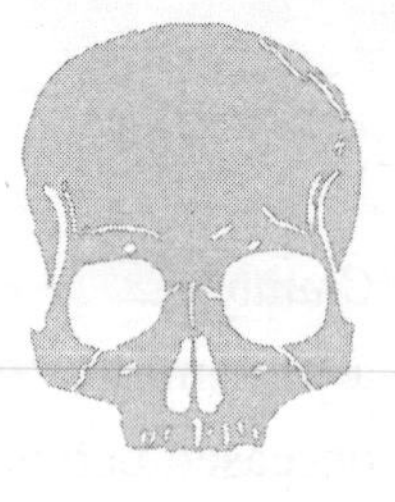

20

Nora put on her best suit for the occasion, and when she entered the FBI briefing room she was immediately glad she had. The room was wall to wall with well-groomed young men and women in immaculate blue and gray suits, polished shoes, and shining faces. This was a far cry from the jeans-and-work-shirt informality of the Institute. Even in New Mexico, it seemed, the FBI were totally buttoned-down. She was especially pleased to be there, as Weingrau had come by her office earlier and praised her for working so well with law enforcement. "What you're doing," she'd said, "is invaluable publicity for the Institute." On top of that, the Institute's press office had issued a release about the pro bono cooperation with the FBI, and the *Albuquerque Journal* had picked it up. Many details, of course, had been left out, including the gold cross, High Lonesome, and the body itself, but it was still a favorable story.

Nora took a seat near the rear as a fellow named Lathrop was winding up a PowerPoint presentation on the facial reconstruction, using pictures of the dead man's face.

"We employed the method outlined by Taylor and Angel in

Craniofacial Identification in Forensic Medicine," he was saying in a pretentious British accent, standing next to an image of the deceased person's reconstructed face. "We think it gives better results than computational forensics. Wouldn't you agree, Agent Swanson?"

Corrie nodded curtly as Lathrop continued clicking through the photos.

"We determined," Lathrop went on, "that our man was an emaciated fellow, in his fifties, balding on top with a fringe of hair, skin weathered from years in the sun. We took all this into account as we painstakingly reconstructed the face, added wrinkles and hair and a leathery tan. We think we've achieved an excellent likeness, and the proof is that we already have a tentative ID."

He looked around. "Any questions?"

Many hands went up. Lathrop picked one.

"Okay, but was it murder?"

Corrie started to answer, but Lathrop interrupted. "Nothing definitive either way," he said. "At least from a forensic point of view."

"But this is an official case now?" someone asked.

This time, Corrie answered. "Yes, it's official and approved by the SAC."

There were a few more questions about how Lathrop had reconstructed the face, what the actual process involved, which the man answered with plummy self-confidence and panache while Corrie stood next to him.

"Thank you, Dr. Lathrop," said Corrie, rather abruptly, as the questions wound down. She took over as Lathrop nodded and retreated, resuming his seat with a satisfied smile. "Yesterday," she said, "Sheriff Watts and I showed these photographs to some old-timers in the Socorro area, and we have a tentative identification of the victim as one James Doolin Gower. So far all we have is the name, but we'll be confirming the ID and following up on the details of his life. Now, I want to introduce Dr. Nora Kelly, a senior curator at the Santa Fe Archaeological Institute. Dr. Kelly excavated the remains and has been studying the artifact found with the body. Dr. Kelly?"

Nora stood up and went to the podium. She had prepared a small PowerPoint presentation of her own, which she now fired up with a remote Corrie handed her. Lecturing at the Institute had become second nature to her, and any nervousness she might have felt at speaking in front of a roomful of government agents quickly fell away.

The first image appeared on the screen: a photograph of the cross, pictured against black velvet. It fairly glowed, and there was a faint murmur from the audience.

"Dr. Orlando Chavez and I have examined the cross, and we have some preliminary findings. It appears to date from the Spanish colonial period, pre–Pueblo Revolt—that is, between 1598 and 1680. It was probably made in the New World, with both the gold and gems having a New World origin."

She went to the next slide: a close-up of the mounted turquoises.

"The turquoise has been identified as coming from the ancient Chalchihuitl mine in the Cerrillos Hills, south of Santa Fe, which was a major source of prehistoric and historic turquoise. It has a very distinctive pale green color and pattern. The other gemstones are harder to source, but the nephrite jade is probably from central Mexico. The cross is of particularly fine workmanship and was probably made by a master goldsmith in Mexico City. There's a good chance it was carried into New Mexico by a padre as a personal holy object."

She brought up the next slide.

"There are what appear to be some unusual assay marks on the cross, which my colleague at the Institute is now researching."

She ended the presentation. "Finally, since you're all law enforcement, you'll be interested to know that there's no documented history or provenance for this artifact. It's not from any public or private collection that we know of, and there's no record of a theft of any object like this. That's all we can say about it so far, but when we identify those assay marks we will know much more. Thank you."

Corrie stepped forward. "And thank you, Dr. Kelly. Any questions?"

A dozen hands went up.

"How much is the artifact worth?" one person asked.

"From a historical point of view, it's very rare. There's nothing quite like it in my experience."

"But on the open market? Can you give us a monetary value?"

"I'd guess somewhere in the six figures."

"What's this Pueblo Revolt you mentioned?" asked somebody else.

Nora had wondered how much historical background the group might need. Looking around the room, she realized most of these agents probably had come from other parts of the country and knew next to nothing about local history.

"A good question," she said. "Let me give you a little historical context. New Mexico was first settled by Europeans in 1598 by the Spanish conquistador Don Juan de Oñate and a group of European colonists, along with a number of friars. Those padres fanned out to all the subjugated Puebloan Indian settlements along the Rio Grande, where they built mission churches. These churches needed ecclesiastical goods—crosses, bells, chalices, statues of the Virgin, that sort of thing. So a lot of workshops in Mexico City began churning out holy items to supply the churches along the northern frontier. Since they had access to plenty of gold, silver, and gems pouring out of the mines, some of these religious articles were quite spectacular. They were carried up from Mexico City and distributed to the mission churches across New Mexico. That, we think, is the case with this cross. It's heavily worn, so we assume it was carried by a padre rather than placed in a church.

"In 1680, the Indians rose up, killed four hundred settlers and dozens of padres, and drove the rest of the Spanish out of New Mexico. This was the Pueblo Revolt. The Pueblo Indians proceeded to erase every trace of Spanish occupation. They destroyed houses, burned churches, smashed the crosses, and ground up the statues. Anyone who'd been baptized was ritually washed clean. All marriages performed by a padre were dissolved. That's why it's rare to find an object that survived the destruction—particularly one made of gold."

"Why gold in particular?" asked another person.

"The Puebloans had come to think of gold as an accursed metal that made Spaniards crazy, the thing most responsible for their enslavement in the mines. They are said to have blocked up and hidden those mines so the Spanish couldn't reopen them if they returned. And when the Spanish did return in 1692, some of the mines did, as far as we know, remain hidden."

The level of excitement and interest in the room had intensified. *Gold*, Nora thought. *The magic word.*

"So why would a guy like that be carrying this cross in 1945?"

"We don't know."

"He must have gotten it from somewhere."

"It might have been passed down in the man's family. He

might have found it or stolen it. As I said, there's no documentary evidence that we've been able to find, except the assay marks I mentioned. It's possible we'll never know where it came from."

More hands were up, and a murmur of excited voices filled the room. Morwood, Corrie's boss, stood up and turned to the group, holding up his arms. A hush fell, and one by one the hands lowered.

"I'd like to remind the group that this is a potential homicide investigation. The gold cross is intriguing, but let's not take our eye off the ball. We've no reason yet to think it's associated with the man's death—even if the death is a homicide. What I find more significant are the signs of violence—the cracked skull, the broken ribs, the mule shot in the head. They, not the cross, have bearing on whether the man was the victim of homicide."

He turned to Corrie. "In your opinion, how serious were the injuries sustained by the victim?"

"None fatal, or even disabling, to be honest. Looks like he might have fallen off his mule."

This elicited a murmur of laughter.

"I wouldn't rush to any conclusions," said Morwood. "He might have been in a fight, and there might also have been internal injuries of a more serious nature. Have you looked into that?"

"Yes, sir. The peritoneal cavity showed no signs of internal bleeding. The organs are still out at the lab, but so far nothing indicates internal damage. The remains are scheduled for a CT scan, which will give us a more definitive answer."

"Good. And, Dr. Lathrop? I commend you and Agent Swanson for that excellent facial reconstruction."

"Thank you, sir," said Lathrop. "Thank you indeed!"

* * *

Corrie walked down from the stage. She couldn't believe that shithead Lathrop had hogged the credit for her reconstruction. Maybe she should have objected when Morwood had suggested, ever so gently, that Lathrop be the one to present the findings. She had agreed—and then he'd flat-out stolen credit for her work.

She saw Nora approaching. "Great presentation," Corrie told her. "Much appreciated, thanks."

"Glad to help." Nora looked at her closely. "Are you okay?"

"I'm fine," said Corrie under her breath as she gathered her files together and put away her computer.

While the room emptied, Morwood came up and shook Nora's hand. "I want to thank you, Dr. Kelly, for speaking today."

"Of course."

"There was quite a lot of interest in the cross, as you saw."

"Gold, gems, lost mines—that gets people's attention."

"Sometimes too much." He turned to Corrie. "A fine piece of work with the reconstruction."

"You should know, sir," Corrie began, "that Dr. Lathrop took credit for work that I—"

Morwood held out a hand. "Dr. Lathrop is the world's expert on telling a horse skull from a mule skull. Is that what you're about to tell me? Because I don't want to hear any complaining."

Corrie fell silent, her face coloring.

Morwood's voice softened. "A bit of advice: let others share credit, even if undeserved. It'll work wonders for your career." He leaned forward. "*I* know who did the reconstruction, and I'm the one who counts."

"Yes, sir."

Morwood turned to Nora. "I'd like a private word with Corrie, if you don't mind."

"Of course."

Nora left the two alone in the conference room. Corrie could see a stern look gathering on Morwood's face. "I need to speak to you about Brad Huckey," he said.

Corrie folded her arms. "What about him?"

"You and I have had several conversations about how important it is to get along with everyone, even those who are difficult. At the FBI, we place a high premium on maintaining good working relationships. It's the nature of our business to come in contact with unsavory, retrograde, obnoxious, and even criminal individuals."

Corrie stared at Morwood, feeling a flush of anger. "So what, exactly, did Huckey say?"

"He said—take this with a grain of salt—that you were difficult to work with, insulting, and uncooperative."

Corrie waited a beat. "Anything else?"

"That you misidentified a bone he recovered and interfered with his search protocol."

"And you believe him?"

Corrie hadn't meant to assume such a challenging tone, and the question seemed to take Morwood aback. "No, I don't, except to the extent that it represents a failure on your part to get along."

Corrie took a deep breath. "I'm perfectly willing to get along with unsavory, retrograde, obnoxious, and even criminal people as part of my job."

"I'm glad to hear it, but—"

Corrie interrupted him. "Excuse me, sir, but what I'm *not*

willing to do is put up with co-workers like that. There's a difference. Right from the get-go, Huckey was loud, insulting, arrogant, and sexist. He disparaged me in front of Sheriff Watts, he treated the site with contempt instead of respect, and when we were inside the mine, rather than acknowledging the tragedy that took place there, he thought it would be amusing to drop an old case of TNT at my feet. His behavior was unprofessional from start to finish." She took another deep breath. "Are you telling me I should put up with that?"

Morwood frowned. "Well, in principle—"

"Then forgive me if I just come out and say it: I won't put up with it. Not from co-workers, and especially not from someone technically subordinate to me. That undermines my authority as a special agent. Wouldn't you agree, sir?"

A long silence filled the room. Morwood gazed steadily at Corrie. At last, he asked: "Was he really that bad?"

"Worse. And I might also point out that *I* was willing to let it go. It was Huckey who complained—not me."

"He reported you called him, among other things, a 'dickless wonder.' That's not exactly professional on your part."

"Perhaps not. But I still maintain that if he'd treated a guy like he treated me, he would've gotten his butt handed to him."

Morwood nodded slowly, his brow furrowed. "Okay. I hear you. I don't want my agents to have to deal with that kind of behavior."

"Thank you, sir." She almost asked him what he planned to do about it but realized that might sound like she was angling to have Huckey reprimanded. Frankly, she didn't give a shit what happened to him, as long as she didn't have to work with him again. A guy like that was never going to change.

Morwood nodded crisply and turned to the door. Corrie

finished packing away her stuff, heart beating like a drum in her chest. Had she just screwed her career? Or was standing up for herself a good thing? She had no idea one way or the other and was filled with confusion. She knew only one thing: she was never going to put up with a bully like Huckey again. It was too much like her miserable high school days.

She emerged from the conference room to find Nora waiting for her in the hall.

"Sorry that took a while," Corrie said.

"No worries."

"What are you doing now?"

"Heading back to Santa Fe. And you?"

"I've got to drive down south to some godforsaken hole and interview someone who might be a relative of Gower's." Then Corrie added, almost without thinking: "Want to come?"

"Me?" Nora said in surprise. "Why?"

"Because it's a long, boring drive... and, well, I could use the company."

Nora hesitated for what seemed a long time. Then she nodded. "Sure."

21

JESSE GOWER LIVED in a log cabin with a tin roof, surrounded by ponderosa pines and looking out over the Magdalena Mountains. A battered chicken coop—still populated, judging from the occasional cackling noise—stood across a dirt yard from the cabin, next to what looked like a shuttered toolshed. It would have been a nice place, Nora thought, if the yard weren't full of old cars, two refrigerators, a washing machine, rolls of barbed wire, a broken cattle gate, and other miscellaneous junk. Since the phone had been disconnected, Watts had suggested they go there and hope to find him at home.

Nora had been struck by Sheriff Homer Watts. He was utterly different from what she'd expected—he was a tall, skinny guy, ridiculously young, with an easygoing, aw-shucks manner. But it was his cowboy hat she particularly noticed. It was glorious, a 100X beaver Resistol in silver belly that she was sure cost well over a thousand dollars. Watts babied the hat, brushing every bit of dust off and keeping it immaculate—and no wonder, because when he wore it he looked remarkably like a young Gary Cooper. She couldn't help but wonder if something might happen between him and Corrie, despite—or maybe because of—the awkward formality of their interactions, all "Agent Swanson" and "Sheriff Watts" and that sort of thing.

He'd been surprised when Corrie suggested that Nora come along but had voiced no objection. They had all gone together in the sheriff's car, and now Watts pulled up some distance from the house. "I think we'd better wait a bit," he said. "Not a good idea to surprise the guy."

So they waited and waited, but nothing happened, save a squawk and some activity from the henhouse.

After a few minutes, Watts shifted in his seat. "Why don't you all stay in the car and I'll go knock on the door?"

"Why don't I go and you stay here," Corrie said. "I'm less threatening. You're big and tall and in uniform."

"Well, now..." Watts didn't finish the sentence, but it was clear he wasn't happy with the idea.

"I'm armed and trained," Corrie said.

"I'm just wondering," said Watts with a laugh, "how it's going to look to people around here if I stay in the car and you get shot."

"All the grievance warriors out there will give you a medal for recognizing gender equality," said Corrie as she got out.

Nora waited with Watts while Corrie walked slowly up to the porch and waited at the base of the steps. "Jesse Gower?" she called. "You in there?"

No answer.

Nora watched while Corrie mounted the steps and knocked on the door. "Jesse, you in there? It's Corrie Swanson."

The door opened slowly, almost as if a ghost were operating it, and a scarecrow of a man appeared: dressed in pale clothes, face hollowed out, lanky yellow hair tied back in a messy ponytail that fell practically to his waist. His nose looked as if it had been broken, then healed imperfectly. Several day's worth of stubble completed the picture of a terrifying wreck of a man. *An addict for sure,* thought Nora. Crank, or smack—or both.

"Who?" the man finally said.

"Um, Corrie Swanson. FBI." Nora watched her lift her credentials, then drop them and offer her hand. The man stared at the hand as if dumbfounded.

"You can't come in," he said, starting to retreat.

"That's okay, no worries, we don't need to come in. We just have a few questions—"

But the door shut, and there was the sound of a lock turning.

Now what? Nora thought.

Sheriff Watts started to get out, but Corrie motioned for him to stay inside. "Mr. Gower?" she said through the door. "We found the body of a man named James Gower. We're here to ask you a few questions."

Nothing.

"He was found with a valuable object."

Still no response.

"Are you a descendant? We're searching for the rightful owner."

At this, after a moment, the door slowly opened again and the specter stood in the doorway. "What object?"

"If you'll allow me and my partners to sit down on this porch of yours, we can talk about it."

He gestured slowly for them to come.

Watts got out of the Jeep and slipped on his amazing hat, while Nora followed. They climbed the stairs to the porch, where a torn sofa and several rickety chairs lay scattered about. They all sat down, and the unsteady Gower took a seat on a stool, his bony knees sticking up through holes in his pants.

It was cool on the porch, and fragrant with the scent of pine needles—a lovely spot, Nora thought once more, as long as you ignored the yard of junk.

She examined Jesse Gower more closely. His pupils were dilated, and he looked strung out. Very strung out. She wondered how he got drugs way out here.

"So tell me about this object," he said.

"First, are you related to James Doolin Gower?"

"I want to know about the 'valuable object.'"

"You'll know about it," said Corrie, "once we've established your relationship with James Doolin Gower, if any."

The official tone, or perhaps the insinuation, seemed to wake him up. He stood. "Fuck you all."

"Okay," said Corrie, "let's go." She turned to Watts. "Obviously, he's got nothing to do with Jim Gower or that gold object."

At this, the man paused. "Gold object?"

Corrie stared him down. "Mr. Gower, I need to know if you'll cooperate."

"I'll cooperate. I will." He eased back down on the stool. After a long silence, he said: "James Doolin Gower was my great-grandfather."

Corrie pulled out a picture. "This man?"

Gower took the picture in a trembling hand. He stared at it. "Where'd you get this?"

"It's a facial reconstruction, made from the skull of a man found in a ghost town several miles from here. A man tentatively identified as James Gower."

"That's pretty good. It's him, all right."

"I want you to be sure. Here's another picture, and another."

He looked through them. "I'm sure it's him. He disappeared long before I was born, but I saw enough photos to know."

Corrie took the pictures back. "Tell us about him."

"Not much to say. He had a hardscrabble ranch in the San Andres. The government confiscated his ranch and everyone else's in the area when they created the White Sands Missile Range."

"The government took his ranch?"

"Oh, yeah. And after those government bastards stole his ranch and paid him almost nothing for it, he spent the last few years of his life trying to make a living. Or so my dad told me. He was sure the government took his land because they wanted something on it—oil, maybe, or gold. My great-grandma left him, and then he disappeared. Nobody ever heard from him again."

"When did he disappear?"

"A couple of years after they stole his ranch." He thought for a minute. "I'd guess in the midforties, based on what my father told me."

"Did anyone search for him?"

"The government people and the sheriff organized a half-assed search party for a few days and then gave up. So you found his body up there in High Lonesome?"

"What makes you think that?" Corrie asked.

"You said the body was found in a ghost town some miles away. High Lonesome's the only one that comes to mind."

"As it happens, that's correct. The body was found by a relic hunter."

"What was he doing up there?"

"That's what we're trying to find out," Corrie said. "Do you have any thoughts?"

He shook his head. "Not a clue. How did he die?"

"We're looking into it. Could be homicide, could be an

accident. Any rumors or stories passed down in your family about him?"

He looked at her with suspicion—or maybe, Nora thought, paranoia. "Not really. So he was carrying something valuable? Was it his gold watch?"

"Gold watch?" Corrie asked.

"Yeah. Pocket watch, with constellations engraved on the spring cover. A flyback chronograph."

"A what?" Watts asked.

"Flyback chronograph. I think they called it a repeater back when it was made, in the 1920s or thereabouts."

"You seem to know a lot about it," Corrie said.

Gower shrugged. "My dad knew something about repairing timepieces. That watch meant a great deal to my great-grandfather. It was worth a lot of money."

After a pause, Corrie went on. "We found something made of gold. But it wasn't a watch. It was a cross."

"A *cross*?" Gower seemed to have difficulty picturing his ancestor with such an object. "How much is it worth?"

"We're looking into that as well."

"I'm the only descendant. It belongs to me. The rightful owner—just like you said."

At this, Nora leaned forward. "It would be helpful to us if you could give us a sketch of your family history and relationships. A family tree."

"My great-grandfather, your dead man, had one child. His name was Murphy Gower. He was taken by his mother to her family's homestead—this place, here—when she left her husband. Murphy Gower was my granddad. He inherited this place and married Eliza Horner, my grandma, and they had one child—my dad. His name was Jesse, too. He spent some time in Culver City, California, then came back here and married my mom, Millicent. They tried to get a ranch going outside of Magdalena. That's where I spent my first twelve years. Then the ranch went bust, my mom left, I got a scholarship to Harvard, my dad died—and I dropped out."

"Harvard?" Nora blurted out.

"Yes, *Harvard*. Full scholarship. Don't look so shocked. I was at Harvard for two years and did very well." For the first time, some color came into his face: the blush of shame.

"Go on," said Corrie.

"So I went to New York, did some writing. Didn't work out. I needed peace and quiet. So I came back here to write my novel. I'm still working on it."

A silence.

"What's the title of your novel?" Corrie asked.

"Lamentable."

This was followed by another silence.

"And then what happened to you?" Corrie asked, a sudden edge to her voice.

Gower's pale face became splotchy with color. "What do you mean? Nothing happened. I'm living off the eggs from that henhouse over there. And writing my novel."

"For ten years?"

He shifted. "James Joyce took seventeen years to write *Finnegans Wake*."

Corrie leaned forward. "What I mean is, when did you become addicted to drugs?"

Gower's face flushed with anger. He lurched to his feet. "Get off my fucking property."

Corrie rose, as did the others. "And you," she said. "Get yourself clean—or you'll die."

"What about my cross?" Gower asked in a cracked voice.

"When it's no longer needed as evidence, there's a process that will allow you to claim it. If you are indeed the only heir—and aren't dead by then."

He stared at them from the porch as they returned to the Jeep.

"Jesus," said Watts, "you were awfully hard on that fellow." He carefully hung his hat on a wire hat rack and got behind the wheel, looking at her curiously—as did Nora. The outburst was so uncharacteristic.

"Harvard—and now this?" Corrie said angrily. "That's a fucking tragedy. And..." She hesitated.

"Go on," Nora said.

"I..." Corrie paused again. "I saw the same shit in my family. I've got no tolerance for it."

22

CORRIE DESCENDED THE concrete steps to the basement of the Albuquerque FO building. It seemed asleep, windows dark, parking lot empty—not surprising, considering it was five o'clock in the morning. She had awoken from a bad dream, a rerun of her missed shot, and after that, sleep had been impossible, and at last she had given up and gotten out of bed. After showering and eating a granola bar washed down with two cups of coffee, black and strong, she'd gotten in her car and driven to work. The mule skeleton had been bothering her—Lathrop had been particularly possessive during his examination of its bones, and she'd barely managed to peer over his shoulder while he worked. At the time, she'd let him have his way, thinking the mule less important than the examination of Gower. But she still had some unanswered questions—in particular, why the animal had been shot—and she wanted time to have a closer look without the interfering old pathologist hanging around.

Using her key card, she entered the path lab and turned on the lights. The cramped entrance was more crowded than usual by the stacks of unopened cartons and boxes that had accumulated. This, she'd learned, was an ongoing problem—the loading dock was just beyond the lab, and the hall and entryway of the lab had become a convenient place to cache newly ordered supplies that people were too lazy to unpack and store quickly. Lathrop himself seemed particularly guilty of this, as Corrie could see many of the labels came from medical and laboratory supply houses.

She threaded her way through the mess to the operating theater. It, too, was crowded, with examination tables with movable hoods, wet gurneys, and forensic equipment. On the far side of the room was a refrigeration unit with several drawers; one was currently occupied by the remains of James Gower, and another by his mule—*hinnie*, goddamn it, she'd never remember that stupid word.

She gowned up, put on gloves, mask, and hood, and began an examination of the skeletal remains. Wheeling over one of the empty tables, she opened the locker containing the animal. Unlike its owner, it was almost completely skeletonized, having been more exposed to the elements. She rolled out the drawer and transferred the bones to the examination cart. Before moving the cart under the lights, she took a moment to open Gower's locker as well, and slid the drawer out. With the refreshing absence of Lathrop she decided to examine those remains again without the pressure of someone breathing down her neck. The mummified corpse, missing some of its internal organs, was still in a fetal-like position, one arm extended. Again she was struck by the unnatural position of the body; it just didn't look like someone, even a person dying in agony, would have assumed that position. And the skin coming off in sheets like that—was that really a product of having spent three-quarters of a century desiccating in an arid environment? It, too, looked odd.

She turned her attention back to the animal bones and decided to start her examination with the hooves and legs. The animal might have been shot because it was injured or lamed. As she worked, the silence of the lab seemed to grow. She was accustomed to morgues and the dead bodies that tenanted them, but she had never been able to shake the feeling—especially at times like this, when she was alone in the lab—that they weren't really dead after all, but only sleeping. And sometimes, not even sleeping... but awake and listening.

She shook off this ridiculous thought and continued the naked-eye examination. There was nothing unusual about the hooves or leg bones, no obvious fractures. The pelvis also looked normal. As she moved on to the rib cage, she noticed something interesting. The third and fourth left posterior ribs had spots that stood out—just shadows, really. She peered at them closely. She turned toward the cabinet that stored microscope goggles, near the lab entrance. Naturally, there were some boxes blocking the door, which she shifted with irritation to open the cabinet. She pulled out a pair of Galilean-type binocular loupes, fixed with 2.5× goggles, and fitted them onto her head. As she was adjusting the straps to make them comfortable, she heard a muffled beeping noise from behind her, faint but regular. Was it a UPS truck, backing up to the loading dock? No—too early. She shut the cabinet and pushed the boxes against it.

Under magnification, she saw that she'd been correct. What had seemed to the naked eye like a shadow on the weathered bone was, with the help of the goggles, two side-by-side hairline fractures in the ribs, with no signs of healing. Another perimortem injury, and oddly similar to the rib fractures she had seen in Gower. Now, this was strange. Had both mule and rider had a bad fall? That seemed the likely explanation. But this would not account for the fact that the mule had been shot.

She now focused her examination to the entrance hole, which was directly between the eyes. Under magnification she could see clear microscopic pitting just around the rim, indicating a point-blank shot; the barrel of the gun had probably been pressed right to the animal's head. The .22 round had not been powerful enough to exit the skull, so it bounced around inside, killing the animal instantly and preserving the round.

Slowly, Corrie straightened up and pulled the magnifying goggles from her head. She still had not found any indication of why the animal had been put down. The legs looked sound, and a few hairline fractures in the ribs would in no way cripple the animal. There might have been internal injuries, but that was doubtful.

Her examination finished, feeling frustrated, she covered the cart and rolled it aside to bring out Gower's remains for examination.

Once again, the muffled beeping noise intruded on her thoughts. This time, she looked around, her irritation mounting. It sounded too close to be from the loading dock—it seemed to be somewhere inside the lab itself. Had somebody left a phone in here, its alarm on? Because that's exactly what it sounded like—low, regular, insistent.

As she looked around, her ear directed her to a stack of recently delivered boxes near the goggle cabinet. The beeping seemed to be coming from that area.

She approached, curious. The examination table on which the hinnie bones were laid out was in the way, and she rolled it aside in order to get a closer look.

The beeping stopped—but not before she was able to zero in on its source: a box atop the stack.

For a crazy moment, she wondered if it was a bomb. But that was silly: bombs only beeped in the movies. Reaching over, she picked up the box and shook it—first gingerly, and then with a little more severity. She held it to her ear.

Nothing.

What the hell?

Box in hand, she turned back toward the examination tables in order to get enough light to read the label. When she did so, the beeping inside the box resumed.

Corrie went still. Then, slowly, she took a step backward, away from the tables.

The beeping stopped again.

Carefully, deliberately, she brought the box up to eye level. It had been sent by a laboratory company in Michigan, and the label read:

FOUR-C SCIENTIFIC
12-PACK/ELECTRONIC RADEX DOSIMETERS
RADIATION DOSE RATES IN μSv/h FOR β-, γ- AND X-RAYS
(Batteries included)

Almost without thinking, she tore the box open, exposing twelve little boxes, each with a dosimeter inside. She ripped open a box and took out the dosimeter—a small plastic device with a tiny LED screen and a clip for fastening it to clothing. Shoving the box aside, she held it out and—with a trembling hand—moved it toward the table that held the hinnie.

The beeping intensified, becoming more rapid.

She took another step, and another, holding it toward the

skull. The beeping became so intense it merged into a single loud hum, with the LED screen flashing red.

"Holy shit," she said, backing away, with the device slowing down and finally ceasing.

Still holding the dosimeter out in front of her, Corrie now walked past the table and approached the open drawer containing Gower's remains.

Again, the noise went from an irritated beeping to a manic castanet to a continuous buzz.

For a second, maybe two, Corrie stood in frozen horror. She took two steps back, then wheeled around and fled the lab.

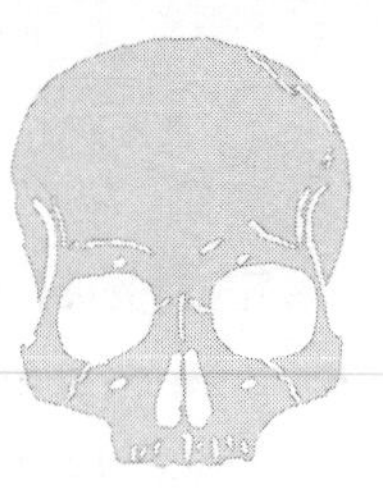

23

In her lab, bending over a table covered with potsherds, Nora Kelly heard faint sirens. She paused for a moment to listen. Sometimes, of course, sirens passed on the street. But these were slowing and growing louder and she realized that they must have turned into the Institute's parking lot.

A minute later a loud knock came at the door. It opened before Nora could reach it. Standing there were Corrie Swanson, Special Agent Morwood, and Dr. Weingrau, her face creased with concern. Behind them stood two people dressed in white radiation suits, with face shields and radiation symbols on the front, one carrying a heavy metal box.

"What in the world—?" Nora began.

"I'm afraid the FBI are here to take the cross," said Weingrau. As she spoke, Digby appeared behind her, rubbernecking.

"We would have called ahead," said Corrie, "but there was, um, a national security protocol that prevented it."

"National security protocol?"

"It appears the gold cross in your safe may be radioactive."

"Radioactive?... Is this some kind of joke?"

"The level is likely very low," Corrie added hastily. "But enough that we have to collect it and take it to our radiological evidence room. May we come in?"

Nora stepped aside and Corrie entered, followed by the others, crowding into the room. At least Digby remained outside.

"Where is it?" Corrie asked.

Nora took a deep breath and glanced at Morwood, whose face was unreadable. "Look, if you don't mind, I need a little more explanation first. How could the cross—"

"We'll explain back in Albuquerque," Morwood interrupted. "Right now, we've got to get that cross into this box."

"It's in the safe over there. I'll open it."

"No," said Morwood. "These men will do it. Everyone else, please stand back."

The goons in suits went to the small safe set into a far wall. Nora told them the combination, and they punched it in. They opened the door, removed the cross in its leather wrapping, and gently placed it in the box—evidently lead-lined—then closed and locked it.

In the meantime, Corrie laid some papers down on Nora's desk. "Here's the receipt and release. Just sign here, please, indicating the item has been collected."

Nora signed the document. Everything was happening so fast. "Now what?"

"We'll take it back to the field office. There we can explain more thoroughly what's going on—if you'd like to come with us."

Nora glanced at Weingrau, who nodded. "Nora, please do go with them and then report back to me. This is alarming—to say the least."

"Okay," said Nora simply.

* * *

Nora rode to Albuquerque in an FBI car. Corrie traveled on ahead in a van with the cross, so Nora wasn't able to get any of her questions answered. Within an hour they had arrived at the FBI offices on Luecking Park Avenue, entering via the back, where the monkey-suited men carried the box into the building at a trot. Nora joined Corrie and Morwood as they followed the men.

"So am I going to grow an extra head?" Nora asked, annoyed and only half joking. "That thing's been in my safe—*and* out of it—for more than a week now, and suddenly everyone's going to DEFCON One."

"You don't need to worry about the radiation," Corrie said. "It's not all that much above background. Sorry about the fuss, but it's protocol, and I had no say. Believe me, I freaked out, too—when I first discovered it. But I'm told the dose is about the same as flying in an airplane at 35,000 feet for a couple of hours."

"Then why all the hysteria?"

"Again: protocol. And an abundance of caution. Even if the radiation is minimal, we've got to follow the rules. After all, we don't know where it came from."

"Those rules didn't get in the way of my taking 'it' to Santa Fe and irradiating the Institute!" Nora said, more hotly than she intended. She took a deep breath. "Sorry. My job . . . well, there's some politics going on just this moment."

"Don't worry about it," Corrie replied.

They walked a few moments in silence.

"I just don't understand how this is possible," Nora said.

"Ditto. All I know is that the bones of the mule, the pack, and everything associated with the body—along with the body itself—are radioactive."

* * *

Following the men in monkey suits, they wended their way through the basement of the FBI building, passing through a warren of cinder-block corridors. At last they stopped before a door, and Morwood punched in a code. The door clicked open to reveal a vast storage room, shelves packed floor to ceiling with containers and strange items wrapped in plastic. Nora could see everything from an ancient car bumper and a section of sawed-up flooring to a window frame riddled with bullet holes. Next to the window frame was an old Tommy gun with a drum magazine.

"The evidence room," Corrie said.

"It's like a museum."

"It *is* a museum," Morwood said. "And, like in a museum, nothing ever gets thrown out."

They passed through the room, eventually reaching a gleaming steel door at the far end covered with radiation hazard symbols.

"We have to wait here," Morwood said.

The door opened with a hiss, and brilliant lights beyond blinked on automatically, revealing a clean, spare room. The two men went in, and the door slid shut behind them.

"After 9/11," Morwood explained, "a few critical FBI offices got radiological evidence rooms such as this. We were one of them." He cleared his throat. "Shall we head up to my office and discuss this, ah, development?"

Minutes later they were taking seats in his office. Morwood settled down behind the desk, clasped his hands together, and leaned forward. "So," he said with a thin smile, looking at each of them in turn. "I guess everyone's first reaction to this news can be summed up quite simply: What the hell is going on?"

A silence gathered.

"Do either of you have any idea how this fellow, Gower, got irradiated?"

Another silence. "The bones, clothing, the mule skeleton—it's all radioactive?" Nora asked.

"Yes," Corrie replied.

"The man disappeared seventy-five years ago," said Nora. "So how is it even possible that his corpse is radioactive? Where on earth . . . ?"

And then, abruptly, she stopped and turned to Morwood. The seed of an idea had taken root in her head. "Might I ask why the Albuquerque office was one of the few to get a radiological evidence room?"

Morwood gave her a faint smile. "Los Alamos and Sandia National Labs, the nation's two premier laboratories for nuclear weapons research, are within our jurisdiction."

"Los Alamos," Nora said. The idea that had begun to form in her head now blossomed into a revelation—one so powerful it almost took her breath away. She turned to Corrie. "What was the exact date Gower disappeared?"

"Let's see." Corrie paged through her tablet. "He was reported missing in July 1945."

Now Nora's heart was hammering. "In 1945, the first atomic bomb was detonated right here in New Mexico, the Trinity test—in the desert just south of High Lonesome. Corrie, look up the date on your iPad."

Corrie brought up a web screen and began to read from Wikipedia. "*Trinity was the code name of the first detonation of a nuclear device. It was conducted by the United States Army at 5:29 AM on July 16, 1945.*"

Corrie looked up. "The same month Gower was reported missing."

"Keep reading," Morwood said.

"The test was conducted in the Jornada del Muerto desert about thirty-five miles southeast of Socorro, New Mexico, on what was then the USAAF Alamogordo Bombing and Gunnery Range, now part of White Sands Missile Range."

Corrie set down her tablet. An electric silence filled the room. And then Nora spoke. "So Gower got caught in the atomic blast."

"Caught—and *killed* by it," Corrie said. "That explains those strange forensic details—the fractured ribs and skull, the skin coming off in strips. And the clothes that looked almost as if they were singed."

"Exactly," said Nora. "Because they *were* burned."

"And also the fractured ribs of the mule! They must have been hit pretty hard by the pressure wave of the blast. Probably knocked them down."

"Right," said Nora. "Gower couldn't have been at ground zero, or he would have been vaporized. But he was close enough to be injured, yet survive—briefly. With a massive dose of radiation. He managed to get back to his camp in High Lonesome before he died."

"And *that's* why the mule was shot," said Corrie. "Gower put it out of its misery before he died."

Morwood sat back in his chair. "Extraordinary. A man, killed in the first atomic test—and all these years, no one knew." He tapped a finger on the desk, thinking. "Since the event occurred on a military reservation during a weapons test, we obviously have to bring in the army. So I would suggest that the next step is to brief army command at the White Sands Missile Range on these findings." He glanced at Nora. "And for now, this must remain absolutely confidential. Don't tell your colleagues at the Institute."

Nora nodded. She wondered how that would go down with Weingrau, when she eventually learned about it.

"But why was he out there?" Corrie asked. "What the hell was he doing?"

Morwood looked at her. "That, Corrie, is the question your investigation must now answer."

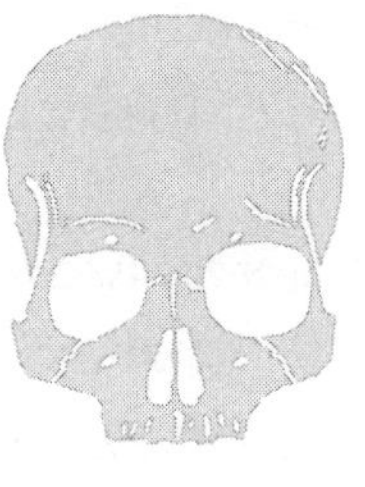

24

THE ARMY COMMAND center at White Sands Missile Range was like a town unto itself, Corrie thought as they passed through a checkpoint into a sun-drenched grid of metal and stucco buildings in a flat expanse skinned out of the desert sands. She, Morwood, and Nora had driven to the base in one of the seemingly endless supply of black FBI SUVs. Following behind was Sheriff Homer Watts in his vehicle. Watts had been briefed, and his reaction had been one of astonishment.

They'd been met at the gate by a pair of soldiers in an open-top jeep, who escorted them past some housing blocks, a water tower, a golf course, and an array of white radar dishes to their destination: a low, flat structure of tan stucco. They pulled into a set of parking spaces reserved for the commander.

As they climbed out, Corrie took a deep breath. An early October heat wave had descended in full force, and it must have been close to a hundred degrees. The heat shimmered off the asphalt, and beyond the residential and operational areas of the base a dust devil twisted across the desert. Although the mountains framing the horizon were lofty and dramatic, it was not what you'd call a pretty place.

They were met at the door by another soldier, along with a welcome blast of A/C. The soldier ushered them through security and led them down a long corridor.

The base commander rose when they entered his office. "General Mark McGurk," he said, coming around his desk and extending his hand. Corrie's first reaction was one of surprise: he didn't match her idea of a general at all. For one thing, he was short, with a round face. And instead of being in dress uniform, he wore rumpled combat camo, the only sign of rank a little black star on his left breast pocket.

"This is my executive assistant," he said as they shook hands, "Lieutenant Woodbridge."

By contrast, Lieutenant Woodbridge was Black, slender, elegant, and at least six inches taller than the general himself.

They all sat down in chairs arranged in front of the desk. The office was functional, with pictures of what Nora assumed to be McGurk's wife and kids on the desk, the walls covered with plaques, commendations, and photographs of missiles in various stages of testing: on the ground, rising into the air, and exploding. The desk was flanked by two flags, the American flag and the yellow flag of New Mexico, with its iconic Zia sun symbol.

"So," General McGurk said, sitting back down, "I have to tell you that your notice came as a huge surprise. Imagine—finding the remains of someone killed in the Trinity test. I've reported it up the chain of command, and there's been a lot of interest. *And* concern. Even though it happened seventy-six years ago, it obviously remains a tragedy—and it just as obviously has the potential for negative publicity. As we're all too aware, anything nuclear is bound to be controversial."

"Exactly our fears," said Morwood. "It's one of the reasons we're keeping this under wraps."

"Very smart. And I just want to add that we in the army appreciate the FBI bringing this to our attention so promptly."

"At least we now know it wasn't a homicide," Morwood said. "But there are still some case details that need to be cleared up."

The general nodded.

Morwood turned. "Special Agent Corinne Swanson is agent in charge. She'll fill you in."

The general's eyes turned to Corrie. Although his expression remained unchanged, she nevertheless sensed surprise. It was, she knew, the usual combination of youth and gender that threw him off.

"Thank you, sir," she said briskly. She removed a thick binder from her briefcase and placed it on the general's desk. "I've copied all the relevant documents and reports."

"Many thanks, Agent Swanson."

She tried to speak confidently, keeping a quaver of nervousness out of her voice as she addressed this powerful, if approachable, individual. "I'll just touch on the highlights of the investigation so far, sir. And then, if you don't mind, I was hoping to ask a few questions."

"Of course."

Corrie proceeded to tell the general about the relic hunter, the shootout with Sheriff Watts, and the initial discovery of the body. "Dr. Nora Kelly performed the excavation," she said. "There were a lot of puzzling forensic details relating to the body, most of which the man's exposure to the Trinity test has now answered." She described the fractures; the skin peeling like a mummy's wraps; the charred areas of clothing.

As she spoke, she flipped through the binder to show various pictures.

"The biggest surprise," she said, "was that he was carrying an item of great value." She flipped to the page containing photographs of the cross, and the general peered at it with interest.

"It appears to be from the early Spanish colonial period, before 1680. It was being examined at the Santa Fe Archaeological Institute by Dr. Kelly here, until we realized its radioactivity."

"An old cross," the general said. "Any idea why it was on his person?"

"No idea," said Corrie. "Not yet, anyway. It doesn't appear to have been stolen."

The general nodded.

"So that's basically the briefing," said Corrie. She glanced at Nora. "Dr. Kelly, do you have anything to add?"

"Yes, thank you. We're trying to identify some unusual hallmarks on the cross, to see if we can't trace its manufacture. It's solid gold and of high craftsmanship. We're fairly sure it was made in Mexico City in the early 1600s and brought up the Camino Real into New Mexico."

The general smiled. "Well, I wish you luck. Meanwhile, have you identified the individual? And, for us on the base anyway, perhaps more to the point: Do you know who he was and what he was doing in the desert on the morning of July 16, 1945?"

"The man's name was James Doolin Gower," Corrie said. "His family owned a ranch where he grew up in the foothills of the San Andres Mountains. They were evicted when it was taken over by the government in 1942. While we don't know what he might have been doing, exactly, he was not all that far from the area of his family's old ranch when the bomb was tested."

As she spoke, a flash of recognition went over the general's face. "Gower? You mean this fellow was from the family that owned the old ranch house not far from the Trinity site? We call it the Gower Ranch."

"One and the same," said Morwood.

The general shook his head. "I'll be damned. That place has some history to it, you know. The Manhattan Project personnel used it as a workshop in the days leading up to Trinity. In fact, Dr. Oppenheimer and a few others slept there the night before the test." He paused a moment, thinking. "I'm pretty familiar with the history of the Trinity test, and there's no mention of trespassers or others who had to be escorted off. Of course, that's pretty wide, empty country. Do you think Gower was on his way back to his family's ranch when the bomb went off?"

"Good question. We know he was upset about the government taking the land."

"Can't exactly blame him for that," said McGurk. "Most of the ranchers who had their land taken weren't happy. And to be honest, the government didn't compensate them fairly at the time. That wrong was eventually corrected, but it took far too long."

"General, do WSMR archives contain any information about the taking of the Gower Ranch?"

"I can't say with certainty, but the government kept good records. I'll get you what we have as quickly as possible."

"And you say there were no trespassers on the range during the time of the test? No one else caught in the blast?"

The general shook his head. "There were a number of lawsuits from people living just outside the range who later got cancer. Those were settled years ago. Beyond that, nothing that stands out."

"Were any members of the Gower family involved in those lawsuits?"

"I can certainly check." McGurk turned to Woodbridge, who had been taking notes. "Please put a high priority on these requests."

"Yes, sir."

"My final question," Corrie said, "is this: Could a visit to the Gower Ranch house be arranged?"

Morwood shot her a glance—she had intentionally not mentioned the request ahead of time, in case her boss shot it down—but the general merely nodded. "I don't see why not. To the best of my knowledge, it's been kept more or less intact—same furniture and so forth. Not for any particular reason; I assume at the time, moving things out was considered an unnecessary inconvenience. None of our personnel have much reason to enter that section of the base at present. The roof has been replaced once or twice, I believe, but essentially it's the same place."

"When would be convenient?" Corrie pressed.

"Why not right now?" The general turned. "Lieutenant, call for two jeeps and drivers from the vehicle pool." He glanced back at Corrie. "It's a bit of a drive, thirty miles each way, but we'll pass through a good portion of the range, including the beautiful San Andres Mountains. This is a place not many get to see."

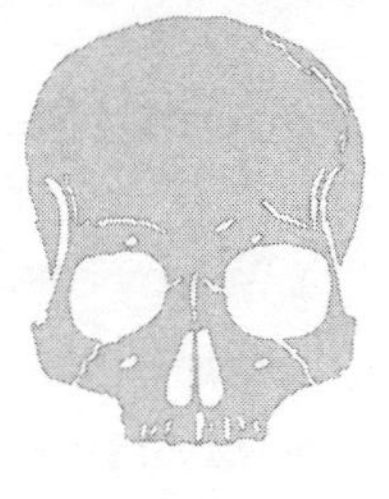

25

THEY SET OFF in two jeeps. Corrie rode in the front of one with the general driving, with Watts and Nora sitting in the back, while Woodbridge and Morwood rode in the other.

They rode northward on a good gravel road along the base of the mountains, through scenery that was not only spectacular but pristine as well.

"Where are all the bomb craters?" she asked.

The general laughed over the rush of air. "This is the largest military installation in the United States—the size of Rhode Island and Delaware combined. The areas used for testing comprise less than one-tenth of one percent. Basically, this is one of the best-preserved landscapes in all of the Southwest."

"How can that be?"

"When we took over the range in 1942, all domestic grazing stopped. The land's returned to its original state. So essentially, you're looking back in time—at New Mexico before the cattle arrived. If you go to the WSMR fence line, you'll see the contrast. On one side is grass as tall as your waist. On the far side, it's mostly cactus, tumbleweeds, and creosote. Two centuries of grazing have been rough on the land."

Corrie shook her head. "It looks like Africa."

"It *is* like Africa," said the general. "You won't find better-preserved grassland in all of the West. If you keep an eye out, you might even see some oryx."

"Oryx?"

"A big antelope with long, straight horns. They escaped from a game ranch in the thirties and thrive here, because they don't need to drink water."

Corrie felt her intimidation evaporating before the general's open, chatty demeanor—and the fact that he was driving himself. "Excuse my ignorance—but what, exactly, goes on out here?"

"That's a deceptively simple-sounding question. Where do I start? This is where we developed many of our short- and medium-range missiles, starting with V-2 missiles appropriated from the Germans right after World War Two, the Viking rockets, the Nike and Patriot air defense systems. These days, of course, there's a lot of drone testing in partnership with Holloman AFB, which is adjacent. We're also home to the White Sands Space Harbor, with two giant runways once used for the Space Shuttle, as well as an emergency orbiter landing site. Among other things, we train astronauts." He paused. "And then, of course, there are the missile dogs."

"Missile dogs?" Watts asked.

The general smiled. "Missiles don't always behave like they should, especially during testing. Sometimes they explode in midair or fall apart, and the pieces that come down will be lost to radar. It can be hell to find them—not to mention that impact speed sometimes buries the parts in the sand. So we spray the critical parts with shark-liver oil. In the case of a loss, we helicopter the dogs and their handlers to the debris area—and they'll have it swept clean before you know it."

"That's amazing," Corrie said. *Shark-liver oil. Who'd have guessed?* The general was a veritable font of information, and it was clear he loved talking about the range under his command. She also knew that there had been friction, at times, between the FBI and the military. She sensed the general was trying to put her at ease, keep the tone light.

The mountains now loomed above them, purple in the fall light, and the road took a turn into a long canyon.

"We're passing through the San Andres now," said the general. "On the other side is the Jornada del Muerto desert, where they tested the bomb. The foothills of the mountains are beautiful, but that's one hellacious desert beyond."

The road climbed a bit, and they came to a pass with forever views before descending into a broad series of grassy foothills. They turned north.

"Here, to the right, is the Hembrillo Basin," the general went on, waving his hand at a range of nearby hills. "That was the site of the largest cavalry battle in the Apache wars, fought against the great chief Victorio in 1880. On our side of the fight were the famed Buffalo Soldiers—Black troopers of the Ninth Cavalry. This whole area used to be the heart of Apache country, but that battle forced Victorio out of his stronghold and down into Mexico, where he was killed."

"You certainly know the local history," Nora said.

"Some commanding officer I'd be if I didn't. But it's true—history, Western history at least, is a hobby of mine. And, let's face it, this is a research site and proving ground, not a forward emplacement. In between the occasional crises I do find some leisure time for reading now and then." As he spoke, his eyes kept drifting toward the battle site he'd just described. Then he shook his head. "History has taught me some hard truths. Those Apaches were just fighting to keep their homeland—no different from what our forefathers did in the Revolution. We were in the wrong with regard to the Apaches, and it's a great shame to our—ah, take a look over there—a herd of oryx!"

Corrie glanced eastward over the grasslands. A herd of antelope stood at attention, watching them, their horns piercing the sky.

"It really is like Africa," she murmured.

"Just as I said. And here's our turn."

He swung left onto an uncertain dirt track and slowed considerably. The unimproved road wound among some low hills before emerging into a small grassy basin. A ranch house stood in its center, surrounded by an eroded adobe wall, with a roofless stone barn and some venerable-looking corrals situated nearby.

"The Gower Ranch," the general said.

They pulled up near the house, and Corrie stepped out. It was cooler here, the altitude higher, with a half crescent of hills on one side and the great upthrust of the San Andres Mountains on the other, together forming protection from wind and weather. A small creek burbled out of the side of the hill above the ranch, then flowed on through the basin and headed out between the hills toward the distant Rio Grande.

Watts joined them, with Morwood, Nora, and Woodbridge.

"I'll be damned," said Watts, taking off his hat and looking around. "What a pretty spot this is!"

"They certainly didn't lack for much," said the general. "They even had their own hot spring." And he pointed toward a group of cottonwood trees on a nearby hillside.

"I can see why Gower was upset about being evicted," said Nora.

"I'll say." Watts shook his head. "This is a little piece of heaven."

They followed the general through a broken gate into the yard and up the portal to the front door. He removed a key and unlocked it, and they filed in, Lieutenant Woodbridge bringing up the rear.

The place was cool inside and smelled of dust and old fabric. The curtains had once been drawn, but the sun had left them hanging in tatters, its beams streaming through the gaps. It was a place somehow dignified in its simplicity. They walked through the foyer into a tiny living room with a rat-chewed sofa, two wooden chairs, and a broken table. The kitchen had an old woodstove in white enamel with chrome edging, along with another table and chair. The only decorations were a few magazine covers and newspaper pictures, framed and hung on the walls.

"It's like a time capsule," said Nora, looking around.

"Look at that," said Watts, pointing to a high shelf in the living room. A moth-eaten cowboy hat lay upside down next to an old Parcheesi board. On a lower shelf were stacked half a dozen *Life* magazines and a *National Geographic*—one of the ancient ones with no picture on the cover.

"Where's the test site, by the way?" Nora asked.

"The Trinity shot took place about eight miles north of here," McGurk said. "As I mentioned earlier, Dr. Oppenheimer slept here the night before. Perhaps on that very cot in the back bedroom."

"So where's the historic plaque?" asked Watts, and everyone laughed gamely.

There was a long silence as they contemplated the old interior, dust motes floating through the bars of light. Corrie looked around, wondering if there were any clues here to Gower and what he had been doing on that fateful day. But the house told no story beyond one of hardscrabble existence and eventual abandonment. She finally mused out loud: "Look at this place. What was a guy like Gower, who obviously didn't have two nickels to rub together, doing with a fabulously valuable cross?"

"He probably found the Victorio Peak treasure," volunteered Watts.

The general and the others chuckled.

"Hold on," said Corrie, startled. "What treasure?"

"It's an old legend," volunteered Lieutenant Woodbridge. "One of many, *many* old legends. Some claim a billion dollars in gold is buried on Victorio Peak. Others, twice as much. We passed it on the way here."

Corrie looked around. "Why didn't I hear of this before?"

Watts shook his head. "I was joking. It was a story made up in the 1930s by a man named Doc Noss, who claimed to have found a vast hoard of gold inside the peak. He spent the rest of his life raising money and blasting and digging, never recovering a red cent."

The general nodded in agreement. "Noss was an old-school swindler. It was just one of his schemes for grifting money out of people, getting them to contribute to his so-called treasure hunts. Although I have to admit, that was one of his better ones. He was eventually murdered by someone he'd victimized—shot to death right on the hillside, in fact."

"But how do you know there's no gold?" Corrie asked.

Morwood now spoke. "Agent Swanson, New Mexico is full of legends of buried treasure. Virtually all of which are false."

"So what *is* the legend?" Corrie felt a little aggrieved that no one had bothered to mention this so-called treasure to her.

"During the Pueblo Revolt," Watts said, "the Spanish padres supposedly gathered up all the wealth from their churches and were transporting it to Mexico when they were waylaid by Apaches. They left the trail and hid the treasure in an old mine somewhere in this area, then blocked the entrance. In 1930 this con artist, Doc Noss, claimed to have found the treasure inside a shaft in Victorio Peak, but he accidentally caved it in while blasting a bigger passage."

" 'Claimed' being the operative word," said the general. "Does anyone here know how much two billion in gold weighs?"

"Sixty tons," said Woodbridge.

General McGurk chuckled. "The lieutenant has heard me rant on this topic before." He threw her an amused glance. "No more answers from you."

Woodbridge stiffened. "Sir."

The general looked back at the others. "She's right, though. Sixty *tons*. If you put that on mules, a hundred pounds to each mule, you'd need a train of over twelve hundred mules! Even if there were that many mules in all of New Mexico in 1680, there's no evidence the Spanish ever mined anywhere near that amount of gold in the entire Southwest. On top of that, there's no abandoned gold mine or shaft in Victorio Peak. Despite the geology being such that no gold *could* be found there, so many people have searched over the years that if the legend had a shred of truth, something would have been found!"

He looked around at the now-quiet group. "Sorry if I sound

vehement. The legend fascinated me, too, when I first got here—it fascinates everyone. But I soon learned that the Victorio Peak 'treasure' has been a thorn in the side of WSMR from the beginning. Noss and his treasure hunters spent a decade blasting away on the peak with nothing to show for it. Ever since 1942, when the land was closed, we've had treasure hunters agitating to get in there and dig. Four or five times, the army tried to put the thing to rest by allowing treasure hunting companies to search the peak and its surroundings. They blasted and dug and probed with the latest instrumentation—and found nothing. They've literally ripped that poor hill apart. You should see what it looks like from the air."

Corrie glanced at Nora. "You know anything about this treasure?"

Nora smiled. "Everyone in New Mexico's heard the story, Corrie."

"Oh," said Corrie, disappointed. "Well, that's too bad, because it might have explained the gold cross rather neatly."

"Let's keep the investigation in the real world, shall we?" Morwood said rather sharply, and Corrie felt herself coloring.

They headed back outside, into the afternoon sun.

"Lieutenant Woodbridge and I are going to close up," said McGurk. "You all go on ahead."

Corrie, Morwood, Nora, and Watts walked back toward the waiting jeeps.

"Agent Swanson's looking dissatisfied," Morwood said as they left the cabin behind. "I'm beginning to recognize the expression."

"It's just an old ranch house," Watts said. "I'm glad I saw it, but I didn't expect to find any surprises after three-quarters of a century."

"I'm glad I saw it, too," Nora said. "It's a piece of history. And the general went out of his way to be both tour guide and historian. Considering he has better things to do, I found him very hospitable."

"Maybe *too* hospitable," Corrie said.

"Aha, that explains the dissatisfied look," Morwood said. "I've never met a junior agent more skeptical than Corrie. It's a good attribute—up to a point."

"Thank you, sir," said Corrie, trying, despite her irritation, to maintain the jocular tone of the conversation.

And with that they climbed into one of the jeeps and the driver took off, leaving the piece of heaven behind.

General McGurk walked back into the house, Lieutenant Woodbridge following. He halted at the window, arms folded, staring through the ragged curtains to the blue mountains beyond. A minute passed as he took in the picturesque vista. And then he turned and said, in a low voice: "We've got to take care of this problem. And I mean take care of it *right now*."

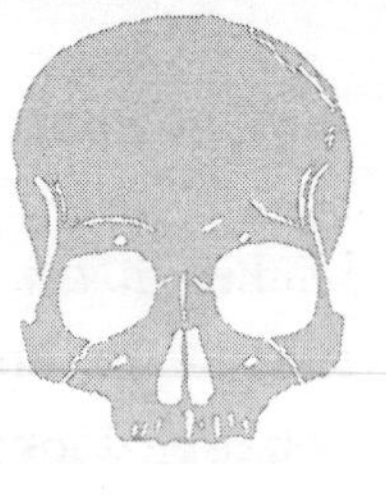

26

THIS TIME, CORRIE jogged, rather than walked, down the crowded third-floor corridor of Presbyterian Hospital, ignoring all obstacles in her way. She slowed as she neared the end, where Rivers's room was. Somehow, Morwood had managed to beat her there, and she could see him standing in the hallway among a knot of people comprising a doctor, a nurse, and two BLM rangers—including the one she'd seen on her first visit, packing a newspaper and cup of coffee. The door to Rivers's room was ajar.

"What happened?" she asked as she came up to them, gasping for breath—realizing a split second later she'd interrupted an intense conversation.

One by one, they looked her way.

"Our prisoner's dead," Morwood told her.

It was as she feared. Word that Rivers—the creep who'd shot Watts—had gone into cardiac arrest had been what had sent her racing to the hospital.

She turned to the doctor. "Any idea why? Obviously it wasn't his leg wound."

The doctor, face gaunt and tired beneath a day's stubble,

blinked slowly. "There were complications, which is why he was still in the hospital. But it appears to be sudden cardiac death."

Corrie looked from one face to the next, hoping someone would be able to provide a more satisfactory answer. "Sudden cardiac death? That doesn't make sense."

"Well," said the doctor in a tired voice, "SCD is the single largest cause of natural death in America."

"But what were these complications? Did they cause it?"

"Infection. And it's possible. But SCD can also come out of nowhere," the doctor replied. "He wasn't on an EKG monitor, so we can't be sure if death was caused by ventricular fibrillation or some other latent arrhythmia. His cholesterol was unusually high, perhaps due to an inheritable condition, so cardiomyopathy is also a possibility. What we can say for sure is that death was caused by loss of heart function."

"Corrie," Morwood said, breaking in, "we've ordered an autopsy, so all these questions will be answered."

Corrie turned to the rangers in their BLM uniforms. "Were you on duty when this happened?"

"I was," said one of the rangers—the one she hadn't met before. He didn't look pleased to make the admission. The name *Akime* was embroidered onto his name tag.

"When was this?"

"About five in the morning. The nurse went into the room to check on some unusual readings from the monitoring station—a minute later, she came running out." He swiveled his eyes toward the nurse standing beside the doctor.

"Cardiac arrest," the nurse said. "The patient was unresponsive."

"Naturally, measures were taken," the doctor added. "Cardiopulmonary resuscitation, electrical stimulation. But I'd guess the cardiac arrest triggered an MI, as well—which sealed the deal."

"MI?" asked Corrie.

"Heart attack. And once blood flow to the brain ceases, well . . ." The doctor shook his head.

There was a brief silence. "He was in a hospital," Corrie repeated. She turned back to the ranger. "You were supposed to watch him."

The man shifted his weight from one foot to the other, then glanced again toward the duty nurse as a drowning man might toward a life preserver.

"This isn't a cardiac ICU," the nurse said to Corrie. "It's not even a step-down unit. The patient was recovering from a bullet wound to the leg, in a maintenance ward chosen specifically because it had a secure room. It was a low-grade infection."

"Convenient," Corrie said.

She felt Morwood's hand on her shoulder. "Agent Swanson? Let's take a walk."

As he began to turn her away from the group, she resisted a moment, looking at the guard. "May I see the visitor log?"

The guard retrieved it from where it was resting against a chair leg. Taking it, Corrie allowed Morwood to lead her down the hall. She glanced into Rivers's hospital room as they went by. The single bed within was rumpled, empty.

They ducked into a stairwell alcove, an oasis of relative quiet in the busy hallway. "You realize what you did wrong back there?" Morwood asked in a tone of mild reproach.

Corrie took a deep breath. "What, sir?" She could guess well enough, but it seemed prudent to let him say it.

"You lost your cool. You were impatient. You called into question the expertise of the doctor and the competence of the BLM rangers. This is not how we gain cooperation and support. Remember, you aren't a lone wolf out here. As long as you carry that shield, you represent the FBI. Even though the cause of death seems pretty obvious, we're going to conduct an autopsy." He paused. "I know you're annoyed you didn't get anything out of the man—I'm a little annoyed with you about that, too. And now, you're upset because you won't have another chance. But you're not going to get anywhere by taking it out on others."

Corrie looked at the floor and took a deep breath. "You're right," she said. "I'm sorry." Was she really annoyed at herself? Maybe—but she could analyze that later. "I know the doctor and the nurse did all they could. But those rangers? I wasn't impressed with them at all when I visited before. I wouldn't be surprised if they were snoozing when—"

"When what? Somebody slipped in and magically caused that dirtbag's heart to stop? It's a wonder he lived as long as he did. Besides, you heard the nurse: Rivers was being kept in a secure room with a locked door. Those guards were there to make sure only authorized visitors signed in and out."

He pointed at the log in Corrie's hand—a clipboard. She glanced at it.

"Those BLM rangers may not be the sharpest knives in the drawer, but you had no reason to call their professionalism into—"

"Hey! Look at this!" Corrie said. As Morwood was speaking, she'd been idly scanning the top sheet on the clipboard. Now she turned it toward him.

Morwood peered at the top sheet. "Sheriff Watts, arresting officer. Laforge, BLM, federal transfer and processing. Swanson, FBI, questioning—we know all about that last visitor, don't we?"

Corrie pushed the clipboard closer. "Look at the final entry."

Morwood frowned. "Bellingame, Military Police, FORSCOM, questioning."

"What's FORSCOM?"

"United States Army Forces Command."

"So he came from White Sands. What was an MP doing questioning Rivers?"

"He didn't come from White Sands. The nearest FORSCOM installation is Fort Bliss, adjacent to the missile range."

"Same goes for Fort Bliss. If they're adjacent, they're part and parcel of the same thing, right? What's their interest?"

"Bliss and WSMR are more like night and day. Fort Bliss houses armored divisions, brigades, and an air defense command. Oh, and an intelligence center for tactical ops. Fort Bliss is the real deal... and they *don't* give tours."

"They had even less reason to question Rivers, then."

Morwood took the clipboard from Corrie. "This speculation is a waste of breath. This MP might hail from Fort Bliss. Then again, he could be from Fort Bragg. *Or* Fort Knox." He stepped out of the alcove and walked quickly back toward the secure hospital room, Corrie at his heels.

The doctor and nurse were still outside the door but had turned away, preparing to leave. They stopped when they saw Morwood approaching. He walked past, to the ranger. "Akime?" he said.

The ranger straightened. "Sir?"

Morwood showed him the clipboard. "The last name on this list of visitors. MP Bellingame. It says he was admitted at eleven fifteen last night."

The ranger stared at the clipboard as he might the head of a gorgon.

"Were you on duty at the time?"

"I was."

"So you saw this man?"

"Yes, sir."

"And you admitted him?"

"He said he had some questions for the prisoner, sir."

"Did he say what base he was from, or who had sent him?"

"He showed me his credentials, which looked good. I... didn't make a note of his base."

"You didn't ask to see his orders?"

"That isn't protocol, sir."

Morwood's jaw worked briefly. "And how long did he stay?"

Akime thought briefly. "About ten minutes."

"Was anybody else in the room with them at the time?"

"No, sir."

"Did you hear anything unusual while the officer was inside? Raised voices, for example?"

"No. Nothing."

"Did you hear the prisoner being questioned at all?"

A long silence. "No, sir."

"Doesn't eleven o'clock at night seem an odd time to be interviewing a prisoner?"

"It isn't my job to question that sort of thing, sir."

"And did you look in on the prisoner after the MP left?"

"Yes." The ranger shifted his weight again. "About fifteen minutes later. Give or take."

"And what was he doing?"

"Sleeping. Like he'd been doing before the MP arrived."

"Don't go anywhere." And turning away again, Morwood walked toward the nurses' desk.

"What are you going to do, sir?" Corrie asked from beside him.

"Do? I'm going to make sure they preserve the security video of this visit from MP Bellingame." He gestured at a camera in the corner of the hall. "I'm going to make sure Rivers gets an even more thorough autopsy than previously envisioned. And no—not for the reasons you brought up. The request should have gone through channels, and I want to know why it didn't. I'd also like to know what questions our MP had for the prisoner." He hesitated, then said, rather stiffly, "I commend you, Corrie, for thinking to examine the visitor log."

Since before she'd even gotten the call about Rivers, Corrie had been trying to figure out a way to ask Morwood something—something she worried he might not approve. Given this unexpected crumb of praise, she figured now was as good a time as any.

"There's something else, sir," she said.

Morwood had already pulled out his phone. "What's that?"

Corrie took a deep breath. "Search the Gower farmhouse."

"I thought that was you there with me, yesterday," Morwood said, dialing.

"No, sir," Corrie said. "I mean, I want to conduct a search of the farmhouse. A formal search."

Morwood stopped dialing and—slowly—lowered the phone. "Now, why the hell would you want to do that?"

"Because I believe it's the most likely place to gather additional evidence about our corpse, sir. Our *radioactive* corpse."

"You saw the place. Any number of people have stayed there since the Gowers were forced out—including, I might add, J. Robert Oppenheimer himself. And you heard General McGurk say the roof has been replaced. Do you suppose that was done at the first sign of a leak? That old cabin has suffered nature's fury, *and* army ownership, for three-quarters of a century."

Corrie knew Morwood wasn't done, so she stayed quiet and let him continue.

"But that isn't what bothers me. What bothers me is that the army, as a pro forma rule, requires a warrant for any FBI search of its property."

Corrie had learned this, as well—and it was the primary reason she'd been hesitant to make the request.

"We've talked about this before, Swanson—as recently as in the jeep, barely twelve hours ago. The general was kind enough to take us out personally, as his guests, to see the old place. How do you think he's going to feel if we repay that courtesy by asking for a search warrant?"

"Sir, I'd think that given the unexpected death of our prisoner, and the still unknown nature of his last visitor, he would understand the need."

"So what, specifically, are you looking for?"

"Gower must have had a powerful reason to be sneaking onto a closed military base to wander near his old family homestead. That reason may still be in that house—letters, papers, things stuck in a drawer."

Morwood paused a moment and finally exhaled in exasperation. "I've got some calls to make. While I make them, I'll consider your request. *Consider* it."

"Thank you, sir."

"Don't thank me yet. And even if I let you file that warrant, and you file it successfully, the general might feel offended, and with good reason. I want you to bend over backward to show your gratitude by not pissing him off. WSMR's a major presence around here."

"I understand."

"Now, go do some calming paperwork. I always find that

soothing. I'll get back to you." And with that he turned away, raising his phone again.

Corrie knew better than to say anything more. After shooting a quick glance in the direction of the room recently occupied by Pick Rivers, now deceased, she made for the elevator that would take her to the hospital lobby.

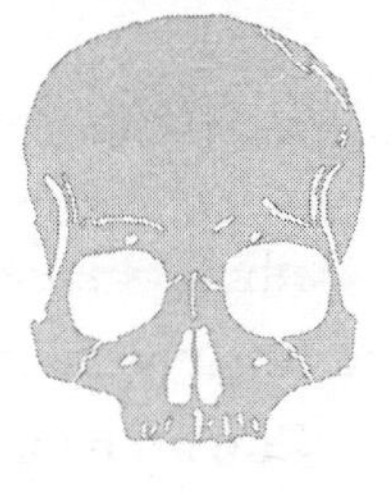

27

CORRIE SAT IN the jeep's passenger seat, feeling the wind whip her hair as they sped across the grasslands. It was the following afternoon, and everything was going as well as could be hoped. Morwood had approved her request for a search warrant—despite his bluster, maybe he'd planned on doing so all along—and General McGurk had apparently raised no objection, because she'd been admitted through the White Sands main post gate with barely a glance at her paperwork. Corrie had hoped to show her gratitude to the general, but she never even caught a glimpse of him in the brief time she spent at the headquarters area. Within minutes of her arrival, a jeep, driven by a uniformed PFC, had pulled up at the visitor waiting area—vehicle and driver practically clones of those from her previous visit—and now, almost an hour later, they were slowing as they approached the basin that contained the ranch house.

The view was as impressive as before, with the flanks of the San Andres rising up behind, and it was a cooler day, with a crisp touch of fall in the air. The driver pulled up in front of the house and yanked back on the parking brake. Corrie thanked him and got out of the jeep.

"I'll probably be a while," she told the soldier.

"No problem, ma'am," the private said. "I'll be waiting on the porch." He climbed the creaky steps, took a seat in a dusty old rocking chair, and opened a magazine he'd kept rolled as tight as a swagger stick, settling in for the long haul. Apparently being her chauffeur was his assigned duty for the day. The magazine, she noticed, was *Boating*—an odd choice, given the arid landscape that surrounded them.

Her pack was heavy with evidence-collection paraphernalia—most of it probably unnecessary—and she hefted it out of the back of the jeep and slung it over her shoulder. She then did a slow 360 of the Gower Ranch. She'd done her share of practice searches at Hogan's Alley and elsewhere in Quantico, along with one real search—the archaeological dig site where she'd first met Nora Kelly—but this felt different to her. It might be the loneliness and desolation... but more likely, she thought, it was the strong possibility that she'd find nothing, that this was a waste of time. Despite how hard she'd fought to get here, Morwood's objections had resonated in her head. Eighty years of abandonment was a long time. Gower had been kicked off the place three years before he died. And in the last eighty years, the house had gone through several incarnations, including bunkhouse for famous scientists, and, finally, an abandoned structure of minor historical interest. Anything of significance had probably been thrown away years ago or crumbled into dust.

In spite of all that, certain facts remained to create in her a lively feeling of suspicion, if not conspiracy. Gower had been lurking in this general area for a reason, caught by chance in the Trinity blast with an extremely valuable cross of gold. Where did he get it? Why was he carrying it? The man who'd found his corpse was now dead, under suspicious circumstances. The FBI had not been able to track down Rivers's final visitor. There was no MP Bellingame on the roster at Fort Bliss, nor anywhere else in the army, it seemed. Hospital security cameras showed an African American man in a natty MP dress uniform, face obscured by a white MP officer's cap. What revved up her suspicion even more was that the man seemed to be aware of the placement of the hospital's security cameras. During his ingress and egress, he could be seen casually turning his head this way or that, or looking down at a clipboard in his hand, in such a way that all they got was a fuzzy image of the lower half of his face. Even Morwood found that significant and had lit a fire under the M.E.'s office to complete the autopsy ASAP—with full tox panels.

Her thoughts returned to the layout of the Gower Ranch and how she would methodize her search. She started with searching the corrals—but there was nothing there, not even historic horseshit. She moved on to the crumbling stone barn, dutifully taking out her FBI-issue camera and shooting a dozen photographs of the outside. Inside, it smelled of dust and hay. There were still some rusting tools hung on a back wall, a stack of crumbling bales of alfalfa, a few empty horse stalls. The floor was dirt, and she kicked at it here and there, finding nothing. Someone had used one of the walls for a dartboard; a couple of darts, so old they had real feathers for fletching, were still rusted into place. But there was nothing of interest.

Time for the house.

She walked over, climbed onto the porch, nodded to the private—at present ogling a twenty-four-foot Boston Whaler—opened the unlocked door, and stepped into the house. As she walked through the foyer into the living room, with the bare kitchen just beyond, she felt an almost overpowering sense of familiarity...and not because she'd been there just two days before. The place reminded her of the old double-wide she'd shared with her mother, growing up in Medicine Creek. There was the same atmosphere of loneliness, of lost hopes and dreams, of the long decline of opportunity, slipping away like sand between one's fingers. As she stared past the living room into the kitchen, one ugly memory in particular returned to her: sneaking in late one night, hoping to creep past her drunken mother's room without her hearing—in vain.

You think you can just live here for free, eat here for free, come and go as you please?...You don't have any skills, what can you possibly be worth?...Don't you walk away while I'm talking to you—!!

Her mother was out of her life now—probably for good. At least she'd reconnected with her father, Jack. He was living near the Delaware Water Gap, working a steady job. They were still rebuilding their relationship, one brick at a time. But already, that foundation felt solid beneath her feet.

She shook these memories away and examined the old ranch house. Was Gower trying to sneak back in here to get something? Had he been deterred, given it was an active bunkhouse for Trinity workers leading up to the test?

She decided to start in the back rooms and work her way to the front. Stepping into the kitchen, she walked around, opening cabinets and drawers. Most were empty beyond some cheap cutlery, a box of salt, and some rusted mousetraps. The enameled woodstove was empty, the floor beneath it thick with dust. There was no electricity, but she opened the refrigerator anyway: inside was an old bottle of milk, its contents reduced to a scaly film. With effort, she edged the refrigerator away from the wall: more dust. The floor was linoleum, faded and hideously patterned, edges curling up.

She moved on slowly, examining first the bathroom, then the small room that had served as a bedroom. This latter had a huge dresser that, she hoped, might prove a gold mine, but all she found was an empty, crumpled-up packet of C-ration cigarettes and—in the bottom drawer—a *Farmers' Almanac* from 1938.

She picked up the almanac. It was foxed with age. As she flipped through it, she found various markings in faded pencil. Some dates were underlined; others had check marks beside them. There were a couple of marginal notes as well, in a crabbed, barely legible hand.

She thought a moment. *Nineteen thirty-eight*. Gower would still have owned the ranch then. Even if those scribblings belonged to someone else, there could be important information hidden in the pages. She took an evidence bag from her carryall, slipped the almanac inside, and sealed and marked it. Then, taking a last look around the room to make sure she had missed nothing, she exited and walked into the living room.

She stood inside the doorway and took a deep breath. This was the last place left. Through the ragged curtains of one dirty window, she could make out the PFC, leaning the chair back at a dangerous angle and flipping the pages of his magazine. She paused briefly to clear her thoughts and then began taking in the room, trying to envision what it had been like eighty years before, when it had been a home instead of a ruin. She let her eye linger on each item in turn: the frayed sofa; the table with its two chairs; the framed pictures hanging on the cracked walls; the shelves displaying various bric-a-brac.

She moved over to the shelves, examining each item in turn: some ancient *Reader's Digest* collections and other books; a few empty wine bottles that must, to some eye, have seemed attractive; the stack of magazines, cowboy hat, and Parcheesi board Watts had pointed out.

Corrie let a finger trail over the spines of the books. It left a line in the dust behind it. There were some Zane Grey titles, a Gideons Bible courtesy of the Sage Brush Motel, and a well-thumbed copy of *Early Legends of the Western Frontier* by one Hyman S. Zim. She took this last book down and flipped through it; though it was battered and obviously well read, there were no notes as there had been in the almanac. Still, it was likely this had been one of Gower's own books, and it might contain references to something that could prove helpful. She slipped it into another evidence bag, made for the couch, then—remembering the likely rat infestation—sat down at the rickety table instead. Its wooden top was as busy as a Keith Haring painting with carved doodles, drawings, and messages—most likely made by bored soldiers, waiting for some drill or test or whatever. There were a couple of dates: *July 1945*, *Sept. '44*. These must have been made by Trinity workers. A few of the carved drawings were crudely anatomical, and the messages of the "Kilroy was Here" variety. Corrie dutifully snapped pictures of them anyway. Then she put her camera away and sat back in the chair—gingerly—with a sigh.

It had been worth the effort to get the warrant, if only so she wouldn't kick herself later, wondering if she'd missed the one step that would have cracked the case wide open. Even so, it seemed likely that when Gower's land was confiscated, the man must have taken everything of value—especially if it had to do with treasure hunting.

Then she paused. *Would* Gower have taken everything with

him? If so, what was he doing crossing the desert near the ranch on July 16, 1945?

She'd done more background research on White Sands and the Trinity test since her first trip onto the base. Despite what the great-grandson had said, when Gower first left his farmhouse, the land was only being leased by the government for the White Sands Proving Ground. It wasn't until later that the parcels of ranchland were taken permanently, and by the 1970s they were all an integral part of the missile range. In 1942, when the Gowers were evicted, Jim Gower had every reason to think he'd get his ranch back before long—nobody knew an atomic bomb was soon to be detonated in the neighborhood—and maybe he hid something awaiting that return.

Maybe. Perhaps. *Woulda, coulda, shoulda.* Time to admit she'd found nothing. She stood up. Time to go.

As she did so, her eye fell on the two magazine covers, framed on the wall across from her. The frames looked rough and handmade, like some her own father had made to decorate their trailer. The illustrated covers had been shellacked into place, the varnish now brown and cracking.

She walked over to them. Once again, her mind went back to her mother's trailer in Medicine Creek. She had put some pretty tacky things on the walls, too—but nothing quite so tacky as this. One of the covers was an ancient issue of *Arizona Highways*, surely the most boring periodical known to man, with a black-and-white picture of Sunset Crater. She recognized the volcanic formation from slides of a trip to the Grand Canyon her class had taken in eighth grade. But not her. Corrie's mother, of course, had nixed the idea as too expensive. God forbid she should run out of money for booze and Kools...

The other frame contained a 1936 cover from the *Saturday*

Evening Post. Its banner informed Corrie it was an illustrated weekly founded by Benjamin Franklin, and that it cost five cents. The painting splashed across the cover was probably a scene from some Western yarn within: a man on horseback, rounding a bend in a high prairie trail to see a tiger rattlesnake perched menacingly atop an abandoned .50-90 Sharps buffalo rifle.

At least this picture promised some action. Corrie took it down, curious to see the framing work close up. As she did so, her fingers touched something attached to the back.

She turned it over. On the back was a piece of paper, held to the frame by cellulose tape almost as age-stained as the varnish.

Carefully, she peeled it away from its hiding place. But even as she did, the tape broke into pieces and the paper fell away. She caught it deftly in midair and—trying to touch it only by the edges—turned it over. It was an old black-and-white aerial photograph of a desert landscape of valleys, canyons, and arroyos, photographed from a considerable height.

More quickly now, she walked over to her carryall, removed a Ziploc evidence bag, and slipped the photo inside. She took several photos of the framed picture, front and back, as well as the stained rectangle on the wall that marked where it had hung for many decades. Then she hung the frame back on its peg and looked around once again. Her gut told her the room had no more secrets to yield. After another moment, she picked up the pack, slung it over her shoulder, and headed for the front door and the ride back to the transportation office.

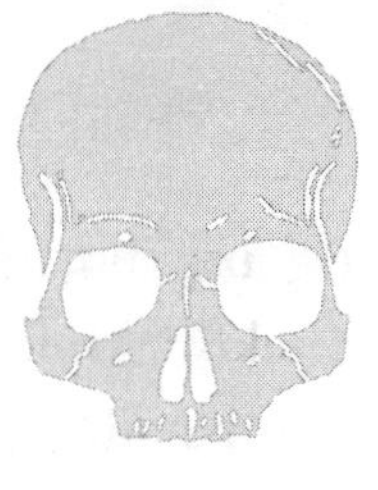

28

IN HER COMMODIOUS, relic-decorated office in the Old Building of the Santa Fe Archaeological Institute, Nora Kelly snapped on a pair of nitrile gloves and carefully slipped the photograph out of its evidence bag.

"This is the original?" she asked, looking quizzically at Corrie.

The FBI agent—who was sitting restlessly on a nearby stool—nodded. "I wanted you to see it, just in case there was something a reproduction would miss."

She turned the photo over in her hands a couple of times, looked at it closely from a variety of angles, held it up to her nose, and took a gentle sniff. "Old-school photographic paper. Even smells kosher."

"Our lab identified it as being seventy to eighty years old," Corrie said. "They'll be able to provide more specifics when I get it back to them."

So that's why she's in a hurry, Nora thought. This time, when Corrie had called, Nora had simply been unable to stop work wrapping up her analysis of the Tsankawi dig site and come down to Albuquerque at a moment's notice. So Corrie had brought the evidence to Santa Fe.

"And this?" she asked, pointing to a small line of old adhesive tape clinging to the back of the upper edge.

"Scotch-brand cellulose tape made by the Minnesota Mining and Manufacturing Company, approximate date of manufacture 1940."

Nora nodded as she continued her examination. "You've got a good lab to be able to date that."

"We have the best."

Nora smiled. "Do you know why 3M called it Scotch tape?"

"No idea."

"Because when it was first being developed, adhesive was applied only along the edges, instead of the entire strip. Someone joked that such parsimoniousness was typically Scotch—the Scottish people being stereotyped at the time for their, shall we say, excessive frugality."

"Hey, I'm Scots and I take offense," said Corrie, laughing.

"In the 1950s, Studebaker even put out a car called the Scotsman, named for its low price and lack of frills."

"Imagine a corporation trying that today," said Corrie. "How is it you know such an odd piece of trivia?"

"We Kellys hail from Dublin, and—" Nora switched into an Irish brogue— "me granda loved to slag them what lived across the channel." She returned her attention to the photo. "Too bad there's no information or legend on the verso to give this photo some provenance."

"Our lab technician in Phoenix was especially disappointed there was no handwriting. They're actually able to identify not only how old an ink formulation is, but how long ago it was written on a page." She paused. "One other thing of interest—there are no fingerprints."

"That's strange, isn't it?" Nora held the image out in front of her thoughtfully. "But you think this was taped up there by James Gower?"

"Yes. Him or one of the Gowers. Based on the age of the tape and the date on the magazine cover. Hidden there, maybe, for their expected return."

"Poor old Gower." Nora glanced at her. "Well, you didn't bring it here for a forensic exam—you were hoping for a location."

"It's a little blurry. But you know the landscape of New Mexico like the back of your hand, so I was hoping you might recognize it."

"Flattery, flattery. But you're right, it *is* blurry—too blurry to be useful in an aerial survey. Maybe the plane, or whatever, encountered turbulence just as the camera exposed the shot. Anyway, let's take a closer look." She cleared a spot on her desk, put the evidence bag on it, then carefully placed the photo atop that, taped edge away from her. "Looks like typical New Mexico, all right—I can see canyons, arroyos, and a scattering of piñon-juniper. Taken from a relative altitude of maybe, what, three thousand feet?"

She looked at the photo for a long time, frowning. Then, hunting around the stuff on her desk, she plucked out an illuminated magnifying glass and held it over the image, moving from top to bottom, left to right, so close she could see her own breath faintly mist the glass. She cursed under her breath.

"What is it?" she heard Corrie ask over her shoulder.

"I don't know. Something's wrong."

"Wrong? I know it's blurry, but—"

"No, not that. I feel I should recognize this, but..." All of a sudden, she stepped back and lowered the magnifying glass with a laugh. "Am I stupid, or what?"

"Sorry?"

"This photo—Gower taped it to the back of the frame *upside down.*" Nora turned the image one hundred and eighty degrees, then bent over it once again.

"That's better—now north is at the top, and everything looks more familiar. That group of low mesas, there, and that canyon, twisting like that..." Abruptly, she straightened up and smiled in triumph. "It's Anzuelo Canyon, and that's Navajo Ridge."

"Where's that?" Corrie asked.

"I'll tell you where it isn't—it isn't close to White Sands or High Lonesome. It's probably a hundred miles away, north and west as the buzzard flies." She looked back at the photo, beckoning Corrie closer. "I recognize it because of the slot canyon, here."

"Slot canyon?"

"You see this narrow, curved line, with that sharp bend at the end? That's a slot canyon. It's an extremely narrow channel of sandstone, hundreds of feet deep but only a dozen or so feet wide. There are quite a few in the Southwest." She tapped the dark semicircle gently with a gloved fingertip. "This section, here, is known locally as El Anzuelo, which is Spanish for fishhook—for obvious reasons. And the ridge curving across the eastern side of the frame is a section of Navajo Ridge."

"I wonder why Gower would hide a rather poor aerial photo behind a picture in the first place?"

"Beats me."

"Is there anything else in the photograph that stands out to you? Historic, geologic, out of place? Anything?"

Nora shook her head. "Anzuelo Canyon is the only thing of interest. Above the canyon is a medium-size Tewa Indian ruin, called—what was that name?—Tziguma."

The two women sat in silence for a long moment, staring at the old photograph.

"One thing's for sure," Corrie said at last. "If it was Gower who hid this—and he's the most likely suspect—he must have done so for a reason."

"Agreed," Nora said. "Let's see if we can figure out what that reason is."

"All right," Nora said, stretching and massaging the small of her back. It was an hour later, and they were in the Institute's small, exquisitely decorated library, a pile of survey maps, atlases, and historical tomes lying on the table between them. "So that Tewa pueblo I told you about, Tziguma, appears to have once been the site of a Spanish mission church."

"Just beyond the slot canyon," Corrie said. "The Fishhook."

Nora nodded. "The Tewa joined the Pueblo Revolt and killed the padre, but when the Spanish returned in 1692, the Tewa resisted, and the pueblo was destroyed and abandoned, and eventually fell into ruin. As far as I can determine, it's never been excavated."

"Never excavated," Corrie repeated. "And yet it's rumored to contain buried treasure."

"Half of the ruined churches in the Southwest, and all of the abandoned pueblos, share that rumor."

"Maybe. But in this case, it's mentioned in not one or two but three separate books—including this one that probably belonged to Gower." As she spoke, Corrie tapped the copy of *Early Legends of the Western Frontier* that she'd taken from the cabin.

"True." Nora began closing the books and straightening the maps. "So what's next? Are you going to take this up with your boss?"

"Morwood?" Corrie shook her head. "He'll say it's too speculative. I've pushed my luck with him just about as far as I can these past few days. I'll have to check it out myself first. If it seems important, then I can loop him in."

"Sounds good," Nora replied. "But that leaves you with one problem. How the hell are you going to get out to Anzuelo Canyon? You'd never find it in a million years. Even your new friend Watts—" Abruptly, she stopped. "Oh no."

"Walked right into that one," Corrie said. Then she laughed. "Why, thanks, I'd be delighted to have you take me there."

Although the library was sparsely occupied, Nora's blistering response nevertheless turned every head in the room.

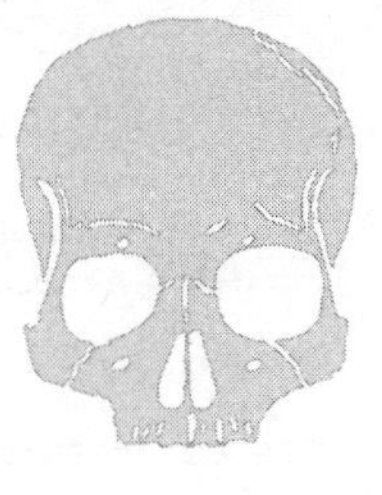

29

THEY PARKED THE car at the end of the track and stepped out. The long dirt road winding through the high desert had ended in a turnaround at the edge of a canyon. The air was crisp with the scents of sagebrush and blooming chamisa, and puffy white clouds passed by in the cool breeze, casting slow-moving shadows on the landscape. It was, Nora thought, a perfect day for a hike. The ridge overlooked Anzuelo Canyon, a broad cut in the sandstone plateau, with spires and hoodoos of white sandstone rising here and there like misshapen snowmen.

They had driven to the canyon in Nora's car, because—since this wasn't official business and it was a Sunday—Corrie wasn't authorized to use her OGV.

"Pretty cool," said Corrie, looking around.

Nora took out her phone and fired up a GPS app. "Looks like we're about two miles from the ruins."

They shrugged into their day packs and set off on a faint dirt trail. It switchbacked down into the canyon and followed a dry wash that snaked along the bottom. As they moved up the canyon, it gradually narrowed, the walls getting higher and more dramatic.

"I've never seen a slot canyon before," said Corrie.

"They're pretty dramatic. But they can also be dangerous. I was once caught in a flash flood in a slot canyon, years ago in Utah. It was probably the most terrifying experience of my life."

"How did that happen?"

"I was leading an archaeological expedition to a prehistoric cliff dwelling. You could only get to it through a single slot canyon. A flash flood came through, loud and violent as a dozen freight trains..." She halted, wondering why she was suddenly telling this painful story, to an FBI agent of all people. "Anyway," she hastily added, "there's no possibility of rain today—I checked. And the ruin we're going to isn't in the slot canyon, but above it."

The canyon walls were now narrowing sharply, throwing them in cool shadow. The air smelled of sandstone, and indirect light filtered down, shrouding them in a warm glow. It was, Nora thought, a bit like entering a cave.

"So what do you know about this place?" Corrie asked.

"As I mentioned, the Spanish built a mission here, at a Tewa pueblo called Tziguma. The Tewas joined in the Pueblo Revolt and destroyed the church. The place was ultimately abandoned, and nobody's paid much attention to it since...except treasure hunters, maybe. It isn't considered an important archaeological site."

Now they were in the heart of the canyon. The sheer stone walls twisted this way and that, polished by countless floods, the floor a clean bed of sand.

Corrie stretched out her hands. "You can touch both sides. This is amazing."

"This section is the so-called Fishhook," said Nora. "When we come out on the far side, there's a trail that climbs up to the top of the mesa, where the ruins are."

A quarter mile along, the canyon spread out again and light once more penetrated the gloom. The canyon walls disappeared and they emerged among a series of low mesas.

"I can't help but think," said Corrie, "that maybe Gower must have found that cross while hunting for treasure. Maybe in the ruins of that mission church."

"I doubt it. We're hell and gone from High Lonesome."

The trail crossed the wash and began winding its way up a ridge to the top of a mesa. It was a short, steep climb, and then they passed through a layer of rimrock before coming out on top.

"This is it," said Nora. "The ruins are over there to the right."

"I don't see anything."

"You see where there's a change of vegetation? Where cactus and saltbushes are growing on those lumpy piles of stone and earth? That's it."

"But where's the church?" Corrie took off her backpack and pulled out a copy of the photo.

Nora peered over her shoulder, toward a large mound of earth. "That's the church; you can tell from the outline."

Corrie put the photo away, and they walked into the ruins. Potsherds and flint chips lay everywhere, mingled with broken building stones, weeds, and scattered anthills.

"Look at this!" Corrie picked up a big painted potsherd.

"Very nice, but I'm afraid you need to put that down," said Nora. "We're not supposed to touch anything."

"Oops. Sorry." She put it back.

They walked toward the larger mound. Closer up, Nora could see a massive wall of adobe that had collapsed and eroded, thickly covered with saltbushes. At the far end stood a pillar of adobe—the only part of the wall left standing. They climbed up the mound, scaring off a bunch of crows, which rose into the air screeching and cawing before landing in a nearby piñon tree.

They peered down into the area that was once the nave of the church. "Hey, people have been digging here," said Corrie. "And some of those holes look fresh."

"I'm not surprised," said Nora. "You get looters at many archaeological sites in New Mexico. Most of them are too remote to protect."

"You think they were digging for treasure? Could be where Gower found the cross?"

"I suppose it's possible he was digging here long ago. There must be a reason that aerial photo was hidden in the house."

A sharp sound cracked through the ruins, and Nora saw a geyser of dust shoot up to their right.

"Down!" Corrie yelled, but Nora was already diving behind the interior slope of the wall. They landed hard on the ground, among the bushes, as more cracks sounded, one shot striking the adobe pillar with a spray of dirt and others clipping a bush on their left.

"This way!" Corrie hauled Nora to her feet, and they ran to the adobe pillar, then threw themselves down behind it.

Nora saw that Corrie had her handgun out. A moment passed while they breathed hard.

"The shots came from that ridge over there," Corrie said.

"What the hell? They *couldn't* be shooting at us."

"They damn sure are."

Nora felt her shock turning to fear and panic. "But why?"

Corrie didn't answer. Instead, she crawled to the edge of the pillar and peered around, through a screen of bushes.

Another shot rang out, and she pulled back. "Shit! We're pinned down." She checked the chamber of her gun, making sure it contained a round.

"What do we do?"

Corrie shook her head. "If the shooter wants to come down here, he's got to expose himself. There's no cover for him."

"Are you going to shoot back?"

"I sure as hell hope not. If I fire my service piece, I have to report it, and you wouldn't believe the paperwork." She didn't mention that she was a lousy shot and the shooter, clearly using a rifle, was too far away anyway.

"So what do we do?"

"Give me a minute."

Nora sat, back pressed against the adobe, trying to control her breathing. She glanced at Corrie, who was now edging out to take another look. Keeping low, she glanced out through the bushes. Minutes passed.

"I think he might have left," she finally said.

"How do you know?"

"I saw what looked like a dust trail thrown up by a vehicle along that ridge. It seemed to be heading away."

"That's a little sketchy."

Corrie took off her backpack, pulled out a jacket, broke off a branch from a bush, and draped it over, putting her baseball cap on top. Then she slowly moved it out from behind the pillar—barely showing at first, then a little more.

Nothing.

"The shooter would definitely have seen that," Corrie said. "I think he's gone." She paused. "Here's what we'll do. You run like crazy across that open ground and down into the arroyo."

"The hell I will!"

"I'll cover you and fire back at him if he shoots. Then I'll follow. Once we're in the arroyo we'll be well covered, and we can loop around and drop down off the canyon rim without him getting a shot. But I really think he's gone."

Nora peered out herself at the terrain. It made sense—if Corrie was right about the shooter having left.

Corrie positioned herself behind the bushes, in a prone position, ready to fire. "You ready?"

Nora nodded. Her heart was pounding in her chest.

"Count of three. One, two, three, *go*!"

Nora braced herself, then sprinted across the short stretch of open ground and leapt into the arroyo. No shot came. A moment later Corrie raced across, joining her. They crouched, side by side, breathing heavily.

"So far so good," said Corrie. "We'd better move fast in case he comes after us."

In silence they descended the arroyo, keeping low and moving along the walls, until they reached the cut into the canyon rimrock. They climbed down a jumble of boulders and pour-overs, and soon were off the mesa. Swiftly but cautiously, they darted behind a range of low hills until they reached the Fishhook. They jogged through the slot canyon, emerged out the other end, and fifteen minutes later were at the car. Nora slid into the driver's seat while Corrie leapt in and slammed the passenger-side door. Gunning the engine, the car slewed around and took off down the road.

Corrie holstered her gun. "That aerial photo. It led us right to this spot—where someone was waiting for us. I think we were ambushed."

"Are you saying that photo was planted? That you were meant to find it?" Nora thought about this for a moment. "The

Gower farmhouse is totally off-limits except to the army. And on top of that, how did they know we were coming here today? Or that we'd come at all? Nobody would station a shooter up there permanently."

"I think the army planted it. I didn't like McGurk from the moment I met him. I wouldn't put it past him to have us followed."

"Followed—*and* shot at?"

"Maybe."

"But why?"

"I don't know."

Nora hesitated. It seemed far-fetched almost to the point of being paranoid. Corrie had an overactive imagination, and she'd taken an unreasonable disliking to McGurk. "It doesn't make sense," she told Corrie. "Think about it. What's his motivation? Killing a fed—that's a huge step to take. It would trigger a firestorm of attention. And *planting* the photo? How did he know you'd look behind that picture, that you'd find it, that you'd figure out the location it displayed, and then decide to check it out? How did he know when? I haven't noticed anyone following us. And finally, if that had been an army sniper up there, we'd be dead. He was only a hundred, maybe a hundred and fifty yards away. But those shots were at least ten feet wide of us. It could have been a myopic hunter, for all we know. Or maybe the person who was digging those holes—trying to scare us off his 'claim.' Or simply a nut. There are plenty of those, you know, hiding in their own little pockets of the wilderness."

Corrie was silent. "Those are reasonable points. I guess I just don't like the general. He seems...I don't know. *Too* nice, in a way."

"Would you rather he was an asshole?"

Corrie shook her head.

"Are you going to report this to the FBI?" Nora asked.

"God, no. It would open up a can of worms—and get me into trouble for coming out here on my day off, unauthorized, with a civilian."

"So what *are* you going to do?"

Corrie pursed her lips. "I'm going to ask Sheriff Watts to come out here. He's an expert tracker, or so he says. Maybe he can figure this out. He's been pretty useful."

Nora smiled. "He's also pretty cute."

"Oh, shut up," Corrie said, and added sarcastically: "You can come, too—as my chaperone."

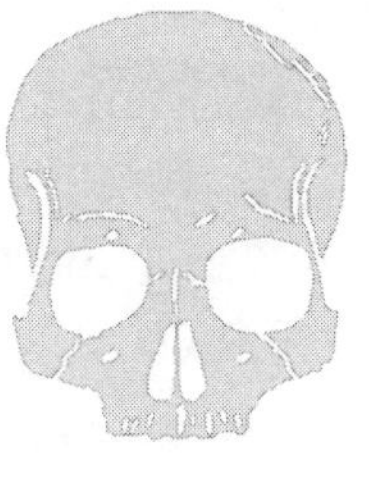

30

There didn't seem to be anyone in the outer office, and the inner office door was almost, but not quite, shut. Corrie led the way and knocked.

"Come on in," came Watts's strong voice.

Corrie opened the door and stepped in. She hadn't actually been in Watts's office before, and she was surprised. The outside of the building was nice-looking, if a bit sterile, but the sheriff's office itself was more like a cabin in the mountains, with knotty pine walls hung with a couple of small Navajo rugs and the head of a bull elk over a bricked-up fireplace. The desk was neat as a pin, and filing cabinets lined one wall.

"Now, this is a pleasant surprise," Watts said, standing up. "Special Agent Swanson. And Dr. Kelly, too. On a beautiful Monday morning, no less. You're just in time—I was about to head out to lunch. What can I do for you?" He ran his hand through his curly hair. "Oh, sorry," he added. "I should be offering you a seat."

"Thanks," said Corrie. They sat down, and he did likewise.

"Any developments?" Watts said.

"Yes," said Corrie. "But... well, can this be kept confidential for now?"

Watts nodded. He folded his hands and leaned forward, an expression of interest and attentiveness on his face.

"Are you familiar with Anzuelo Canyon?"

"I've heard of it. Out by Pie Town?"

"That's right," Nora told him. "There's a pueblo ruin above the canyon called Tziguma."

"Never been there."

Corrie hesitated, then removed the photo from a manila envelope and placed it in front of Watts. "That's an aerial photo of the area."

Watts picked it up. "Looks old."

"We've dated it to roughly 1940."

"So this is Anzuelo Canyon?"

"Yes," Nora said, pointing at the photo. "And that's the location of the old Tziguma mission church. Destroyed during the Pueblo Revolt."

He nodded. "Where'd you get this?"

"I got a warrant to search the Gower farmhouse," Corrie told him. "It was tucked behind an old picture."

"Interesting."

"So yesterday afternoon," Corrie continued, "we went there."

"Find anything?"

Corrie swallowed. "We didn't have time. We were shot at."

Watts almost stood up. "Shot at?"

Corrie told him the story. Even before she had finished, Watts had gotten up from his desk and was reaching for his hat. "Let's go."

"What about your lunch?"

Watts waved this away. "You saw where he was shooting from,

right? You can bet he left tracks and maybe other evidence, as well. We need to get out there while the sign is still fresh." He fitted the hat to his head, lifted his revolvers and holsters from a hook, buckled them on. "We'll take my vehicle."

They arrived at the edge of the canyon as the sun passed the meridian, casting small puddles of shadow below the rock formations.

Watts examined a digital map on his cell phone. "We'll approach indirectly, above the canyon. It's a little longer, and a bit of a bushwhack, but safer." He took off hiking along the rim, while they followed, circling around through the sparse piñon and juniper scrub. After half a mile he suddenly stopped, spreading his arms to halt the others.

Slowly, he knelt and examined the ground. Then he gestured for them to come over.

"See that?" he said, pointing to fresh marks in the sand. "Someone came through here. Large foot: maybe size eleven. A man. Heavy. These are no more than twenty-four hours old, probably less."

"So you think it's the shooter?"

"Let's follow the tracks and see where they go."

He moved forward, keeping to one side. The sections in sand were easy to see, but Watts seemed able to follow the footprints across areas of hard gravel and even bare rock.

Even Nora was impressed. "How do you do that?" she asked.

"It's sandstone, so a walking man leaves faint abrasions. Here, take a look."

Corrie dropped to her knees and looked, with Nora peering from the other side.

"I can't see anything," Corrie said.

Watts ran a finger lightly over the sandstone surface. "There are loose grains here, but not here."

"I still don't see it."

"It's not hard when you spent half your childhood looking for lost cows." He laughed. "That's why I became a cop instead of a rancher. I don't ever want to track a cow again."

The man's trail followed the top of the canyon, circled around past the slot, then climbed up the back side of the mesa, arriving at a rimrock plateau.

"That's it," said Corrie. "Over there is where he was shooting from."

"You two stay back," Watts said. "I'm going ahead. I'll call out when I'm finished."

Bent over, Watts followed the tracks until he disappeared behind some boulders. Five or ten minutes passed, then they heard him shout. "Come in!"

They followed his trail around the boulders. He was standing to one side, taking photos with his cell phone.

"Circle around here and let me show you something."

They came over.

"Okay, here's my reconstruction. The man came in here the way we did—there are his prints. He's got a rifle—you can see where he set it down temporarily, leaning it against that rock, where the rifle butt made a mark in the sand. He was here for a while—just hanging out, it seems. Then he took the rifle up again, walked to that other spot, and knelt. He then fired seven shots."

"Seven shots." Corrie thought back. "That's right. How did you know?"

"Seven casings. See them, stuck in the sand?"

"Right," said Corrie, embarrassed she hadn't noticed them herself.

Watts went over and bent down, picking one up with the tip of a pencil. He fished a Ziploc bag out of his pocket and dropped it in. "Going to fingerprint these," he said as he picked up the rest.

"Those are big casings," said Nora.

"Damn right they are. It's a .56-.56 rimfire cartridge from an old Spencer repeating rifle."

"Wasn't that some kind of Civil War weapon?" she asked.

"Exactly. It was a heavy-caliber, short-range rifle that fired a low-velocity round. It's a terrible weapon if you want to kill someone from a distance." He tucked the Ziploc bag away. "So then, after firing, he stands up and walks back over that way, and leaves. Goes back a different way than he came, I think, because I only saw ingoing prints, not outgoing."

"Why would some crazy guy be taking potshots at us with an antique rifle?" Nora asked.

Watts shook his head. "I think it's a lot more likely this was just some jackass plinking in the mountains without a proper backstop. He didn't see you."

Corrie stared at him. "Are you kidding? The rounds were hitting all around us!"

"How close?"

"Like ten feet."

Watts smiled wryly. "Ten feet? Come over here."

Corrie came over, and Watts said: "Here's where he was kneeling when he fired. You kneel down right here, too." He placed his warm hands on her shoulder and steadied her as she knelt. "Now, hold your arms up like you're firing a rifle and sight down to the ruins." He helped adjust the re-creation with his hands, arms around her back. "Like that. Now: What do you see?"

Corrie looked toward the ruins. "Not much but that pillar of adobe."

"That's right. He was shooting at that pillar, which makes for a prominent target. You just happened to be hiding behind it, out of sight."

"Bullshit. He was shooting at us."

Watts turned to Nora. "What do you think?"

Nora hesitated. "It's hard to say." It was clear to Corrie the archaeologist didn't want to openly disagree with her—but it was also clear that she saw Watts's point.

"That Spencer," said Watts, "holds seven rounds in a tube magazine. He shot seven rounds. Seems like he came out here to try out the gun, fired a full set of rounds, then left. Those antique rounds cost thirty-five dollars each. You can't buy them new. This guy was a serious gun collector, not a sniper."

"Do gun collectors often fire their weapons?"

"Oh yes. A true collector buys working weapons and wants to fire them at least once, just to have the experience. That's part of the romance of collecting a fine old weapon. Maybe I'll get lucky with the prints. Unless you want to take them to the FBI lab?"

"God no," said Corrie. "I don't even want them to know I was out here. And getting shot at by some dumbass cowboy firing a gun?" She shook her head.

Watts grinned. "So you're coming around to my point of view?"

"I guess so," said Corrie grudgingly. "But if he was such a serious collector, why didn't he take the shells?"

"They aren't worth anything."

"But you'd think he'd collect them, if only as souvenirs. Unless he *wanted* us to find them."

Watts shook his head. "You're overthinking this, Agent Swanson. If you don't mind me saying so."

Corrie did mind, but she said nothing. Just then, her cell phone rang.

"Amazing to get cell coverage out here," she said, pulling it out and seeing it was Morwood.

"Corrie?" Morwood's voice sounded wrong. She was instantly on the alert.

"Yes, sir?"

"We've just gotten a report: Huckey's body was found up in High Lonesome. At the bottom of an old well. It looks like an accident, but we've got the ERT up there."

"What was he doing?" Corrie asked, amazed.

"It seems he was, ah, looting the place." Morwood paused. "I'm heading up now. Meet me there as soon as possible."

31

It was a long, bone-rattling drive from Anzuelo Canyon to High Lonesome. By the time they arrived, Corrie was heartily glad to get out. It was already late in the day, and the sun had sunk into a pile of distant thunderheads, turning them into towers of blood and casting a strange reddish light over the landscape. The entrance to the ghost town had been blocked with crime scene tape, and several cars and vans were parked just outside.

Beyond the vehicles, the place was swarming. Corrie could see Morwood talking to the Evidence Response Team, standing around the well. As she approached, she could hear his voice—uncharacteristically loud. When he saw her, he broke off and came over.

"What's this?" he asked with annoyance, staring at Nora and Sheriff Watts. "I was hoping to keep this incident under wraps!"

Corrie was surprised by his vehemence. "Sir, when I got the call, we were investigating an unrelated aspect of the case. It would have required a major detour, and delay, to drop them off."

Morwood didn't reply to this, but it seemed to mollify

him somewhat. He looked at the group. "This is all strictly confidential."

"Understood," said Nora.

"Come with me," he told Corrie. Then he glanced at Nora and Watts. "You might as well come, too."

Morwood led them to the site. A winch with a bloody stretcher dangling beneath it was still hanging over the well. The wooden well cover, old and worm-eaten to begin with, was broken in half, and next to the well, stretched out in an unzipped body bag, lay Huckey's corpse. His head was covered with a folded plastic sheet.

"Smell that?" Morwood said, gesturing at the body.

Corrie hesitated. Smell what—the dead body? This was an odd request.

"Come closer."

When Corrie did so, a movement of air brought the sudden strong smell of alcohol to her nostrils.

"Was he drinking?"

"He stinks of it, doesn't he?" said Morwood. He gestured over his shoulder. "He was camped over there. The spot was littered with Southern Comfort miniatures, with more in his damn pack. We've taken blood to find out just how impaired he was."

"How was he found?" Nora asked.

"He didn't show up at work this morning. His wife was frantic, said he was supposed to be home Sunday night. We triangulated his cell phone pings. Hell of a job, too—the signal keeps cutting in and out this far from civilization; we were lucky to do it." He turned to one of the ERT techs. "Tom, where's that stuff you found on him?"

"In the evidence locker, sir."

"Take a look at this." Morwood went over to the locker. Inside, laid out in compartments, were several evidence bags. "We found all this in his pockets." He pulled up some bags. "A gold coin, a ring, some old keys. The larger stuff is at his campsite. The guy was looting everything he could get his hands on. He had a metal detector and was digging holes all over."

Watts shook his head. "Why did the FBI keep a guy like this on payroll? I knew from the first he was bad news. He came in here, breaking down walls, no respect for the place."

Morwood turned to him. "Keep your opinions to yourself, Mr. Watts," he said acidly.

Watts coolly removed his hat, smoothed his hair, and fitted it back on. "That's not my style, Agent Morwood."

Morwood turned away brusquely and said to Corrie, "Come with me." He headed away at a fast walk. Corrie followed, Nora and Watts tagging along. God, she hoped the sheriff wouldn't make any more antagonizing remarks. She had never seen Morwood in such a state.

The wall of a small outbuilding had been freshly knocked down, and Huckey had dug several holes under the adobe foundation of the small church. As Corrie looked around, she could see that while he had done some damage, fortunately he hadn't had time to cause any real destruction before he fell down the well. They continued past the church to an area outside the town, peppered with holes.

Nora knelt among the shallow holes. "This area," she said, "was probably the garbage dump of the town—judging by all the broken crockery and bottles."

"Let's check in with Alfieri and hear the latest." Morwood charged across the old main street to where Alfieri was just stepping out of his Tyvek suit, red-faced and sweating.

"Fill us in, Milt."

"It's pretty straightforward," Alfieri said. "The evidence seems clear that Huckey came up here alone. He had a metal detector and was sweeping the ground, locating objects and digging them up. Drinking all the while, it seems. We found his empty miniatures lying almost everywhere. At some point, judgment impaired by alcohol, he walked across that covered well. The rotten cover gave way and he fell a hundred feet to his death. We think it happened at night, because his broken flashlight was found at the bottom with him."

"The well's dry?" asked Corrie.

"Yes," said Alfieri. "Dry as a bone. He, ah, struck the bottom headfirst."

No wonder they covered his head with a sheet, Corrie thought. "Where was he camped?" she asked.

"Follow me," said Morwood.

Huckey had pitched his tent in the lee of the wall of the old church. There was a small circle of stones where he'd built his campfire, a cooking pot, an empty can of Dinty Moore beef stew, more Southern Comfort minis, cigarette butts, and other trash. Lined up on an old plank were the other things he'd evidently found: a horse bit with silver engraving, a brass Spanish stirrup, old bottles, a china plate, a few pieces of flatware, locks and fixtures pried off doors, ivory piano keys, more coins.

Nora, who had lagged behind, now appeared as they were looking the campsite over. She knelt to examine the evidence.

"Could I please have a pair of nitrile gloves?" she asked.

Alfieri handed her a pair, which she snapped on. She picked up one of the old bottles. "Rich and Rare," she said, reading off the bottle.

"That's the same brand Gower had in his pack," Corrie said.

Nora examined some of the other items, then picked up a buffalo nickel. "Nineteen thirty-six," she said. "That also could be an item left by Gower. These are important clues."

"In what way?" Corrie asked.

Nora rose. "It might mean that Huckey found Gower's old campsite. I'd like to look around at some of these holes he dug, if you don't mind."

"I think that's a good idea," Corrie said quickly. She glanced sideways at her boss.

"Mr. Alfieri will show you where the holes are," Morwood said. "Milt?"

"My pleasure." The technician took out a sketch of the town, on which he'd marked the locations where Huckey had been digging. Corrie and Watts tagged along behind the others. Following the rudimentary map, they started at the far end of town and worked their way back toward the police tape.

Nora knelt to examine each hole carefully before moving on. "He was a busy little gopher," she murmured.

As they approached the livery stables, Nora paused at one particularly extensive area of digging. "This looks promising."

It was a flat spot not far from the old corral where they'd found the remains of the mule. Nora knelt and picked up pieces of a broken bottle. "Another Rich and Rare," she said. "And here's a circle of stones where he had his campfire." She moved aside a crusted tumbleweed. "Look at this!" she exclaimed, easing a chewing tobacco tin out of the detritus of the stone circle. It was rusted, but the stamped legend *Pat. Pending 1940* was still visible along its edge.

Nora stood up. "This was almost certainly where Gower camped. Do you see that rotten canvas in the sand over there? I'll bet that was his tent." She looked at Corrie, then Morwood.

"This should be excavated. There might be important clues here. And..." She hesitated. "If Gower did find more treasure, this would have been a likely place to bury it."

Morwood looked at Corrie. "Thoughts?"

"I agree."

Morwood nodded. "I do, too." He turned to Nora. "In retrospect, I'm glad you were here," he told her. "And I apologize for my lack of welcome. We should get this dig going as soon as possible. When can you start?"

Corrie held her breath as she watched Nora consider this question. She knew the archaeologist was under a lot of pressure at work, and quite honestly had no idea what the answer would be.

Nora finally spoke. "I'll need a day to get my gear together and review my assistant's progress at Bandelier. That means the day after tomorrow. This looks like a two-day job, so I'll have to camp overnight. If there are no objections, I'll bring along my brother, Skip."

Morwood frowned a little, but to Corrie's surprise he did not object.

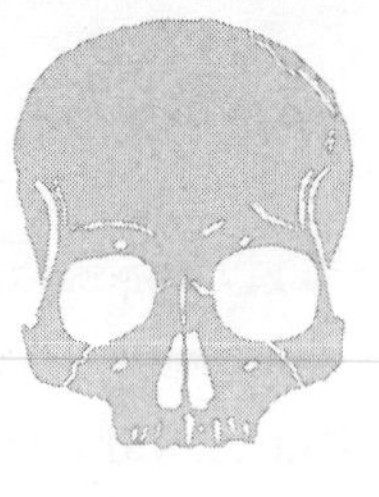

32

First Sergeant Antonio Roman sat in the driver's seat of his M1079 van, staring out the dusty windshield at the empty terrain around him. It managed somehow to be both drab and rugged: dust and sand and stubbles of prairie grass, with low peaks in the near distance. Surrounding him was a small circle of other vehicles: two M1113 shelter carriers, two M1123 cargo loaders, and an M1079A2 base platform. In front of the vehicles, a temporary command shelter had been erected, and within it half a dozen members of his platoon were finishing up the assignment that had come down to them so abruptly. Beside them was a trailer with a pneumatic catapult, currently empty.

His radio squawked. "Tango One, Tango One, this is Victor Nine Nine, over."

That would be Specialist Third Class Hudson, remote piloting the Nightwarden. Even out here in the Missile Range, with no hostiles for thousands of miles, Hudson liked to play soldier. Roman picked up his radio. "This is Tango One, copy."

"Final pass negative. Request permission to set return course."

"All acquisition data received in proper order?"

"All acquisition data properly received, sir."

"Very well, Victor Nine Nine, permission granted. Land and secure. Tango One, over."

"Copy, Tango One, land and secure. Over and out." And the radio faded into silence.

Roman made some notations on his tablet, then slowly looked out again across the landscape. It was after four, and the sun hung low over the distant mountains. Although he wouldn't tell his team, he was eager to wrap up this bullshit exercise and get back to base. The last episode of the *Westworld* season was going to drop this evening, and he didn't plan to miss it.

For the thousandth time, Roman wondered why the old man had suddenly gotten such a bug up his ass. Like any other army base, White Sands had its share of drills and tests, scheduled or unscheduled. But over the last few days, it felt like the place had been mobilizing for Omaha Beach. There had been scouting missions for impending bombing runs; air-conducted updates of strategic survey maps at ultra-high resolution; and even manual searches for ERW. Roman knew that over the years White Sands had seen its share of munitions testing, but careful sweeps had been done, and explosive-remnants-of-war searches seemed unnecessary make-work in the twenty-first century. But most surprising of all had been today's mission: his team had been tasked with using an RQ-7 tactical reconnaissance and surveillance drone to search for a malfunctioning missile that had impacted in the area of Victorio Peak. And not just any RQ-7-type drone, either, but a Nightwarden, the very latest, equipped with synthetic aperture radar, low-frequency sonar, and a satcom link for beyond-line-of-sight control. It was the only such drone on the base, and—Roman was pretty sure—not intended for mundane tasks like this. Another drone, a more garden-variety RQ-7A Shadow, sat in a trailer behind one of the Humvees as a redundancy measure.

Roman put the tablet aside and glanced toward the horizon, where the small speck that was the returning Nightwarden slowly grew larger in the fading light. Maybe something was going on at levels far above his pay grade. Maybe all bases were conducting unusually high volumes of drills and tests. At least, that's what he'd told himself until today—politics in the outside world didn't interest him much. But this search for a missing MIM-23 . . . that misfire had happened several months ago, and the conclusion was that it had self-destructed intentionally while in the air. Besides, he was fairly sure the Hawk hadn't been headed in this direction to begin with.

The Nightwarden was close now—that mother sure could move—and he saw Specialist Hudson in the command shelter, both hands busy with controls as he maneuvered it in for a landing. As he supervised from the Humvee, Roman put his speculations aside. The general was a good sort, as far as COs went—Roman had never heard of one who didn't have some peculiarity or other. Maybe that was a requisite for command. McGurk wasn't a petty tyrant, and he didn't swagger around like some tinpot Hitler. Roman had never heard him speak a word in anger. If his eccentricity was a passion for nuclear history, there was nothing wrong with that. In fact, it would explain the rumors that McGurk had specifically requested the post of base commander about eighteen months before—not exactly a smart career move, since such positions were usually assigned to colonels. But Roman would rather have someone who—

His thoughts were interrupted by movement in the side mirror. It was a small convoy—two jeeps, apparently—approaching from the direction of the Main Post. *What the hell?* His idle curiosity turned into something else altogether when he saw the star stenciled on the door of the lead jeep.

He leapt out of the M1079 as the two jeeps came up beside him, creating a roiling cloud of dust when they braked to a sudden halt. The Nightwarden had landed now, and Roman's team paused in the act of bringing up its trailer to stare in surprise at the sight of General McGurk's vehicle.

Roman noticed two MPs were in the second jeep. Behind the wheel of the first was McGurk's executive assistant, Lieutenant Woodbridge. She stepped out of the jeep with almost imperial gravity, then turned her tall, slender form slowly until she faced Roman. With her high cheekbones, perfect copper skin, amber eyes, and full lips that never seemed to smile, she reminded Roman of an Egyptian queen. And like a queen, her mere presence inspired fear—the yin to McGurk's yang. She stood still as a statue in the dying light. The two MPs remained in the second jeep, engine idling.

The only person moving quickly was General McGurk. He'd gotten down from the lead jeep and was rapidly approaching. His face wore an expression Roman didn't recall seeing before. Roman quickly came to attention and saluted, but McGurk walked right past him and stopped before Specialist Hudson.

"Report," he snapped.

Hudson, not used to being addressed directly by the general, had scrambled to his feet. "Sir?"

"Report!"

Hudson swallowed. "Sir, recon pattern finished without any positive results. Sir."

"Let me see that grid." McGurk took the tablet from the specialist's hand, peered at it, tapped it a few times. "You only covered sections C-12 to F-14."

"Yes, sir, those were the operational orders."

"That's less than half these formations!" the general said, waving his hand in the direction of Victorio Peak.

"Sir, ballistics stated that if the MIM-23 missile had crashed, it could only have been on this side of the—"

"I'm not interested in what ballistics said!" the general said. He had not raised his voice, but a suffusion of red had crept up his face until it reached his hairline. "Can a computer predict the path of a missile gone haywire?"

"No, sir."

"Can you tell me, *for certain*, that missile didn't crash on the far side of that formation?"

"No, sir."

"Then search the far side, damn it! And increase the target radius by two miles. Send the results to me directly."

"Sir—" Hudson began. But McGurk had already turned on his heel and was returning to his jeep. He glared briefly as he passed Roman.

It had happened so suddenly, unexpectedly, and quickly that Roman hadn't had time to intervene. The general got back into his jeep; Woodbridge followed; and then the two vehicles turned and began speeding back to headquarters. Roman watched them recede in a kind of daze. The general's angry presence here, micromanaging a routine mission, was unusual. This wasn't just a bug up the old man's ass—this was more like a horned rhinoceros.

Roman felt a presence come up behind him. "Sir?" It was Hudson. "We've completed the parameters of the sweep, as indicated by—"

"You heard the general," Roman interrupted. "The parameters have changed. We return here tomorrow at six hundred hours and extend our sweep, per the new orders."

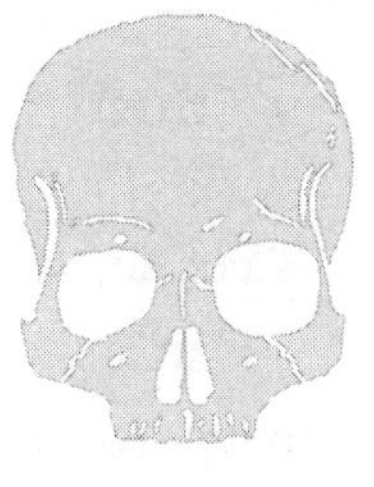

33

THIS TIME, WHEN Corrie Swanson drove up to the log cabin with the tin roof, Jesse Gower was waiting for her on the front porch. She got out of her car, navigated her way through the detritus in the yard, and paused at the base of the first step.

The man—as far as she could tell, still dressed in the same shabby clothes as the last time she'd seen him—looked back at her from one of the ancient chairs on the porch. It might have been her imagination, but it appeared as if his blond hair had been washed and combed. He'd definitely shaved.

"I got your messages," she said. "Both of them."

Jesse Gower had left the voice messages at her office, each time asking about the progress of the investigation—and the gold cross. He said nothing in return.

"Can I come up?"

He waved her up onto the porch, and she took a seat on a stool.

They sat for a minute in silence, looking at each other. She thought back to her harsh parting words the last time they'd met. They had bubbled out of someplace deep within her, unexpectedly. Maybe it was the fact that, in Gower, she could see a bit of her mother: addicted, self-absorbed, angry at the world. More troubling, she could see herself... or, rather, herself as she might have become.

"Listen," she said at last. "I'm not here to interrogate you or search your place or turn you in. I'm here as somebody looking into what happened to your great-grandfather. We're after the same thing. There's no need for us to be adversaries. And..." She paused. "I'm sorry about the things I said. When I left, I mean."

Jesse Gower took this in without changing his expression. "And the cross?"

"That cross is still evidence. It was found with his body, on public land. There's nothing I or anybody else can do about that for the moment. When this investigation is over, we can see about the possibility of giving it to you. That's complicated, too—there are laws governing such things. And..." She hesitated and wondered if she should tell him it was radioactive. But that information was strictly embargoed. "I promise to do what I can."

Gower took this in, too. She sensed that, between phone calls, he'd had some time to think things through as well.

"And I didn't mean to come across as such an asshole," he said. "It's just..." and he waved vaguely over the dust-bowl yard, the rusting implements, the oppressive and overwhelming sense of lost dreams. Corrie understood immediately. Going off to an Ivy League school after such a difficult upbringing must have seemed like ascending to a better world. But that world had fallen apart, and now he was back here—worse off than ever.

"I grew up in Kansas," she said. "In a town not much bigger, and only a little less ugly, than this place." She caught herself. "I didn't mean—"

"No. You're right. It's ugly." Jesse paused. "Cambridge was a revelation to me. I had no idea the world could be so green."

"Green isn't always so great," Corrie replied. "I grew up surrounded by fields of corn. As a kid, I thought they went on and on and on, without end. A green hell."

They were silent a moment. Then Gower stirred. "Do you want a glass of water or something? Sorry, I really don't have—"

"I'm fine. Thanks, though." There was another brief silence as they looked out over the desolation. Then Corrie took a deep breath, having made a decision.

"Your great-grandfather was killed in the Trinity test," she said. "We think he was out searching or hunting—for relics, perhaps—out in the Jornada del Muerto desert. He got caught in the blast. He made it back to his camp at High Lonesome, but he died soon after."

"Jesus." While she'd spoken, his face had turned to a mask of shock and disbelief. "And you're saying he's been buried out there—since the day they tested the bomb?"

"Yes. We believe we've discovered his campsite. It's in the process of being examined."

"Have you learned more about the cross?"

Corrie hesitated. She didn't want to arouse too much interest, since it was still anyone's guess whether Jesse Gower could ever claim the artifact. "It was irradiated, too—he was carrying it with him when the bomb went off. We don't have much information about it, beyond that it's old and valuable. It may have been the property of a Spanish friar carrying out missionary work across the Southwest."

"How irradiated?"

"Not much now. About what you'd get from flying at 35,000 feet."

Jesse sat back with a sigh. "So you didn't find a pocket watch on him?"

"No. Why do you ask?"

"It seems strange he'd be carrying the gold cross and not his watch. That was one of only two possessions he really cared about. It was kind of a famous heirloom in the Gower family, passed down for several generations. But it disappeared with him, so they say." He paused, ruminating. "A gold cross. Spanish. That sure sounds like treasure. You think he might have found the Victorio Peak treasure just before he died?"

Corrie didn't answer. Jesse Gower was putting the pieces together very quickly—maybe too quickly. Why, exactly, had she come out here again? Partly it was in response to his calls. But something in her gut said he knew more than he'd already told them.

Into the silence came a cackle from the direction of the henhouse.

"Pertelote!" Gower cried. "Way to go!" He turned to Corrie. "There's my supper."

"Pertelote?"

"Sure. I can tell all the hens by their cackles. They're eccentric little beasts."

"But where on earth did you get that name?"

Gower went quiet for a moment. "The residual effects of my education. I've named lots of things on this old ranch after bits of English literature, sitting out here on this porch. Not much else to do. Chaunticleer and Pertelote were a rooster and hen from Chaucer's *Canterbury Tales*. Pertelote was my rooster's favorite—until he vanished. I think a racoon got him. I've named all the other hens, too. And the henhouse is Canterbury. And that old blasted tree is Childe Roland, from Byron's poem—

to me it sort of looks like a knight that hasn't fared too well. And all that space between the road and the fence is the Waste Land." He paused. "Guess you don't need to have read Eliot to figure that out."

Corrie listened to this sudden rush of words with surprise. Jesse Gower clearly did have a brain. She had an unexpected urge to ask him about his novel, but that subject hadn't gone over so well the last time. Instead, she pointed idly at the shuttered old toolshed, its windows nailed over with ancient boards. "And what do you call that?"

"Nothing," Gower said abruptly. He shut down so quickly Corrie sensed that she'd accidentally said something wrong. Changing the subject, she went on: "That pocket watch you mentioned. Can you tell me more about it?"

"It was a gold flyback chronometer."

"What's that?"

"It's what in horology is known as a 'complication'—something a timepiece can do other than just tell the hours and minutes. Among other things, chronometers can count seconds very accurately. Basically, a flyback chronometer is one where the second hand resets automatically, without the need to push a button."

"Horology? Sounds like something a pimp might study."

For the first time, Jesse smiled. "Like I told you, my dad knew something about watches and watch repair. He usually got crappy Timexes to work on. But once he got an old Patek Philippe to clean and regulate. I remember him letting me see the inside of it. There was an entire little world in there—levers, springs, rotors, even jewels. I've never seen my dad so excited. It was the only time he got to work on one of the Holy Trinity."

"The what?"

"The three oldest and greatest Swiss watchmakers. Patek Philippe, Vacheron Constantin, Audemars Piguet. Each of their watches containing hundreds of pieces, made with the most meticulous care. And all hidden from view, working quietly and perfectly together."

As he spoke, a shine had come into Jesse's eyes.

"What about Rolexes?" Corrie asked. "I thought they were the best."

"They have some iconic designs. But they're basically tool watches. They aren't made with the same fanatical care, and they don't have things like perpetual calendars or..." He stopped talking, apparently noticing how Corrie was staring at him.

"Go on," she urged.

He shrugged. "Why bother? I could never afford a watch like that in a million years. Not even if I sold—" And here he went silent again.

Corrie decided to let her silence match his own for a minute. Here was a man who spent all his time alone with his thoughts. He wasn't used to sharing them with others.

"You said your great-grandfather only cared about two possessions," she said casually after a while. "What was the other one?"

He looked at her a minute, as if balancing an innate suspiciousness with an urge for companionship. "An old drawing," he said at last.

"Why was it so precious to him?"

"Who knows? It was another one of those things passed down in the family, like some holy book or something. My mom wore a cameo her whole life, even though it turned out to be a fake. People grow fond of things." He hesitated. "Besides, it's long gone."

Corrie could feel him withdrawing, closing up. At the same time, her mind was working, putting together some of the things Gower had just said. *Even though it turned out to be a fake...*

She looked around, her gaze stopping at the toolshed. There was something defensive in the way Gower had responded to her question about it. And the padlock on that shed looked suspiciously new, compared to everything else around the place.

"That toolshed—would it be possible to take a look inside?"

"Why?" Gower asked, his voice rising in pitch. "That's the second time you've mentioned the shed."

"It's curious-looking, I just thought—"

"You just thought. You just thought you could come out here, tease me with vague promises about that cross, and then ask more questions. What do you think is in there? A meth lab, maybe?"

"No, I—"

"All these bullshit implications about being a kindred spirit, about Kansas, pretending to be interested in watches... what you're really trying to do is pump me for information! You fucking cops are all alike!" He was on his feet now, shouting, eyes watering. "And to think I almost bought it! Get out! Get the fuck away and don't come back!"

Corrie realized there was nothing she could say. He had flown into a sudden, irrational rage, bipolar style. She had seen it in others before, and there was only one way to respond. And so, while Gower was still yelling, she stood up, descended the steps, and walked briskly back to her car.

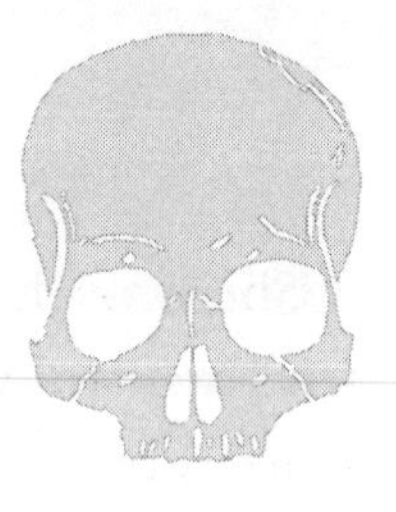

34

Nora sat back on her heels and contemplated the completed excavation of Gower's old campsite at High Lonesome. She'd opened six square meters, encompassing the heart of the campsite, uncovering Gower's firepit, his trash, a rotten tent, and an alarming number of empty bottles of Rich & Rare. It had been a strange and unpleasant day: a high screen of clouds had covered the sun, and strong gusts of wind blew tumbleweeds about the ruins, depositing a thin blanket of dust over everything, including her hair and eyes.

The excavation, on the other hand, had gone beautifully and much faster than she'd expected. She was glad of that. While Weingrau hadn't objected to her taking more time off from the Institute, she seemed a little less enthusiastic about Nora's absence than previously. Adelsky had done an excellent job at the Tsankawi excavation, but without her he had inevitably fallen somewhat behind. And she felt uneasy about all the time and attention Connor Digby was getting back at the Institute, where he had temporarily taken over some of her administrative duties and seemed to be doing a fairly competent job.

She shook her head and banished those thoughts. She'd spent ten years at the Institute; Digby had a few weeks. He was five years younger than her, with a publication record that, while fine, couldn't compare with hers. There was no way he would be promoted above her. It was small-minded and even a little paranoid of her to worry about it.

She turned her attention back to the dig. Most of the items she had uncovered had been photographed and packed away, including a very unusual object wrapped in leather that she recognized as a Native American medicine bundle. In eleven hours, she and Skip had managed to complete the work that she'd initially estimated would take two days. On top of that, the results had been spectacular. What they had found was going to completely overturn their previous ideas. It was, she thought with some satisfaction, going to blow the case wide open.

Skip packed away the last of the tools, then closed and latched the lid of the equipment box. "How about a couple of frosty ones to celebrate?"

Nora had to smile. Skip never missed a chance to crack a beer, but she had to admit this evening seemed especially appropriate. "Don't mind if I do."

"Coming right up."

"Let's close this up first," she said.

"You're the boss."

They rose and together pulled a large plastic tarp over the excavated area, pegging it down carefully. Then they retired to their own campsite, fifty yards distant. Nora was glad the wind had finally abated and they could enjoy the evening without breathing dust.

Skip rummaged in the cooler and returned with two bottles of Dragon's Milk, chips of ice still clinging to the sides. He opened them both with a flourish, handed one to Nora, and sat down next to her, cross-legged. He raised his bottle in salutation. "Here's to an amazing dig."

They clinked bottles and drank.

"So," said Skip, "what's your take on all this?"

"Well," said Nora, "first thing, it's clear that Gower had a partner—given there were two bedrolls in that rotten old tent. And I'd guess, from the amount of charcoal in the firepit and all that trash in the dump, they were here for quite a while—perhaps two weeks."

Skip nodded. "And the medicine bundle?"

They had found the medicine bundle inside the collapsed tent. It was made of fringed buckskin, much shriveled by age and rain. Nora had carefully unwrapped it and removed the items in it—a prehistoric bird point, a small agate fetish of a wolf, braided sweetgrass, a bundle of small feathers and sage, and five tiny leather pouches of dried earth.

"I think it probably belonged to his partner," she said, "which would mean he was Native American. I would guess Apache."

"How do you know?" Skip asked.

"It's what's called a mountain soil bundle. Four of those inner pouches contain earth gathered at the summits of the four sacred mountains, and the fifth would contain soil from the person's home area. Only Apaches and Navajos make bundles like that. I wouldn't be surprised if Gower's partner was Mescalero. All this land here was their traditional homeland."

"So where'd the partner go?"

She fell silent a moment, musing. "The partner must've cleared out fast. To leave that mountain soil bundle behind makes me think he was in a panic. And he never came back for it." She paused to take another sip of stout. "With today's discoveries, I think we can put together a clearer account of Gower's last day alive."

Skip rubbed his hands together melodramatically. "Goody."

The sun had sunk behind the Azul Mountains, and a purplish mist filled the desert floor below. Dark clouds were swiftly moving in, leaving only a thin band of lighter-colored sky above the mountains, which was soon extinguished. Nora could see lightning flickering beyond the mountains, too far away for the sound to reach them. It was one of those evenings that felt dark and ominous, as if the end of the world were approaching. With the setting of the sun, the temperature was declining rapidly.

"Let's build a fire and then I'll tell you my theories."

"Deal." Skip cut some grass and sagebrush with his knife as a starter, and a moment later a fire flared up, casting a warm pool of light in the rising darkness.

Nora began. "The date is July 15, 1945. Gower and his partner—"

"Wait. We need to give his partner a name. Otherwise, what kind of a story would it be?"

"Okay, let's call him X."

"No, that's no good. Too clichéd." Skip paused. "Let's call him A, for Apache."

Nora rolled her eyes. "So they'd been camped up here for a couple of weeks. They were looking for something out there in the Jornada del Muerto or the foothills of the San Andres."

"Treasure!" said Skip, cracking another bottle.

"Maybe. Or a lost mine. Or something of value left in the old Gower farmhouse. Anyway, they were camped here. A was probably looking out over the same landscape we're looking out at right now. It might have been an evening just like this one, with dark clouds moving in and a storm approaching. I read up on the Trinity test, and it turns out the firing was delayed because a lightning storm passed over."

"Must've worried them, the bomb getting hit by lightning and all." Skip's eyes gleamed in the firelight.

"It did. So Gower is out there in the desert, riding his mule. A is back in camp, waiting for him to return. Meanwhile, unbeknownst to either of them, the Manhattan Project is about to culminate its top-secret work by testing the first atomic bomb.

"Night falls, and the hours pass. By chance, Gower's route takes him near ground zero. The bomb is sitting on top of a hundred-foot metal tower, wired up and ready to go. The scientists are in their bunkers, waiting out the passing thunderstorm. Finally, just before dawn, the weather clears. At five twenty-nine AM they push the button and the bomb explodes. The test is a great success—except that Gower is caught by the fringes of the blast. Back in camp, A has a ringside seat to the explosion: a *direct view* of the Trinity site, twenty miles away. You have a line of sight to Trinity from here—right there."

She pointed into the indistinct expanse of nothingness between the mountains, filled with purple shadows. It gave her the creeps, looking into the empty, demon-haunted desert, where one of the most significant events in human history had taken place.

"Must've scared the crap out of him," Skip said.

"That's an understatement. Can you imagine what A felt when he saw a flash of light brighter than the sun? And then that monstrous fireball, the size of a city, punching up into the sky, along with the searing heat. A minute later, the wave of overpressure would have hit him, along with the terrible roar of the explosion. Nothing like this had ever been seen before in the history of the world. Even the scientists who knew what to expect were awed beyond belief and rendered speechless. Oppenheimer compared it to the radiance of a 'thousand suns.' "

She paused, still looking out toward the desert. "Gower was badly hurt. He's lucky his eyes didn't melt, which happened to so many at Hiroshima who were looking up when the bomb went off."

"So what do you think A did after he saw the explosion?"

"What can he do? He waits for his partner to return. Think of the guts *that* took. It was probably ten hours or more before Gower struggles back to High Lonesome. And what does A see then? Gower: bleeding, his skin burned red and coming off in sheets, his hair and clothes singed. The mule, too, was probably bloody, its hair burnt. Both received a massive dose of radiation and were dying. One of the symptoms of radiation poisoning is severe mental confusion and a raging, unquenchable thirst. So Gower's raving mad. A probably tried to help him, but Gower soon died, most likely screaming in agony."

"Jesus."

"I can't even imagine what that partner must have thought: witnessing the blast and then seeing his partner transformed into a gibbering, flayed monstrosity. It must have seemed like the work of the devil."

"How do you know A didn't split the moment he saw that blast go off?"

"Like I said: He wouldn't abandon his partner. And he was a religious man: not Christian, but a believer in the Apache tradition, as evidenced by that medicine bundle. In Apache belief, you must bury the dead. It's a sacred obligation. So A had no choice but to bury the body of his friend and partner, which he did."

"So you think Gower was deliberately buried?"

"Yes, and I'm kicking myself for not realizing it earlier. A doesn't search the body, so he doesn't realize Gower is carrying a gold cross... or if he does know it, he's beyond caring."

Skip tossed a few more sticks on the fire, and it flared up, beating back the encroaching darkness. "So he buried him in the cellar."

"Yes, because that's where the wind-blown sand had drifted in and was soft and deep and easy to dig. Now I understand why the body was in that strange hunched, quasi-fetal position: that's the traditional flexed position of Apache burials. The one arm sticking out probably just flopped out that way when A dumped the body in the hole. As soon as Gower is in the ground, A flees. He did his duty, but that doesn't mean he wasn't terrified. So terrified that he leaves everything behind—the mountain soil bundle, tent, bedrolls, and the rest of that stuff we uncovered in the campsite. Except... he does one other thing before he leaves. He puts down the mule to relieve its suffering. And he never returns—or dies before he can. Otherwise, that mountain soil bundle wouldn't have still been here."

"So what happened to him then?"

Nora was silent for a moment. "This happened seventy-six years ago, so A is probably dead. Doesn't take a mind reader to guess it probably changed the course of his life."

"I wonder if he ever told anyone."

"I doubt it. They were illegally trespassing in a closed military area. Gower's disappearance was never explained. I'm sure he took his secret to the grave."

"Yikes." Skip finished his beer. "You know, creepy stories always make me hungry. Dinner?"

"Sure."

An almost full moon just peeked over the ridges to their left, above the mountains, struggling through a brief opening in the clouds.

"Another beer?" Skip asked.

"No. Actually, yes. What the hell."

They sat by the fire in folding chairs. Skip prepared the coals and tossed a couple of steaks on the grill, along with some poblano chilis and corn. They watched everything sizzle for a few minutes. Then Skip forked the steaks over and turned the chilis. Suddenly he paused, then stood up, facing the rising moon.

"I just saw a shape," he said quietly. "Moving on the ridge up there, against the moon."

Nora stood and looked. "What kind of shape?"

"A person."

"Sure it's not an animal?"

Skip squinted up at the fuzzy moon, already disappearing back into the scudding clouds. "Maybe. But it seemed too tall and thin for an animal."

Nora scanned the mountain ridges, now black in shadow. "No one in their right mind would be up there at this time of night."

"Well, if they decide to pay us a visit, I'll say hello with my Remington 870."

"Don't let your trigger finger get too itchy," Nora said. "But keep that shotgun loaded and in your tent."

"I'll cuddle it all night," Skip said with a laugh.

The steaks were now done, and Skip served out dinner. Nora

ate with gusto. Skip, as usual, had prepared the food to perfection, the steaks juicy and pink, the poblanos charred just right, the corn roasted in the husk, shucked and slathered with butter. A few times she glanced up at the mountains above them but saw no light or trace of life—nothing but blackness.

"Hey, Skip," Nora said when they were finished. "Bring out your Gibson and give us a song. Let's chase away the gloom. I managed to give myself the creeps telling that story."

"'Old Chisholm Trail,' coming right up." And Skip ducked into his tent.

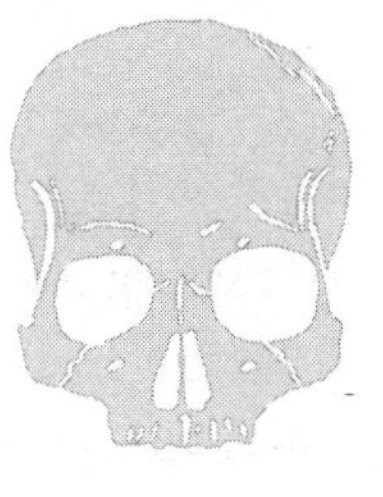

35

NORA WOKE IN the middle of the night, her heart suddenly pounding. It was pitch black, the moon having been obscured by clouds.

"It's me," murmured Skip, hovering just outside her tent flap. "Talk in a whisper."

She sat up. "What's going on?"

"There's someone out there in the dark."

"Are you sure?"

"I heard voices. Get dressed."

Nora quickly pulled on her jeans and shirt. She poked her head out of the tent. Skip was crouching by the tent, hidden in the dark, holding the twelve-gauge. The fire had gone out, and the blackness was complete.

"Where are they?"

"There," said Skip, pointing. "Listen."

She listened intently, but all she could hear was the faint sound of wind stirring the fabric of the tent. She stared into the darkness, and then, suddenly, she saw a brief flare of light, as if someone had lit a match and then immediately snuffed it.

"Shit, you see that?" Skip whispered.

"Yes."

They waited. Nothing. Nora's heart was pounding harder in her chest now, so hard she was having trouble focusing on the sound out in the darkness. The seconds ticked by.

There was a faint crack of a broken twig.

Nora held her breath, trying to get her heart rate down. Skip raised the barrel of his shotgun and aimed it into the unbroken sea of darkness against the mountains.

"They can't see us," he whispered, "unless they're wearing night vision. Which I doubt."

"What do we do?"

Skip was silent, still aiming the shotgun. Nora heard—or thought she heard—the sound of a faint whisper. She touched Skip, and he nodded that he, too, had heard it.

"I'm going to ease over there," he said, "and circle around to flank them."

Another crackle or rustle came from the darkness.

"And they're creeping up on us." He lowered the gun and cradled it, getting ready to move off. "We have no choice but to go on the offensive. Do nothing, make no sound. Keep in mind they're as blind as we are."

Nora answered by squeezing his arm, then letting her hand slip away.

Skip crept, with immense caution, into the darkness. Nora waited, staring in the direction of the sounds. Even as she did so, she heard another faint crunch of a footfall. It couldn't be more than twenty feet away. Skip was right—this was a deliberate, vigilant approach.

Skip's warning may have been wise, but Nora realized she couldn't wait there, helpless, like a sitting duck. Silently, she turned and reached back into the tent, fingers probing in the darkness for her folding knife, stored in a tent pocket along with her flashlight. She found both and slowly withdrew them. She laid the flashlight at her right foot and unfolded the blade of the knife—a blacked-out Zero Tolerance 0888. It locked in place with the faintest of clicks. If anyone came at her, she'd make damn sure they regretted it.

Another whisper came: breathy, closer. Jesus, it was dark. She extended her hand, gripping the titanium handle, crouching and tense and ready to thrust and slash. The balance and heft of the weapon—a limited-edition blade, mailed to her anonymously after she assisted Corrie Swanson at Donner Pass a few months before—was reassuring.

What was Skip doing? She could hear nothing of his movements, which was probably a good thing, but it left her feeling abandoned nonetheless. She could hear the blood pounding in her ears. The darkness was so absolute that the intruder, or intruders, might be mere inches from her and she wouldn't know. She arced the knife through the darkness before her, slowly. Nothing.

More seconds ticked by. Could she turn on the flashlight and toss it, as a diversion? No—as soon as she turned it on it would reveal her location, make her a target. Her mind went through various other scenarios, but none of them seemed to have much chance of success. She simply had to trust in Skip. He was the one with the shotgun.

...A whisper in the darkness, so close she almost believed she could feel the brush of the person's breath. She reached out with the knife again and swept it in front of her—nothing.

She was now so tense it was an effort just to draw breath.

And then she felt rough fingers brush her face.

With a scream she thrust out with the knife, slashing back and forth, the blade encountering resistance and biting in. There was a cry of pain. Still flailing, she scrambled backward, falling into her tent—and at that same moment she heard the monstrous crack of the twelve-gauge. Its muzzle flare briefly lit up the scene, illuminating three men: two right in front of her and a third behind, carrying rifles, with Skip off to one side, shotgun pointed. He fired again, another massive boom that caromed off the mountains, mingling with shouts and cries and the scrabbling sound of men retreating in haste.

Nora seized her flashlight and turned it on, just in time to see the last two figures disappearing into a nearby ravine. Skip came rushing over and put a steadying arm around her.

"Are you all right?" he asked.

Nora nodded. "I'm fine," she gasped. "Did you see them? Did you hit one?"

"There were three of them—but it all happened so fast I didn't get much of a look. I fired over their heads. I mean, I didn't want to kill anyone unless I had to. I still had three rounds... if they'd kept coming."

Nora got her hyperventilating under control. "You did right." She held up the knife. "I think I slashed one of them."

"Christ, I'll say you did."

Nora glanced at the knife in the reflected glow of the flashlight. Its blade was dripping blood.

"Fucking scumbags," Skip said. "You know, I've been saying you were crazy, carrying around that ZT like it was an ordinary pocketknife—but I'm sure glad you had it with you tonight." He paused. "What the hell were they doing, sneaking up on us like that?"

Nora swallowed. "I've no idea. Let's get the hell out of here."

"No argument there."

They packed in great haste, Nora putting everything into the back of the vehicle while Skip stood watch with the shotgun and flashlight. She slowed down when it came to the artifacts, making sure they were properly packed in archival-quality boxes, while Skip urged her to hurry. As soon as she was done they tore out of the ghost town, Nora behind the wheel, and began the long, jarring ride in the dark back to civilization.

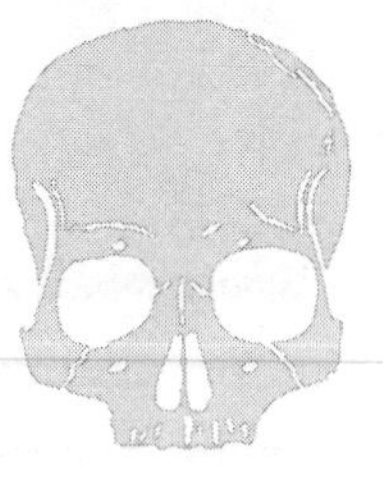

36

You said you cut one of them?" Corrie asked. It was almost five in the morning, and she'd been awakened by the phone call out of a sound sleep.

"I'm damn well sure I did," came Nora Kelly's voice. "Deep, too."

"You know where? Face? Arm?"

"No."

"Well, maybe we'll get lucky with hospitals or emergency clinics." Corrie paused. "And you don't know what they were doing there? If they were intentionally coming after you?"

"They were armed. But I wonder... If coming after us was their intention, I'm not sure we'd be talking now. My guess is they were headed to High Lonesome in search of something and were surprised to find us. Perhaps what happened was an attempt to scare us away. I can't be sure."

"Well, you two will have to come in and make a statement."

"I figured as much." Nora hesitated. "Look, Corrie. We made some important discoveries during the excavation."

"Such as?"

Briefly, Nora explained about Gower's partner in treasure hunting; the unusual burial position of Gower's corpse; the medicine bag that had been left behind.

"A what?"

"A medicine bag. A bundle of shaped stones, herbs, other things that possess supernatural or healing qualities. It must have belonged to Gower's partner. It's a very precious object and strange that he left it behind."

"Just as strange as leaving the gold cross." Corrie sat farther up in bed.

"Yes. Normally, I would have left the pouch in situ... but with those guys out there in the dark, I couldn't take the chance." A silence on the line. "Corrie, I think there's a possibility I can track down Gower's partner."

"What? After all these years? He's probably dead."

"Probably. But even finding out what happened to him in later life will help us. Look, a mountain soil bundle like the one I found is unique. No two are going to be exactly alike. It will help me narrow down who the Apache was, learn if he really was Gower's partner, and maybe understand what it was they were looking for."

"But that bundle is evidence."

"If we find the partner, and he's still alive, he could tell us what really happened. Fill in the rest of the story. He might even be able to lead us to the treasure."

Corrie opened her mouth to object, then sighed instead. "All right. You and Skip come in later this morning, say eleven. We'll get your statements. And I'll try to get you photos and a detailed list of the contents of the bag."

"No. No photos, no list of contents. I need the medicine bundle itself."

"You're kidding, right? You can't just take the bundle. That's part of the chain of evidence."

"Look, you were the one who came out to my dig site, practically begging for my help. You're the one who got me interested in all this—at just the wrong moment in my own career. Now we're going to do the right thing, uncover the history of what happened. Or I'm done."

"Jesus." Corrie let her head fall back on the pillow. "I'll figure something out, okay? Meanwhile, get some rest. And be careful. Looks like we both have our work cut out for us." She hung up.

About twenty miles to the southeast, in a small soundproofed room full of electronic equipment, General Mark McGurk watched as Lieutenant Woodbridge clicked a mouse button, pausing the audio and recording software that were running on her computer. She then saved the file and looked up at him.

"Five by five?" he asked.

She scrolled back through the recording—the scrubbing needle on the screen moving quickly over the digital waveform—then played back a section at random. Nora Kelly's voice sounded through the monitors: *He could tell us what really happened. Fill in the rest of the story. He might even be able to lead us to the treasure.*

"Outstanding, Lieutenant," the general said. "Outstanding."

"And if they learn the location, sir?"

"If they do," McGurk said, his voice going low and soft, "I know just the way to make sure they keep that knowledge to themselves."

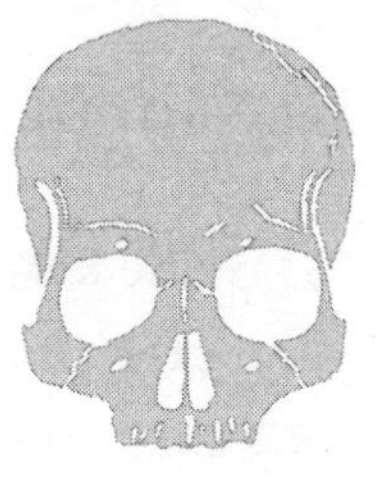

37

So a second person was working with Gower," Morwood said. "A partner."

"Yes, sir," Corrie replied. It was shortly after lunch; Nora and Skip Kelly had come by her office as requested, given their statements, along with partial descriptions of their attackers, and then left. Morwood, his eyes red-rimmed, was now paging through Corrie's initial report and its accompanying photos.

"A partner who hadn't been with Gower that day but who—when he saw the dying man come back to camp—made tracks like a bandit."

"That's what Dr. Kelly believes."

"And yet he had time to bury Gower, shoot the mule—and leave the gold cross behind."

Corrie sighed inwardly. It was true, this made little sense to her... and probably even less to Morwood.

"But these discoveries—suppositions—of Dr. Kelly's don't seem related in any direct way to the assault on them last night."

"No direct link has been discovered, sir."

"We'll see about that." He froze, looking at one of the photographs. "Sweet mother of God. Is that a Zero Tolerance blade?"

"Yes, sir."

"And the archaeologist was packing it?"

"Yes, sir."

"Looks like a limited edition. Belongs behind glass, not in somebody's pocket."

"Well, she used it to take a good slice out of whoever came at them. We've taken blood and tissue samples off the blade, along with a full battery of photographs." She didn't mention that, beyond these steps, Nora had declined to submit the knife as evidence.

"Well, if she's fast with a knife, that's a good kind to have at hand. We shouldn't have any problem following the blood trail." He put Corrie's report to one side and picked up another. "I'll be sending a team out to secure the entire site."

"What site do you mean? High Lonesome?"

Morwood nodded tersely.

Corrie almost asked a question but then suppressed it. But Morwood already seemed to know what she would say. "Yes. I'm taking over supervision of the case."

In the stunned silence that followed, Morwood opened the second report. "The full autopsy report is back on Rivers, and an analysis of his blood chemistry and other indicators show persuasively that he died of—" he consulted the report—"Brugada syndrome."

Corrie found her voice. "Brugada syndrome?"

"I've never heard of it, either. 'Brugada syndrome, brought on by injection of carbamazepine.' As best I can make out, people in questionable health, or with latent cardiac issues—and our friend Rivers ticks off both those boxes—can have malignant arrythmias induced by an injection of epilepsy sodium blockers. Of which carbamazepine is one. There are lots of other big words in this report, too: polymorphic ventricular tachycardia; myocardial voltage-gated sodium channels; dilated cardiomyopathy. You're welcome to read it for yourself." He tossed the report back on his desk, where it landed atop Corrie's. "What it all adds up to is homicide. Rivers was murdered, probably by someone who knew him well enough—or was well connected enough—to know his general state of health. Rivers was also involved in various unsavory kinds of work, including fraud and the sale of antiquities, illegally acquired or otherwise. We're pretty sure that figure in the hospital video is the killer. With Rivers's death being a homicide, the canvas—Gower, Rivers, Trinity—has suddenly grown larger, and far more complex. That's why I'm getting involved."

"You're taking the case from me?" As soon as she spoke, she realized how pathetic and whiny the question sounded and regretted asking it.

"Don't take this personally, Corrie," he said. "It's standard procedure that any case handled by an agent during their probationary period be assumed by their supervisor if certain criteria are met. In this case, those criteria have been met—in spades." He smacked the papers on his desk in emphasis. "You should be proud of this work. A lot of the early heavy lifting, particularly when it comes to Gower, was done by you. And your gut instincts, especially in the hospital, have been proven right, in more ways than one. But the fact is, even now we're still not sure if the two dead men are connected—but to find out, we have to escalate the investigation. Do you understand?"

"Yes, sir," Corrie heard herself say. Her voice sounded oddly far away.

Morwood smirked, shook his head. "Sure you do. But you hate it nonetheless. I would, too. Try to look at the bright side: You're involved in a much larger investigation than you ever dreamed of that first day you went out to High Lonesome. And you're still going to be in charge of vital investigative avenues—the forensics, the irradiated corpse, the origin of the gold cross: avenues that, you've reminded me several times, are where your expertise lies. You're going to find your hands full."

The bright side. But Corrie nodded and said, "Thank you, sir."

"Don't thank me yet. We've got a long road ahead of us."

"But—" Corrie began. Despite her shock at this announcement, she still had things to say: the possibility Rivers was working for someone else; where White Sands and General McGurk figured into all this; if she could have permission to temporarily sign out the medicine bundle to Nora Kelly. But when Morwood looked up impatiently, Corrie heeded the warning bells in her head and simply nodded, turned, and exited the office.

The medicine bag and the rest of it would just have to wait.

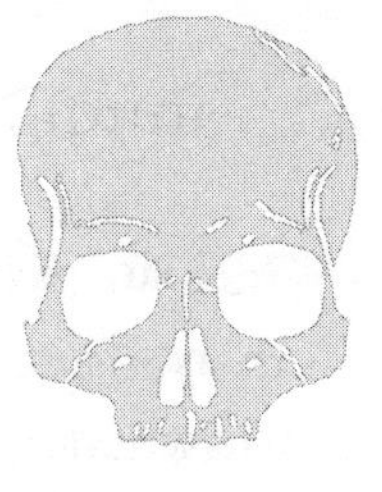

38

Corrie Swanson parked down the street from the Space Harbor Bar in Alamogordo. She got out of her car and took in the place. Alamogordo had turned out to be a much bigger place than she'd imagined, spread out at the base of the Sacramento Mountains. It had the feel of a government town, charmless and functional.

She'd heard that the Space Harbor Bar was supposed to be a favorite hangout of soldiers posted to WSMR and air force personnel from Holloman AFB. As she stood in the street, with the last of the evening light dying in the empty sky, she almost decided to get back in the car. This was a stupid idea, she told herself; it was throwback behavior. On the other hand, Morwood hadn't forbidden her to look into the WSMR angle—as long as she was quiet about it. She had nothing fresh to go on—the almanac she found had been carefully examined and determined to be of no value to the investigation. And there was nothing illegal or unethical in a young woman going into a bar and having a few drinks, FBI agent or not. If someone said something, and she accidentally overheard it—so much the better.

Since Morwood hadn't seemed open to further conversation on the subject, she might as well go on a fishing expedition of her own—a fishing expedition in the middle of the desert.

She took a deep breath, smoothed down her skirt, shook out her hair, and headed toward the bar's blinking neon sign: a depiction of the Space Shuttle taking off. Pausing inside the door, she looked around and pondered again whether she should proceed. It was eight o'clock, and the place seemed busy, especially for a Thursday night. There were many soldiers in uniform, and she was glad to see a surprising number of them were women. It wasn't very cozy—an unfortunate mixture of chrome and Naugahyde—but it was clearly a respectable joint, the atmosphere lively but restrained.

She pushed in and headed over to the bar. A soldier immediately slid off his stool.

"Offer you a seat?"

Corrie gave him an encouraging smile. "Well, sure. Thanks." She took a seat on the still-warm stool.

"Name's Billy." He held out his hand like a kid, and Corrie shook it, amused. He *was* just a kid, barely twenty-one, with the usual whitewall cut. She reminded herself that she wasn't all that much older.

"Corrie."

"Nice to meet you, Corrie. Can I buy you a drink?"

"Well, why not?" She glanced at the row of beers on tap. "I'll have an Alamogordo Pilsner."

The soldier ordered the beer, dropping a twenty on the bar, and ordered another for himself. He had obviously had several already.

"Do you live around here?" Billy asked, turning to her and standing a little too close.

"Albuquerque."

"Albuquerque. You're a ways from home. Whatcha doing down here?"

"Work."

He nodded, draining his beer and ordering another.

Corrie had hardly sipped hers. She quickly shifted the subject. "You based at WSMR?" she asked, pronouncing it "wizmer" as the locals did.

"Sure am. I'm an EOD technician."

"EOD?"

"Explosive ordnance disposal. We dismantle and destroy bombs and IEDs, using blast-proof suits or robots. I'm in training at WSMR, and then I'll be assigned somewhere else."

"That sounds fascinating."

Billy had now waved over another beer and sank his mouth into it. Corrie had never seen anyone drink so fast.

"It is, it is." He leaned toward her. "You staying around here?"

That didn't take long, thought Corrie. "I'm staying with my father."

"Oh. So you have family down here?" He chugged down his glass.

"Yes." She had to get this conversation focused, and fast. "EOD, huh? What's it like working at WSMR? You ever have any contact with the commander, General McGurk?"

"General McGurk?" The soldier seemed confused for a moment. "Oh, no, we don't have any contact with him." He raised his hand and fluttered his fingers in the air. "He's way up there, a mucky-muck, you know?"

"I thought there were a lot of rumors about him."

"Nobody talks about him that I know of. But listen, Corrie." Again he leaned in, beery breath washing over her. "Listen, we can talk about McGurk or whatever else you want. But maybe we could do it someplace, you know... quieter?"

He swayed forward as he said this.

"I like it here."

"Come on, my truck's just—"

Corrie finished her beer, placed the glass back on the counter, and stood up. "No, thank you."

"Come on, darling... hey, wait, don't go!" He swayed forward again and pitched facedown, as Corrie neatly stepped back to avoid him.

There was a small commotion, then a man in an officer's uniform smartly stepped up and came between her and Billy, who was struggling to get up.

"I'm sorry," he said to her, placing a hand in the small of her back and guiding her off. "Let's get away from him."

Now Billy's friends were crowding around and dusting him off, while the bartender was telling them to get him the hell out.

The man continued to steer her expertly toward a table. "Will you join me for a drink?"

"Sure."

She took a seat, and he sat down opposite her. He had a silver bar on each lapel of his shirt, which was khaki, not camo, and a little different from most of the other outfits people were wearing in the bar. Intense blue eyes, late twenties, fit and handsome, ramrod military bearing. This was more promising than Billy.

"Name's Ben. Ben Morse."

"Corrie Swanson."

He shook his head. "That guy's really a disgrace to the military. Maybe I should report him."

"Please don't. He's harmless." That was the last thing she needed: to be dragged into some sort of disciplinary situation.

He looked at her and smiled, eyes crinkling. "Okay. For your sake."

The waitress came by, and Corrie ordered another beer, while Morse ordered a gin and tonic. Corrie realized this beer had better be her last if she was going to drive home, so she decided to cut to the chase. She gave him her prettiest smile. "I'm kind of ignorant about the military, but those bars—what rank is that?"

"Lieutenant. Lieutenant Morse, at your service." He gave her a mock salute.

"Oh, you're an officer, then?"

"Yes, I am. Just a JG, but I'm due for promotion to full lieutenant. In fact, I'm leaving for San Diego the day after tomorrow."

Lieutenant JG... "Wait. So you're navy?"

His smile broadened. "Of course. What else would I be?"

"I don't know, I..." Corrie stopped. "Well, this is an army and air force base. And we're in the desert. The nearest navy ship must be hundreds of miles from here."

"We do other things besides sail the ocean," Morse said. "For example, I work at the VLF array."

"The what?"

"The naval radio station. It's in the northern part of the range, about six miles northeast of the Trinity site. West of Abajo Peak."

The drinks came. He raised his glass and clinked hers.

"Radio station? What do you play: Oldies? Top Forty?"

Morse chuckled. "We only have one class of listener: submarines."

"You're joking."

Morse shook his head. "Low-frequency radio waves can

penetrate both the ground and seawater. That lets us forward orders to submarines. The conditions here are close to ideal—that's why we're a tenant command on an army base." He paused a moment. "Sorry, I really shouldn't say any more about it."

"That's okay, I totally understand." She understood something else, too: the way he'd said "tenant command" in a bitter tone he couldn't fully conceal.

"It must be rough duty, though," she said. "I mean, I'm just guessing. But far from sea, on a little patch of turf in the middle of army types who probably look on you guys as trespassers."

"It's not that bad," he said, but again his tone held the whiff of disgruntlement.

"Do you ever, ah, run into General McGurk?" she asked, in a way that she hoped sounded like she was intentionally switching subjects for his benefit.

His glass paused on the way to his lips. "You know him?"

"No, not at all." She thought fast, sensing a fresh edge to his tone. "It's that I had a friend, an officer, who didn't have a lot of good things to say about him."

He nodded. "Not surprised."

"Why do you say that?"

"I don't like to talk out of school, but…"

Corrie waited, her heart accelerating. All of a sudden, it seemed like this crazy, stupid mission of hers just might work.

"These WSMR commanders come and go. Most of them have respect for how things are done, understand the routine is there for a reason. But since McGurk's father was posted at WSMR as a lieutenant back in the sixties, he seems to think that gives him legacy rights to do whatever the hell he wants."

Corrie was surprised to hear this: The father was also at

WSMR? She quickly covered up her reaction. "That explains what my friend was saying. What kind of stuff, for instance?"

Lieutenant Morse took a quick sip. "He's been here just over a year, but he completely upended the test and training schedules. He moved some of the bombing targets as well. Just to assert himself."

"Why would he want to do that?"

He looked at her, his eyes suddenly narrowing. "Why the interest?"

Looking at him, Corrie realized she had pushed too hard.

Quickly, she made a decision. Good or bad, it was a decision. She reached into her jacket pocket, took out her FBI shield with her photo ID, and laid it on the table. He stared at it for a long moment, then looked up at her.

"Is this for real?"

"Special Agent Corinne Swanson."

He looked at her with complete astonishment, and then flushed, trying to cover up his surprise. "Excuse me—I'm just floored. You don't..." He stopped.

"I don't look like an FBI agent? Don't worry, I hear it all the time." As she spoke, she thought about how she might use this to her advantage. "In fact, this is one of my very first cases," she said, lowering her voice conspiratorially. "If you could help me out, I'd be really grateful."

He took a deep breath. "What's this about?"

"Can I ask you if you're willing to keep our conversation strictly confidential?"

"Not until I know where the conversation's going."

Okay, time for a different approach. Corrie put on her best crisp, official-sounding voice. She'd been practicing her presentation and interrogation skills, but it was hard to get the right balance between serious and bitchy. "We're investigating a death connected with WSMR. I wish I could say more. Let me just assure you that General McGurk is not suspected of any wrongdoing, nor is anyone at WSMR. I'm just trying to fill in some information about the general. If you'd be willing to answer a few questions, strictly in confidence, that would be really helpful to me—to us."

He thought for a moment. "Let me see if I can explain something first, just so you won't take what I'm about to say in the wrong way. As you guessed, there's some friction between my unit and the army—McGurk treats us like we're squatters. The air force contingent at Holloman isn't too happy with him, either. He's trod on his share of toes. And Woodbridge—that lieutenant he picked as his personal attack dog—she's a stone-cold operator, smart and ambitious and about as friendly as a rattlesnake. Put all that together, and you can imagine a lot of trash-talking about McGurk goes on—true or not, sometimes it's hard to say."

"Thanks for explaining the situation. So what do you know about McGurk's father?"

Lieutenant Morse glanced around and leaned toward her. "I don't *know* anything, really. Just rumors that I probably shouldn't be repeating."

"You can speak freely. This is all off the record, for my own information only. I won't even take notes."

The lieutenant looked a little relieved. "Some of the rumors are a bit absurd."

"Those are the ones I'd like to hear."

Morse hesitated again. "Where are you based? Albuquerque?"

"Yes."

"You been in this area long?"

"No, not really."

"Well . . . have you heard about the legend of Victorio's gold—the Spanish treasure hidden in the peak?"

Corrie felt a charge of electricity jolt her spine. "A little."

"When Lyndon Johnson was president—so the story goes—he somehow heard about the Victorio Peak treasure. He and the secretary of the army teamed up with the governor of Texas, and they organized a secret project at WSMR to investigate the peak with the latest technology and find the treasure—if it was there. They put together a select group of military officers at WSMR and Holloman to work on the project. That rumor, by the way, has been around for decades—never proved or disproved."

"And McGurk's father? Was he one of them?"

"So the rumors go."

"And . . . did they find anything?"

"Some people claim they did, but most say nada. They probed the peak, sounded it and drilled it, set off explosives. Total bust. And the reason they found nothing is that nothing's there." He finished his drink. "There *is* no treasure. The whole legend is bogus."

"And General McGurk?"

He shrugged. "They say he wangled the appointment at WSMR so that he could find the treasure his father couldn't. Which is why he's been altering bombing runs and such. According to the grapevine, he's using bombing runs as a cover for a treasure hunt. You see, when the EOD teams locate dud ordnance from those bombing runs, they go out and detonate it in place. The rumor is that they're screwing with some of the ordnance to create duds, then using that as cover for seismic blasting to locate the underground cavern supposedly holding the gold."

"Jesus," Corrie murmured. Suddenly McGurk's father having been posted to the base didn't seem so coincidental after all.

"Exactly. I told you the stories were absurd. And that's all I know—or all I'll admit to knowing, even to an FBI agent." He tapped her beer glass. "Now—would you like another? I've just got time for one more before I have to hit the road."

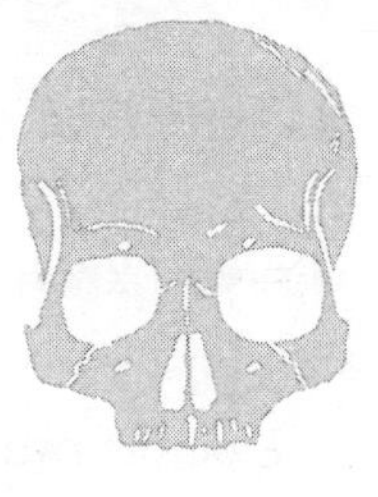

39

I'm afraid it would be better if you went in alone," said Watts, sitting behind his ancient, scuffed desk. "If you go in there with a cop like me, that won't start you off on the right foot."

"You know people in Mescalero," said Nora Kelly. "Can you at least give me an introduction? I can't walk in cold."

Watts nodded. "Sure, I can give you a name." He leaned forward and flipped through an old-fashioned Rolodex on his desk. He copied down a name and address and handed it to her. "Emmeline Eskaminzin. She's on the tribal council, and she's an attorney who's been involved with missing indigenous women cases. I've helped her, following up on leads in Socorro County."

"Thanks."

"She also happens to be the great-great-great-granddaughter of Geronimo."

"Wow."

"But don't mention that unless she brings it up." Watts placed his hands behind his head and leaned back, the old wooden chair creaking in protest. "That's sacred stuff in that medicine bag, you know. It might be pretty hard to get anyone to talk about it."

When Nora didn't reply, he continued. "If you want my advice, this strikes me as a wild-goose chase. It'll be a miracle if you can find out who that bag belonged to. And even if you do, what then? The man's long dead."

Nora gathered up the photos and put them back into a manila envelope. "At least it will get me away from here."

Watts's smile turned to a frown of concern. "Still no word on those guys that tried to ambush you at High Lonesome?"

"Not that I know of. From what Corrie tells me, they covered their tracks like professionals."

"I heard you gave one of them a souvenir. Maybe one that will never go away." Watts paused. "You're getting awfully involved in this case, aren't you? I mean, this isn't exactly archaeology."

You think I don't know that? Nora managed to swallow this remark instead of say it. Time was running out on her permit at the Tsankawi site; Adelsky, her graduate student, had finished all the work he could do without her supervision; and for a senior curator, she'd spent remarkably little time at the Institute recently. "I'd take this as an object lesson, Sheriff: when Corrie Swanson asks for your help, be careful what you promise. This whole thing started as an afternoon visit to High Lonesome. Now I'm hip-deep in it." She paused. "I'm intrigued as well."

Watts's smile returned. "Good luck, then."

The town of Mescalero lay in the mountains east of WSMR, in a pretty river valley surrounded by pine-clad hills. It could have been in Wyoming or Canada, thought Nora as she slowed down on the approach to town. Hard to believe the brutal desert was only twenty miles away.

She turned off the main road into the parking lot of a modest tribal building and community center. Grabbing her backpack, she entered the building and was greeted by a receptionist in a small lobby and waiting area.

"I'm here to see Emmeline Eskaminzin," Nora said.

"Third door on the right."

She went down the hallway, trying to suppress feelings of nervousness. The door was open, and a woman, sitting behind a desk in a small office, rose to greet her. She was strikingly tall and athletic-looking, dressed in a conservative suit and silk shirt straight out of a corporate law office. The only nod to Apache culture was her hair, pulled back in two braids, their ends tied with colored twine. She appeared around thirty.

"Dr. Kelly, right? Please, have a seat."

Nora sat down in a chair opposite the desk.

"What can I do for you?" The woman folded her hands with a smile. "You were a bit mysterious on the phone."

Her voice was quiet and low. In her mind, Nora had run through several ways to spin this delicate request; but now, facing this no-nonsense person, she decided to lay it out as straightforwardly as possible. "I'm an archaeologist," she said, "and I've been doing some consulting work for the FBI. I'm trying to identify the owner of a particular medicine bundle that we found during a recent excavation. I think it belonged to an Apache."

"A medicine bundle?" Eskaminzin asked. "How do you know it's Apache?"

"I'm not sure, but the objects inside appear to be Apache. And the Mescalero are the tribe closest to where it was found."

"Do you have it with you?"

"Yes." She took the container out of her backpack and put

it carefully on the table. This woman, she thought, would never know how much wheedling, cajoling, and threatening it had taken to convince Corrie Swanson to let her borrow the evidence.

Eskaminzin eyed the box but did not touch it. "May I ask where you found it?"

"In a ghost town called High Lonesome, in the foothills of the Azul Mountains at the north end of the Jornada del Muerto. Do you know the place?"

"I've heard of it. You mentioned the FBI. Is this a criminal investigation?"

"No," said Nora, "at least not yet. The bundle's owner is not implicated in a crime at all, and besides, it's at least seventy-five years old."

Eskaminzin pursed her lips, staring at the box, and a silence settled in the small office. Nora had the feeling she was one of those people who didn't speak until she had carefully gathered and considered her thoughts. "In Apache culture," she said slowly, "the medicine bundle is considered private. It's not meant to be shown to anyone. It's very unusual to find one abandoned."

Nora nodded. "I understand."

"Perhaps you could tell me why it's important to identify the owner?"

"There's an unusual story connected to it. It has to be kept strictly confidential."

Eskaminzin said, "Understood."

"Back in July of 1945, the bundle's owner and a man named James Gower were camped in High Lonesome while looking for something in the Jornada. That's the mystery—we don't know what they were looking for. Early on the morning of July sixteenth, Gower was crossing the desert on his mule when he was caught in the atomic blast of the Trinity test. Are you familiar with the test?"

"I am acutely familiar with the Trinity test," said Eskaminzin. "The bomb was set off on our ancestral lands, and it spread radioactive contamination over a large area. Please go on."

"Gower made it back to High Lonesome, but he'd received a fatal dose of radiation and soon died. His partner buried him in the traditional Apache fashion, in a flexed position, and then fled, leaving behind this medicine bundle."

"To do that, he must have been extremely afraid."

"He saw the blast," said Nora.

"He *saw* it?"

"Ground zero was in direct line of sight from where they were camped."

"How terrible."

"A few weeks ago, Gower's body was found up in High Lonesome, where it had been since the day of the test. Since it's on federal land it triggered an FBI investigation. I was asked to excavate the body, and later dig their old campsite. That's where I found the medicine bundle."

Eskaminzin remained silent for a long time, her face betraying nothing. Finally she said: "Please open the box."

Nora unbuckled the container and took out the bundle. Eskaminzin took the shriveled buckskin in both hands, handling it gingerly. She carefully opened it and slid the items out one by one, lining them up on her desk. Once they were arrayed, she picked each one up and examined it, turning it around, then placing it down for the next one. When she put the last one down, she looked up at Nora.

"Nantan Taza."

"I'm sorry?"

"This medicine bundle belonged to Nantan Taza."

"How do you know?"

"I'm sorry, I can't tell you how I know, beyond saying that every medicine bundle is unique and contains items that tell of an individual's clan and family. Nantan Taza was my grandfather's brother. That may sound like an odd coincidence, but we're a small tribe."

Nora could hardly believe her luck. "What else can you tell me about Nantan Taza?"

Eskaminzin folded her hands. "What you've just told me, about his witnessing the atomic blast, explains a great deal. We long wondered why he was the way he was."

"How so?"

"Everyone said that as a boy, Nantan was a dreamer, a happy-go-lucky type, full of plans. But then something happened . . . and he became a strange, dark, and silent man."

"And this thing that happened—it was around the time of the atomic test?"

"Yes. He never married, had no family. He earned a small living from a grazing allotment where he ran cattle, and he was a good hunter. He stood out from others not only by his solitary ways but also what some considered to be his visionary powers. Or so they say. Sometimes, people in great need would go to him to understand the future, or to ask for a vision or spiritual guidance. Even so, he was a forbidding person. Laughter and humor are a big part of Apache culture, but I never saw him so much as smile. Ever. He looked as if he'd stared the devil in the face. And from what you tell me, I guess he did."

"What happened to him?"

"About ten years ago, he departed."

"You mean he passed away?"

"No, I mean he left."

"Left to go where?"

"We don't know."

"He just left? How old was he?"

"Eighty-five. Let me explain. For a long time, as I've implied, he was regarded with a certain amount of awe. But in his later years, younger people became skeptical of the idea that he had special powers. They saw him only as a grumpy, off-putting old man. Some made fun of him. Finally, people stopped consulting him. I think perhaps he felt he'd outlived his usefulness. So one day he filled a sack with his possessions, took his rifle and ammo, got on his horse, and rode off into the mountains."

Nora paused a moment. "Why would he do such a thing?"

"In the days when we were a nomadic people, an old person would sometimes decide to go into self-exile rather than become an encumbrance. This was especially true when we were fighting the Mexicans and Americans and had to move like the wind. What he did was anachronistic, perhaps—but not unusual."

"So he just went off and—then what? Did he die?"

"Maybe. Or maybe he simply decided to live apart. Our reservation covers almost five hundred thousand acres. There's good hunting and plenty of water. He could have lived in some remote canyon and nobody would ever know."

"He'd be in his midnineties now," Nora said. "Alone in the wilderness for a decade...it's hard to believe he might still be alive."

Eskaminzin smiled indulgently. "We are the people of Geronimo, Cochise, and Victorio. We are survivors."

"If he is still alive, is there... well, any way of knowing where he might be?"

Eskaminzin was silent a long time before at last she spoke. "In his last years here, a young boy used to go by his cabin to bring groceries, chop wood, and help work his cattle. In return, I think Nantan would tell him stories. When Nantan left, that boy was the only one who seemed surprised—and upset."

"Could I speak to him?"

"He's a young man now, and you'll find him in Albuquerque, where he's got a job in a bank." She jotted on a piece of paper and handed it to Nora. "His name's Nick Espejo."

Nora rose. "You've been extremely helpful. Thank you." She gathered up the items from the medicine bag and began putting them back in the container. As she turned to leave, Eskaminzin said, "Be very respectful, please, with that medicine bundle."

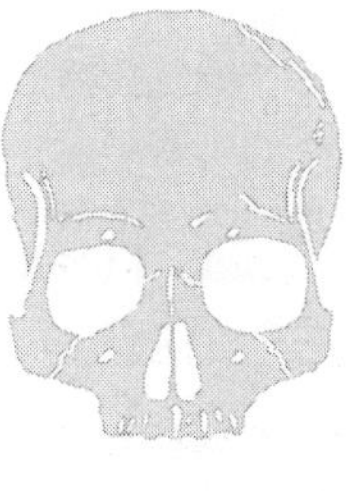

40

DON'T HANG UP!" the voice said the moment she answered the phone. "Please, just... don't."

Corrie recognized the voice, of course. Normally she would have hung up, but not before giving Jesse Gower a detailed explanation of how in her history of meeting countless losers, addicts, lowlifes, scumbags, assholes, and perverts in a remarkably short span of years, he took the prize. But she reminded herself it was an active case; he was a person of interest; and, if nothing else, she would have to make a note of his contacting her.

So instead she remained silent.

"Look. I've apologized before. Saying sorry again isn't going to help any. You know how... messed up I am. That's not an excuse, it's just an explanation. It's really hard for me to trust anybody in authority. I got that from my dad, who got it from his dad. Anytime a cop says something to me, I have to analyze it to see if there's some trap. You know, that was probably the longest talk I've had with anyone in maybe half a dozen years. That shows you what a pathetic life I lead. And, you know, the questions you asked, the interest you showed,

I guess I'm not used to it. I got paranoid. When people ask me questions, it's usually 'Where the hell's my money?'" He laughed mirthlessly.

Still, Corrie didn't say anything. As apologies went, it was a pretty good one. It had the ring of truth, at least. But since he'd ordered her off the ranch, she'd done some thinking, too. He had revealed more than he realized during their conversation. It was clear that, at the very least, he'd been pawning stuff—and the offhand remark about the cameo implied he'd learned a thing or two about estimating value. She wouldn't be surprised if he sold relics, too, and given how touchy he was about the toolshed, she imagined that's where he kept them. And then, there was that other sentence he'd started but not finished—which led her to another suspicion entirely.

She realized he had stopped talking. "Yes?"

"I was asking, will you accept a peace offering?"

"Like what? A baggie full of crystal? I'm not into biker food."

"That's not fair." He sounded genuinely hurt.

She sighed. "What kind of a peace offering did you have in mind?"

"I can't tell you over the phone. It would spoil the surprise."

"Look, Jesse. I've driven all the way over there twice, only to be run off both times. You're going to have to do a little better than that."

"All right." A moment of silence. "I wasn't exactly telling the truth about my great-grandfather's other precious possession. When I said it was long gone, I mean."

When Corrie didn't reply, Jesse said: "Well?"

"Well, what?"

"Aren't you going to thank me? I mean, that's a clue."

"A clue to what? But I knew it, anyway."

"You did?" A pause. "Do they teach you FBI agents to read minds now?"

"No. We're just trained to pick up on certain things. Statements that don't add up, or that strike you as wrong. *Or* that are interrupted in midsentence."

"I'm a novelist. I'm careful to always finish my sentences. Except when I'm swearing, but even then I try to be grammatically correct."

"Maybe so. But you did leave a sentence unfinished in our last conversation."

"Yeah? What was that?"

The sentence had been "Not even if I sold..."—but Corrie was not going to tell him that. "Let's just say that when I put it together with the fact your great-grandfather had something of value besides that gold watch, I get the feeling that maybe you were thinking of pawning something. But you didn't. Which means it's still in your possession. And it probably isn't just any 'old drawing' but something really valuable."

Then Jesse did something unexpected. Instead of gasping in awe at her deductive powers, he burst out laughing. Corrie, frowning to herself, did not interrupt him. Finally, the laughter subsided into infrequent eructations of amusement.

"I'm sorry," he said. "I'm not laughing at you. I mean, you were doing so well there for a minute."

"Oh yeah?"

"Yeah. You see, you used the word 'value'—when the actual adjective was 'precious.' Didn't pick up on *that*, did you?" Another irruption of laughter. "The watch went missing the same time he did—but he left the other thing behind. Nobody could ever figure out why he'd made such a big deal about it. But he treated it like a holy object. Wouldn't let anybody else touch it.

And so, over the years, it's been passed down: with the watch gone—it was first a sort of family curiosity. But so many years have passed that now it's more like an heirloom." He paused. "So—what do you think of that?"

"I'm not sure what to think," said Corrie, struggling to follow his ramblings.

"You were on the right track, though," Jesse went on. "In my great-grandfather's time, most people would have thought his precious item fit only to line a henhouse with. But over the years it's gained value. Maybe a *lot* of value. Even if Pertelote is still the only one who can enjoy it."

"And so you refrained from selling this precious thing, even while you sold all the other relics in that shed?"

"Are you trying to make me mad? Here I am, making a peace offering to you. An important one, at that."

"So tell me why this thing is important."

"My great-grandfather, carrying a fabulous gold cross, dying of radiation from the Trinity test... This other treasure of his was important to him, so surely it must be important to *you*."

Corrie tried to suppress her irritation at his coy teasing. Was this just another come-on, where she'd drive all the way out only to find him turning from Jekyll to Hyde yet again?

"You're saying this object could help further my investigation?"

"I don't think it could hurt."

Corrie sighed. "Why don't you just *tell* me what it is, Jesse, instead of all this bullshit."

"You have to see it. Really. I can't explain."

She thought about this. It was just worth a trip. "All right. I have some paperwork to finish up here. I'll try to leave within an hour."

"I'll fry up some eggs for us. If you want anything to drink besides water or malt liquor, you'll have to bring it yourself."

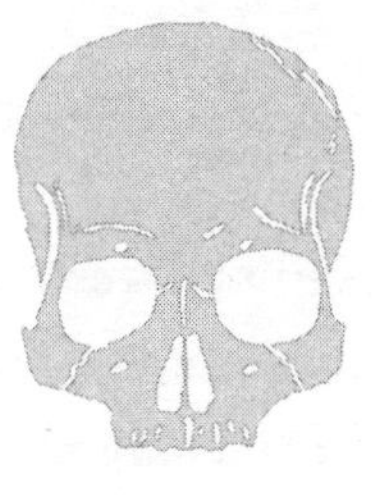

41

Corrie ended up wrestling with her casework for two hours, rather than one. It felt strangely pleasing to be working with documents involving one's own case…even if Morwood was in the process of taking it over. At last she rose from her desk, trotted downstairs, got into her car, and drove out of town. She wondered if this "precious object" wasn't just more bullshit.

The drive was as long as she remembered, but she was relieved that—although the sun had set and the roads had no lights—she found the way without getting lost. On one of the last stretches of dirt road, a big F-250 passed her going the other direction at high speed, which really pissed her off. She tried to catch its license plate in the rearview mirror, but the truck was so filthy with dust and dried mud that the plate was obscured. Men and their trucks—they were like boys playing with Tonkas. It raised a huge cloud of dust, and she had honked in annoyance, but the burly vehicle had been moving so fast it was gone and out of hearing. She spat out a mouthful of dust, then closed the windows and put the air-conditioning on recirculation mode. One thing she'd never get used to was the damned dust. Southern New Mexico made Kansas look like a tropical oasis by comparison.

She slowed as she approached the ramshackle Gower farm, then turned in at the spavined, tilted mailbox. Beyond the large collection of objectionable lawn art, the house looked dark. Surely this wasn't going to be Jesse's attempt at a candlelit supper?

She got out of her car, looked around slowly. All was silent.

"Gower?" she called out.

Nothing.

"Jesse? You there?"

When there was still no answer, she reached into the car and took out her flashlight, checked her gun to make sure a round was chambered, and then cautiously approached the house.

"Jesse?" she called again.

Where the hell was he? The property was small enough that he'd be able to hear her calling from any location. He didn't seem the type to play some kind of practical joke. Was he in the house, high on crank, headphones blasting, having totally forgotten the conversation they'd had a few hours earlier? She sniffed the air, but there was no odor of ammonia or weed—only the faint stench of bird shit from the henhouse.

When she called out again and there was still no response, she fell silent.

The old treads squeaked as she ascended the porch. Shining her light around, she noted nothing different. The screen was long gone, and the door itself was hanging ajar. She pushed it open with her foot, stepped inside, and then paused, slowly sweeping her flashlight beam over the living room as she took it all in.

The place looked like it had been hit by a tornado. Old

sofas were overturned, their stuffing torn out; bookshelves pulled away from walls, contents flipped through—she could see little notes, probably Jesse's, peeping here and there from the pages. A dresser stood askew in one corner, empty drawers grinning in her beam of light, the contents scattered. Manuscript pages covered everything like bunting. Pictures were torn from the walls, standing lamps sprawling, the TV staved in and knocked over.

She stepped carefully through the maelstrom of destruction, her flashlight continuing to roam. She considered turning on a light to see if there was power, then thought better of it.

She'd never seen the inside of the place, but she knew one thing: however Jesse lived, it wasn't like this.

Reaching the far end of the living room, she scanned the kitchen that lay beyond. It, too, was a whirlwind of devastation. One thing caught her eye—four eggs, broken, on the floor in front of the old stove.

I'll fry up some eggs for us. If you want anything to drink besides water or malt liquor, you'll have to bring it yourself.

She turned and made her way back out to the front porch. Some instinct told her that wherever Jesse was, he wasn't in the house. What was this—a drug shakedown? Maybe he owed someone money, and they'd come for it. It looked like there had been a furious tussle, followed by a violent and thorough search. Maybe he'd escaped out the back and taken off into the gathering dark—or, God forbid, been kidnapped.

She thought of the truck that had passed her on the road.

Stepping down off the porch, she let her light range over the property. The henhouse looked untouched, but even from this distance, she could see that the padlock had been cut from the toolshed door.

Now she pulled her gun from its holster. Except for the beam of her light, and her own footfalls on the dusty ground, silence and darkness were absolute. Corrie got a good fix on the location of the shed, then turned off her light and stood motionless, allowing her night vision to return. Once she could see its outline, she began creeping forward again—slowly, slowly—until she reached the broken lock.

Her heart was beating like a hammer. Still silence. She readied herself, and then—moving fast—kicked open the door, dropped to a defensive stance, and covered the room with her Glock, bringing up the flashlight to support her right hand with the "ice pick" Harries grip she'd been trained to use.

"FBI, nobody move!" she barked.

There was nothing but the echo of her voice and the faint squeaking of the door.

Slowly, Corrie straightened up. As she did so, her elbow brushed against a light switch—the old-fashioned kind you toggled on and off by pushing. If she hadn't provoked a reaction yet, she wasn't likely to now.

Lowering the flashlight but keeping the gun ready, she pushed the button.

A naked bulb in the ceiling came on. It revealed a space full of the same furious carnage as the main cabin. Jesse Gower sat in a chair near the back wall. He was hog-tied, ankles and wrists bound together behind the frame of the seat. His head was flung back at an unnatural angle, but nevertheless she could see his face was a mask of blood. His shirt and ragged shorts were sodden with blood; more spatter encircled the ground in front of the chair, along with a couple of teeth. It was obvious he had endured a methodical, savage beating.

"Jesse?" she called out quietly. Then she approached the chair.

But she already knew what she'd find. Gower's eyes were open and filmy, and he wasn't breathing. She touched his neck and found no pulse, the flesh cool.

She stepped back, feeling slightly sick, and glanced around the shed. Half of it had been lined with rude wooden shelving. The other part held piles of old tools, auto parts, rusting tin cans, highway signs, and other detritus, apparently once covered by oily tarps. This was merely a mental reconstruction, however, because the interior of the shed was now such a storm of debris that it was impossible to be sure of anything. Except for the obvious: this was the result of a fierce search.

And one other thing: given the level of destruction, if they hadn't found whatever they were searching for, then she wouldn't, either.

42

AN HOUR LATER, at ten o'clock, the Gower Ranch had become a crowded and bustling crime scene. Portable floodlights bathed the house and toolshed in pitiless illumination, and Evidence Response Team workers in uniforms and gowns went to and fro with cameras, evidence bags, and forensic equipment of various sorts.

Corrie Swanson stood back from the fray, leaning against the side of the ERT van. To one side of her was Morwood, and to the other was Sheriff Watts, who had arrived a few minutes earlier while Morwood had been questioning Corrie about what she had seen.

Watts took off his hat, brushed a speck of invisible dust from it, and fitted it back on. "And what, exactly, was he going to show you?"

"He called it his great-grandfather's 'other precious possession.' He said nobody else knew why he treasured it so much, but over time it became a kind of family heirloom."

"Was he bullshitting you?"

"Didn't sound like it to me."

"Okay." Morwood called over the medical examiner, his gowned figure glowing unearthly in the bright light. "What have you got?" he asked.

The man nodded. "Prelim. The victim probably died of a traumatic cervical fracture, caused by radical hyperextension."

"A broken neck?" Morwood said. "He seems to have been worked over pretty goddamned well."

"We'll know more after the postmortem," the medical technician said. "It's possible another injury might have been the fatal one, but I would put my money on the cervical fracture as the proximate cause of death."

"Very well. Thank you."

Morwood turned to Corrie. "I want to commend you, Agent Swanson," he said. "You handled an unexpected and difficult crime scene with care and precision."

"Thank you, sir."

"Tomorrow, I'd like a full report on this matter. I'm particularly interested in the conversations you had with Jesse Gower and what brought you back out here this evening."

"Yes, sir."

"I wonder if the killers were looking for the same thing," Watts said, "and they tried to beat its location out of him."

"That beating," said Morwood, "sure looks like an attempt to get *something* out of Gower. But we have no idea *what*. Maybe he was selling antiquities to finance his drug habit. We haven't yet done a complete inventory of that shed, but it was full of artifacts, many worthless, and others that seem to have been, ah, dressed up to look otherwise."

"Fakes?" Watts said.

"It seems so. The point is, there might be many reasons

for someone to want something out of Gower: money, drugs, information, whatever."

"But we can't be sure they got it," Corrie said.

Morwood turned to her. "How so?"

"It's possible Gower's death was an accident."

"Accident?" Morwood repeated. "You want to know how many molars I counted in that shed?"

"What I'm saying, sir, is it's possible they didn't mean to break his neck. Shooting him would have been a more sensible way of killing him if that's all they wanted to do. Isn't it possible they accidentally killed him before he caved?"

"It's possible. We'll see what the M.E.'s report says about that." He turned to the sheriff. "Well, Sheriff Watts, it looks like we've got quite a homicide on our hands—in your county. The FBI is going to take the lead, but we're going to need your help. Jesse Gower, the land he lived on, and the people he associated with are your jurisdiction. *And* your expertise. I know you've already been liaising with Agent Swanson, and she tells me you've been a great help. We're going to need you even more now. You and I are going to be working together on this one."

"I'm happy to help. It's been a pleasure working with Agent Swanson."

"Good. I look forward to it. Now you probably want a tour of the crime scene." He shook the sheriff's hand and called over an ERT technician, who took Watts off for the tour, leaving Corrie with Morwood.

Corrie watched him go, absorbing this fresh shock and mightily annoyed that Morwood had not only taken over the case, but now had taken over the sheriff. "So the sheriff is no longer working with me?" she asked. "You're reassigning him to yourself, just like that?"

"It's been a rough evening for you, Swanson," Morwood replied. "So I'll pretend I didn't hear that."

Corrie colored when she realized the tone she had taken with her boss. "I'm not complaining about Watts being put on the case, sir. It's just that we were working so well together, and I've come to rely on his local contacts and knowledge."

"You can still consult with him, after going through me."

It took a tremendous amount of self-control for her to keep her mouth shut after that one. Finally she managed to say, in a calm voice, "I sense I may be losing your trust, Agent Morwood."

Morwood closed his eyes a moment, as if he was counting to ten. When he opened them again, he spoke. "It has come to my attention from General McGurk that your warranted search of the old Gower farmhouse yielded some items. And yet I've heard nothing about it, and nothing has been logged as evidence."

Corrie felt the blood rush into her face. "I didn't want to log the evidence until I was sure it connected with the case."

"What was the evidence?"

"An aerial photograph, an almanac, and a book."

"And what was the significance of this evidence?"

"Well, the photograph was hidden behind a picture, the almanac had some notes in it, and the book was entitled *Early Legends of the Western Frontier*, which had stories of buried treasure and such. I thought it might contain clues to what Gower was searching for."

"I see."

"So the general has been in touch with you?" Corrie asked.

"Today I received a call from him asking about it. And I knew nothing."

"Isn't it sort of convenient for him to be calling you?"

Morwood looked at her steadily. "What do you mean by that?"

"I think the general is trying to undermine me."

"Why?"

"Why would he be interested in the evidence I might have collected?"

"It's a reasonable follow-up for him to do."

"I don't know. Think about it, sir—we're dealing with a potential scandal in that the Trinity test actually caused a fatality, a fake army MP murders one of our suspects, we've got irradiated human remains, and now somebody tortured and killed one of our informants. It all seems to point to WSMR involvement in some way, and McGurk's the guy in charge."

Morwood shook his head. "General McGurk, as a suspect? You can't be serious."

"I'm not saying he's involved," Corrie said. "Directly. But White Sands remains a large piece of the puzzle..." She halted. She had been about to tell him of her meeting with the navy lieutenant, but the look on his face made her realize she'd better shut up.

Morwood shook his head. "You know, Swanson, rookie agents tend to overthink their first cases. I'm usually the last one to discount a theory, but this one..." He looked at her appraisingly. "You take the cake, Agent Swanson," he said in a low, neutral tone from which she could glean nothing. "Whether that cake is angel food or a cow pie remains to be seen. But one thing's certain: if the slightest whisper gets out that the FBI finds General McGurk a person of interest, we're all sunk—unless we've got ironclad proof. Go ahead and follow your leads. But keep it absolutely quiet. And I want daily reports. No—make that weekly reports. Until further notice. Is that understood?"

"Yes, sir."

"Good. Then go home and get some sleep. Your formal writeup on tonight's events can wait until the morning." And before she could say another word, he turned away and went toward the hive of activity that surrounded the toolshed of the late Jesse Gower.

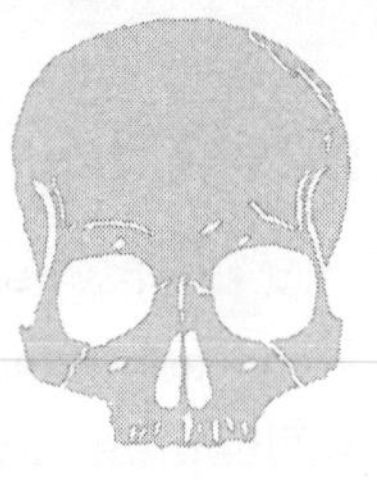

43

Nora found Nick Espejo in a small office in the Bank of Albuquerque building, the sign on the open door announcing him as a loan officer. He was exactly what Nora expected from a young banker: blue suit, polished shoes, crisp haircut. He looked to be in his early twenties. She knocked on the door, and he waved her inside with a big smile.

"Please have a seat, Dr. Kelly."

She sat down. She hadn't told him on the phone what she wanted, and she could see now that had been a mistake, as his warm greeting and fake smile announced that he assumed she was a customer.

"Now, what can I do for you? Rates are at rock bottom—"

"I'm not here as a customer," she said. "I'm an archaeologist with the Santa Fe Archaeological Institute."

The look of heartiness faded a little, replaced by something more wary. "Oh, I'm sorry, I thought you were here to take out a loan."

"I've come at the suggestion of Ms. Eskaminzin. She said you might be able to help me."

At this his face softened. "Well, of course. Please go on."

"It's about Nantan Taza."

This time, the transformation in his face was dramatic. An expression of mingled surprise and sorrow flickered through his black eyes. "Oh. Is he . . . What's happened?"

"Nothing that I know of. Would you mind if I explained? I'll make it as brief as possible." With a warning that it was confidential, she gave him an abbreviated account of the discovery of Gower's body, the Trinity test, the old campsite, and the medicine bundle belonging to Taza. The young man listened with close attention, his face registering surprise more than once.

"So," Nora said once she'd finished, "I was hoping that you might have heard stories from him about Gower, or—well, anything, really, that might shed more light on what happened that day."

Espejo looked down. "It's painful just thinking about it. He told me a lot of stories, but they were Apache stories. Mescalero fables and legends. He was a good man, but he had a gloomy view of things. Not cynical—dark. He seemed to feel our species was doomed. And now I know why. My God—and you really think he actually *saw* the bomb go off?"

Nora nodded. Eskaminzin had used the same word to describe the old man: dark.

Espejo thought for a moment. "I was eleven or twelve. Nantan lived outside Mescalero, up by Graveyard Spring in an old log cabin. He was self-sufficient, hunted for his meat, dried it, had a little garden watered from Graveyard Creek. I ran into him by accident—I was riding up the canyon and disturbed some of his cattle. They were half-wild anyway, but he was angry. To make up for it I chopped some wood for him, and somehow that became a regular thing. At first I was scared of him: he was so stern, never smiled and almost never talked. But gradually I got used to him and he had me run other errands. He treated me like an adult—an equal."

"You said that he told you legends and fables. What else did you talk about?"

"Traditional Apache beliefs. How to live a good life. He talked about the importance of treating everything in the world as sacred."

He paused. "Once in a while, as I got to know him better, he'd talk about going away, but he never said why or when. I thought it was just talk. But then, I came by one day and he was saddling his horse, tying a sack of stuff behind the cantle, rifle in a boot. I asked him where he was going. He told me the time had come to go into the mountains. I was really upset. I couldn't understand, and when I asked more questions he refused to answer them. I cried, I pleaded, but he'd made up his mind. So I ran off to saddle my horse and go with him, but he stopped me dead in my tracks. He made me promise not to follow. And he left."

"I'm sorry," said Nora. "It must have been like losing a father."

"A father—and best friend. I didn't understand how much it all meant to me until he was gone. I still try to believe that he's here with me, in a way—because of his teachings, you know—but it's hard."

Nora hesitated. "Do you know where he went?"

"He wouldn't tell me."

"But... you have a sense?"

At this, Espejo paused. "Why are you asking?"

"I just wondered if he might still be alive."

"He'd be ninety-five."

Nora nodded.

"Ten years of surviving alone in the mountains," Espejo said. "You think that's possible?"

"Do you?"

Espejo didn't answer for a moment. Then he said: "If he's passed on, then he's returned to the spirit land. If he's alive, he won't want to be found. I made a promise never to go looking for him."

"But if he's alive, he might be able to help us solve the mystery. Of what exactly happened that day. Of what he and Gower were looking for."

Espejo didn't respond for a long time. Finally, he stirred. "So if I tell you where I think he went, what will you do?"

"I'll go there, if I can."

Espejo sighed and shook his head. Another lengthy moment passed while he looked down at his desk, thinking. "There was a place he mentioned—mentioned only once. When he was a teenager, he told me one evening during a bad storm, he'd had to purify himself of the taint of some kind of evil. He told me that it was clinging to him, clinging with a grip like death, and that only a spiritual journey would rid him of it. Now I know he must have meant that bomb. Anyway, he told me he'd gone out into the wilderness, wandered around until he found his power place—Ojo Escondido, he called it—and spent five days there, fasting. He said he experienced a powerful vision. But he wouldn't describe it to me and told me never to bring it up again."

"And he didn't say anything more about that experience?"

"No. He implied it had given him some unique insight into the world—but that it was too potent, maybe too dangerous, to be passed on to a boy."

"But you believe this place of power was where he went back to when he disappeared?"

"I always figured that's where he returned."

"You said he called it Ojo Escondido. Do you know of any place with that name?"

Espejo shook his head again. "I remember a few of the elders mentioning it in passing, a long time ago. Supposedly, it was a place near Sierra Blanca, way up at the northern end of the rez. But the way they spoke of it, I could never be sure whether it was real—or mythical."

"Ojo Escondido," Nora said slowly, almost to herself. "Hidden Eye."

"In New Mexico Spanish," said Espejo, "Ojo also means 'spring.'"

Nora took a deep breath. "Can you take me there? Or at least, to where you think it might be?"

A long silence followed this question—long enough to make Nora feel uncomfortable.

"I'm sorry," she said. "Maybe I've overstepped my bounds."

"I'd like to help you," Espejo said. "But I can't. I made a promise."

"Even knowing what you do now?"

The young man looked down at his hands. "That knowledge doesn't change anything."

For a moment, Nora remained still. Then she picked up her backpack, unzipped it, took out the evidence case, and placed it on the desk.

Espejo looked up. "What's that?"

Nora unlatched the box and took out the medicine bundle. As she did so, Espejo jerked abruptly, as if he'd been hit by an electric current. "Where did you get that?"

"It's Nantan's medicine bundle."

But it was clear Espejo had already guessed this. "Where did you get that?" he repeated.

"He left it at their campsite in High Lonesome."

Espejo let out a long, slow exhalation. "That one night he spoke to me about his vision quest, he said something strange. He said he had once been 'spiritually orphaned.' I never knew what he meant. I wasn't even sure I'd understood his words." He looked at the medicine bundle. "I wonder why he never went back to get it."

"He was too frightened by the atomic explosion he'd witnessed."

"But from what you told me, he wasn't too frightened to stay with his dying friend. And he wasn't too frightened to bury him in the required manner." He paused. "It wasn't fear. I don't understand. Nobody would leave that behind."

Again he fell silent for a long moment. Then he said slowly: "One of the things Nantan taught me was that everything has a reason. Nothing is random. So you being here, carrying that medicine bundle—there's a reason for that." He straightened in his chair. "Very well. I'll take you there. Or rather, I'll take you as far as I can without breaking my promise. If we find him—dead or alive—you'll have to go the last mile alone."

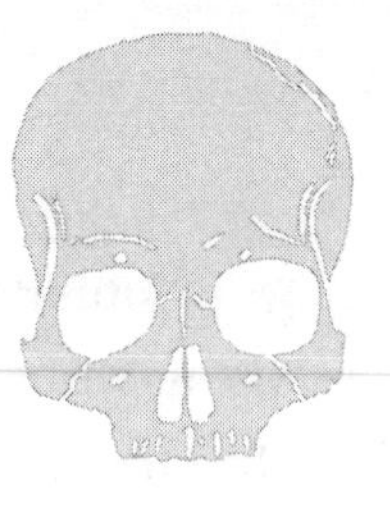

44

CORRIE LAY IN bed, staring at the ceiling. Although she was weary, she could not manage to go to sleep. She was too restless. Restless and frustrated.

She'd barely gotten any sleep after Morwood sent her home last night. She'd spent the day listlessly, getting little done. And now, here she was—staring at the ceiling again. It was no more of a soporific than it had been the night before.

She reached for her phone and turned off the background music she'd put on to make her drowsy: *Deep Frieze*, by Sleep Research Facility. If she was going to lie awake, she might as well think.

There was no mystery to her restlessness—it stemmed from her last trip to Jesse Gower's. Was she feeling guilty for treating him brusquely over the phone? Maybe a little, but he'd certainly warranted such treatment. Was it the grim, brutal, pointless finality of what she'd found? She didn't think so: it wasn't fear or trauma that she felt. She'd seen a lot of awful stuff at Quantico, and besides, nothing could compare to that terrifying figure that had appeared in her Medicine Creek trailer doorway: that huge, white-moon face spattered with blood, the one good arm reaching for her...

She closed the box on that memory and started over.

Jesse had been tortured and killed for a reason. Everyone agreed: someone wanted something from him. But cash, drugs... what?

Yet again, she mentally reran their conversation of yesterday afternoon. He'd practically begged her to come out to the ranch, and as a carrot he'd dangled his great-grandfather's mysterious other prized possession—the one Jesse had initially dismissed as an "old drawing." *He treated it like a holy object,* Jesse said.

Had it been some messed-up joke of his, some way to lure her into taking the long drive to his place, just so he could curse her out again? She didn't think so. Jesse hadn't seemed the kind of person to trouble himself with games like that—and besides, if that was all it had been, he knew full well he'd never see her again... unless she had a pair of cuffs and a warrant in her hands.

Could somebody have been outside the house and heard him on the phone with her? But no, that would be too much of a coincidence. Besides, Jesse himself had said the item was more precious than valuable. Could the phone have been tapped or hacked into? That seemed possible but far-fetched.

More precious than valuable. What the hell did that mean?

She lay in the darkness, trying hard to recall what exactly Jesse had said about this thing—whatever it was—his great-grandfather had left behind. *In my great-grandfather's time, most people would have thought his precious item fit only to line a birdcage with. But over the years it's gained value. Maybe a* lot *of value. Even if Pertelote is still the only one who can enjoy it.*

At least, that was as best she could remember. Jesse—it was

still hard to process the fact he was dead—had had an annoying way of rarely saying anything directly…Everything was an ironic digression, or a rambling allusion to that aborted English major he was so proud of…

Now she wished she'd paid more attention to his digressions. Lining a birdcage? And who was Pertelote?

Pertelote. That rang a bell. He'd said that word before—the last time she'd been out with him at the ranch. She thought back to that earlier conversation—the one that ended so abruptly with him ordering her off his property. He'd talked about expensive Swiss watches, other stuff she couldn't remember without consulting her notes. But that wasn't what was gnawing at her. It had been something said, she felt sure, early in the conversation, during the first time he opened up.

The residual effects of my education. She remembered him saying that. And something else: *I've named lots of things on this old ranch after bits of English literature.*

But who the hell was Pertelote?

Then she remembered. As they were sitting on the front porch, a hen had cackled, and Gower had brightened and smiled. "Pertelote! Way to go! There's my supper."

There's my supper.

I can tell all the hens by their cackles.

I've named lots of things on this old ranch after bits of English literature.

In an instant, Corrie was out of bed.

In ten minutes, she was dressed and in her car.

At 2 AM she was pulling into the Gower Ranch.

She turned off her lights and killed the engine, sitting in the car, waiting for the dust to settle and her night vision to take effect. Except for the crime scene tape, and the missing door on the toolshed—the old structure gaping wide, as if it had lost a tooth—the place didn't look all that different than it had the night before, when she'd arrived to find all the lights off.

When she was sure she had the scene to herself, she picked up her flashlight, checked to see that her weapon had a round in the chamber, then got out of the car.

Keeping her flashlight off, moving by the light of the moon, Corrie ducked under the tape, walked past first the house, then the toolshed—more crime scene tape—and approached the henhouse. All remained silent, and nothing moved in the darkness. She drew a little nearer, then stopped again.

She'd never been close to a chicken coop before and had only the vaguest idea of how they operated—mostly from watching Foghorn Leghorn cartoons. It was a miniature shed-like structure, shingled, with a peaked roof, one tiny window, and a door with a ramp. She turned on her light and let it play briefly over the latched main door, the henhouse itself, and the chicken run beyond. What she particularly noticed was the odor. For the first time, she understood why *chickenshit* was such an offensive term.

...Even if Pertelote is still the only one who can enjoy it...

So maybe whatever it was was hidden in the henhouse. Nothing else fit. The structure didn't look as if the police or anyone else had given it any attention. It was her only lead, and Corrie was going to check it out. She owed that, at least, to Jesse.

Taking a deep breath, she lifted the wooden latch and stuck her head in through the door, shining her light around again. The opposing walls were lined with nesting boxes, about half of them full, with more hens sleeping on perches. Six or seven pairs of beady eyes swiveled toward her accusingly, and there was a spasm of unhappy, nervous cackling.

"I don't much like this either, ladies," Corrie said as she scanned the interior. Which one was Pertelote?

One hen, the closest one on the right, seemed larger and less cowed than the others, and her nesting box appeared to have seen the heaviest use. Corrie guessed she had a personality to match her bulk; she could imagine her as Jesse's favorite. She reached into the straw beneath the hen and received an outraged squawk and a peck on the wrist for her trouble.

"Hey!" She'd had no idea how hard those fuckers could peck. Nevertheless, she had enough time to feel chicken wire beneath the bed of straw. Nothing hidden there.

She ducked back out the main door, checking her wrist with her flashlight. It looked like she'd been hammered with a nail set. There was no way she was going to get pecked again.

The henhouse was, essentially, on a low frame of stilts, with wooden latticework running around beneath, presumably to keep out predators. Kneeling, Corrie shined her light through the latticework, precipitating another chorus of fretful complaint. Beneath each nest was a litter tray, and—judging by the contents—someone had been delinquent in cleaning them.

"Thanks, Jesse," Corrie muttered. Taking a deep breath, she squeezed her throbbing hand through the lattice, located Pertelote's litter tray, and—gingerly but thoroughly—sieved its contents between her fingers. The result was disgusting and without evident result.

"Jesus!" Corrie turned her face to one side, trying not to gag. Was this just another half-baked deduction of hers, some crazy hope that her conversations with Gower—and his death—were not in vain? If Morwood saw her now . . . She pulled her befouled hand out of the litter tray with a curse. And as she did, the tray shifted ever so slightly in its casing.

Corrie paused. Then, grasping the near end of the tray, she pulled, pushed, then lifted.

It was the lifting that did it. The end of the tray moved up about an inch, and Corrie quickly felt beneath. Something was affixed there, protected by a second tray. It was too dark to identify for sure, but it felt like folded canvas. It would not fit through the latticework, and rather than risk damaging it, she raised the entire section of lattice and pulled it out from beneath.

She spent the next few minutes washing her hands in Jesse's wrecked kitchen. Then—flashlight and the mysterious discovery in her lap—she sat out on Jesse's front porch and took out her cell phone, preparing to make a call.

Fingers on the touchpad, she hesitated a long moment. And then she shoved the phone back into her pocket, walked briskly to her car, got in, put the bundle carefully on the passenger seat, and drove off into the night.

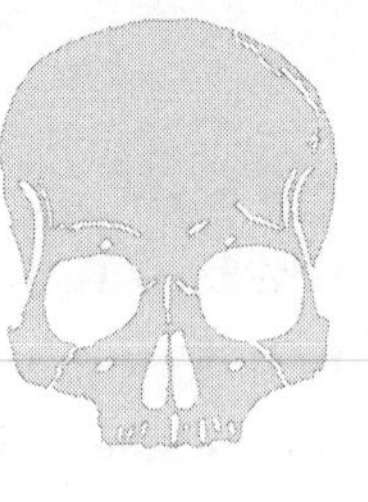

45

THEY HAD LOADED two horses into a trailer at dawn, at the home of Espejo's parents, and then they had driven two hours northward through the mountains of the Mescalero reservation, on a maze of dirt roads that went from bad to worse, until the road ended at a tiny settlement called Muleshoe. It appeared to be abandoned. As they unloaded the horses, Nora could see the mountain range of Sierra Blanca looming above them, nearly twelve thousand feet high, covered with snow. They mounted up and set off, following a trail that wound through fir-clad foothills.

Being on the back of a horse reminded Nora of the dig she'd directed in May in the Sierra Nevada of California. She and her team had discovered and excavated a nineteenth-century campsite from the ill-fated Donner Party. While that had ultimately been a traumatic experience, to say the least, she loved riding, and being on a horse again was a pleasure. The landscape they were passing through, cathedral stands of Douglas firs alongside a burbling creek, was inspiring, and the air was fragrant with the scent of pine and wild geraniums. Espejo was a silent rider, which Nora appreciated. She had ridden with people who liked to talk, and being on horseback, that meant turning around in the saddle and shouting back and forth, which for her spoiled the experience.

But when her thoughts turned to the quixotic journey itself, she wondered what the hell she was doing. Despite the best that Adelsky could do, the work at Tsankawi had fallen behind and there was no covering it up. She'd had to ask Weingrau for yet another day off, and this time the president had not seemed pleased. She'd questioned Nora rather pointedly about what, exactly, she was doing for the FBI now. Nora found herself evading and hedging and explaining. She had to admit to herself that she'd been so drawn into the case that she was losing perspective. On top of that, the trip was a wild-goose chase. It was crazy to think Nantan was still alive. They were going to find nothing more than the remnants of his camp, if that, and maybe his bones. Watts was right: she was becoming too emotionally involved in the investigation. Corrie was a bit green, and could be a pain, but she was perfectly capable of handling things without Nora's continued help.

By noon, they were well above ten thousand feet. The trail petered out, and the creek had turned into a runnel of water through a series of high alpine meadows filled with fall wildflowers. The Sierra Blanca peaks were closer now, rising above them like a wall. They finally emerged from the tree line on a beautiful grassy ridge. At the top, a sprawling view of the White Mountain Wilderness came into view, mountains beyond mountains as far as the eye could see. She doubted there were any other human beings within twenty miles—unless, of course, Nantan was still alive.

Here Espejo halted. Nora rode up beside him.

He pointed. "See those steep parallel canyons down there? Escondido Spring is supposed to be in the middle one, maybe five miles down."

"Doesn't look passable by horse."

"From what little I remember of Nantan telling me about this place, it isn't. We'll ride as far as we can."

He eased his horse forward, and they descended the far side of the ridge, the horses cautiously picking their way. The human trail had long vanished, but the horses instinctively followed a web of elk trails that led back down through broad meadows into the mouth of the canyon. Gradually the land became steeper and rockier, the walls closing in.

"We'd better continue on foot," said Espejo.

They got off their horses, and Espejo, instead of tying them up, hobbled both of them and put a bell around the neck of one, turning them loose to graze in the meadow. When he was done, he looked at her. "Well, you're on your own now."

Although he'd already said as much, Nora had only half believed him. "You're really not coming?"

"This is where I stop. You just keep going down the canyon. It's probably no more than a mile or two to Ojo Escondido."

Nora shouldered her pack and set off down the ravine. Soon the granite walls had closed in tight, creating a gloomy, claustrophobic atmosphere. There was no stream in the bottom, only a dry bed of rocks with scattered brush, with some battered tree trunks washed down in flash floods. It was getting on toward afternoon, and Nora wondered if they were going to make it back to the horse trailer by dark. At least, she mused, it would be the night of the full moon.

The terrain got rougher still, and in a few places the canyon became so tight Nora could almost span the walls with her arms. And then, quite abruptly, the walls opened up into a spacious grassy hollow, perhaps a hundred yards across, shaded with massive cottonwood trees, their leaves backlit like stained glass in the slanting light. A small pool, crowded with willows and greenery, indicated a spring at the base of the cliffs. Beyond the spring, against the far wall of the canyon, stood a rough log cabin, a small outbuilding, a privy, and a sheep corral. There was no sign of life.

Nora stopped, heart in her throat. Was this it? It couldn't be more hidden or remote, and it looked abandoned. It amazed her that a man as old as Nantan had lived long enough to build the cabin and outbuildings. She suddenly feared what she might find in the cabin. But there was no turning back now.

"Hello!" she called, her voice echoing and re-echoing from the soaring canyon walls.

Silence.

"Nantan Taza?"

Still no answer.

She approached the cabin cautiously. The door was ajar. She paused, then knocked.

No answer.

"Hello?"

Silence.

She pushed open the door with a creaking sound and stepped inside. It was dim, and it took her eyes a moment to adjust. It was the simplest one-room cabin imaginable, built of logs chinked with mud, with a dirt floor, stone fireplace, rudimentary table, chair, some flat rocks for plates—and a rough wooden bunk in the far corner. It took a few moments for Nora to realize that a man was lying among the dirty animal skins. He was of almost unfathomable age, his hair long and white, in striking contrast to the dark brown face. Nora felt her heart pounding. Was he dead or alive?

"Mr. Taza?"

The head slowly turned toward her, and a withered hand rose, making a faint gesture for her to come over. She approached in silence and stood over the bed, taking off her backpack and placing it on the floor.

The old man gazed at her. "Who...?"

Nora tried to formulate her thoughts. The man looked so withered, so moribund, she was stunned he was still alive. "I'm Nora Kelly."

"Why have you come?"

"I'm an archaeologist." She hesitated. "James Gower's body was found," she blurted. "I excavated it." She stopped.

The expression on his face changed in a way she couldn't quite identify. "How did you find me?"

"Your friend Nick Espejo guided me. He's still a few miles up the canyon. He didn't want to break his promise to you. I'm alone."

"*Why* have you come?" the old man repeated. His voice was little more than a slow whisper of wind.

"I was hoping," she said, "that you might tell your story. And..." She hesitated.

The cabin went silent.

Nora's instincts told her the old man was waiting for something—but for what, exactly, she didn't know. Her eyes strayed to the backpack, propped up next to her. And then, suddenly, she understood.

Corrie would be furious. Nora might even be charged with a crime. But now—as Nora struggled with a decision that, on some level, she'd known since the trek began that she would face—the importance of such things seemed to fade away under the old man's gaze.

As she struggled with uncertainty, the old man closed his eyes. "I knew, someday, this would happen."

At last—before she could change her mind—Nora unzipped her pack and took out the box. She unbuckled it, lifted out the medicine bundle, and held it out to him.

The old man's eyes opened, then grew wide. He reached out with both hands, and she put the bundle in them. He held it for a moment, then reverently placed it on the bed beside him and tucked it close, almost like a child might grasp a teddy bear. His gaze moved from the bundle back to her. "I've been waiting for a messenger. All these years, I've been waiting. I never thought . . . it would be someone like you."

"A messenger?"

"Yes. I've been punished with long life because I would not tell the story . . . But you've come, and now I know it is time."

He raised his hand and pointed across the room. "Bring me that wooden chest."

She rose and brought over a small wooden box, hand-adzed and pegged, with an ill-fitting cover.

"Open."

She did so. There were two items in the box: an object wrapped in buckskin, and a parfleche-like envelope made of rawhide.

"Open," he repeated.

Untying the leather thongs, she unwrapped the buckskin, revealing a heavy gold pocket watch, with engravings of constellations visible on its worn cover. The parfleche opened to expose an ancient sheet of parchment. On it was an Apache drawing of four horses with riders.

"Those are now yours," he said.

Staring at them, Nora's mouth went dry. "What are they?"

A long silence ensued while he closed his eyes again and took several long, deep breaths.

"I will tell you what it is you came to hear," he said. "And then—then I can finally go."

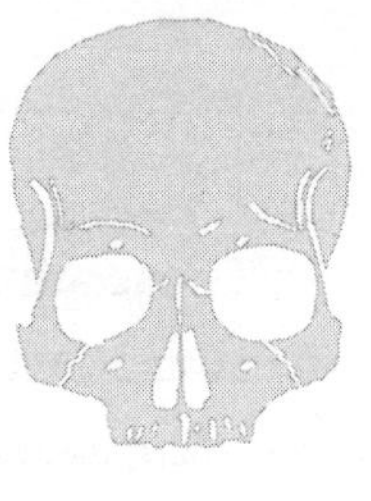

46

Sitting at her kitchen table as afternoon turned to evening, Corrie Swanson carefully laid out the piece of tinfoil she'd prepared on returning home the night before. She pulled on a pair of nitrile gloves, opened the evidence box, and took out—yet again—the piece of parchment and the bundle it had been wrapped in and placed them side by side on the table. She moved a bright light over to it and picked up her magnifying glass.

The wrapping was an old-fashioned oilcloth, stiff with age. She had spread it out, looking for writing or designs. Though it had been hard to see through the dirt and stains of the years, it appeared to be free of any marks.

Now she turned her attention to the parchment. It was stiff and square, about eight inches on a side, and was covered with ancient lettering. Age had turned it a dark honey color. Three of its edges looked old and worn, but the fourth had been cut at a more recent date: under the glass she could see marks of a knife scoring back and forth in the parchment. The faded old lettering on that side had been cut off—clearly, this had once been a larger document divided in half.

She turned the parchment over and examined the other side. On it was a picture, drawn in color with what looked like crayons. Areas here and there were filled in with watercolor. It, too, had been cut. The section on her half showed two indigenous people wearing leggings, galloping, one on a black-and-white spotted horse and the other on a roan. They both carried bows and were chasing a cavalry officer, who was fleeing from them on horseback. The drawing had a childlike simplicity and clarity of exposition: every detail had been painstakingly rendered, including streaks of paint on the Indians' faces, the bridles and reins, and the cavalry soldier's uniform. It was lively and engaging and, despite the passage of years, still remarkably fresh.

On the other hand, the strange lettering on the other side—which she didn't recognize but assumed was Spanish—looked very much older, so faded as to be barely legible. There were crossings-out and blots of ink that made her think it had been written in haste. The script was indecipherable to her. It was even hard to make out individual letters among all the curlicues and flourishes.

She sat back, speculating—as she had been doing all day. This was clearly the item that Jesse had spoken of. Nothing else made sense. But had his great-grandfather treasured this parchment for the drawing, the Spanish text—or both? A quick computer search had told her Indian drawings like this, known as "ledger art" because old army ledgers had often been used as drawing pads, were valuable. Usually, they were drawn by warriors who wanted to depict important battles or courting scenes. The Indians had valued parchment because of its toughness and durability. It was remarkable Jesse had held on to it, despite needing money for drugs. It was hard to imagine an addict not cashing it in; it was that important to him. Or possibly he didn't realize its value. But no, he'd said it himself: *In my great-grandfather's time, most people would have thought his precious item fit only to line a henhouse with. But over the years it's gained value. Maybe a* lot *of value.*

She sighed. This was clearly evidence. Her responsibility was to bring it in to Albuquerque to be logged and examined in the lab. And the Spanish, or whatever that old calligraphy was, needed to be translated by an expert. But such was her annoyance with her supervisor that, though an entire day had passed, she'd hesitated to report it.

Maybe she wouldn't ever. Morwood would probably just dismiss it, as he had her suspicions of the general, and give her another of his fatherly lectures about not going off on a tangent. But finally she shook off such thoughts. That was the old rebel thinking, not the new FBI agent. She *had* to follow the rules, and that meant notifying Morwood—even though it was six o'clock on a Sunday evening. Damn, she should have done this earlier.

She picked up her phone and called Morwood's cell.

He picked up on the second ring. "What is it, Corrie?"

She told him about her hunch; about going up to Gower's place; about finding the parchment. She didn't mention exactly when she'd done it, and he didn't ask. Instead, a long silence followed. As she waited, she prepared herself for the dismissive, perhaps even irritated, response. But instead, when Morwood spoke again, his voice had taken on an unexpected edge. "Can you send me some pictures? Just take a few with your cell phone while I wait."

"Yes, sir."

She photographed both sides of the parchment, the oilcloth

wrapper, and the waxed string used to hold it together, and shot them off to Morwood.

"Okay," he said, "got them."

Another long silence followed. "And how much did you estimate the drawing is worth?"

"Looking around on the web, I got the sense they sell for a lot of money. Like ten thousand dollars."

Another silence. "And the Spanish script on the other side?"

"I have no idea what it is."

"This could be a significant piece of evidence, Corrie. Did you log it yet?"

"Not yet. I collected it using all the evidence protocols, though, and documented everything."

"Very good. We need to get that Spanish script translated. First thing tomorrow, bring it down to the evidence room and we'll log it in. Ultraviolet light or multispectrum imaging ought to make the script more legible. Then get in touch with Dr. Kelly and see if their Spanish expert at the Institute will look at it and make a translation. We might also get an expert in ledger art to examine the drawing."

"Yes, sir."

A hesitation. "Good work, Corrie."

She was surprised and gratified. "Yes, sir. Thank you, sir."

After he had hung up, she looked once again at the document, with its curly faded script. She dialed Nora's cell phone number, but it went immediately to voice mail. Nora had gone to the Mescalero reservation, trying to trace the old Apache; she probably wasn't back yet. Corrie swallowed at the thought. The fact that Nora had insisted on taking the actual medicine bag they'd found at High Lonesome with her—her certainty that no substitute would do, and anything else would doom her investigation before it even began—made the compliment Morwood had just given Corrie seem almost ominous. If Nora didn't get that back to her soon... In a sudden hurry, she packed everything back into the evidence box, then carefully sealed it, making note of the date and time on the lid. She was going to make damn sure the chain of evidence on this item was rock solid.

She thought back to her conversation in the bar. If General McGurk was really looking for the Victorio Peak treasure, she'd need to have evidence for it beyond hearsay. She knew enough about Morwood to mentally hear his little speech about the danger of rumor and innuendo in an investigation. Despite that, she could feel the pieces of the puzzle coming together. Gower and his partner had been looking for treasure, and Gower found it: that gold cross was proof. Gower's great-grandson was tortured and killed, his place ransacked, by people trying to find something. Could that thing be this piece of parchment? Jesse knew it was precious to his great-grandfather... and he had died keeping its secret. Was the general really involved?

The general was about forty-five, so he hadn't been born yet when his father was at WSMR in the early sixties. But maybe he grew up hearing stories. She wondered how she could find out more about the general's father—not rumor, but fact. The FBI could easily request his military records. It was done all the time. But she'd have to go through Morwood, and he'd hit the roof. He was busy looking into the death of Rivers, and he'd already warned her to keep her own investigation below the radar.

Rivers... he was another piece of this puzzle, she felt sure. Why else would he have been killed? Was he up there at High

Lonesome, digging for the Victorio Peak treasure? It seemed everyone was hunting for the same jackpot.

She sighed. Enough speculation. Tomorrow she'd log the evidence, get in touch with Nora, and have the parchment translated—but not before retrieving the medicine bag and returning it to evidence storage, where it belonged.

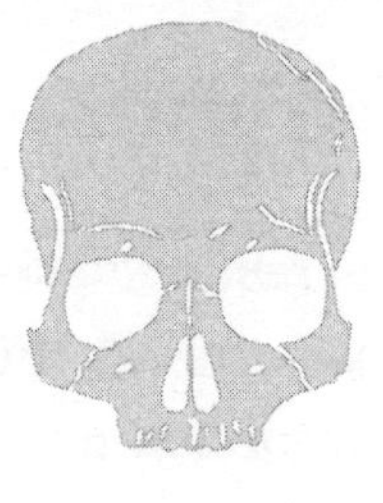

47

Charles Fountain, Esq., had a fine office in an old Territorial building in town, occupying the floor above the Sage Diner. But everyone knew that instead of sitting in his grand office, he could usually be found in the diner itself, tucked into the corner booth in the back, drinking coffee, meeting friends, and doing business. And this was where Watts and Morwood found him, even on a Monday afternoon, by himself, with a big pot of coffee and the table spread with papers.

As they approached, he gave them a smile and an outstretched hand. "Hello, Sheriff. And you must be Special Agent Morwood. I hope you don't mind if I stay seated—I'm afraid in my middle age, I've developed a serious medical condition known as a *potbelly*." The slight bulge around his waistline barely qualified for the term, but he chuckled at his own little joke and invited them to sit. "Coffee?"

"Please."

He waved over the waitress, who brought two mugs. Fountain served them himself, then sent the pot back for a refill. "I apologize for the clutter," he said, gathering up papers and stuffing them willy-nilly into an already bulging accordion briefcase. "A messy desk is a sign of contentment. I read that in a fortune cookie, so you know it must be true."

Watts realized he still had his hat on, and he removed it, checked that the table was spotless, and gently placed it upside down. Morwood had asked him to take the lead in the conversation, since he, like everyone else in town, had known Fountain most of his life. Watts slipped out a steno notebook on which he'd jotted some questions. "Thanks for meeting with us, Mr. Fountain."

"How many years have I known you? Charles, please. Same goes for you, Agent Morwood."

Watts acknowledged the informality with a nod. "We've got some questions related to the Gower homicide. A search of the place revealed he was probably dealing in antiquities—relics and the like. Possibly selling them to support his drug habit."

Fountain nodded. "Just like his great-grandfather. To buy alcohol instead of meth."

"Right. A lot of those relics, in fact, would appear to be stuff his great-grandfather collected. There's an old shed up at the ranch where the junk's been sitting forever. Gower's father or grandfather may have added to the collection as well. The kid was selling it off, little by little, to finance his habit."

Fountain shook his head. "And to think the Gower boy started out at Harvard. That's a long way to fall."

After a brief pause, Watts continued. "I'm sure you're aware that, despite little obvious evidence of recent lootings, there's been a notable upsurge in unprovenanced antiquities hitting the market. It's been going on long enough now to make me concerned. Given the lack of provenance, it would seem that the looting of historic and prehistoric sites *is* involved... except in this case, done with painstaking care and research. Sophisticated. Most looters just leave their holes, but maybe these guys fill them in and make it look like nothing happened."

"Interesting theory." Fountain took a sip of coffee. "In order to work, the racket would have to be well organized. I'd speculate that such a group would stay away from the Gower boy. Too big a risk. Besides, these black market antiquities you mentioned are valuable. I'd guess that most of the stuff in that old Gower shed isn't in that class."

Watts smiled grimly. "We were wondering if you had any insight into who the kid might have been selling to."

Fountain leaned back in his seat. "Exactly what kind of relics did you find up there, Sheriff?"

"Civil War bullets and buttons, bottles, arrowheads, old magazines and books, a couple of busted banjos—that kind of stuff."

"No documents? Receipts?"

"No."

"Too bad." Fountain pursed his lips. "You don't think Gower had anything of real value? The great-grandfather was a junk dealer—not to put too fine a point on it."

"What was junk seventy-five years ago might have become valuable today."

Morwood now broke in. "Speaking of that, among the finds up there was a nineteenth-century Native American drawing, hidden in the chicken coop."

At this, Fountain's eyebrows, bushy as mustachios, shot up. "Ledger art? How interesting."

"So I'm told."

"That, at least, might be worth a lot. Did he know it was there? I can't imagine why he didn't sell it."

"And another thing," Morwood said, "which we're keeping confidential for now. Turns out the Rivers death was a homicide."

For the first time, Fountain's face lost its usual expression of glib jocularity in place of real shock. "Murdered? In the *hospital*?"

"Yes. Someone injected a deadly drug into his IV drip. A guy wearing a phony MP uniform. We got a video of him."

"Did you ID him?"

"No," Morwood said. "African American, tall, thin. He probably knew where the video cameras were and was careful to hide his face. The point is, both Rivers and the Gower kid seemed to be involved in the relic business...and both were murdered. We're wondering how it might fit together."

Fountain took another swig of coffee and set the mug down. "You may recall that several prehistoric graves were dug up in Bonito Canyon a few months ago?"

Watts nodded. "I remember that."

"I don't think anyone would have known if a photographer hadn't compared two pictures he'd taken a month apart and noticed some discrepancies. That was a professional job—the kind a sophisticated, organized group like the one you're talking about might have pulled off. Like I said before, you really think such a group of professionals would get involved with an addict like Gower—or an ex-con like Rivers?"

"It's an avenue we're exploring," Watts said. "You haven't heard any rumors that might give us a lead?"

"Not specifically," said Fountain. "But I'm pretty sure that if this gang does exist, they're not local."

"Why do you say that?" Morwood asked.

Fountain chuckled. "As a defense attorney, I've come to know pretty much every shady character—lowlife and otherwise—in Socorro County. Hell, I saved some of their asses from prison. If this were local, I would have heard something." He finished his coffee and poured himself another. "I'll certainly put out some feelers. Gower's meth would have come out of Albuquerque, and the kind of group you're postulating would probably operate from a large city, too." He contemplated his fresh cup for a moment. "I can think of one lead you might find useful. There's a bar down in San Pasqual called the Cascabel Tavern. Rivers used to hang out there before he cleaned himself up, and he had a big mouth. It's a long shot, but you might see if anyone heard anything."

"Thanks."

"Just be careful—the Cascabel is a notorious hangout for doomsday preppers and anti-government types."

"Thanks for your time and your advice." Morwood nodded and rose. "We'll add the Cascabel to our list. Along with High Lonesome."

"High Lonesome?" Fountain asked.

"Whatever's going on here, High Lonesome seems to be at the center of it. Since we're starting to pile up more bodies than clues, the FBI has decided to send the ERT up there again, in force, to do a proper search. Comb every inch of the place, maybe even take it apart if we have to."

"That would be a shame," Fountain said, while Watts looked aghast.

"Yes, it would. Let's hope it doesn't come to that." And Morwood turned to leave. "Thank you, Mr. Fountain."

"There you go with that 'Mister' again. Good luck. You too, Sheriff."

Watts didn't answer as he followed Morwood out the door. He was thinking about what he could do to stop the destruction of High Lonesome at the hands of the feds.

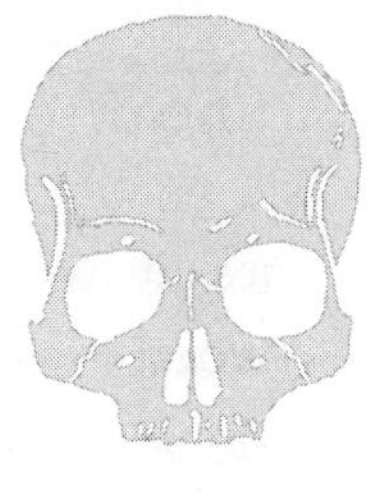

48

IT WAS ELEVEN o'clock on a Monday morning at the Institute. Orlando Chavez sat in a rolling chair in his laboratory, Nora seated next to him. They had been there ever since Nora had roused Chavez from bed at six in the morning and persuaded him to come into the office early. Both were staring at a large computer screen with an image of the text on the parchment Nantan had given her.

"Finally, we can read it clearly," said Chavez. They had spent hours photographing the parchment under UV light and digitally enhancing the faded script to bring out the details. "So: what we have here is a classic example of Cortesana Castilian script from the seventeenth century. It looks like gibberish to the unpracticed eye, but the challenge isn't the language—Spanish hasn't changed that much in the last few centuries—it's reading the script. I can read it, but for the uninitiated it's practically impossible. Fortunately, there are online alphabet charts of old Spanish scripts." His voice had become almost professorial. "Here, let me show you."

Moving to a second computer screen, he typed in some commands and brought up a website displaying numerous charts. Each showed a letter of the alphabet with all the old Castilian script versions of it, both upper- and lowercase.

"Take the capital letter *A* for instance," he said. "Here are all the ways it is written in Cortesana script. A remarkable variety, and some don't look anything like an *A*! Now, *B*..."

Controlling her impatience, Nora gently interrupted. "That's fascinating. Now, can we move on to the text?"

"Of course. Now that it's legible, let's see what it says..." Chavez fell silent and peered at the image on the first computer screen, while Nora waited.

After a few minutes he sat back in his chair. "*Madre de Dios,*" he said under his breath.

"What does it say?" Nora was bursting with eagerness.

"It's hard to know exactly what it *says*, since roughly one-half of the text has been cut off. But I can translate the half that's here."

"And?" Nora asked.

"Let me translate it for you, line by line," Chavez said. "I don't mean to keep you in suspense, but I'd rather not add my own summary, because...well, you can see for yourself."

"'*S.C.C. Majestad,*'" he read, then paused. "That's shorthand for *Sacra Cesarea Cathólica Majestad*, or Holy Roman Catholic Majesty. Intriguing. It indicates the letter was addressed not to the viceroy in Mexico City but to the emperor of Spain himself, Charles II—clearly this correspondence was very important. Okay now, let me go line by line:

On the 20th of August 1680 I write in haste—
along the Camino Real. On the 10th of Aug—

He stopped. "The tenth of August was the first day of the 1680 Pueblo Revolt. I'll resume:

many of the holy fathers. Having foreknowl—

"He probably means foreknowledge of the Revolt. One of the Pueblo plotters betrayed his fellows and told the friars about the revolt just before it started:

Angelico, and Fray Bartolomé and soldiers—
of the cathedral, the churches and the miss—
with treasure and fled southward. Along the Ca—

Nora interrupted. "You said treasure?"

"Yes. The Castilian word is *tesoro*. 'Along the Ca—' must mean "Along the Camino Real,' which was the Royal Road from Santa Fe to Mexico City, down which the friars fled during the revolt."

He went on:

beset by savage Apachu Indians and forced east—
the treasure in the old Reina de Oro mine in the—
Sierra Oscura. We concealed the south entrance—
a stone five paces to the right. At the base of E—
on a large stone directly below. We conce—
We are yet pressed by the Apachu and I—
you receive it, and that the holy treas—
Catholic Majesty upon the recapture—

Humble servant and vassal of Your Majesty, who—

Fray Bartolomé de Aragon

He stopped and peered through his thick glasses. "Nora, do you see the significance of this? What we have here appears to be an actual historical account of the Victorio Peak treasure."

"Not only that—it appears to include directions to where the treasure was hidden."

"And look here, it mentions the Sierra Oscura. That's the range of hills *north* of Victorio Peak." He exhaled. "This is incredible. It means Doc Noss was a fraud and con all along, claiming he'd found the treasure on Victorio Peak!" He paused. "'At the base of E—'...That could refer to a hill or landmark in the Sierra Oscura—the *real* hill."

"Is that still on the White Sands Missile Range?" Nora asked.

"Yes, but near the north end, on the Jornada del Muerto side of the mountains, not far from the Trinity site."

Not far from the Trinity site. "Have you heard of this Reina de Oro mine?"

"No. It was clearly one of many pre-Revolt mines, of which all historical documents were lost during the rebellion." Chavez took off his glasses and wiped them with a handkerchief. "There's something I wasn't going to tell you yet, but—well, this document changes everything."

"What's that?"

"It has to do with the gold cross found on the body of James Gower. At first I thought it was mere speculation on my part, but now..."

He placed the glasses back on his nose. "A little background first. In 1519, as you know, Hernán Cortés landed on the coast of Mexico and eventually conquered the Aztec capital of Tenochtitlán, the largest city in the New World. It was ruled by the emperor Montezuma, who had staggering amounts of gold, silver, and other precious objects in his treasury. The Spanish destroyed Tenochtitlán in 1521 and carried away its treasure. Almost all of it was melted down into bars to ship back to Spain. But some of that gold was reworked into holy objects for use in the New World."

He tented his fingers, voice deepening.

"Montezuma wore a large gold forehead ornament with the likeness of the god Quetzalcoatl on it, studded with precious stones. It was the fundamental symbol of his divine authority. After Montezuma's death, the Spanish pried out the stones and melted down the gold—and remade it into a cross. It was a highly significant action, you see. They did it for the same reason they built churches on top of Aztec temples and sacred places: to transform the symbols of pagan worship into Christian ones."

"And that was the cross Gower was carrying?"

"I believe so." His eyes shone. "The very cross scholars long believed was lost to history—or just a legend."

"But how do you know it's *that* cross?"

"Those little stamps I've been scratching my head over? The ones I thought were hallmarks or maker's marks? They were not. They were, in fact, Nahuatl glyphs: one for the name Montezuma, and the other a syllabic glyph for Jesus. When I saw that, I wondered if it might be *the* cross. But that's an extraordinary claim, and I was searching for corroborative evidence. This letter is that evidence. The cross was believed to have been carried up into New Mexico around 1600, so it would naturally be found with the ecclesiastical treasure." He tapped the computer screen with a long finger. "*This* treasure."

A soft knock came at the door, and the president's assistant came in. "Sorry to bother you, but, Nora? That FBI agent called your office phone. I heard it and picked it up. She's been trying to reach you."

"My office phone?" Nora pulled her cell from her pocket. During their session with the Spanish letter, it had gone dead. "Thanks." After congratulating Chavez and promising him a bottle of Dom Pérignon, she went to her office and called Corrie from her landline.

"Nora, I've been trying to reach you all morning!"

"Listen, Corrie, I've got some incredible news. I found Nantan Taza, the old Apache. He's alive. And he gave me a—"

"Hold up, Nora," Corrie said sharply.

"What is it?"

"The phone...might not be good. We need to meet. In person. Somewhere safe."

"Can you come to the Institute?"

"Yes." A pause. "No. Not safe enough. Come to my apartment in Albuquerque."

"When?"

"Around six, please."

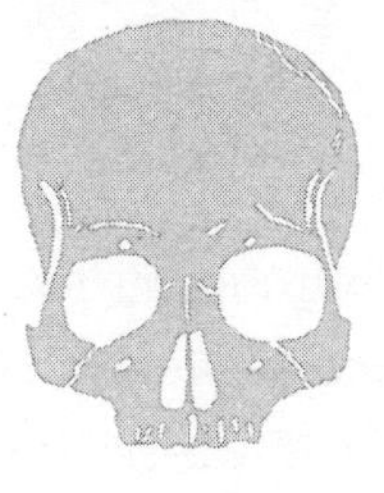

49

"I warn you," said Watts, as he and Morwood stood in the parking lot outside Cascabel Tavern, the light of a blinking neon cactus framed against the evening sky. "This place isn't too friendly to law enforcement."

"So you said." Morwood pulled out a glossy of Rivers and another glossy, blurry and indistinct, of the guy in the MP uniform who had killed him and handed both to Watts. "I'm going to let you do the talking. You look like one of them, and I don't."

"Well, damn, Agent Morwood, I told you to wear a cowboy hat and jeans," said Watts with a grin.

Morwood snorted. "Hell will freeze over first."

Watts heard some yelling, followed by a woman's shrill voice at the other side of the dirt parking lot. Two guys appeared, swinging their fists at each other while the girl hollered, thoroughly enjoying the fight.

"Kind of early for that, don't you think?" Morwood said. "It's barely six."

"Never too early at the Cascabel. Besides, I'd much rather go in there now than wait until midnight." Watts tugged the brim of his hat and strode across the lot, Morwood following. He pushed open the saloon doors and entered the bar, fragrant with the smell of cheap perfume and spilled beer—and choking with cigarette smoke, even though it had been against the law to smoke in a New Mexico tavern for fifteen years.

Watts glanced around as they headed to the bar but didn't see anyone he knew. He ordered a cup of coffee while Morwood ordered a glass of seltzer. The bartender was enormous, well over six feet, solid as a cast-iron boiler. He had a big black beard and a ponytail, and his facial expressions made it clear that he didn't approve of their drink choices.

Watts took out his sheriff's star and placed it on the bar.

The man eyed it, then looked up at Watts. "So?"

"I was hoping to ask a few questions about a guy who used to come in here. Pick Rivers."

The bartender looked at him steadily, then turned to Morwood, staring at the ID hanging on a lanyard around his neck. "You a fed?"

"FBI."

Another long stare at each of them. Then the bartender said: "You guys look smart. If you want my advice, I'd finish your drinks and go on out. This isn't a good place for you, I guarantee it."

"How about answering a few questions first?"

"No thanks."

"Aren't you curious to know why we're interested in Rivers?" Watts asked.

"Not particularly. He's a loudmouth asshole."

"We shouldn't speak ill of the dead."

At this the bartender fell silent. Watts could see he wanted to ask how Rivers had died, but he didn't.

"He was murdered," Watts added.

Now he could see the bartender was even more intrigued. He stuck out his hand. "Sheriff Homer Watts."

The bartender, taken by surprise, took the hand. "Bob Glen."

"Yeah," Watts went on. "Rivers was assassinated. In the hospital, if you can believe it. Some guy came in and injected a deadly drug into his IV."

Glen said nothing.

Watts removed a glossy of the killer. "This guy."

Glen looked at it. "Shitty photograph," he said. "Can't see his face."

"That's the problem. Look, Mr. Glen, we're not here to bust anyone's balls or get into politics. We want to find out who killed Rivers. That's all."

Glen leaned forward and spoke in a low voice. "Look, if I answer a few questions, will you guys get out? I've had enough trouble in here already, and I don't want my place trashed again."

"Sounds like a deal," said Watts. "Do you know if Rivers was involved in looting or selling of relics?"

"Yeah, he used to brag now and then about how he'd dug up some ruin, found pots and shit like that."

"And did he ever say who he was selling to? Or working with?"

"I got the impression he was working for himself. He was too fucked up back then to work with anyone. But after he got out of the Graybar Hotel, he stopped coming around. I sort of got the idea he'd straightened himself out—"

"Fee-fi-fo-fum!" came a drunken voice from behind them. Watts turned to see three guys in full cowboy regalia coming up, boots thumping, spurs jingling. All three had the rough red faces of the drinking class, and he recognized them as the

Sturgis brothers. They had a ranch out in Arabela, where they had set up concrete bunkers, shooting ranges, obstacle courses, a solar panel array, a ten-thousand-gallon fuel tank, and an arsenal of weapons, all ready for the coming apocalypse. They weren't real cowboys, just a bunch of doomsday-prepper assholes who illegally overstocked their federal grazing allotments, for which they paid almost nothing—anti-government guys on the government dole. They rounded up their cows with ATVs and airhorns and didn't even own horses.

"I smell the blood of a fed," the drunken man finished, coming up to Morwood, the other two crowding around his stool. Morwood looked the man up and down, saying nothing.

The bar had gone quiet, and the other patrons were looking their way, some standing up to get a better view.

"Hey, Sturgis," said Watts, "we don't want any trouble, okay? We're just asking a few questions about a homicide. This guy." He pulled out the glossy of Rivers.

Sturgis swiped the glossy out of his hand and flicked it away like a Frisbee.

Morwood stood up. Watts could see all three of the Sturgis brothers were open-carrying, as usual. Everyone in the bar, it seemed, had a piece strapped on. He was glad he was wearing his brace of six-guns.

Morwood remained surprisingly cool for a guy in his late forties and not in especially good shape facing a giant gorilla of a man. "Do you really want to go there, Mr. Sturgis?"

"Yeah, I do. I *really* want to go there."

There was a long silence while the two of them looked at each other. Then Sturgis reached out and plucked Morwood's shield hanging on the lanyard. "Remember Ruby Ridge," he said, and leaned over and spat on it.

Now the silence in the bar was total. Watts waited, tense, ready to reach for his Peacemakers. He had no idea what Morwood would do next or what might happen.

Slowly, almost leisurely, Morwood pulled the lanyard over his head, and then—hands out at his sides in a nonthreatening posture—he walked still closer to the gorilla. "Well, I really *don't* want to go there. So we'll be leaving now. Maybe we'll see you boys another time."

All eyes were on the faces of the two men staring each other down. Only Watts noticed that as Morwood was speaking he was also deftly and quietly polishing his badge on Sturgis's loose shirttail.

After a tense silence, Morwood turned and walked to the saloon doors, Watts following. Behind them, catcalls and whistles erupted. At the entrance, Morwood looked back.

"Remember Oklahoma City," he said in an iron voice.

They crossed the parking lot and Morwood got into his truck, Watts sliding into the passenger seat. When they were out on the highway, Watts turned toward Morwood. The FBI agent's face was neutral, collected, smooth, showing no sign of what had just transpired.

"That took self-control," Watts said.

"Yes. It did."

"That was assault, cut-and-dried."

"Absolutely."

"If you don't mind me asking," Watts said, "what are you going to do about it?" He didn't add that he, personally, would likely have punched the lights out of the son of a bitch; but, he had to admit, that would have taken them all into unknown territory.

"Suffice to say, a rain of shit is going to fall down on Mr.

Sturgis—I just have to decide how hard. But we've got more important things to do right now. Besides, my badge needed polishing."

They turned on Highway 380 and headed east. The sun was almost touching the horizon as they cleared the pass through the Azul Mountains. To the south, Watts caught a glimpse of a tiny trail of dust, illuminated in the setting sun. He stared. That was the start of the BLM road to High Lonesome.

"Hey, Agent Morwood?"

The agent looked over.

"Are your people doing any work over at High Lonesome?"

"Not yet."

"Well, then, I think we've got a problem."

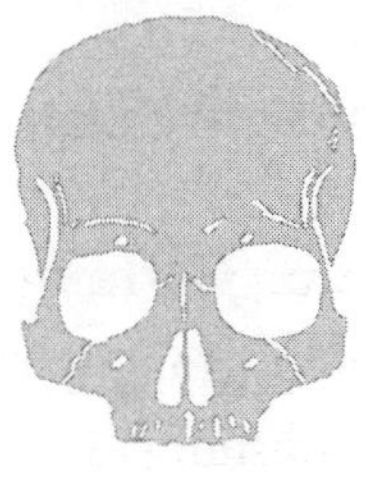

50

Nora arrived at Corrie's apartment just as the sun was setting over Sandia Crest. Corrie was waiting at the door, and she ushered her in. Nora was eager to deliver her news, but Corrie stopped her from speaking and led her into a second bedroom she had turned into an office, with a computer on a table and piles of manila folders and paper on the floor. A nearby trash can was overflowing with more paper.

"Sorry," Corrie said, shifting the stacks out of the way. "I've been so busy with this case, I can't find time to do anything else. You wouldn't believe the paperwork an FBI agent has to do. There's even more at the office."

She pulled a chair up and positioned it next to the desk, in front of a tripod where she had set up her cell phone as a video recorder. "Sit down, Nora. I'm going to take notes and videotape your statement."

"I always wanted to be a social media star," said Nora, trying to lighten the mood.

Corrie didn't smile. "I'll sit here and ask questions." She turned on the cell phone video and sat down. "Okay. Tell me about your journey to Nantan Taza and what you discovered. Everything you say is going to be logged as evidence in the case."

This was a side of Corrie that Nora had rarely seen. She began by describing the horseback journey, finding the dying Taza, and giving him the bundle.

At this, Corrie abruptly paused the recorder. "Wait. You *gave* him the medicine bundle? You're kidding, right?"

"No."

"But..." Corrie could barely choke out the words. "That was evidence. *Evidence*. You *knew* that. Do you have any idea how hard I had to fight just to get that damned dirty old sack out of the frigging building?"

At this, Nora's excitement faded behind an upwelling of irritation. "That 'dirty old sack' just happened to belong to someone. And I had to give it to him in order to get something in return. Something valuable."

"Just how the hell am I going to explain this to my boss?" Corrie asked, raising her voice. "I'm already on his shit list. Your waltzing off with this piece of evidence—which I signed off on, remember?—is going to be the last nail in the coffin."

"So now you're trying to lay this on *me*?" Nora said, her own voice rising accordingly. "I didn't ask you to show up at my dig site, with your sob story about how you'd messed up, begging me to drive halfway across the state to help you. I should have known better. I'm the one doing you the favor."

"That doesn't justify what you did. I *trusted* you with that evidence. I expected you to act within the law. And besides, once you saw the site I could barely drag you away from it!"

"That's like a drug pusher blaming a buyer for getting addicted!" All the pent-up frustration and annoyance she'd been holding back—more than she'd realized—came tumbling out at once. "Well, guess what? You're not the only one with work troubles. By wasting all this time helping you, I've put myself totally behind schedule on my dig...and I've risked losing a really important promotion. And that's on *you*." She stood up. "Whatever. I'm done. I'm out of here."

"Nora—wait."

"Go to hell." She turned to leave the room.

"Nora, I'm sorry. I didn't realize this was causing you such problems."

Nora hesitated, breathing heavily.

"You said you got something valuable in return."

"Yes."

"Maybe I can use that as an excuse, keep us both out of trouble."

Fury vented, Nora felt herself cooling down. It wasn't like her to blow her top—that was more Corrie's department. She wondered if she should demand an apology and realized she wouldn't get one. Anyway, she'd been out of line as well.

Corrie continued. "It's not considered unreasonable for an FBI agent to give something in exchange for information of value."

Nora forced herself to turn and sit down again.

"All right," Corrie said, "if you're ready, let's resume." She turned the recorder back on.

Nora took a deep breath. "After I gave him the medicine bag," she began once more, "Taza asked me to fetch a wooden box. Inside were two items: a heavy gold watch decorated with constellations, and a piece of parchment with a Native American drawing on one side and faded Spanish script on the other."

"A piece of parchment?" Corrie asked, leaning forward with an astonished expression. "Was it cut in half?"

"Yes. How did you know?"

Corrie didn't answer the question, instead asking another. "What did the old man tell you about it?"

"He said that the Jornada del Muerto and all the surrounding land, all of WSMR, once belonged to the Apaches. Many centuries ago, he said, his ancestors encountered a group of friars hurrying down the Spanish trail with soldiers and mules. They attacked the pack train and pursued it into the foothills, where the Spanish fled, looking for a defensible site. They took refuge on a small peak. The Apaches surrounded them, but the Spanish soldiers kept them at bay while the mules were unloaded and their cargo placed in the mountain. The Spanish defended themselves for a while longer, but they had no water and eventually the Apaches prevailed and killed them all. A day later, the Apaches caught a boy from the pack train, carrying a letter down the Camino Real. He had escaped from the peak during the fight. The Apaches took the letter from him. The boy said it was terribly important and was written to the high chief of Spain himself. The Apaches kept the parchment, not knowing what it was but believing it to be of great significance to the Spanish. At some point many years later, one of the keepers of the parchment drew pictures on its back. Sacred pictures, he said, of a battle where Geronimo defeated his enemies. The pictures were to counteract the negative power of the written words on the other side.

"Taza went on to say that, through inheritance from his father, he became the keeper of the parchment. He was only seventeen, he said, and didn't take it very seriously. He'd developed a youthful curiosity about the white man and his ways. He struck up a friendship with a man named James Gower, much older than he was, and the two of them spent a lot of time hunting for relics and treasure in the mountains and desert Taza knew so well. Taza had lost both his parents, and Gower became a kind of surrogate father. At some point, Taza showed Gower the document, and Gower immediately understood its significance."

"Gower was able to read the letter?" Corrie asked.

"The language, it turns out, isn't hard to translate. It's the script that's difficult. Gower apparently knew how to read that old script and was also fluent in Spanish. He may not have been educated, but he was clever."

"Go on."

"So the two decided to become partners and find the treasure described in the letter. As a way to seal the bond, they gave each other their most precious possessions. Taza gave Gower his medicine bundle, and Gower gave Taza his gold watch. And they cut the piece of parchment in half, each keeping a piece as a symbol of their partnership.

"Taza knew, deep down, that hunting for the treasure was wrong: the lands they scoured were sacred, and there was evil attached to the Spanish hoard. But the lure of gold was great. They established a camp at High Lonesome, obtained a mule, and began searching the Sierra Oscura for the hill mentioned in the document. They kept at it for a number of weeks... and then something unthinkable happened.

"They'd decided to split up temporarily, in order to cover more territory. When Taza returned to camp that night, Gower and the mule were still gone, searching in the foothills to the south. Then, just before dawn the next morning, Taza saw it—a sudden light brighter than the sun. There was no sound at first, he told me. The light expanded with unbelievable speed, until it was like a gigantic eye, and he described how it rose into the dark sky, shimmering with every color of the rainbow. And only then did the sound come. It was, he said, the roar of the devil—nothing else could have been so powerful, or so terrible. Moments later, a wind like a hurricane threw him to the ground. When he managed to struggle to his feet, he saw a dirty pillar rising to the heavens, spreading in all directions, dropping rain and flickering with lightning, while the mountains and deserts echoed and re-echoed with thunder."

"Jesus," said Corrie.

"Frightened almost out of his wits but unwilling to desert his friend, Taza waited at the camp for Gower to return. At sunset, he finally did. His skin was hanging from his body like rotten leather; he was injured, bleeding and scorched; his eyes were as red as blood. And he was raving mad. The mule, too, was half-crazed. Gower babbled about the devil, gold, and Armageddon. He lived only half an hour, Taza said, and then Taza buried him and shot the mule. He left that evil place, never to return, unfortunately overlooking the medicine bundle in his panic and haste to get away. And he never did return, or even speak of it again—until now."

Nora stopped. The emotional toll of telling the story had drained any residual anger from her. And what she'd said clearly had the same effect on Corrie.

After a silence, Corrie said: "Can you show me the parchment?"

Nora took out her leather portfolio and removed a clear archival sleeve containing the parchment. She laid it on the desk.

For a moment, Corrie stared at it. Then she took the evidence packet from her briefcase and removed her own piece of parchment. She placed it on the table beside Nora's. The two cut edges fit perfectly together.

Nora stared in disbelief. "My God. Where did you get that?"

"Up at the Gower kid's place. Hidden in the henhouse."

"Do you know what it is?"

"No. I was hoping you could tell me."

"It's directions," Nora told her. "Directions to the Victorio Peak treasure."

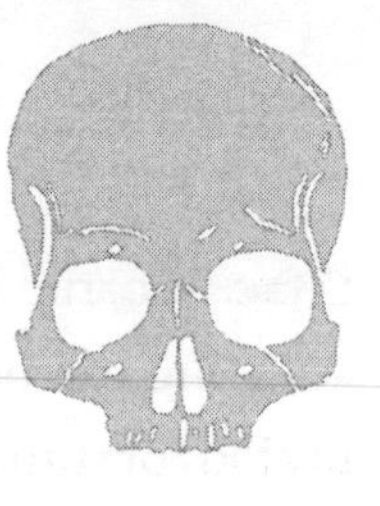

51

Nora stared at the two pieces of parchment, now placed together on the desk. "I have a translation of my half," she said. "Done by Orlando. We have to translate your half."

"How are we going to do that?" Corrie asked, peering at the parchment. "Not only is it a squiggly mess, but some of the letters are so faded I can't read them."

"Back at the Institute, Orlando photographed my section in UV light and then digitally manipulated the photo to increase contrast. Maybe we could do the same. Do you have anything that's blue and transparent?"

"I have something better: a handheld UV examination light. Standard FBI equipment." Corrie rummaged around in her office supplies and pulled out a small black penlight.

Nora took it. "You shine it on the parchment and I'll take a picture with my cell phone."

Corrie positioned the light and switched it on, illuminating the document. Nora could see that in the eerie purple glow, the script stood out much better. She took a series of photographs with her cell phone and transferred them to Corrie's iMac. Corrie loaded the photos into an image editor and, selecting the best exposure, started working with it. In a short period of time, by cranking up the contrast and adjusting the brilliance, the script on the screen became clear enough to read.

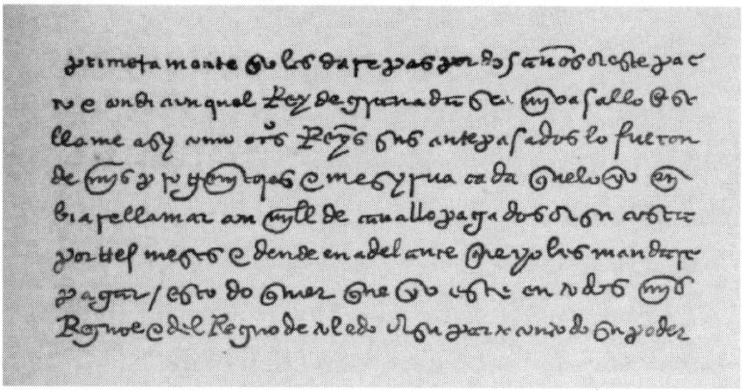

Corrie peered at it. "It doesn't even look like letters."

"Watch and learn." Nora, suddenly grateful for Orlando's pedantry, loaded the website of old Castilian scripts and pulled the alphabet chart for Cortesana. "I'll use this."

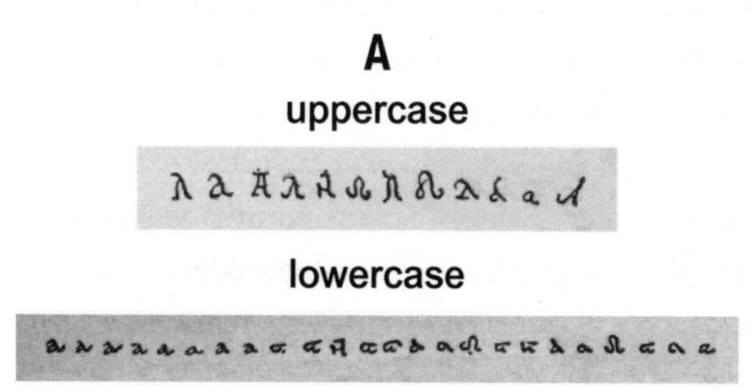

"See? Those are all the variants of *A*."

Corrie stared. "Very cool. I had no idea you could find something like this on the web."

"It's just going to take a while."

Nora started to work, taking Corrie's piece of parchment one letter at a time, looking it up on the chart, and then seeing which modern letter it represented. It was laborious at first, but after ten minutes she started to recognize the letters from memory. An hour later, she had transcribed Corrie's half of the document. She sat back. "There it is."

"Can you translate it?"

"You bet." She took a blank piece of paper and began with the first line, working slowly and sometimes having to check unusual words with Google Translate.

—to Your Majesty from the province of New Spain
—ust the various Pueblos rose in revolt and martyred
—edge of said revolt, Fray Marcos, Fray
—rescued much of the holy ecclesiastical treasure
—ions. We burdened sixty-two mules and horses
—mino Real in the vicinity of Senecú we were
—ward, where we were so pressed that we hid
—peak called El Aguijón del Escorpión in the
—to the mine and made the mark of the cross on
—scorpión we made a second mark of two crosses
—aled the northern entrance to the mine with no mark.
—send you this letter through a messenger and pray that
—ure may be rightfully returned to Your Holy Roman
—of Your Majesty's northern possessions.

—kisses your Royal feet and hands,

Nora finished the last sentence and pushed the paper toward Corrie. "Done."

"And the first half?"

"Right here." Nora took out the paper on which Orlando had written his translation of the other half of the document. She put the two translations together on the table with trembling hands, and they both looked down to read the letter in full, in English.

S.C.C. Majestad:

On the 20th of August 1680 I write in haste
to Your Majesty from the province of New Spain
along the Camino Real. On the 10th of Aug
ust the various Pueblos rose in revolt and martyred
many of the holy fathers. Having foreknowl
edge of said revolt, Fray Marcos, Fray
Angelico, and Fray Bartolomé and soldiers
rescued much of the holy ecclesiastical treasure
of the cathedral, the churches and the miss
ions. We burdened sixty-two mules and horses
with treasure and fled southward. Along the Ca
mino Real in the vicinity of Senecú we were
beset by savage Apachu Indians and forced east
ward, where we were so pressed that we hid
the treasure in the old Reina de Oro mine in the
peak called El Aguijón del Escorpión in the
Sierra Oscura. We concealed the south entrance
to the mine and made the mark of the cross on
a stone five paces to the right. At the base of E
scorpión we made a second mark of two crosses

on a large stone directly below. We conce
aled the northern entrance to the mine with no mark.
We are yet pressed by the Apachu and I
send you this letter through a messenger and pray that
you receive it, and that the holy treas
ure may be rightfully restored to Your Holy Roman
Catholic Majesty upon the recapture
of Your Majesty's northern possessions.

Humble servant and vassal of Your Majesty, who
kisses your Royal feet and hands,

Fray Bartolomé de Aragon

They read in silence, and the stillness in the room continued as they looked up at each other.

"This is incredible," Corrie finally murmured.

"Yes," said Nora. She shook her head as if to dispel a dream. "Which peak is this Aguijón del Escorpión—the Tail of the Scorpion?"

Corrie leaned over the keyboard, and soon Google Earth popped up on the screen, showing the Sierra Oscura at the northern end of the missile range, west and south of the Trinity site. The range ran north-south for twenty-five miles and encompassed hundreds of hills, peaks, buttes, and ridges.

"You're asking which one is the Scorpion's Tail?" Corrie asked, peering. "It took Gower and Taza weeks to find it."

"They didn't have twenty-first-century technology," Nora said. "Think about the strange name of the peak. Could it look like a scorpion's upraised stinger? Or is it called that for some other reason?"

Corrie shrugged. She expanded the view, zeroing in on the northern end of the Oscura range, nearer to the Trinity site. There were almost too many peaks and ridges and hills to count.

"Here's a thought," Nora said. "After Gower found the treasure, he would have made a beeline back to High Lonesome, carrying that cross as proof of his find. High Lonesome is here on the map. His route must have taken him within about a mile of ground zero on either side of the Trinity site, here, to have been caught in the blast. So let's draw lines from High Lonesome to within a mile on either side of the Trinity site, and see which hills they intersect."

Using Google Earth's line-drawing facility, she drew the two lines. The lines cut through the Oscura foothills, crossing a dozen or so peaks. Nora and Corrie leaned forward to peer closely at the screen.

"Whoa!" said Nora. "Look at that hill. You see that?"

Corrie zoomed in. The hill was named Mockingbird Butte on the map.

"I don't see it."

"Not the hill itself," said Nora. "The little canyon just below it, cutting into its base."

Corrie stared. The little canyon curled up from below, shaped very much like the raised tail of a scorpion with a bulbous stinger at the end. "Holy shit."

"Holy shit is right," Nora said, tingling with excitement, heart pounding. "*That's* the peak. *That's* where the Victorio Peak treasure is hidden! Not in Victorio Peak at all, but there!"

An hour later, Corrie and Nora each held an empty glass of wine they had drunk to celebrate. The precious parchments had been carefully sealed back up in the plastic evidence envelope and stored in the FBI-issue safe in Corrie's home office. She had tried to call Morwood but gotten only voice mail.

Nora rose. "I'd better get back to Santa Fe," she said. "Skip will be holding dinner for us, and he gets cranky if it dries out in the oven."

"Okay." Corrie rose, too. "Meet me in my cubicle at eight o'clock tomorrow morning. We'll take this in to Morwood together."

"I can hardly wait."

Corrie smiled at the thought. "It's going to blow his mind."

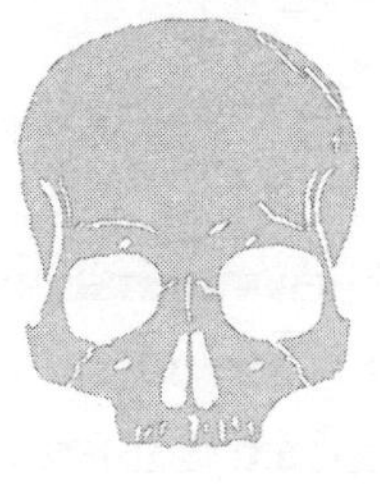

52

AS THEY APPROACHED the crest of the pass leading down to High Lonesome, Morwood pulled the vehicle to one side of the road. "We'd better not let our headlights show over the ridgeline," he said. "Let's have a look and see what's going on."

Watts got out, put on his hat, and buckled on his six-guns. Morwood didn't say anything during this ritual but was privately amused. He took a pair of binoculars out of the glove compartment, and they walked into the ponderosa forest and climbed to the ridgeline.

Below, the town of High Lonesome came into view, a thousand yards away. There were lights. Morwood peered down with the binocs and could see two pickup trucks parked at right angles to each other, their beams illuminating a work scene. Several men were busy taking apart the second-floor wooden wall of the building in which Gower's body had been found. Two others, armed, stood nearby, apparently on guard.

"Son of a bitch," said Watts.

Morwood counted the men and confirmed there were five visible. "We need to call in backup," he said.

Watts grunted. "How long is that going to take?"

"Hours, but the alternative is to apprehend them ourselves, which is suicide."

After a moment, Watts nodded. "Backup it is."

They returned to the vehicle. Morwood pulled down the radio, but they were out of range, and there was no cell coverage. He started the truck. "All we can do is head back until we find coverage and call it in."

Watts pursed his lips. "Can I make a suggestion, Agent Morwood?"

"Sure."

"Let's approach a little closer and see if we can't ID some of them, or at least get a plate number. By the time we drive out, call for backup, and return, those guys are going to be gone."

Morwood thought about this. It entailed risk—but also reward. Even a plate number would be crucial information.

"Okay," he said. "Not a bad idea."

Morwood eased the truck forward, headlights off. The moon hadn't risen, but there was a desert azimuth glow in the sky: just enough to see by. He eased the truck over the pass, and they proceeded down the switchbacks, slow and quiet, brakes only, in neutral to prevent the sound of gears. Reaching the far end of town, Morwood snugged the truck up behind an adobe wall where it would be well concealed. They got out. Watts took out one of his .45s and slowly spun the cylinder while Morwood checked his own weapon.

"We're going to get close enough to ID a plate and that's it," Morwood said.

"Right."

They crept out from behind the adobe wall. The town was sunken in darkness, with a bright glow from the headlights at the opposite end. Keeping adobe walls between them and the lights, they worked their way closer.

About halfway through town, as they came around the wall of a ruined building, two additional lights suddenly switched on, pinning them in the glare. They must have been hidden, awaiting just such an intrusion: their beams seemed to come out of nowhere. Morwood heard a simultaneous racking of weapons.

A voice said: "Easy now, keep your hands visible. We've got three weapons on you, so don't do anything stupid."

Morwood froze. He could see the tiny red dots of laser sights playing on their chests.

"Keep your hands well away from those guns, Sheriff."

"Yes, sir," said Watts.

Now a tall man strolled out of the darkness, halfway between the two lights. He wore a duster and cowboy hat and carried a rifle and sidearm. When he reached the middle of the street, between the newcomers and the activity at the far end of town, he stopped. Morwood stared at him. Something about the man was familiar, although the voice was not. Two other figures partially emerged from the shadows on either side, rifles aimed, flashlights in hand. When one of the lights briefly flickered across the first man's face, Morwood suddenly realized who it was.

The man wearing the duster was the MP in the hospital video.

"All right now, gentlemen," the man said in a laconic drawl. "Sheriff, you first. Just ease out those two six-guns from their holsters, slow as molasses, just two fingers on each. Hold them out arms-length and let them fall to the ground. You understand me, pardner?"

"Yes, sir."

With just thumb and forefinger, moving with great slowness,

Watts crossed his left arm over the right, plucked the two revolvers from their holsters, and held them out, dangling.

"Now drop them."

"Drop and roll left," Watts murmured to Morwood out of the corner of his mouth.

Morwood tensed.

"I said *drop* them, pardner."

Watts began to release the guns, but then—with a lightning-fast flick of both wrists—caught them and brought them back up, firing in two directions simultaneously, elbows tucked in. He struck both men on either side, sending them spinning into the dirt. Watts broke left and rolled, even as the man in the duster raised his rifle to fire. Morwood followed the sheriff, pulling his Glock as he rolled and fired at the man still standing.

But Morwood missed, and the man in the duster got off a shot that hit him in the right hand. It was like being clobbered with a bat, his gun spinning away. Dazed, in the dust, Morwood could hear more shots and shouting, and he felt himself grabbed and violently dragged into a small ruin. There was more shooting and the dull thud of rounds striking the adobe walls.

Watts crouched down over him, holding Morwood's gun.

"Damned good shooting," Morwood managed to say.

"You're hit," said Watts.

"Yeah."

Watts was already tearing a strip of cloth from his shirt, which he used to bind up Morwood's hand. By now the FBI agent's head was clearing and the shock of the injury was turning into pain. Which, in its own way, was good. "Give me that gun. I can still shoot with my left hand," he said.

"Damn glad of that," said Watts.

"I just can't hit anything," Morwood said. There was an

eruption of more gunfire, bullets whining overhead or smacking into the wall. Judging from the places where the rounds were hitting, they were pinned down in cross fire. Then came a sudden, concentrated sound of shots, not directed at them—followed by the hissing of tires and the sound of a vehicle horn, quickly silenced: the men had found their vehicle and neutralized it.

"How many?" Morwood asked.

"I'd guess half a dozen. Not counting the two guys I shot."

Morwood grunted.

"I've got twenty-four rounds of ammo in my belt plus six in the cylinders," said Watts. "You?"

"Fifteen." Morwood took a deep breath, keeping his mind off the pain. "We've got to scope out their cover, locations, and fields of fire. That means putting our heads up."

"Right."

"Some of them have rifles," Morwood said.

"Yeah. That's going to be tough."

Another fusillade of rounds slammed into the walls around them.

"Here's what we do," said Morwood. "We both rise and engage in suppressing fire just long enough to see what's what. Fast, less than a second."

"Understood."

"On three." Morwood counted, and they popped up, firing furiously, then dropped back down. Another monster fusillade followed in response.

"Don't know about you," Watts said, "but what I saw is, they've got good cover all around, clear fields of fire, we're surrounded, and they're advancing."

Morwood grunted again.

"I'd say we're fucked," Watts said.

Morwood closed his eyes, mastered the pain as best he could, then reopened them. "I was thinking the same thing." He took a deep breath, let it out. He had to focus.

"Maybe," Watts said, "we should be shaking hands and wishing each other goodbye, like they do in the Westerns."

Morwood grimaced. "Not yet."

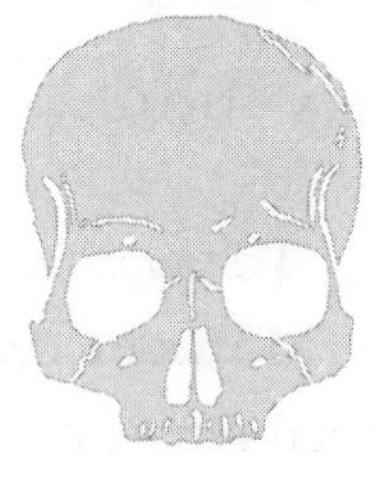

53

Now that the treasure—and its location—seemed a reality, Corrie knew that sleep was going to be almost impossible for a third night in a row. There was a chance, of course, that the treasure was gone, someone having found it years ago. But she doubted it—a treasure like that would be hard to keep secret, especially on a missile range. *Sixty-two mule loads*. A mule, according to Nora, could carry about a hundred-and-fifty pounds max, so one-fifty times sixty-two equaled over nine thousand pounds of treasure. Not anywhere near the sixty tons of legend, but the historic and artistic value alone would be immense. Tomorrow, she thought with satisfaction, it would all be over: there would be an immediate, public, and official search, and the treasure would be found and secured. And the general, if he was involved, would be shit out of luck.

Her cell phone rang. Nora was on the other end.

"Corrie?"

"Hi, what's up?"

"I've made a discovery that changes...changes everything. You've got to come over."

"What?"

Nora sounded almost tense. "The phone isn't good, just like you said. We have to do this in person. You've got to come by my place in Santa Fe."

"It's eleven o'clock. It can't wait till morning?"

"Please come. And bring the parchment. I've got to go now."

And she hung up.

Corrie put down her phone. That was a strange call, for sure. What could she have found? It must've really upset her, judging from the tone of Nora's voice. But then, her own voice probably sounded the same way, under the circumstances.

Corrie opened the safe and took out the evidence envelope containing the two pieces of parchment. She glanced at her service weapon, remembered Morwood's lectures that carrying it always should be second nature, and holstered it. She went to her car for the drive to Santa Fe.

Nora's condo was on Galisteo Street, just south of Paseo de Peralta. Her car was in the driveway and the lights were on, curtains drawn. Corrie parked behind Nora's car, went to the door, and knocked, holding the envelope.

"Come in," Nora called. "Door's unlocked."

Corrie entered and immediately felt herself seized and immobilized in a hammerlock. She struggled, trying to scream, and was hit hard against the side of the head.

"Get her weapon," someone said.

She was disarmed with great efficiency, her purse and ID taken, her wrists handcuffed behind her back, and she was shoved, half-stunned, from the hall into the living room.

There was Nora, taped to a chair. Lying on the floor was Skip, hands cuffed behind his back, face bloody. There were a handful of soldiers in the room, along with Lieutenant Woodbridge and General McGurk. One soldier had an M16 pressed to the back of Skip's head.

Without a word, the general tore open the envelope and removed the two pieces of parchment, looked at them, shoved them back in, and handed them to Woodbridge.

"He was going to kill my brother," Nora sobbed. "I'm so sorry, he was pointing that gun at Skip's—"

A soldier smacked her across the face. "Shut the fuck up."

"Where's the translation?" the general asked.

Corrie stared at him. His calm control frightened her more than anything else. She realized that he hadn't just tapped her phone—he must also have bugged her apartment. What exactly had they said and not said? Had they spoken the name of the Mockingbird Butte? She wracked her brains, trying to remember.

"I don't have it," she replied.

The general considered this a moment. He looked at Corrie. "But you know where the treasure's hidden."

Corrie didn't answer. The general made a gesture, and the soldier with the M16 to Skip's head gave him a jab with it.

"Your last chance to answer."

"Yes," said Corrie. "We know where it is." Despite everything, her initial panic was being replaced by a feeling of scorching clarity. The bastard wasn't going to get away with this.

"If you kill him," she said calmly, "you'll never, ever get the information you want from us. You'll have to translate that old Spanish document on your own, and, believe me, it won't be easy. It will require experts. Experts have questions. And they don't know the desert like Nora does. But if you let him live, we'll tell you where the treasure is."

The general gazed at her. "Tell me? No, thank you. You'll *lead* me to it."

Corrie returned the stare. "And then?"

A long silence ensued, and then the general said, "You're a cool little bitch, considering the circumstances. We're not going to kill anybody if you cooperate. If the treasure's where you say it is, you'll be fine."

Bullshit, thought Corrie.

McGurk turned to Woodbridge. "Lieutenant, call in the transportation."

She got on the radio, and three jeeps soon pulled up. Everyone got in, and they drove south out of town a few miles on I-25, to the U.S. Army Reserve National Guard base. A helicopter was waiting on the tarmac. All three hostages were silenced with gags and tape; the soldiers pushed them into seats, and the chopper took off into the velvet night.

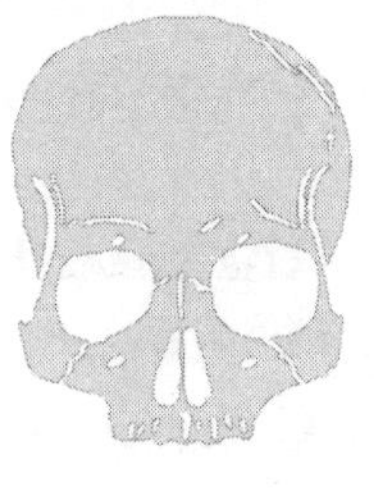

54

HUNKERED DOWN AGAINST the wall, Morwood struggled to forget about the pain. The cloth wrapped around his hand was already soaked with blood.

Watts had been keeping the shooters at bay by shifting back and forth behind the wall and popping up at unpredictable intervals to fire a round. The idea was to keep them behind cover, making it difficult for them to advance. But the strategy could last only so long, and meanwhile it was depleting their ammo.

There came a lull in the firing, and then a voice called out. "Sheriff?"

Morwood was startled. That was a voice he recognized: *Fountain*. He could see the shock in Watts's face.

"Sheriff? It's Charles Fountain."

"I know who it is," said Watts. "And you're a goddamned lying son of a bitch."

"It would be foolish to deny such an obvious statement," said Fountain. "But more to the point: You're in a heap of trouble. Maybe I can help you get out of it."

"Bullshit."

"I'd hate to have to kill you, Homer. Let's talk."

Watts was about to reply, but Morwood touched his arm and said, in a low voice: "Keep him talking."

After a hesitation, Watts nodded. He turned and yelled, "So talk."

"You don't have to die. We can work something out."

"Like what?"

"A share in the spoils. We could use a county sheriff on our payroll."

"Spoils? You mean like the Victorio Peak treasure?"

At this Fountain chuckled. "No need to play games with me, Sheriff. We don't bother with fairy-tale treasures. We go for the real stuff. And I mean *real*."

"Like what? Something up here?"

"Oh yes, something here. Something of tremendous value—our research is crystal clear on that. Now: Would you like to join us?"

"What about my partner?"

"We could use an FBI agent as well."

Morwood doubted this. They might think they could turn a county sheriff, but not an FBI agent. They were going to kill him, of course, as soon as they could. And likely Watts, too.

"So what's in it for me?" Watts asked.

"A lot more than your crappy county salary."

"What do I have to do?"

"Toss your guns over the wall and come out of there with your hands up. We'll treat you real nice. We'll find what we're looking for very soon. You'll get your fair share, I promise."

Your fair share of a bullet between the eyes, thought Morwood. He and Watts exchanged glances, which told him Watts wasn't taken in, either.

"What do you say?" Fountain pressed.

"Tell me more about this thing you hope to find," Watts asked.

"Enough talk. I'll give you sixty seconds to make up your mind to join us—or you're dead. Starting now."

Watts leaned in to Morwood. "You know they're going to kill us," he said.

Morwood nodded.

"Thirty seconds!"

"My only thought is we rush them and take as many of the bastards out as we can," Morwood said.

"You mean like Butch Cassidy?"

"Ten seconds!"

Watts swore under his breath, popped up, and fired in the direction of the voice. He was back down just before the guns roared all around them.

"You lost your chance, Watts!" called Fountain. "You and your family always were a bunch of self-satisfied prigs! Hear those crows? They're going to be pecking out your eyes like maraschino cherries."

Morwood looked at Watts. "What about it? If we rush Fountain together, we'll get him, at least."

Watts shook his head. "Let me give this a think."

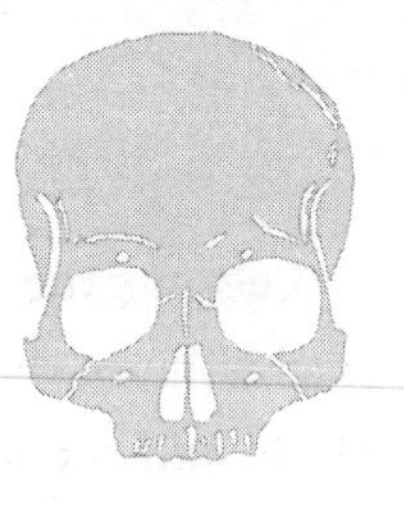

55

THE HELICOPTER THUDDED through the night. They were flying south: Nora could see the glowing thread of towns along the Rio Grande, a wandering ribbon of light in the darkness of the desert. They passed to the east of what Nora assumed was Socorro and headed toward the vast well of blackness that made up the White Sands Missile Range. Woodbridge was the pilot, and the general sat next to her in the copilot's seat, while the three of them were jammed together with three armed soldiers in canvas jump seats behind.

Nora glanced over at Skip. He returned her gaze, his eyes filled with apprehension. They had broken his nose, and blood was crusting all over it and down his shirt. Corrie, on the other hand, kept her expression carefully neutral. The soldiers were alert. It was clear from their shining, eager faces that they were anticipating a big payday. And Lieutenant Woodbridge, piloting the chopper, was chilling in her efficiency and competence.

The general, Nora thought, had chosen his people well. A small, elite group, handpicked for a very secret, very unusual assignment.

Leaving the Rio Grande behind, the chopper followed the backbone of the Oscura mountains. As it came over their crest, she could see an illuminated landing zone on the desert floor. The helicopter circled and came in to land on an asphalt pad near two heavy, canvas-covered trucks. A single crew member stood on the pad, gesturing the chopper in. A moment later they had settled, the rotors thudding down. The general got out and the soldiers followed, yanking the three by their cuffs and marching them out beyond the rotor wash.

"Line up there," said a soldier, pushing them alongside one of the trucks.

The soldiers stepped back, and the general came forward. Woodbridge exited the chopper and joined the general.

"Remove the gags and restraints," said the general.

The tape over their mouths and bindings were removed.

"You realize that—" Corrie began, but Woodbridge quickly stepped up and slapped her hard across the face.

"You will speak when asked a question, and at no other time," the general said. "Consider that we're in the middle of the largest military reservation in the country—three thousand, two hundred square miles. This area is uninhabited, closed, surveilled, and patrolled. I am the commander in charge, and I have a thousand personnel at my beck and call. In preparation for this evening, I have ordered an MQ-9 Reaper and an RQ-7 Shadow drone, along with their support platoons, to be ready on the flight line at a moment's notice. As you can see, cooperation is your only choice. Fail to cooperate, and you will be terminated. Is that understood?"

No one said anything. The general said calmly, "When I do ask a question, I want a *yes sir* or *no sir* out of each one of you. Or there will be consequences. Now, *do you understand*? Dr. Kelly?"

Nora hesitated, and Woodbridge struck her across the face so hard she staggered.

"Yes, sir," said Corrie and Skip.

Nora gasped, trying to collect herself from the blow, face burning, tears springing into her eyes. "Yes, sir."

"Good. Now let us begin by your telling me the name of the peak in the Oscura range where the treasure is located."

Silence fell.

The general said, "I will ask the question again, and if I don't get an immediate and correct answer, Lieutenant Woodbridge will fire a round into that individual's head." He pointed to Skip.

"Once you shoot him," said Corrie, "you'll lose all leverage with us, and you know it."

The general looked at her. "You're right." He made a gesture, and a soldier stepped forward and slammed the butt of his rifle into Skip's solar plexus, dropping him to the ground with a gasp of pain.

"Wait," said Nora. "Corrie?" She stared at the FBI agent. "We're going to cooperate." She turned back to the general. "Mockingbird Butte."

Corrie said nothing.

The general smiled. The soldier who had hit Skip now helped him to his feet. He was clutching his stomach and gasping.

"Mockingbird Butte," the general repeated. His eyes glittered. "Such an insignificant little hill. Who would have guessed? Let's go."

Nora and the others were pushed into the back seat of one of the trucks and surrounded by armed soldiers. Both trucks started up, and they drove off down a warren of dirt roads winding through the foothills. At a certain point, the trucks left the road and began crashing through brush and tall grass, stopping from time to time while soldiers got out and reconnoitered. Finally, both trucks stopped.

"Out," the general said.

They complied. The trucks had come to a stop at the edge of a dry wash. On the other side a hill rose up, black against the starry sky. It was a low hill, no more than a hundred feet high, with a knob of rock on top.

The general stopped in front of Nora. "Now what?"

"At the base of the hill," said Nora, "on the south side, is a large rock with two crosses carved onto it. From there, you go straight up the hill to another rock with a cross. The entrance . . . the entrance is five paces to the left."

The soldiers began searching the base of the hill with powerful headlamps. There were many boulders to examine, but it didn't take long for one soldier to shout out a discovery.

"Bring them along," said the general as they headed toward the location. At the base of a square block of basalt, in the beam of several headlamps, Nora could see a small cross chiseled into the rock, partially obscured by tall grass.

"Find the second marker," ordered the general.

The soldiers walked up the side of the hill, fanning out, examining each boulder as they went. The entire hillside was strewn with rocks, and the minutes ticked by. Finally, about two-thirds of the way up, a soldier cried: "Here!"

They walked up. The soldiers had already moved five paces to the left and were removing rocks from a depression.

"You," said the general, pointing at Skip. "Get in there and help."

Skip limped over and, still in obvious pain, began moving rocks.

Soon the outline of a mine entrance was exposed. It wasn't

well hidden. Seventy-five years ago, Gower had probably uncovered most of it, Nora assumed, only lightly re-covering it before embarking on his fateful journey back to High Lonesome.

In another ten minutes the opening was fully exposed—a crude black hole, about five feet in diameter, boring straight into the mountain.

"Go," said the general.

Woodbridge gestured with her M16, and Nora, Skip, and Corrie went into the mine, following the four soldiers, with the general and Woodbridge behind.

They're not going to let us leave this place alive, thought Nora, feeling curiously detached. She glanced at Corrie and saw the same blank expression she'd noticed before. And poor Skip...her heart almost broke thinking of what they'd done to him, how they'd terrorized him. She hoped the end would be quick.

The tunnel began to slope slightly downhill, forcing them to stoop. There was a scent of dust, and the narrow space was filled with the hollow echo of their feet.

The soldiers in front stopped. "General?"

Their lights illuminated an inscription scratched on the tunnel wall:

J D GOWER
JUL 15 1945

Nora could see, just beyond the inscription, a makeshift door made of juniper limbs lashed together with rawhide. It was ajar, and it opened into a dark chamber.

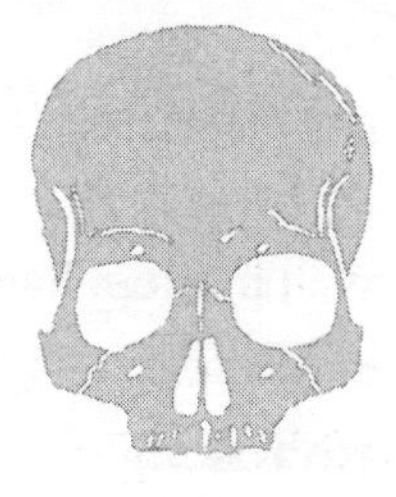

56

Morwood lay on his back, head swimming. Watts had continued to keep the attackers at bay, more or less—but with every shot, Morwood winced at the thought of one less round. The attackers had managed to move from cover to cover during the cross fire, and now the two were surrounded, only a short dash across open ground from their foes. But Watts was a hell of a shot, and so far that was the only thing preventing the final, inevitable rush. Morwood had his Glock in hand and—when they came over the wall—he was determined to take at least one out.

"How're you doing?" Watts asked.

"In the Westerns, the odds are always worse than this," Morwood replied.

"This ain't no Western," said Watts. "But there was once a guy, one of my predecessors as sheriff of Socorro County, name of Elfego Baca. He held off forty cowboys singlehandedly for thirty-three hours, killing four and wounding eight. They made a movie out of that standoff."

"He must have been sitting on an arsenal. We don't have one handy—and they're waiting for us to run out of ammo. Where are you at?"

"Got eight rounds left, four in each cylinder."

"I'm at seven."

A silence. "Maybe," said Watts slowly, "we should *let* them think we've run out."

"How so?"

"If I pull the trigger on an empty chamber, it makes a distinctive click. We might just fool them that way."

Morwood nodded slowly. "And after the last round is fired from my Glock, the slide ejects the spent round—but it makes a different sound from when the slide strips another round from the magazine and chambers it. If they know firearms, it's a sound they might recognize."

"I'd say it's a safe bet they know firearms."

Morwood's concentration was interrupted by more shooting.

"It's worth a try," said Watts.

Watts opened the cylinders in both guns and took three rounds out of each. He then shifted them one place over in the cylinder so there was a single empty chamber between the next round and the last three. Morwood, for his part, ejected the Glock's magazine, leaving a single round chambered, thumbed out the rounds, and slid the empty magazine back in.

Watts popped up and—waiting for a moment of relative silence—fired a double shot, the second pull falling on an empty chamber, eliciting return fire. He stumbled back down. "Shit!" Blood was dribbling down the side of his head. "The fuckers got my other ear."

"At least you're back in proportion."

Watts took off his hat, spattered with blood, a piece of the brim torn off. "And worse, they ruined my hat."

"My turn," Morwood said, crawling along the adobe and—like Watts, waiting for a moment of quiet—raising his head, firing the last round with his left hand. A flurry of shots followed. He quickly pushed the rounds back into the magazine and reinserted it. He didn't dare rack a round—the sound would tip them off.

"We'd better wait a bit," said Watts. "They might be thinking we've only got one or two rounds left. So they'll probably do something to try to provoke us."

"Probably a feint, baiting us to fire."

Watts nodded. They waited tensely... and then Watts heard the thudding footsteps of someone running.

He popped up and pulled the trigger twice on a figure running from one piece of cover to another. The second pull was on the empty chamber.

He ducked back down as more shots followed.

"Now," said Morwood, "we engage them in negotiations. That's what they'd expect if we'd run out of ammo."

Watts nodded and called out, "Hey, Fountain!"

"Too late, Sheriff," came the reply. "You had your chance!"

"Look, let's talk."

Silence.

"We've had time to think it over. We can help you!"

"Not with the crows pecking out your eyes, you can't."

Watts's voice took on an almost pleading tone. "There's no need to do anything stupid like killing a sheriff and an FBI agent. That'll bring down law enforcement on you like a ton of bricks. You know that."

"Not likely. We've got a thousand square miles of mountains

and deserts where we can disappear your remains. Say adios. Maybe our next sheriff will be halfway decent—not a snot-nosed poseur who likes to show off his six-guns."

"Bring it on," said Watts, feigned bravado growing genuine at this insult. "We'll shoot your ass to pieces."

"Sure you will."

Morwood heard the rush of feet, and he instantly racked a round into the chamber.

"This is *it*!" Watts muttered urgently.

The two leapt up and began shooting. The six remaining men, who had just started to rush them, were completely stunned by the sudden outpouring of fire. They broke and scattered, heading for cover. Every last shot of Watts's found a mark, including Fountain: Morwood saw the lawyer spin away under the bullet's impact, a gout of crimson blossoming before he collapsed into the darkness and out of sight. Firing with his left hand, Morwood was more noisy than he was dangerous, but Watts's shooting made up for it.

And then, just like that, it was over. Watts was back down, crouching next to Morwood.

"We got five, but did you see that guy—Bellingame, or whatever his name is—escape?"

"I did. Christ, that was some shooting." He popped out his magazine, examined it, slapped it back in. "I'm out."

"I've got one round left—for Bellingame. Let's go get him."

Morwood peered over the wall. The headlights from the two trucks still illuminated most of the town, casting long shadows. There were many areas of darkness in which a man could hide.

Morwood shook his head. "It's going to be hell smoking him out without calling in the cavalry."

"The bastards shot up our car," said Watts. "So we'll have to take one of theirs. And I'll bet that's exactly what Bellingame's anticipating. He can't let us go. The shootout ain't over yet."

And he holstered his empty Colt, then patted the other affectionately.

57

A SOLDIER MOVED TO the old juniper door and gave it a push. With a crackle of dry rot it swayed inward, splintered off its hinges, and fell to the ground with a dull clatter.

"Wait," said the general.

The soldiers paused while the general pushed past them, his flashlight beam probing the cloud of dust disturbed by their entrance. As he stepped over the fallen gate, his light played about the room. Nora saw, between pale sheets of falling dust, dazzling flashes of gold and gemstones as the beam roved back and forth, revealing what lay within. There were audible gasps. The general stepped inside, Woodbridge following. Everyone else remained still.

Nora watched the general move deeper into the treasure chamber. His face glowed golden from the light reflected off the glittering heaps. It was a fantastical sight: golden chalices, crosses, monstrances, vestments spun through with threads of precious metal, miters, reliquaries encrusted with gems—all hastily stacked together, without any organization. And surrounding it all sat rotten boxes and burst leather sacks, spilling gold doubloons and palm-size gold and silver bars.

The general finally looked back at the group, slowly, as if emerging from a dream. "What are you doing, standing around?" he barked. "We've got work to do!"

The soldiers snapped to attention and moved in, pushing Nora and the two others in with them.

"Put them in the rear with a guard," the general said. "Well away from the exit. We need to move all this—*now*!"

A soldier ushered the three past the heap of treasure to the back of the chamber, then stood guard before them. Nora took in the almost incredible quantity of riches around them with a strange dispassion. But she would never have the chance to study any of it.

The general and Woodbridge wasted no time organizing the soldiers. Three of them left briefly, then returned with a rack of batteries and a bank of bright lights, along with canvas stretchers to carry out the treasure. They also brought in a small wooden box with lettering stenciled on the side in military fashion. Nora could see this was a well-planned, well-rehearsed operation. They were going to empty the chamber right then and there.

It was also clear to Nora that she, Skip, and Corrie were very soon going to be killed and their bodies left there. Something was tugging at the back of her mind, like a voice whispering over and over. She had faced death before, but never like this—cold-blooded, with no chance to fight for her own life. She looked at the stenciled box. It probably contained explosives. They would be shot sooner or later—probably sooner; the mine would be emptied; and then all traces of it, and them, would be dynamited into oblivion, never to be seen again.

There was no hope of escape, no hope of rescue. She glanced at Corrie, whose eyes remained strangely empty. Skip's head was bowed.

The bank of lights was quickly erected and hooked up. The glittering heap of gold and silver was set ablaze in sudden light, and for a moment everyone seemed stunned all over again. Nora took advantage of the light to glance around the chamber. It was much bigger than necessary to hold the treasure. It was so large, in fact, that from where they stood—near the back of the cavern—the bright light faded off behind them into shadow and darkness.

There it was again—that odd tugging sensation at the back of her mind.

And then, quite suddenly, Nora recalled the text of the Spanish letter.

> We concealed the south entrance to the mine and made the mark of the cross on a stone five paces to the right... We concealed the northern entrance to the mine with no mark.

The northern entrance to the mine. She glanced again at Corrie, then Skip, and then their guard. The guard wasn't paying any attention to them at all; his gaze was riveted by the heaps of gold suddenly afire in the lights. The general was shouting orders to start loading the stretchers.

Nora edged up to Corrie. "Remember the letter?" she whispered. "'*The northern entrance to the mine.*'"

Corrie looked at her blankly for a moment. Then, understanding blossomed in her face. She, too, glanced at their guard, but he remained mesmerized by the frenzied activity of loading the treasure. He wasn't considering the possibility of another exit behind him.

Nobody had considered it.

Nora nudged Skip, then started slowly edging backward, into the shadows. The other two followed suit.

"Go!" whispered Nora.

They turned and slipped into the darkness, moving as silently as possible, and then running. Once it became too dark to see, Skip pulled out his lighter and briefly flicked it on. In the wavering light, Nora could now make out the rear of the chamber: a blank wall of stone. She felt a sudden despair. But no; about eight feet up was a single small opening. They rushed toward it and, noiselessly, Nora helped Corrie up first, then Skip. They grasped her hands and pulled her up behind them. Skip flicked the lighter on again, and they ran at a crouch down a low stone passageway. There were no branching tunnels. In a few minutes they saw, looming up before them, a sloping heap of rocks—the tunnel ahead was blocked.

And now shouts echoed down the passageway, the voices distorted. These were followed by shots. Their escape had been discovered.

"Move these rocks!" Nora cried.

They scrambled to the top of the pile and began shifting rocks, pulling them from the top and sending them rolling down. Behind them, there was more shouting, growing closer now.

Suddenly, Nora felt a rush of cool air, and a patch of stars appeared above the rock pile. Pulling out several more rocks created an opening large enough for them to wriggle through. Nora went first, then helped pull Corrie and Skip out onto a steep hillside.

Gunfire erupted again, and Nora could hear rounds smacking and ricocheting off the rocks.

"We have to block it!" she said.

As she picked up a nearby rock, intent on jamming it into the hole, Nora noticed a much larger boulder, perched on the hillside half a dozen feet above the hole. Corrie saw it at the same time. "Let's use that!" she cried, climbing up and positioning herself, feet first, to push. Nora and Skip grappled with it, trying desperately to keep it from moving in the wrong direction, and at last the boulder shifted, then rolled, thudding to rest in the hole and filling it like a countersunk screw.

They could hear more gunfire and shouting filtering up through the stone.

"Let's go!" Nora cried, and the others followed her down the hill. There was no moon, but the starlight was so bright in the high desert air they could see just enough to navigate. At the bottom of the hill they paused.

"Where now?" Corrie asked.

"Into the mountains," said Skip. "They've got soldiers. They're going to be sending up drones. Out in the desert, exposed, we'll be dead meat."

He led the way from the base of the hill, across a hollow, to the opening of a ravine that headed into the mountains, now and then using his lighter to help illuminate their way. As they moved into the ravine, Nora glanced back and could see several lights dancing along the base of the treasure hill.

"They're coming after us," Nora said.

"Of course," said Skip. "All that gold is useless to them if we survive to talk about it."

"We'd better lose the tail, do something unforeseen," Corrie said, looking around. "Like . . . climb up this cliff."

"Are you kidding?" Skip said. "I can't even see the top."

Nora looked up. The cliff was black as night, no detail at all. They'd have to feel their way up it. It seemed crazy—but they were short of options.

"I'll go first," Nora said, and before she could think better of it she laid a hand on the rough rock, found a handhold, then a second, secured a foothold, and pulled herself up. "Skip, you follow me. Do what I do."

"I'm not going up that," said Skip. "No way. Not doing it."

She pulled herself up another step, and another. "Corrie will help you."

"Get going," said Corrie in an unfriendly tone.

"Jesus, just give me a moment."

Nora glanced over her shoulder. Corrie was bending down, murmuring and helping Skip place his hands on handholds, then one foot, then another. He hoisted himself up with a grunt.

"Go slow," warned Nora.

She turned and continued climbing, waiting between each move for Skip to catch up. It was a horrible sensation: clinging to a sheer wall of darkness, feeling around for each handhold, unable to see how high the cliff was—or where this nightmare would end.

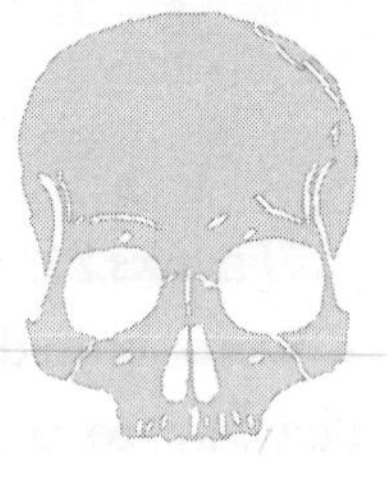

58

Watts took a deep breath, as if consciously enjoying the sensation of inhaling sweet, fresh air. Morwood realized that was exactly what he was doing—in case it was destined to be his last. Then he vaulted out from their place of cover and sprinted to the next building, scooping up one of the dead men's firearms as he went. Morwood followed a moment later, grabbing a weapon as well. No shots were fired, and they peered out. The old main street was deserted, with no sign of Bellingame. The two pickup trucks were still in position, headlights pointing at right angles.

"We've got to cover those trucks," said Morwood. "And I'm sure he's doing the same."

Watts checked the gun, a Beretta 9mm. He ejected the magazine, then swore. "One round in the mag, one in the chamber." He reinserted it.

Morwood tossed away his empty Glock and examined the gun he'd grabbed, a Ruger .357 Mag. He opened the cylinder. "Four rounds. We've got to move closer, cover both vehicles. You move first, I'll cover."

"Thanks."

Watts bolted from behind the building and ran across the alleyway to a stone wall. A shot rang out; Morwood saw the flash and fired back at it. Watts gave him a thumbs-up and positioned himself to cover Morwood as he made his move.

Morwood decided he'd better go in a different direction. He crouched, moved to the other side of cover, then broke, running across the main street. This time a pair of shots rang out, but he managed to dive down behind the corner of a ruin without further injury.

Recovering his breath, he crouched, peering around the edge, trying to forget his throbbing hand. He now knew approximately where Bellingame was. Despite his gun hand being out of commission, it was still two against one, and Bellingame's odds were not good.

"We're closing in," Watts called out. "There's two of us, with fresh guns and ammo. You can surrender, or we can kill you. Your choice."

The silence stretched out for a long moment. Then Bellingame called out: "Or I kill the both of you."

"Tell that to your dead pals. All six of them. Or was it seven? I've lost count."

A bitter laugh. "Then come get me, asshole."

"I'll bet you fancy yourself quite a shot," called Watts.

No answer.

"Not a good shot, then?"

Morwood wondered what Watts's game was, goading Bellingame like this.

"Better than you," came the response.

"Well, then, I've got a proposition," said Watts in a boastful tone. "Let's settle this Old West style. You and me, right here in the street. We draw and see who's the faster."

"And have your partner shoot me down? No, thanks."

"He's a man of honor. If he gives you his word, you can trust him. Anyway, his gun hand got shot to pieces."

Morwood could hardly believe what he was hearing. Had Watts gone crazy? He opened his mouth to protest, but then Bellingame's voice rang out.

"A right old-time shootout. And what if I win?"

"Then I'm dead and you can help yourself to a vehicle and take off. But you ain't going to win, because I can tell you're one of those cowboys who's all hat and no cattle."

"You're a big talker there, mister."

"It's your only option. Unless you want to just give up. No doubt the government would be happy to offer lifetime accommodations."

This was insane. What was Watts thinking? But Morwood decided to keep holding his tongue.

"All right," said Bellingame. "If your pal gives his word of honor. We both holster our guns and come out into the street. I give the count and we draw."

"Agent Morwood," Watts called out. "You okay with this? Word of honor?"

Morwood didn't answer right away. It was crazy, it was stupid, and yet the alternative was more shooting—and God only knew how that would end up. Watts had something up his sleeve... and rather than mess it up, it seemed better to let it play out.

"I give my word," he called out.

"Okay, Bellingame! Let's do it."

Morwood moved around the corner to where he had a good

view of the street. He saw Bellingame emerge from behind a wall, 1911 in its belt holster and the duster flapping behind him in the wind. And now here came Watts, from the other end of town, moving out into the street, in his cowboy hat and two six-guns strapped crosswise around his hips, grips facing inward above the tooled Slim Jim holsters. Christ, it was like a time machine. But they were fifty yards apart, and that was a hell of a distance with a revolver, even with time to aim through sights. But here they were, shooting from the hip—and Watts with only one round left.

"Ready to fill your hand?" Watts yelled.

Bellingame nodded. "On three. One. Two. *Three!*"

Bellingame drew and—in the same moment—Watts skipped away unexpectedly, pivoting to one side with the athleticism of a ballet dancer. The shot missed.

"What the fuck—!" Bellingame went to fire again, but in the moment of delay Watts drew and fired with astonishing speed, fanning the Peacemaker's hammer with his palm, and Bellingame's curse was cut short by a bullet in the mouth. He bit down with a gargled cry, toppled backward, and lay still.

After a moment of shock, Morwood stepped out from behind the wall and walked over, staring down at Bellingame. The man's eyes were wide open in surprise, blood spreading across the dirt below.

"Damn," said Watts, holstering the Peacemaker. "Bad shot."

"Bad shot?" Morwood cried. He'd never seen anything like that in his life.

"An inch too low. I was hoping for the bridge of his nose."

"You've been practicing that maneuver?"

"Most of my life."

"And back there, when you drew on those two simultaneously? That too?"

"Ever since I was five," said Watts, "I've wanted to be the fastest gun in the West. I practiced all the old moves, even though I knew they were just a part of history." He paused. "Nice in a way—getting to use them for real, I mean."

And, as they started off in the direction of the trucks, Morwood saw the sheriff smile to himself.

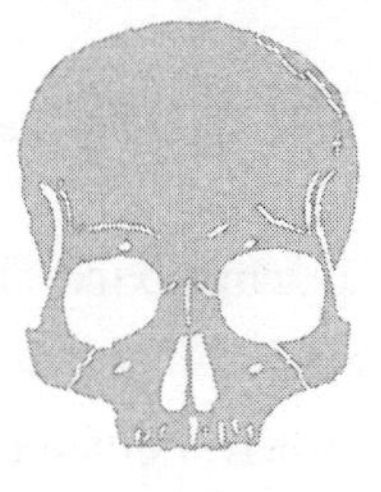

59

Nora soon got into the rhythm of climbing, making one move at a time and then waiting. The cliff gradually got less sheer until at last she was able to scramble over the rim. Skip followed, crawling, and rolled on his back. "Son of a bitch," he said, gasping.

"Where are we going?" Corrie asked. "We can't just run away aimlessly."

"The closest inhabited town has got to be San Antonio," Nora said. "Forty miles, at least."

"We can talk while we move," said Skip, rising to his feet.

They set off, running along the ridgeline. It curved to the north, carrying them deeper into the mountains, which loomed up like black sawblades above them.

"Pretty soon the general's going to unleash all sorts of shit on us," said Corrie. "We can't hide for long, even in the mountains. We've got to have a plan."

"Agreed," said Skip. "But *what*?"

Nobody answered. There was no plan, except to keep

moving, Nora thought. Forty miles to San Antonio? That was absurd: they'd have to cross the Jornada del Muerto desert on foot to get there, one of the worst deserts in the country. They wouldn't survive that without water, even if not being chased by drones. But where else could they go?

They continued along the ridge, as fast as they dared given the darkness. Within a quarter of an hour, Nora—glancing back—noticed lights begin to appear.

"See that?" she said.

"Let's drop down into the next valley," Skip said. He headed down a sloping hillside and the two women followed, trying to maintain their footing in the darkness and loose scree. They reached the bottom of the draw, a sandy wash lined with prickly scrub. Skip turned and headed downstream.

"We're not that far from the old Gower Ranch house," said Nora.

"Could we take refuge there?" Corrie asked, but then answered her own question. "No—too obvious."

Nora glanced back again. The lights were maybe a half mile away.

"We're not going to outrun them," Corrie said.

"We keep moving," said Skip. "And lose them. If we don't, we're dead."

The narrow valley broadened into a small plain dotted with hills and piles of rock. The lights appeared behind them once again. Suddenly, Nora heard a *zing!* followed by the report of a rifle. They threw themselves down in the grass as more rounds snapped and whined around them.

"The bastards must have night vision scopes," said Corrie. She ran at a crouch, and Nora and Skip followed. Another volley of rounds struck around them, but the distance was too great for an accurate shot. In a moment they had taken cover behind a hill, gasping for breath.

Nora looked up. With no light pollution and no moon, the sky was bedazzled with stars. From their vantage point she could see out over the Jornada del Muerto, a vast pool of blackness... with just one tiny cluster of lights off to one side, at the base of a mass of mountains.

"Hey—you see that? Those lights?" Nora asked, pointing.

"It looks like some sort of outpost," said Skip.

"Outpost?" Nora repeated. "Way out here at the end of the Sierra Oscura? That has to be Abajo Peak. Even for a place like WSMR, that's the middle of nowhere."

Corrie stared. "Wait. What did you say?"

Nora frowned in confusion. "Huh?"

"Go over that geography again. Quickly."

"Sierra Oscura. Abajo Peak—"

"That's it. You remember I told you about that navy guy I met in a bar?"

"Yes," said Nora.

"He said he worked at a small communications station inside White Sands, west of Abajo Peak."

Nora squinted into the dark mass of mountains. "If so, that must be it."

"A *navy* station?" Skip asked dubiously. "Here, in the desert?"

"They use it to communicate with nuclear subs. What did he call it? ELF station, or extremely low frequency. The radio waves go all the way through the Earth to subs even on the other side."

"Wow," said Skip. "You learn something every day."

"Okay. That's where we'll go." And Corrie gathered herself to run.

"And what will that get us?" Nora asked. "We'll just be turning ourselves in."

"They're navy," said Corrie. "On army land. The two don't get along. If we can make it there, perhaps we can blow the whistle on the general."

Nora shook her head. "Fat chance. You think the navy would believe us—over the commanding general of the whole damn place?"

"You got a better idea?"

Skip interrupted. "Look. It's not like we have a choice. We go there, try to explain what's going on. Take our chances. It's better than having a drone turn us into wet spots on the desert floor."

"Agreed," said Corrie.

Nora shrugged. It was, she admitted, better than getting hunted down—*if* they could reach that little cluster of lights.

"This way," Corrie said. She led them at a run toward a series of ravines coming down from the mountains. They entered a boulder field, a complicated braid of alluvial deposits and channels, which made for slow going but at least provided better cover. Looking back, Nora could no longer see the lights.

Corrie and Skip continued leading the way, trending northward by a circuitous route. And then Skip stopped. "Listen," he whispered.

A faint hum could be heard to the south, sounding like a distant lawn mower—or, perhaps, several.

"Drones," said Skip.

The three cast around, but there was no place to take refuge—just brush and large boulders. The sounds got louder.

"Low flying," said Skip. "They're going to see us."

And then several black outlines appeared out of the south,

moving slowly across the night sky: no lights, visible only by their blotting out of the stars. Just the sight turned Nora's mouth dry.

"Flatten against a rock!" Skip urged.

They did so. The drones passed low overhead. At first they appeared to keep flying on, but then the sounds of their engines changed as they began to loop around.

"They spotted us," said Skip. "Move!"

They stumbled through the boulder field, weaving this way and that as the drones homed in. There was a flash, followed by a deep whooshing sound.

"Down!" Skip cried.

Nora threw herself down next to a large boulder, cramming herself against its underside. There was a bright flash, then an ear-popping roar of overpressure. Shrapnel zinged and snapped among the boulders.

"Keep moving!" Skip screamed. They leapt up and ran, stumbling and half-blind, through the dark boulder field as the remaining drones again disappeared beyond the hills. But from the sound, Nora could tell they were turning for another pass.

They came around a hill, and the Gower Ranch house abruptly came into view, spread across a dark basin below them.

"Shit," said Corrie. "We're sitting ducks."

"The hot spring!" Skip cried a moment later. He turned to Nora. "You said there was one on the hillside above the ranch."

Nora turned toward the tall cottonwoods where the general had mentioned the spring was. The drones were now approaching again, moving low and slow. She was about to protest, but Skip and Corrie were already scrambling along the hillside, heading for the trees. They entered the grove and there—

coming out of the rock—was a steaming rivulet of water, rimmed and crusted with travertine. It flowed into a man-made pool, crudely constructed of rocks, with more tendrils of steam hanging above it.

"In!" said Skip.

"What—?" Nora began, but Skip grabbed her hand with a curse, pulling her into the hot water.

"Lie down," he said.

The steamy water enclosed Nora in a sweltering embrace, only her head above the surface. The drones passed overhead with a nasty buzzing sound and continued on.

"Wait," Skip warned in a low tone.

The drones made another pass, this time farther apart. Then they flew past yet again, widening their search pattern.

"Their thermal cameras can't make us out," said Skip. "Not in all this heat."

The drones flew on, their search pattern drifting west, and soon the sound of their engines had vanished.

"They've lost us," Skip said. "Let's go while we still have time."

Emerging from the hot springs, steaming in the cool fall air, they jogged northward, keeping within the complicated maze of foothills and dry washes. They had made an abrupt turn to reach the springs, and it appeared the pursuing soldiers had lost them, too.

They topped the next ridge and scrambled down the other side, Nora scraping her hands badly in the process.

Reaching the bottom, they sprinted across a ravine, which soon turned into a warren of steep canyons choked with boulders and tributaries. Corrie was now leading, and at every turn she picked the most difficult way, but always trending in the direction of the north star. It was a nightmare trek, moving in the dark among boulders and fallen trees, brush and landslides—one of the nastiest landscapes Nora had ever been in, at times almost impassable. But what was hard for them would be hard for their pursuers, and she couldn't imagine better country in which to lose a tracker.

An hour later, scratched, exhausted, and bleeding, Corrie finally stopped. Nora was nauseous, physically shattered. Pure adrenaline was the only thing that had been keeping them going.

"I think we've lost them," said Skip. "Really lost them this time."

"Let's not count on it," said Corrie.

"We should be east of the navy station," said Nora. "I think we should turn west, head down and out of the mountains, and make a beeline for it, hoping to get there before we're cut off." She was aware that neither she nor the others had the energy for further evasive tactics in that rough country.

"They may already know we're headed there," said Corrie.

Skip shook his head. "We've got no choice. Literally."

Two minutes later, after the briefest of rests, they turned and headed down a narrow ravine choked with junipers. After another half hour of pushing through the brush, the endless ribbons of washes and ravines opened into grassy foothills—and there, half a mile away on the flat, was the cluster of lights of the navy station.

"Looks quiet," said Skip.

Venturing out onto the plain, they had to come out of cover. The desert was flat and featureless, dotted with creosote bushes, sparse clumps of grass, and low, sprawling prickly pears.

"I can hardly move," groaned Corrie.

"You've got to," Skip told her.

They started off at a run, which soon deteriorated into a shambling jog. Nora's lungs were burning, and the feeling of nausea returned.

And then, overhead, the sound of the lawn mowers returned.

"Keep going!" Skip urged. "They're not going to fire close to a navy station!"

Nora was so exhausted and frightened that she could hardly think. The desert was hard-packed gravel and they walked onward, stumbling through the low bushes. The buzzing grew louder, and once again the big black shapes passed overheard, like cruising torpedoes—but none fired a missile.

The birds came back around. The station loomed ahead, a collection of ugly, low concrete structures beside a cluster of communications towers. On one side, spreading out over a vast acreage, were a web of wires on short posts—some sort of gigantic antenna farm.

The drones were now doing tight circles above them, and over the sound of her gasping for air and pounding heart Nora could make out the thud of a helicopter. Rising over the mountains came a chopper, brilliantly lit. And at the base of the mountains, the bobbing lights of the pursuing soldiers appeared, heading their way.

The three reached a fence surrounding the antenna field. They ran alongside it toward the buildings. Behind them, the helicopter was fast approaching a landing zone just beyond the navy station. Nora had no doubt that the general and Lieutenant Woodbridge were in it.

They'd run out of time.

Now they reached the closest building. Light streamed out a small window, and Nora could make out a few figures inside, sitting around a table. They hesitated, uncertain, as the helicopter banked in for a landing.

And then Skip picked up a heavy rock and heaved it through the window with a terrific crash.

"What the hell are you doing?" Corrie cried.

"What the hell do you think? Getting our asses arrested!"

There was no time for any more talk. The door flew open, and several sailors came out, weapons drawn. Skip raised his hands. "Don't shoot. We're unarmed!"

"Down! Face down! Hands behind your heads!"

They threw themselves down in the dirt and were immediately surrounded. An officer in a commander's uniform came running over. "What's this?" he cried. "Who are these people?"

"Intruders, sir."

"Good God, way out here?" He looked down at them. "Who are you?"

Corrie spoke. "Special Agent Corinne Swanson, Federal Bureau of Investigation."

"What? FBI? Show some ID."

"No ID, sir."

"They threw a rock through the window, sir," one of the seamen said.

"Oh, for Christ's sake. More nuclear protestors. You wouldn't think they'd tramp all the way out here." The officer sighed with irritation. "Search them."

They were quickly patted down for weapons and then pulled to their feet.

"You're under arrest," the officer said. "Master-at-Arms, cuff them."

"Aye-aye, sir."

Their hands were pulled behind their backs and cuffs slapped on. Nora saw the helicopter settling down on the landing zone a few hundred yards away, dust billowing upward.

"It's General McGurk, sir," said a sailor, bringing the commanding officer a radio. The CO listened, spoke briefly, handed the radio back.

"Bring them inside," he said. "We'll wait for the general."

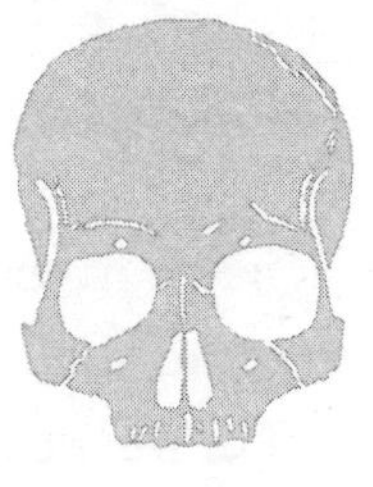

60

THEY WERE MARCHED inside to a small, bunker-like room where the sailors had been playing cards. A few minutes later, Nora could hear the general's barking voice and the door opened again. McGurk stepped in, followed by half a dozen army soldiers. Lieutenant Woodbridge came last, as cool and controlled as ever.

The general turned to the CO. "These are the spies I told you about," he said in a loud voice. "I'll take them now."

"Wait," said Corrie. "The general is engaged in illegal activity. I'm an FBI agent with the Albuquerque FO. Call them for verification. Special Agent Corinne Swanson."

The CO looked at her again with naked disbelief. And no surprise—they were filthy, sticks in their hair, clothes torn and wet, faces bloody from scrapes and cuts.

"Call the FO—" Corrie began again.

"Quiet!" said the navy CO. He turned to the general and said in a cold voice, "Our master-at-arms has placed these intruders under arrest. They are in navy custody."

Only now did Nora realize the genius of what Skip had done in getting them arrested.

"I'm the commanding general here," McGurk said. "I *order* you to turn them over, Commander."

"General, with all due respect, I'm in command of this station, and that decision is mine. Will you please tell me exactly what is going on here?"

The general made a visible effort to control himself. "Commander, we've been pursuing these intruders. They're spies."

"What kind of spies?"

"We don't know yet. Possibly nuclear saboteurs for a foreign government."

"We're not spies!" Corrie said. "The general and these people are in the process of stealing a valuable Spanish treasure from Mockingbird Butte—"

The general stepped forward. "Shut up," he said. "How long are we going to listen to this?"

"Treasure?" the commander asked incredulously.

"That's right!" Corrie cried. "He's been searching for it for years! Our investigation uncovered where it was hidden, and he forced us to take him to it! His soldiers are emptying the treasure chamber right now as we—"

The general smacked her across the mouth. "I told you to shut up." He turned. "Commander, I appeal to your sanity, if nothing else. FBI? Spanish treasure? Do you really need any more evidence to show these are intruders at best, and spies at worst?" He took a deep breath and continued in a more reasoned tone. "And now, Commander, would you be so kind as to turn them over to me? This is an army problem that has taken place on army land, and I think you'll find it difficult to explain why you disobeyed my direct order."

The commander, who had frowned disapprovingly when the general struck Corrie, hesitated. Then he turned to the master-at-arms. "All right. Turn them over."

"No!" cried Skip. He started struggling with the handcuffs behind his back.

"He's got a weapon!" somebody cried.

But even as they spoke, Skip managed to shove one hand into a pocket and pull out of fistful of something. There was a sudden glitter of multicolored brilliance as a half dozen gemstones clinked and bounced and rolled across the floor, along with several gold doubloons.

The silence was electrifying. All eyes had swiveled to the gold and precious stones.

"The treasure," he explained. "I, um, swiped some earlier tonight."

The silence continued a moment longer. Then the commander cleared his throat.

"What is this, General McGurk?" he asked, gesturing toward the now-glistening floor.

The general had gone pale, but when he answered, his voice was even. "I have no idea. Some trick."

The commander gestured to the master-at-arms. "Belay that last order." He removed his cell phone.

"What are you doing?" McGurk asked.

In a calm voice, the commander replied: "I'm calling our emergency FBI liaison number, to check on the existence of a Special Agent Corinne Swanson."

"Of *course* you'll find there is! This woman's obviously an impersonator!"

The CO punched in a number.

"I'll have you court-martialed, Commander!" McGurk

turned to his men. "I order you to take the prisoners into custody!"

But the soldiers hesitated while the commander, with steely coolness, briefly spoke into the phone, listened for a long moment, then thanked the person he was speaking to and returned the phone to his pocket. "There is indeed a Special Agent Corinne Swanson working on a case involving WSMR—and she meets the description of this young woman."

"As I said—an impersonator."

"Perhaps," the commander said quietly. "Or perhaps not. But the fact is, she's in *navy* custody. I have decided not to turn over the prisoners at this time. If you wish to take custody, General, there's a process, as you well know, and it involves paperwork."

The general pulled his sidearm. "*Paperwork*, you son of a bitch? You turn them over or I'll take them from you by force!" He turned to his men. "Soldiers, ready arms!"

The soldiers drew their weapons. In response, one or two of the seamen raised weapons of their own, forming a defensive posture around their CO.

"General," said the commander, "are you aware of what you're doing?"

The general's gun hand began to tremble.

"Men," the CO said, "stow arms."

The sailors lowered their weapons. But the tension in the air remained almost unbearable.

The commander took a deep breath. "We—that is, the navy—are going to verify the identity of these individuals. And then we will decide the next steps—not in an ad hoc manner, but following the established protocol."

The general's hand shook more violently, the barrel trembling.

Lieutenant Woodbridge had drawn her weapon, and it was still pointed at the commander. Now, suddenly, she pivoted, pointing it toward the general. "Sir?" she said. "Lower your weapon."

The general gaped at her, uncomprehending.

Weapon still trained, she spoke to the CO. "Commander, your investigation will find that these people are who they say they are. The Spanish treasure is real, and the general is having it removed right now. We were forced, by orders and threats, to obey him."

The general stared at her. "What? You...traitorous, back-stabbing *bitch*."

"*All* of us were required to do the general's bidding," she continued, and turned to the soldiers. "But it's over now. Lower your weapons, gentlemen."

The soldiers complied.

"General," she said in a voice that to Nora seemed impossibly cool, "you, too."

But instead of obeying, the general backed toward the open door of the hut, trembling weapon still trained on the naval CO. He reached the door, ducked out of it, and disappeared into the night.

"Let him go," said the CO.

A silence. And then the CO said: "Lieutenant Woodbridge, contact WSMR's second in command. Explain the situation, and get your men to halt the looting of that..." He swept a hand across the floor, where the gold and gems continued to gleam. "And get them to call off those damn drones circling overhead."

"Yes, sir."

Nora watched her turn and leave. What had at first seemed

an incredibly stupid move was, she decided, actually incredibly clever: in a moment, the lieutenant had transformed herself from a willing accessory to a loyal army officer.

The CO turned to Corrie. "And you—you're really an FBI agent?"

"What do you mean, *really*?" Corrie said angrily. "You heard Lieutenant Woodbridge! Get these handcuffs off us right now, and let me call my supervisor!"

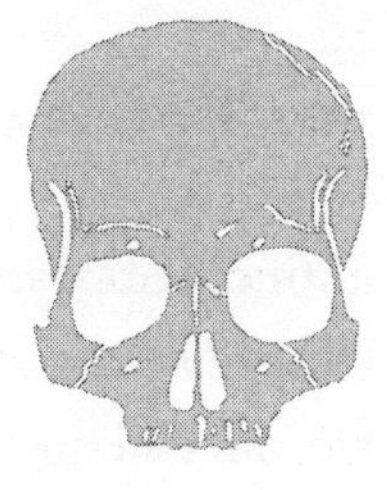

61

THREE DAYS LATER, at ten o'clock in the morning, in the evidence collection room, Special Agent Corrie Swanson had carefully laid out everything the FBI team had recovered at the residence of Charles Fountain. It was quite a haul. Fountain, it turned out, had been running a sophisticated looting operation for more than three years, using a select group of the very same criminals he had defended as an attorney. Fountain was the only member of the group up at High Lonesome to survive the shooting—Watts had wounded him in the arm and, being no gunfighter, he'd lain low until it was all over. He hadn't spoken a word since—not one word—even after lawyering up.

And so it was up to them to figure out what exactly Fountain and his gang had been searching for up at High Lonesome. Even a cursory look over the mass of documents showed that it wasn't the Victorio Peak treasure, as Fountain had confirmed to Watts during the gunfight. No: there was something else, something of great value, hidden up there. But what? The documents recovered from Fountain's walk-in safe were as voluminous as they were confusing.

In preparation for stepping back and letting Corrie take full control of the investigation, Morwood had asked her to assemble all the documentary evidence for a group review. It was a common FBI trick for analyzing large amounts of confusing evidence—lay it all out and get everyone in the same room looking at it.

Corrie was nervous. This was a big deal. She glanced over and saw the coffee was on and fresh, and everything else was in its place. It was 12:55. The group would be arriving in five minutes. She had set it up before lunch.

She adjusted her suit, straightened the lanyard holding her badge—and just then, she heard voices in the hall. Morwood entered, his hand heavily bandaged, followed by Nora Kelly, Sheriff Homer Watts, Milt Alfieri, Don Ketterman, and Nigel Lathrop. And coming in last was someone Corrie rarely saw: Special Agent in Charge Julio Garcia, head honcho of the Albuquerque Field Office.

"This is quite a spread, Corrie," said Morwood, carrying a clipboard with the master evidence list. While he hadn't actually said anything to her yet about discovering the gold and unmasking the general—or, for that matter, the medicine bag's disappearance from FBI custody—her gut told her that she'd pulled off a major coup. "Let's see if we can make some sense out of it, shall we?"

"Yes, sir."

Morwood consulted the list. "Why don't we start with the master plat of High Lonesome itself."

Corrie quickly located it, drawing it out of the mass of evidence and spreading it on a second table. They all gathered around.

"Excellent," Morwood went on. "The aerial photos would be useful as well, for comparison purposes."

Corrie glanced over to where she had laid out the pictures and started searching through them. "Which aerial photos, exactly?" she asked, a sinking feeling in her gut.

"The blow-ups. The ones with the most detail."

Corrie searched, then searched again, while a silence fell. "I don't seem to have them."

Morwood raised an eyebrow but said nothing. "Okay," he resumed a few seconds later, "how about the plat showing the interior of the structure?"

"Yes, sir." Corrie went to where she'd placed it that morning. It, too, was gone.

She swallowed. "It's not here."

Another silence fell. "What do you mean, not here?" Morwood said. "Are you saying that evidence has gone missing?"

Corrie felt her face flaming with chagrin. "It seems so."

"Who's been in here?" Garcia asked sharply. "Who has access?"

"I don't know," Corrie said. "I laid out all this evidence this morning. The plat was here then. But now..." She swallowed.

"It must be a mix-up," said Morwood, trying to cover for her. "Corrie, why don't you look back on the shelves and see if you inadvertently left out a box?"

Corrie knew she hadn't, but she didn't want to disagree. "Yes, sir."

She walked back into the storage area with her copy of the evidence list, but the shelf that contained the Fountain haul was bare. She had taken everything. And there was no other place it could be.

"I'm sorry," she said as she returned, "there's no evidence there. This is all of it."

"How can this be all of it," asked Garcia, his voice climbing, "when key pieces are missing?"

Corrie stared at him, flushing in confusion. "I don't know, sir."

"You don't *know*?" Garcia said, staring at her.

Corrie felt like dying. All her hard work, all the danger she'd endured, the plot she'd uncovered, the treasure...

Somewhere behind her, she heard the faint sound of a door opening, and then a honeyed voice spoke in disdain. "May I inquire when this coffee was made?"

She turned, as if in a dream... and there was the tall figure she knew so well, in the severe but flawlessly tailored black suit, with the silvery eyes and pale chiseled face.

"Who the devil are you?" Garcia demanded.

"Special Agent Pendergast." He glided over and extended his hand. "So good to meet you."

Garcia stood as if thunderstruck. "Pendergast?" he repeated, shaking the hand robotically. "*The* Agent Pendergast?"

"I believe so, yes." He turned to the rest of the group. "Ah—hello, Nora. Corrie."

"This... this is unexpected..." Garcia stammered. "What, ah, brings you to Albuquerque, Agent Pendergast?"

"I've taken a small interest in the case that my protégée, Agent Swanson, has been working on. Forgive me for borrowing some of your evidence. I was delighted by how much she's accomplished and, ah, intrigued by what few gaps still remain."

"Your protégée?" Garcia said.

"Well, I suppose that, technically, she's Agent Morwood's protégée now. Nevertheless, I have a few thoughts. Would you care to hear them?"

"Well, yes. Of course."

"I borrowed this little empty room over here, if you'd care to follow me?"

Still stunned, Corrie followed the rest as Pendergast, moving smoothly as a cat, led them to what almost looked like a disused broom closet. A table filled the entire space—and there, on the table, lay the missing evidence.

"I've brought myself up to speed," Pendergast said with a cool smile. "So we can skip the background. I believe we all agree Fountain and his group were not after the Victorio Peak treasure. But whatever they were searching for, it had to be of great value—so valuable it was worth killing a peace officer, as you learned, Sheriff Watts, when you surprised Mr. Rivers digging in the basement of this building here."

He tapped an old plat of the site with a spidery finger.

"It has been mooted that this structure was a house of prostitution. However, it was not. It was merely a boardinghouse with a downstairs saloon. You can see the names of various people written here and there on this plat—in Fountain's handwriting. He wanted to know who was living in each room. Based on the evidence, it seems his interest focused on one individual in particular: a certain Houston Smith."

He slid the plat toward the group. "Here is his name, in this little room here."

They all peered at the name scribbled on the plat.

Pendergast straightened. "And who was Houston Smith? Not surprisingly, a miner. As you will see from this mining company employment list, here, many of these miners came from the Fourth Cavalry, headquartered near Socorro. That was the cavalry troop that pursued and captured Geronimo, the Apache war chief. After his capture, the members of the Fourth Cavalry were discharged. Several went to work at High Lonesome, because gold had just been discovered there and mining was ramping up fast."

Corrie listened, wondering where this was going. She

remembered Fountain saying much the same thing when Watts first showed her the ghost town.

Pendergast pulled another document forward. "Here are Smith's discharge papers. He was once a lieutenant in the Fourth Cav and right-hand man to Captain Henry Ware Lawton, commanding officer of the Fourth. Lieutenant Smith played a decisive role in the capture of Geronimo—or I should say 'voluntary surrender,' since Geronimo was never captured. He was deceived into surrendering."

Now Pendergast slid out a photo. "And this is the famous picture taken of Geronimo and his band of warriors as they came in to 'surrender.' Note how heavily armed they were. They had long ago laid aside bows and arrows for the latest and deadliest rifles."

His spidery hand fetched another document. "Here is Smith's death certificate. You will note he was one of those unfortunates trapped in the cave-in. His body was never recovered. And *here*," Pendergast continued, "is a document that dates back almost a decade from the present day. It's an auction record. Captain Lawton's Winchester Model 1886 rifle sold at auction for 1.2 million dollars—the highest price ever paid for a gun up to that time. Curious it should be among Fountain's papers. Or, perhaps, not so curious."

Pendergast cast his eyes over the group. "All very suggestive, don't you think? It now seems quite clear what Fountain and his gang were looking for."

Corrie said nothing. It wasn't clear to her at all. None of this confusing welter of evidence seemed to connect.

A smile creased Pendergast's face at the silence that greeted his pronouncement.

"Agent Pendergast," said Morwood, "perhaps you might go

into a little more detail on the connection you see among these facts you've recited?"

Pendergast's eyebrows shot up in mock surprise. "*More* explanation?"

"For those of us lacking your remarkable perspicacity," Morwood said drily.

Corrie could see Pendergast was thoroughly enjoying himself. "Very well. What is the first thing that happens to an armed man when he surrenders to an enemy?"

"He's disarmed," Corrie blurted out. She was suddenly beginning to see how the pieces fit together. "So Lawton took away Geronimo's rifle... and then, perhaps, gave it to Smith as a reward. You said Lieutenant Smith played an important role in the capture. When he was discharged, Smith would have taken the rifle to High Lonesome. He wouldn't have entrusted it to anyone else. But then, he was killed in the cave-in."

"And he wouldn't have taken the rifle into the mine with him," Nora said.

Corrie nodded. "Which means the rifle could still be there—somewhere—at High Lonesome."

"Brava, Agent Swanson!" Pendergast cried, putting his hands together. "And if Lawton's rifle was worth 1.2 million dollars, what do you think Geronimo's rifle would be worth?" He tapped the plat of the old boardinghouse where Smith had lived. "He would have kept that prize close. So it's in those ruins somewhere. Perhaps we should go take a look?" He paused. "And shall we bring Charles Fountain, Esq., with us? I feel confident the discovery of that rifle would be just the psychological impetus needed to get him talking."

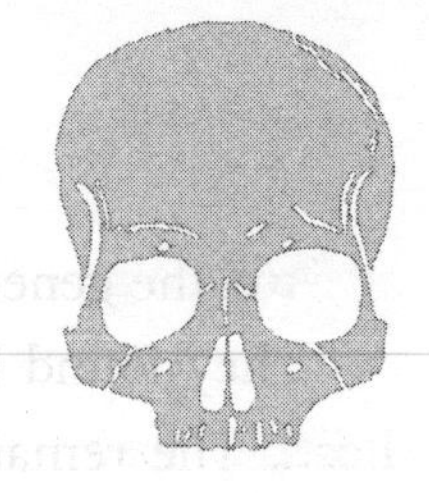

62

NORA KELLY HAD no interest in participating in the search, nor was she asked to. Pendergast was obviously not going to dirty his impeccable suit, either. As a result, the two of them stood side by side, watching the FBI Evidence Response Team, directed by Corrie and Morwood, searching the old ruined boardinghouse—the same building from which she had excavated the body of James Gower. Some team members had metal detectors and were sweeping the grounds and interior. It was a fall day of stunning perfection, the air crisp and cool, the old ghost town flooded with golden sun. Between them—at Pendergast's request—stood Charles Fountain, arm bandaged, shackled and silent.

"Tell me, Nora," Pendergast said, "what happened after the general fled into the desert? I still haven't heard the details."

"The navy delivered us to the FBI, where we were debriefed. And then let go—thank God."

"I understand your brother's covetousness turned out, ironically, to be a stroke of genius."

Nora smiled. "Serendipity, more like."

"And the general?"

"They found his body a day later. He'd shot himself in the head. The remaining soldiers were caught trying to drive the two trucks full of treasure out of the range. It was all recovered. We'll be studying it—and its historical importance—for years to come."

Pendergast shook his head. *"Every man now worships gold, all other reverence being done away.* So said an Augustan poet about the Roman Empire. The same could be said today." He turned to Fountain. "Wouldn't you agree?"

The lawyer did not reply.

"It was a very clever setup," Pendergast continued. "You and a cadre of like-minded men—well-to-do, pillars of the community—had the resources and knowledge to research the most likely spots where valuable artifacts might be found in ruins and historic sites. The background work would be scrupulously done. And then, you'd make a surgical strike—at night, with heavy vehicles or even a helicopter—plunder the site, and leave. Usually, you'd be careful to leave the site looking untouched... untouched but strangely empty. When that wasn't possible, you caused a lot of damage, to disguise the clever theft as an act of mindless vandalism. And then, you'd sell what you recovered on the black market to a circle of oligarchs, sheikhs, and billionaires with a passion for collecting certain things."

"For an FBI agent, you have a very active imagination," Fountain said.

"Except that, as time went on, the sites that could be found by research alone began to thin out. And that's when you'd stoop to a little slumming—paying for tips that couldn't be traced back to you. Even, at times, buying items of dubious value... from people like Jesse Gower."

"Just try to pin his death on me," Fountain said.

"Why would I, when you had nothing to do with it? That was the general's doing—he'd hacked into Agent Swanson's phone using advanced, classified army methods, and he thought young Gower had the last piece of the puzzle. His men got a little overzealous in their interrogation. Ironic, really, because a gang like yours would be the obvious suspects. But you'd allied yourself with Pick Rivers. I imagine you used him, at one remove, for making initial sorties into new projects of yours. Projects you felt insulated from; that gave you deniability. No wonder Rivers seemed to have come into a bit of money recently. Except Sheriff Watts caught him—and Rivers panicked and drew his gun. Rivers didn't confess, of course—he knew that was more than his life was worth—but your associate who called himself Bellingame didn't want to take the risk of letting him live. More proof of the value of the artifact hidden here."

Fountain smiled thinly but did not reply.

"Do you really think they'll find the rifle?" Nora said. "If it *is* a rifle. Maybe someone took it long ago."

"Why, Nora, the doubt in your voice wounds me. I have no doubt it is Geronimo's rifle."

"If it really is, who would it belong to?"

"An interesting question. After its use as evidence in criminal prosecution, I would think it should be turned over to one of Geronimo's descendants, if any should exist. It would be quite a windfall, I would imagine."

Nora couldn't help but smile. "I know at least one exists."

He nodded toward the searchers. "But whether *they* can find it is another matter. No doubt it's well hidden." He paused to examine the progress of the evidence team. "As it happens, I believe they're getting rather warm."

Nora looked at him curiously. "Are you saying you know where it is?"

"I have a guess."

"But you've never even been here before!"

"And what, pray, does that have to do with it?"

Nora was silent a moment. "Okay, I'll bite. Where?"

"The first question to ask, Nora, is: Where is it *not*? It would not be in Smith's room—he was gone all day in the mines, and in his room it would be insecure. Nor would it be hidden in the saloon: that area was too busy. The same for the kitchen. It would not be hidden elsewhere in the town—too risky—or in the surrounding hills, because people would see him going up there and wonder what he was doing. And left outside, it would be exposed to the elements. That leaves only one place: the basement."

"But the basement was thoroughly searched! First by me and then by Huckey and those other two FBI guys."

"Yes. Poor Huckey." He looked at Fountain again. "I suppose dropping him down the well was your work. After all, you couldn't have somebody—especially someone trained in uncovering evidence—wandering around the ghost town and possibly finding your precious rifle."

When Fountain still said nothing, Pendergast looked back at Nora. "In any case, knowing the basement had already been carefully searched was a great help to me. It sharply narrowed down the possible hiding places."

"But where, then?" Nora asked impatiently.

"The basement walls are made of adobe—dried mud—and very thick. Hiding something in them would be quite a simple matter, actually. You hollow out a space in the wall big enough to fit a rifle, put it in, and then mud it back up. A little touching up would disguise the cavity and make it look like the rest of the mud walls. But nineteenth-century mud cannot resist twenty-first-century metal detectors."

Just then, a shout came from the site, and Nora could see everyone rushing into the basement. Through the door she could see one of the team was kneeling at the far wall, above where Gower's body had been found. They began scraping at the mud and soon had broken through to a cavity. Now they were taking pictures and then—finally—a long rifle was removed from its hiding place as all the agents broke into applause.

Nora looked at Pendergast. "I don't know how you do it."

"I simply extrapolate the facts farther than most. That's all. It's like chess: a good player may think three plies ahead. A better player will think five." He turned to Fountain, who was staring at the scene with astonishment and fury. "Well, Mr. Fountain, since your silence has done you no good—as you can see, we found what you've been searching for—you might consider if talking to us will serve you better."

Fountain stared at Pendergast. "You're the very devil."

"Coming from you, sir, I'll take that as a compliment." And Pendergast gave the lawyer a small, formal bow.

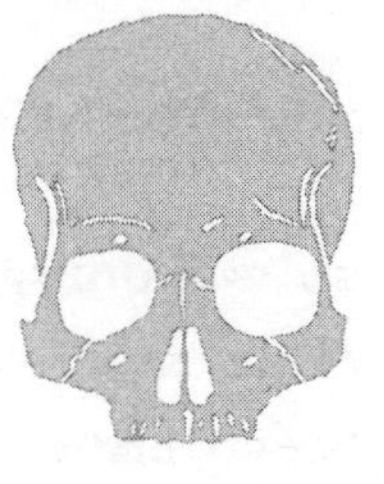

63

PENDERGAST, HAVING DESCENDED deus ex machina on the scene as was his wont, had performed his minor miracle and returned to New York City. Corrie was back in Albuquerque, and Nora had just received a call from the president's office. Dr. Weingrau, she was told, would like to see her as soon as it was convenient. It was convenient immediately: Nora jumped to her feet and—still holding the envelope she'd been about to open—went out from behind her desk and into the hall at a brisk walk.

The office of Dr. Marcelle Weingrau looked much as it had before, with the addition of a Salvador Dalí print on one wall. Nora took a seat in one of the leather chairs. She knew what this meeting was about, of course, and her heart was beating like crazy. She kept telling herself there was no reason to be nervous; in fact, there was if anything less reason, with all the accolades she'd received for her part in assisting the FBI in bringing the case to a close.

"Nora, so glad you could come," Weingrau said, in a warm

and welcoming voice. "Have you recovered from all the recent excitement?"

"Yes," Nora said. "It's embarrassing to recall how I asked you for two extra days to excavate that body at High Lonesome, and it ended up being weeks—"

Weingrau waved this away with her hand. "It ended up being nothing short of heroic. That was remarkable help you gave the FBI... and the publicity was invaluable for the Institute."

"Thank you."

Weingrau folded her hands on her desk. "I asked you here to speak to you about something else."

Nora braced herself. This was it. This was about her promotion.

"As you know, Dr. Winters is retiring, and the position of chief of archaeology will be opening up."

Nora nodded.

"Although I suppose I'm personally an exception to the rule, no doubt you're aware that the Institute has a tradition of promoting from within. We don't normally like to reach out beyond our family, so to speak, to fill positions, especially when we have the talent right here."

"I think it's a good policy."

"Yes. Now, I've been in close consultation with the vice president and our board. The decision to fill this position is not mine alone, particularly since I've only been here for two months. A great deal of thought and discussion has gone on behind the scenes."

Nora nodded again. She managed to contain her excitement. *Chief of archaeology*. It was a big deal, with a substantial increase in salary—but most important, it was tangible recognition of her hard work, years of service, and respected scholarship.

"We have made our decision." At this Weingrau paused, and her face took on a serious expression. "I asked you here because I wanted to tell you the news in person."

Nora nodded. Of course she did.

"I know this is going to be disappointing to you."

At first Nora thought she hadn't heard correctly. But she had. She felt a sort of freeze take hold inside, as if she were falling into suspended animation.

"It was a difficult decision, with much back-and-forth. But in the end, it was the opinion of myself and the board that the position should be awarded to Dr. Connor Digby."

Weingrau paused, but when Nora didn't respond she went on in a hearty voice. "Again, I know this is disappointing news, and I feel you're owed a clear explanation. The position involves not just administrative tasks, you understand, but also a great deal of public and community interface. A *great* deal. It requires not only a person who has impeccable academic credentials, but, well, someone who is personable, articulate, charming—in more coarse terms, a schmoozer. Not that you aren't those things, of course—but you're first and foremost an archaeologist. Absolutely first-class. Your work is brilliant. And what you've done for the Institute has been stellar, and we are so, *so* grateful to you. But administrative work is not your forte. The Tsankawi project is behind schedule—I understand the reasons for that, of course, but still, we will have to renew the permit next year, when we hadn't expected to. Nora, we want to keep you where you shine, where your strengths are so evident—in the field and in the lab. Not in the boardroom or at the fund-raiser."

She was speaking rapidly and nervously now. "That's where Connor comes in. He was a graduate student of mine, you know, and I got to know his family rather well."

No: Nora hadn't known. But it made sense. If she'd taken a look at Digby's CV, as she'd intended to, no doubt she'd have seen he had gotten his doctorate from Boston University—and made the connection.

But Weingrau was still talking. "…He's from that sort of background, you know what I mean: old New England and all that. It's just something you're born into, really. That's no comment on you. It's just the way it is. We're making strides—every year, we're making strides—but it's those old-money, East Coast family connections that still make the difference."

Weingrau finally stopped talking—realizing, perhaps, that she'd already said too much. Nora felt a certain tightening around her eyes and the corners of her mouth, and to her great mortification realized she might cry. But she would never, ever let this woman see that happen. So she stood up with as much dignity as she could muster, and—because she didn't trust herself to speak—simply turned and walked out of the office. She heard Weingrau call her name once before she rounded the corner and hastened back to her office, shutting and locking the door and thanking God Digby wasn't around. He had probably made himself scarce, knowing what was coming down.

She sat there in the dim light, breathing hard, but in the end she didn't cry. She realized this must have been the plan from the very beginning. Weingrau had brought in Digby for this very promotion. It was preordained. Nothing Nora did, didn't do, or could have done would have made a difference. The newspaper articles highlighting her prominent role in the White Sands conspiracy and related murders must have made it awkward for Weingrau to push this through the board. But the board was weak, mostly retired businessmen, and no doubt it had been easy enough in the end.

Nora shook her head. She needed to pick herself up and dust herself off. Life was unfair—she'd already learned that lesson many times over. Losing the promotion was certainly not the worst thing that had happened to her—not by a long shot. As much as she hated to admit it, there was some truth in what Weingrau had said. The job of chief archaeologist, for all its prestige and high pay, brought with it more politics than academics. The chief managed the dirt herd but didn't do the actual work or get her hands dirty. This was something that, in her eagerness for advancement, Nora hadn't really considered.

She heaved a deep sigh. No doubt this was all just rationalization. The entire charade—and that's exactly what it was—stung badly, and she knew it would rankle for a long while. Digby, she supposed, wasn't really at fault—Weingrau had been the mover and shaker. Still, Nora knew she couldn't ever look at either of them in quite the same way again.

It was then she realized that something was clasped in her right hand. It was the envelope she'd been about to open when she'd gotten the news that the president wanted to see her. In her emotional reaction, she had reflexively crumpled it. She now placed it on her desk and smoothed it out. There was no return address on the envelope, just U.S. DEPARTMENT OF JUSTICE in embossed letters. With the kind of day she was having, it was probably a notice of audit from the IRS.

Nora tore it open with the back of an index finger, pulled out the single sheet, and read the missive within. After she had finished—it was a short letter—a deep silence gathered. For a long time she didn't move. Finally, she raised her head and gazed out the window, which had a view of the Institute's rose garden, beyond which stood the piñon-clad outline of Sun Mountain, bathed in the golden light of afternoon. She brushed away some moisture from the corner of her eye, then smiled faintly to herself. Life was indeed unfair—but sometimes when you least expected, it stacked the deck in your favor. As she looked down once more at the letter, a shaft of light fell upon it, and she read it again.

OFFICE OF THE DIRECTOR

UNITED STATES DEPARTMENT OF JUSTICE

FEDERAL BUREAU OF INVESTIGATION

WASHINGTON, D.C. 20353-0001

PERSONAL

Dr. Nora Kelly
c/o Santa Fe Archaeological Institute
4212 Camino Campanas
Santa Fe, NM 87507

Dear Dr. Kelly:

I am pleased to take this opportunity to inform you that you have been selected to receive this year's Director's Medal for Exceptional Achievement.

Once per year, each of the 56 field offices of the FBI selects, by votes of the highest-ranking agents, a civilian who has demonstrated qualities of courage, selflessness, and patriotism, frequently at the risk of personal safety. You have been chosen by the Albuquerque Field Office to receive this award.

In addition, one other field office has—uniquely, in the experience of this Bureau—elected to name you as well.

While I am not at liberty to disclose the identity of this office, you may rest assured it is one of our most significant. In light of this extraordinary development, your medal will be presented to you with a star of commendation for bravery.

We look forward to your presence at FBI Headquarters, 935 Pennsylvania Avenue NW, on the first of next month, at 10:00 AM, where—along with the 54 other recipients—you will receive your award. It will be my great privilege to confer it upon you.

Sincerely yours,
Marissa Greeley
Director, Federal Bureau of Investigation

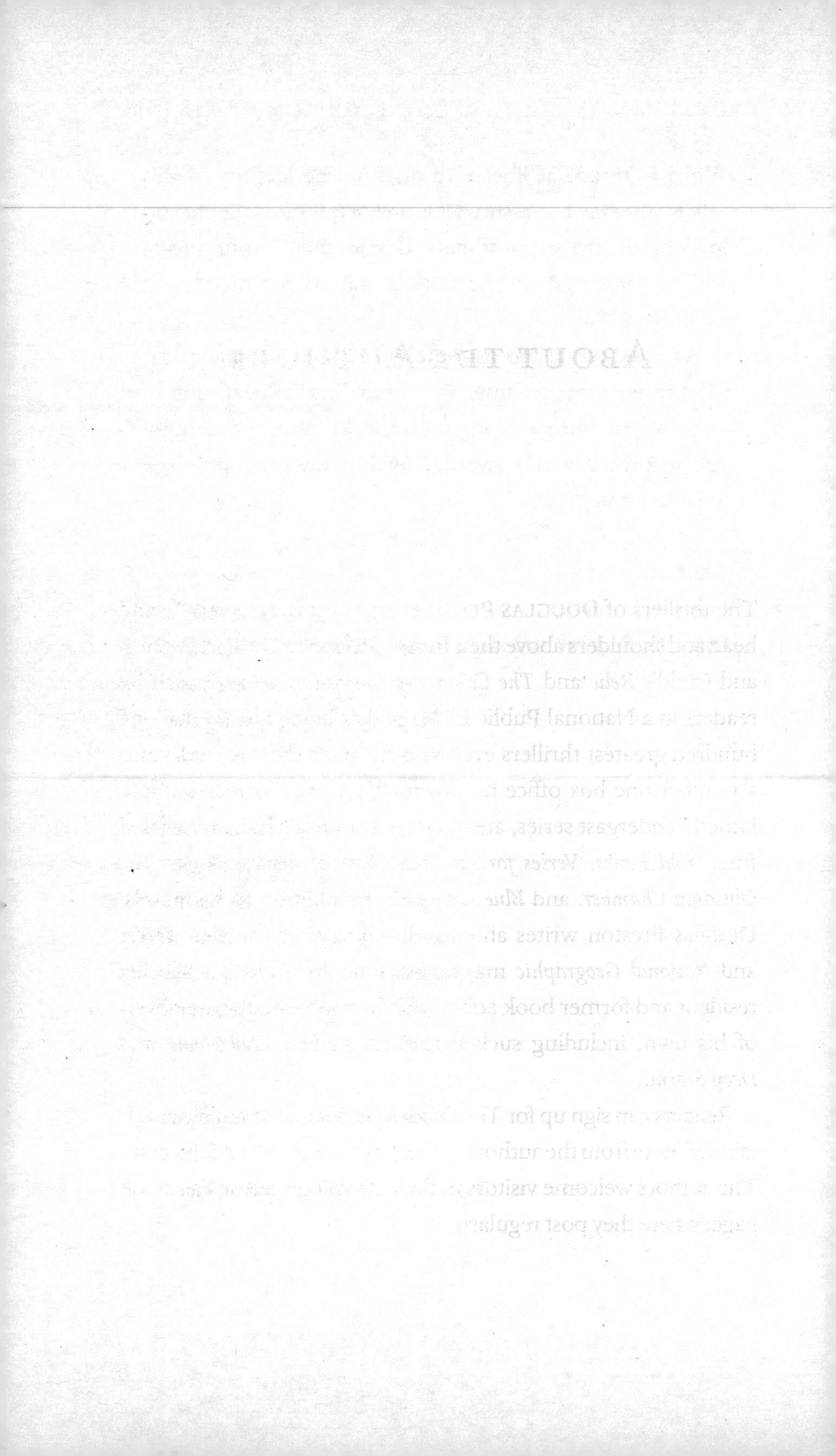

About the Authors

The thrillers of **Douglas Preston** and **Lincoln Child** "stand head and shoulders above their rivals" (*Publishers Weekly*). Preston and Child's *Relic* and *The Cabinet of Curiosities* were chosen by readers in a National Public Radio poll as being among the one hundred greatest thrillers ever written, and *Relic* was made into a number one box office hit movie. They are coauthors of the famed Pendergast series, and their recent novels include *Crooked River, Old Bones, Verses for the Dead, City of Endless Night, The Obsidian Chamber*, and *Blue Labyrinth*. In addition to his novels, Douglas Preston writes about archaeology for the *New Yorker* and *National Geographic* magazines. Lincoln Child is a Florida resident and former book editor who has published seven novels of his own, including such bestsellers as *Full Wolf Moon* and *Deep Storm*.

Readers can sign up for The Pendergast File, a "strangely entertaining" note from the authors, at their website, PrestonChild.com. The authors welcome visitors to their alarmingly active Facebook page, where they post regularly.